VENGEANCE IS PERSONAL

A Colton James Novel

BY

TOM DEPRIMA

Vinnia Publishing - U.S.A.

Vengeance Is Personal

A Colton James novel – Book 2
Copyright ©2015 by Thomas J. DePrima
15.k.16

ISBN-13 (print):   **978-1-61931-027-8**

ISBN-10 (print):   **1-61931-027-9**

ISBN-13 (ebook):   **978-1-61931-026-1**

ISBN-10 (ebook):   **1-61931-026-0**

Cover by: Uniquedesignxx

To contact the author, or see additional information about this and his other novels, visit:

http://www.deprima.com

Dedication

This book is dedicated to the more than one million law
enforcement personnel who have devoted their lives to
keeping the law-abiding public safe. The few bad actors who
get all the press represent just a miniscule fraction of the law
enforcement community.

Acknowledgements

A novel, even one produced by an independent author and
publisher such as myself, is rarely the work of one individual.
I'm deeply appreciative of the developmental editing and
valuable suggestions offered by my good friend and fellow
author A.B. Curtiss, and the developmental suggestions and
very thorough copy editing of Myra Shelley and her team of
proofreaders.

Novels by the author:

Colton James Novels...

A World Without Secrets
Vengeance Is Personal

A Galaxy Unknown®...

A Galaxy Unknown®
Valor at Vauzlee
The Clones of Mawcett
Trader Vyx
Milor!
Castle Vroman
Against All Odds
Return to Dakistee
Retreat And Adapt
Azula Carver

AGU:® Border Patrol...

Citizen X
Clidepp Requital
Clidepp Déjà Vu

AGU:® SC Intelligence...

The Star Brotherhood

When The Spirit...

When The Spirit Moves You
When The Spirit Calls

Table of Contents

CHAPTER ONE

As a child I was terrified of the night. Darkness, like the heavy heat and humidity of the tropics, would wrap itself around me and squeeze the breath from my lungs. I felt that way now.

I'd known that my parents would protect me at all costs, so I had learned to control my irrational fear of the dark long before I reached my teens. But this was different. This was not an imaginary monster or zombie hiding under the bed ready to leap at me. This was very real. And it was compounded by a second inner turmoil— anxiety over not having the *slightest* idea where I was.

My eyes were wide open as I lay on my back, but there was only blackness in every direction. It seemed apparent I wasn't outdoors because not a single sound was reaching my ears. Not a mechanical noise or even a cricket chirp.

And the air was perfectly still, not to mention nauseating. I couldn't remember where I'd been or what I'd been doing to land myself in this predicament. I held my breath and strained to hear the slightest noise, but it was as quiet as— a tomb. A new fear suddenly filled my mind. *I must be in a tomb*, I thought. *I had been buried*— buried alive if the extreme pain in my head and the sensation of a beating heart were proof of life. The surface on which I rested had the cold, hard feel of polished marble, and when I tried to stretch out my left arm, it encountered something vertical, flat, and cold after traveling no more than a few inches.

Most people had enemies, many of whom might work to tarnish good names through rumor and innuendo, or possibly even flatten the tires on a car in the dead of night. But my enemies were the sort who would gleefully make me dead in an instant if they had the opportunity. I couldn't stop myself from hyperventilating, even knowing it would more quickly use up whatever oxygen was available in the confined space.

I knew I had to get my breathing under control, so I forced myself to calm down and breathe normally. *Okay,* I thought, when I'd accomplished that difficult task, *first things first. Determine the size of your tomb.* I slowly moved my hands and arms upward, expecting they would quickly encounter whatever covered my resting place. When they met no resistance, I became even more perplexed.

Since there appeared to be space above me, I decided to make an attempt to stand and learn the limits of my confinement. But first I had to turn over. When I tried to roll to my right, I was again blocked from movement. The obstacle was cold to the touch.

But unlike the blockage on my left, the one on the right side wasn't perfectly vertical. In fact, it was unusually shaped. I cautiously ran my right hand over it in an attempt to identify the reason for such unusual construction. When recognition came to me, I almost laughed, but stopped myself immediately because I realized my situation might still be extremely grave, even if I wasn't yet *in* a grave. The object my right hand had encountered was the base of an ordinary toilet, which most probably meant I was lying on the floor of a bathroom. *But whose bathroom?* I pondered. *And how did I get here?*

Just knowing I was alive and in *someone's* bathroom removed much of the anxiety and confusion from my mind, but I still had more questions than answers. I managed to turn over, and while accomplishing that simple feat, discovered I was clothed only in a tee-shirt and shorts. I also learned that I was covered with some kind of slippery and obnoxious liquid.

My hands slipped out from under me as I tried to get to my knees, and I pancaked back down onto the floor. On my second attempt, I managed to get to my knees and then climb to my feet, all the while feeling around in total darkness. I discovered a sink, then began running my hands along the walls. Once I located a door it was a simple matter to find the room's light switch.

As I toggled the switch to the 'on' position, spasms of excruciating pain stabbed at my eyes like red-hot pokers, causing me to shut them as tightly as I could. I was tempted to turn off the light, but I knew my eyes would slowly adjust if I kept blinking, allowing a little more light in each time.

My dilated pupils finally began to adjust and the pain lessened somewhat with each quick, partial blink. When I was finally able to see through squinched eyes, I peered around the bathroom. Nothing in the blurry image seemed familiar— for a few seconds. Then it dawned on me. I was in the hotel room I'd rented because my apartment was cordoned off as a violent crime scene.

At the very least, the blood and brain tissue that embellished the walls and floor in and around my home's bathroom had to be thoroughly cleaned away before I could return. The bodies were long gone, of course, but the horrific mess and the considerable damage from gunfire remained.

As full vision returned, I surveyed the hotel bathroom in an attempt to discover where the god-awful smell was coming from. When I glanced towards the mirror over the sink, I learned the source. It was me. Or more specifically it was coming from me— although the floor was making a significant contribution. At some point I had apparently upchucked all over the front of myself.

Then, during my recent attempt to rise, I had further spread the mess all over my body, plus the walls of the bathroom. My hair was thickly matted with vomit, and it covered the floor near the toilet bowl. I assumed I'd been attempting to reach the ceramic depository when my stomach decided it could no longer wait to regurgitate its contents. I remembered then that I'd been drinking pretty heavily. Distillery and winemaker advertisements showing people drinking alcohol and having fun wisely never exhibited the aftermath of extreme excess.

This was the first time since my college days I'd gotten sick from alcohol consumption. I wasn't even this drunk the night I learned my parents had been killed in a car accident—perhaps because, although I mourned the loss of my mom and dad, they had been killed on the other side of the country and I hadn't actually seen the bodies at that point. This time I had seen the mutilated body of my best friend. In vivid Technicolor.

It wasn't the first time I'd seen violent death. As a direct result of my new career, I'd occasionally been forced to make some small reductions in the world's population. But this time was different. I have plenty of enemies. I don't have that many close friends.

After washing the spew from my face, hands and arms, I hydrated as much as possible with cold water using one of the plastic cups on the sink. I was on my third cupful before I realized I hadn't yet removed the sealed plastic bag around the cup. I then removed my vomit-saturated tee-shirt and shorts, and rinsed them repeatedly in the sink. Turning my attention to the bathroom itself, I used my just-rinsed tee-shirt as a cleaning rag and began wiping the walls wherever I'd touched them. After several additional rinses of my tee-shirt and a like number of cleansing swipes, the walls looked clean, so I turned my attention to the disgusting mess on the toilet and floor.

After flushing the bowl, I used the shirt to wipe the floor and remove most of the mess, depositing the spew directly into the bowl and flushing. I wiped the floor three more times before all trace of the regurgitation was gone. Lastly, I used a bath towel to dry all surfaces. With the former contents of my stomach removed and flushed down the sink drain or toilet, the overhead fan began to make headway clearing the air of the foul smell.

My underclothes then got a thorough cleaning in the sink with soapy water before being rinsed, squeezed, and left on the ledge of the sink to dry while I climbed into a steaming hot shower. The spray felt so wonderful that I didn't want to get out but finally turned off the faucets and pulled back the curtain.

My head was still throbbing when I emerged from the stall, dripping water all over the floor I'd recently dried, but I felt significantly better overall, until I looked at my reflection in the mirror and saw my face and hair. I had several days' beard growth, but that was understandable. I hadn't shaved since the morning I left my hotel in Amsterdam, The Netherlands. My hair was squeaky clean from several treatments of shampoo but looked as if someone had dropped a wet pile of dark straw on my head. My shaving kit was on the sink counter, so I took care of that chore first. Unfortunately, the comb was missing from the kit, and I assumed it was out in the bedroom. I realized as I stood there contemplating my next move that I was actually dreading leaving the small, now clean, room. I didn't believe for a second that the rest of the suite was neat and orderly. But it wasn't going to clean itself, so I opened the door and stepped out into near-darkness. The only light was coming from the windows, and it was dim at best.

When I flicked on the wall switch in the bedroom, I was relieved to see I was alone. I didn't remember having— or even wanting— company, but then I didn't remember anything after the first two bottles of wine. I must have been so distraught that I lost all focus for a while.

The bedroom was a mess, of course, but not quite the disaster I'd been expecting after seeing the bathroom. At least I didn't vomit out here. I retrieved some clean underwear and slacks from my suitcase and clothed myself, not realizing until then how badly wrinkled everything was from having been jammed into my suitcases for several days. I shrugged and located my comb so I could tend to my wet hair before picking up the assorted apparel and other items strewn about the small suite. When I was finished, the room was presentable. The six empty wine bottles I'd found scattered around the suite, including the one I'd found sitting upside down amid the dying flowers in a vase on the coffee table, were now in the wastebasket. Five of them bore a label that declared their vintage as 1997 Mascarello Barolo, while one was a '98. The 1997 was a vintage I had recently become particularly fond of. The thought was both a happy one and a sad one because it reminded me of Mia. My Mia. My beautiful Mia— the young Greek beauty whom I'd met while on a short voyage from the U.K. to the Netherlands. She was only the second woman I'd ever taken completely into my heart and one of the loveliest women I'd ever met. I'd fallen in love with her the first day of our encounter. Several days later she'd professed undying love for me as well. That was just two days before I'd witnessed her hopping into bed with another man.

I recalled buying the first three bottles of wine but not the latter. However, there was a receipt on the dresser that included a delivery charge. I'd probably ordered the second allotment of wine from the same Rare Spirits Liquor Store where I'd gotten the first batch, and they'd sent it over to my hotel. It appeared they must have run out of the '97 and substituted one bottle with the '98. By the sixth bottle, I wouldn't have known the difference. At several hundred dollars a bottle, it had been an expensive drunk.

The hands of my watch indicated it was just after four twenty a.m., and the date function showed it had been a little more than two days since the firefight in my apartment. I remembered every second of the event and of the debriefing that followed. I also remembered the six hours after the debriefing was over, more or less, but not much after that.

◆ ◆ ◆

It had been early morning by the time the initial crime-scene work was wrapped up at my apartment following the *incident*. The FBI had immediately assumed responsibility for the investigation. In case I'd forgotten to mention it, I'm FBI. Taking responsibility for a case was standard practice when-ever an FBI Special Agent was involved in a shooting that might be related to a criminal investigation.

I'd been told to report downtown to give a statement regarding the events of the evening. I learned much later that the New York State Police, NYC Police, and New Jersey State Police had been invited to attend the interview, watching from behind a two-way mirror in the interrogation room. The Jersey police were there because one of the dead thugs had admitted to having killed a scientist who lived and worked in New Jersey. The Jersey police had been investigating that death ever since the body had been found floating in the Hackensack River a couple of weeks before I returned from Europe. The early morning traffic had made travel downtown an exasperating experience.

When I'd arrived at Federal Plaza, I looked as if *I'd* been a victim of the shooting, but it was only because the clothes I wore had been heavily splattered with the blood of the two thugs I'd shot at extremely close range and had then been thoroughly saturated with the blood of my friend whom I'd held in my arms as he died. The guards at the first-floor entrance stared at me with wide eyes as I put down one of my suitcases, held up my identification, and then walked through the metal detector. I was still carrying my two Glocks, so the equipment beeped loudly as I passed through.

Since I'd had the presence of mind to bring the two packed suitcases that had just accompanied me back from Europe, I'd been given time to clean up. After taking a long shower in the locker room next to the Bureau's gym and putting on clean clothes, I felt ready for whatever they planned to throw at me.

"I told you to stay out of that investigation," ADIC Sobert said loudly as soon as I'd entered the interview room and taken my seat. The timbre of his voice indicted he was plenty upset.

"Sir, you told me that less than an hour before I entered my apartment and was jumped by two goons from Staten Island. I assure you I had not begun *any* investigation on my own in the interim."

"How do you know they were from Staten Island?"

"They said they were working for Delcona. Everyone knows that's his turf."

"So you never mentioned the case to *anyone* between the time we spoke and when you were attacked?"

"No one. After I left your office, Osborne and Snow gave me a lift home. They can confirm we never spoke about it. And once I arrived home, I didn't speak to *anyone* about anything before I entered my apartment and got jumped by the big one called Diz."

"Okay, James. Tell your story to the interviewer."

"I can probably type it faster than I can say it, sir."

"Do it our way, James."

"Yes, sir."

"Philbin will conduct the session," Sobert said, then left without another word.

◆

Special Agent Philbin had entered the interview room a few seconds later. I assumed he'd been watching from behind the two-way mirror where cameras, sound recorders, and various other types of monitoring equipment were already recording every micro-second of the interview.

"Why don't we start with you telling me exactly what happened from the time Osborne and Snow dropped you off at home last night," Philbin said.

So I started with the moment I'd entered the outside door of the building and finished with the arrival of NYC cops responding to numerous 911 calls from neighbors reporting a gun battle. The entire incident had lasted less than ten minutes, so it was almost a second-by-second description.

"That's your *whole* story?" Philbin asked, looking at his own scrawled notes.

"Yep," I said. I hadn't lied about anything. I had *omitted* several minor points though. I'd said that Diz was apparently looking for something, which was true, but I never mentioned that he'd found a small matchbox in my pocket, or that he had ordered me to activate the piece of paper he'd found inside. And there was one thing more I hadn't fully divulged.

In relating the events in my apartment, I'd said that my friend had blindsided Diz's companion, then knocked Diz backward against the apartment door with a shoulder to his chest before jumping into the bathroom and locking himself in. That was all true. But I had omitted that my friend had grabbed the paper out of Diz's hand, then flushed it down the toilet. Since I was the only survivor of the shootout, there was no one to contest the accuracy of my statements.

"What's this *thing* Diz was looking for?" Philbin asked.

"He said Morris Calloway had reported giving me *something* when I went to Paramus. He also said he had killed Calloway."

"How?"

"He didn't say, and I was in no position to perform an interrogation. I was too busy trying to figure a way to survive the night. Diz only said he had 'offed that geek.'"

"Offed?"

"Those are his words, exactly."

"What was it Calloway gave you?"

"Morris gave me nothing. I went there seeking information and left with nothing more than I arrived with. He couldn't answer my question."

"He didn't give you a package or anything?"

"How many ways would you like me to say the same thing? Morris gave me nothing. Morris didn't give me a package. I received nothing from Morris. Morris never even offered me a jelly donut. Morri…"

"Okay, James." Philbin said, interrupting. "I get the picture. So why do you think Calloway would have told them he gave you something?"

"You want me to speculate?"

"Yes. Speculate."

"Perhaps he knew they were going to kill him and figured I was equipped to take them down. A sort of 'revenge from beyond the grave' motive."

"Was Calloway that calculating?"

"Who's to say what *anyone* would be capable of under those circumstances?"

"Why did you refuse to accept the package when Morris offered it to you?"

I sighed loudly at Philbin's poor attempt to use the Reid interrogation technique by hitting me with a question that contradicted a previous statement I'd made in order to confuse me and trip me up. I picked up where I had left off a few seconds earlier. "Morris never offered me a jelly donut. He never offered me a cup of coffee. He never offered..."

"Okay, okay, James. Enough."

"Rephrasing a simple question altered to add an implicit suggestion that I'd committed perjury earlier isn't going to get you a different answer, Philbin."

Philbin glared at me, then calmed and smiled. "Sorry. You know all the tricks, don't you?"

"I received the same training at Quantico that you did. I don't claim to know *all* the tricks, but I don't need to. I've been completely honest about the meeting with Morris. We can remain here all day and into the night with me answering the same questions over and over, and the answers won't change. Morris gave *me* nothing, and I gave *him* nothing, despite what anyone might suspect. All we did was talk for about an hour, and then I left. What he might have told someone else, and for what reasons, won't change that."

"Preliminary reports suggest that both of Delcona's men had already suffered fatal wounds when you decided to decorate your apartment walls with their brain matter. Why?"

"Fatal doesn't mean dead until their hearts stop beating. Both were down but not out. Yes, they probably would have died from the first wounds, but before that happened they might have been able to take me with them. They were trying to do exactly that when I administered the final wounds."

"Administered the final wounds? Is that how you describe murdering two men?"

"It's a better description than the one you used. I was protecting my life. I make no apologies for that. If they hadn't continued to make an effort to kill me, I wouldn't have had to 'decorate my apartment walls with their brain matter.'"

"You always shoot to kill, don't you?"

"Always?"

"You killed a man on the North Sea a few weeks ago with three forty-caliber slugs to the chest and another in Spain a week ago with two slugs to the chest *after* shooting him in the shoulder, a wound that left him unable to even hold his weapon. You don't take prisoners, do you?"

"I do what's necessary to survive. The encounter with the assassin in Spain wasn't our first meeting. He had tried to kill me in a hotel bathroom in Amsterdam. On that occasion I'd been able to incapacitate him without shooting him, and disarm him. And, for the record, after I shot him in the right shoulder and he dropped his pistol, he picked it up with his left hand. He might have been ambidextrous."

"Or you just didn't want him coming at you a third time, so you finished him off at your second encounter."

"What's this about, Philbin? The British police and the Spanish police agreed that I was only defending myself. Neither filed charges against me."

"I've been a Special Agent for fourteen years and have never once had to fire my weapon in the line of duty."

"Bravo. Your point being?"

"Perhaps you didn't have to use yours either. Perhaps you just like killing people when it can be justified."

I knew what Philbin was doing now. He was trying to make me so angry I'd slip up and tell him something I didn't intend to. I said calmly, "I get no satisfaction from taking the life of another human being. I only do what's necessary to preserve my own."

Philbin knew I was onto his game. Bad cops and former cops *were* the most difficult to catch and prosecute because they *did* know all the tricks and procedures. Philbin scowled at me, then stood up and left the interview room.

◆ ◆

I'd been left sitting alone in the interrogation room for about twenty minutes, and I assumed the various law enforcement groups wanted to discuss the information I'd just reported. I had nowhere else to be, so I leaned back in the chair and thought about where my life was going from that point forward. The more I'd thought about it, the more depressed I became. The loss of close friends or family, either from death or simply the breakup of personal relationships, could create an enormous void in a person's life. I sometimes felt as though *everyone* was suddenly gone.

It wasn't true of course; I still had many friends. But the sense of loss could be so acute at this point that some people decided they didn't even *want* to go on. I believed I was stronger than that, and I also knew the overwhelming sense of loss would diminish with the passage of time and as I established new relationships. Hell, I was only thirty-one-years-old.

I would just pick up the pieces of my life and continue. Even if I was to be separated from the FBI, I still had my writing career, as weak as that had been, with a slightly distant-but-solid relationship with fans of the free stories I posted online. Most importantly, my finances were rock solid. The recovery fees I'd received from my sideline work had enabled me to begin seriously looking for a co-op in New York City. As everyone knows, buying property in Manhattan doesn't happen without a sound financial footing.

My reverie had been interrupted by the return of Philbin. "Okay, James, ADIC Sobert says you can go for now."

I'd left without saying anything further, but I wondered how I'd done with the stress-monitoring equipment. There could be no doubt that I was under stress. I *had* just killed two human beings, after all, or at least what passed for human beings in some places these days, so I imagined any stress level of my testimony would be acceptable as long as there were no serious spikes during the questioning.

After retrieving my suitcases from the locker room, I'd headed for the elevators. The security folks in the lobby again stared at me as I passed them and crossed to the exit doors. I managed to hail a cab at the curb, and the cabbie popped the trunk but didn't offer to assist me with my suitcases.

I'd instructed the cab driver to head to a wine shop where I knew they handled the better vintages, and I learned I was in luck. The proprietor said he had the Mascarello Barolo I was looking for. He disappeared into the back and was gone for what seemed like five minutes, but when he returned, he had three bottles of the wine in his arms.

After paying for the spirits, I'd returned to the waiting cab and asked the driver to take me to a midtown hotel. I wanted to forget the day's events for a few hours. At least as much as possible.

I hadn't really intended to get blind stinking drunk, but that's apparently what happened. I couldn't help but wonder if I'd stayed in the hotel for the entire time or possibly gone out and done something I'd deeply regret later. I wished I could remember.

CHAPTER TWO

Two days of insobriety continued to impose its expected physical toll on my body. After straightening up the hotel suite, I tried to sleep, but the little man wielding a sledgehammer inside my head made that impossible. I continued to hydrate, pop aspirin from the small bottle I always carried in my shaving kit, and stare up at the ceiling as I lay on the bed, trying to mentally block the pain.

I wanted to think about something more pleasant, but my thoughts kept returning to that terrible night in my apartment. Had it really been only three days ago? I had never met Delcona or even seen him in person, but the television news image of his smiling face as he'd left the courthouse a free man the year before kept playing in my head. The government's latest effort to convict him on racketeering charges had failed when all eyewitnesses suddenly developed amnesia regarding their previous knowledge of Delcona's activities.

I realized that my mind wasn't going to allow me to lose myself in some more pleasant distraction, so I focused on the events in my apartment. I reviewed everything in minute detail from the moment I'd arrived at my building, trying to determine how the outcome might have been different—better different. But everything pointed to an outcome that could only have been worse. The New York City government had done an effective job of disarming law-abiding citizens while leaving weapons in the hands of criminals who didn't bother to obey the law. Fortunately, not everyone had bowed to the government's conviction that they must adopt a persona of impotency and humble submission when they came face to face with an armed criminal. If Billy hadn't taken the action he had, my death at the hands of those two thugs had been almost assured. His efforts definitely saved my life. I wished I could have saved his.

It was after eight a.m. when I first realized my headache was almost gone. As I stood at the tenth-floor window, staring down at the growing snarls of traffic on the streets far below, the tragic events of three days ago seemed like a nightmare from which I couldn't awaken. Right then, my best friend should have been starting his workday in his cab instead of lying on a slab at the morgue with a tag hanging off one of his toes. The thought made me want to get some wine and start another drunk, but it would be all too easy to slip into a sort of permanent daze. I couldn't let that happen. And besides, I had far too much to do.

My first call was to the morgue. At first I received the standard response that I should call later and speak to a clerk, but when I identified myself as an FBI Special Agent, the morgue attendant made a small effort to check the files. He reported that Billy's body was still awaiting the required autopsy.

Whenever there was suspicion or evidence of violence or foul play, when the death may be the result of a mysterious disease, when an otherwise healthy person died while unattended by a physician, or under any circumstances where a physician was uncomfortable signing a death certificate without an investigation, an autopsy was required.

There was no doubt that Billy and the two underworld thugs had died as a result of violence, and the backlog of autopsy cases meant that it could be five to seven more days before the morgue was ready to release Billy's body to a funeral home.

Billy's family lived in or near Binghamton, N.Y., so I would need my computer for my next call. As I opened my suitcase, I saw the box containing the beer stein I'd purchased in Amsterdam, but which I'd never had a chance to give to Billy. I was sure he would have loved it. My first impulse was to smash it against the wall. But that wouldn't change past events, so I carefully removed the stein from the box and pulled off the packing material to see how it had fared on the trip. It still looked as good as the day I'd picked it up at the secondhand shop. The store owner had done a fantastic job of fixing the chip in the top rim. If I hadn't known exactly where to look, I would never have known it had been damaged.

The man had also done a fantastic job with the old cigarette lighter I'd purchased there. Lengthened by two centimeters, it was now a better fit in my large hand. During World War II and through the nineteen forties and fifties, probably seventy percent of men carried a Zippo lighter. Back then, most people probably would have noticed my lighter's increased length. But that was then. I was betting that few would ever recognize today that it had been lengthened. The shop owner had also polished and buffed the exterior silver surface to a brilliant luster. It looked almost as good as the day it had been manufactured. I removed it from my pocket and flicked open the top. Using my thumb to spin the rough steel wheel, I saw sparks jump towards the wick and watched as a flame flared into being. I stared at the small fire for a couple of seconds before closing the lighter and returning it to my pocket.

After carefully repacking the stein in the cardboard box and placing it on the desk, I removed my laptop computer from the suitcase. As an IT professional, I had come to rely on my computer like people used to rely on their day planners. Most folks these days used a smartphone to keep track of everything, but with the built-in GPS, smart phones allowed other people to track all movements of the smartphone holder. That both bothered me and frightened me. Some people, upon hearing that, called me paranoid, but I preferred to think of myself as being security aware. If I wanted people to know exactly where I was, I preferred to tell them.

My immediate need was for the address file that served as my link to the world. I hoped the phone number of Billy's familial home in upstate New York was in there, but if it wasn't, I could probably find it on the net.

I was in luck. The address record for Billy contained his parents' names, address, and phone number. But now that I had the information, I hesitated to place the call in case they were late risers. I decided to wait until after nine a.m. In the meantime, I unpacked both of my suitcases because I didn't know how long I was going to be staying at the hotel. I knew I would look like an unmade bed if I went anywhere right now, so I called down to have a valet come retrieve my suits so they could be cleaned and pressed. I considered having the valet take and discard my blood-soaked suit as well, then decided against it. I didn't want to give the wrong impression to the hotel staff, which was probably already aware that I had holed up with enough wine for a dinner party.

The ruined clothes, already wrapped in a plastic evidence bag I'd gotten down at FBI Headquarters to protect my other clothes, went back into my suitcase. Then I sat down to wait until I felt it was late enough to call Billy's family. I let my thoughts drift to the days ahead. Delcona had sent his thugs to retrieve me and the gizmo, but I had survived and his people were dead. I didn't believe for a second that would be the end of it. But the firefight in my apartment, combined with the reappearance of Morris's body in the New Jersey swamp, had turned another, even brighter spotlight in his direction. For a while at least he would probably be a good little mob boss and not start any shooting wars. As long as I stayed in the hotel, I was reasonably safe— first because no one knew where I was, and second because there were far too many witnesses around. But I couldn't hide here forever.

After a valet had picked up my clothes, I placed the call to Billy's folks. They had already been notified of his death and were naturally grief-stricken, but they had received few details and were anxious to hear anything I could tell them. In as gentle a manner as possible, I related the events of the night. But as I relived my last minutes with Billy, my voice choked up and tears began welling up in my eyes. Okay, so the hard-bitten persona I'd been trying to project in recent months hadn't fully taken hold— yet. Perhaps in time I'd be able to appear as indifferent as Osborne and Snow, but I also hoped I never completely lost touch with my gentler side.

Once we made it through the tragedy of the event, it was time to make funeral arrangements. I offered to pay for accommodations at my hotel for all family members coming to the city for the services, but Billy's folks said they preferred to have the wake and funeral in Binghamton. Billy's body would then be interred in the same cemetery where other family members had been laid to rest for generations. I told them I'd pick up all expenses for bringing the body to Binghamton and cover all the expenses of the coffin, wake, and burial. They tried to argue but I refused to budge. I knew they were nearing retirement age, and I didn't want them draining their retirement savings to pay for the funeral. I owed Billy big time, and this would be a small down payment on that debt. They finally agreed to let me pick up all the costs. I asked them to make arrangements with a local funeral home to accept Billy's body, and I would have it taken there when it was released by the morgue officials.

When we'd had a couple of awkward silences, I decided it was time to end the call. I promised them I would take care of all the arrangements once they named the funeral home and be in touch as soon as Billy's body was on the way to Binghamton. As the call ended, I took a deep breath and released it slowly, then tried to relax my tense muscles. I hadn't realized until then just how much I'd dreaded making the call.

My next call was to a local funeral home so I could make arrangements to have the body transported upstate. The mortuary would alert the morgue that they would be claiming the body on behalf of the family when it was ready to be released and should be the one to be notified when that happened.

Now that I had finished all of my unpleasant chores and my headache was mostly gone, I realized I probably hadn't eaten in three days. There was a gnawing sensation in my midsection that I knew could only be satisfied one way. I couldn't go out until my clothes were returned by the valet service, so I called room service and ordered enough eggs, home fries, sausages, and pancakes for three people, plus a pitcher of OJ and a pot of coffee.

A number of large hotels in the U.S. had discontinued their room service operations in recent years, so I had chosen this particular hotel for its amenities as much as anything else. I had the money now to live a better life than at any time in the past, and my time at the wonderful hotels and B&Bs in Europe, and especially Amsterdam, had spoiled me a bit. The switchboard operator, or whoever had taken my order, told me it would be about thirty to forty minutes, so I reclined on the bed to await the food.

◆

The order arrived on two carts pushed by two waiters. I think they were surprised to see just one person in the suite, but I gave each a generous tip and they seemed to forget about the food being for just a single occupant.

I wasted no time digging in as the door closed behind the waiters. It was the most delicious food I'd had since my return from Europe. Okay, it was the *only* food I'd had since my return. But it really *was* tasty and properly cooked. The 'over easy' eggs were perfect, the toast wasn't burnt, the sausages were well cooked but not dried out, and the pancakes were just the way I liked them— thick, but light and fluffy.

◆

By the time I'd eaten my fill, the gnawing pain in my stomach had changed to one experienced after a slight over-indulgence in food, but it was a considerably better feeling than the former. I had no place to be, nothing to do, and no energy to do anything anyway, so I decided to take a nap. I didn't have to put the 'Do Not Disturb' sign out for housekeeping because I'd realized it was already out when the valet came. It had probably been out since I arrived. The bathroom could really use a going over, not to mention clean towels, but it would have to wait until my clothes were returned so I could go out and let housekeeping have the suite for a while.

◆   ◆

It was dark again outside when I awoke. I knew I would probably be unable to sleep through the night if I didn't get out of bed and do something, but I still had no energy to do anything except feel sorry for myself. I had to find a way to emerge from my depression, so I began to think about life after Billy's funeral. I had killed the two men who 'offed' Morris and shot Billy, but not the man who had given the orders.

Since finding the gizmo intermixed with private papers from my auto after the building across the street from my third floor walkup exploded in the middle of the night, my life had changed in ways I never would have imagined. The gizmo, resembling an ordinary sheet of copier paper, had allowed me to see anywhere in the present or the past. When I placed it against any vertical surface, it became like a window in time. I had learned to manipulate the image and had been using the gizmo to solve cold cases for the FBI while also occasionally solving recovery cases privately.

My private work had lifted me out of poverty by quite some measure. I supposed that if life were a comic book I would have been Gizmo Man, fighting crime in all its forms. But I would have an advantage over most comic book heroes in that the gizmo also provided a very handsome living while enabling me to fight crime. The problem was that this was real life, and I had no super powers. Anyone could manip-ulate the gizmo, a radically-designed computer with billions of nano-circuits that made it, without a doubt, the most advanced computer on the planet, and one that allowed someone to see through time. Without the gizmo I was reduced to just an ordinary private citizen again.

Besides myself, only Morris and Billy had actually *seen* the gizmo. Billy had been my best friend in the world, and I knew he'd never tell anyone about the gizmo, so the leak had to have come from Morris. Morris was a scientist whom I knew from my days as an IT person when we both worked at the same startup company. I had believed I needed to know where the gizmo had come from and enlisted his aid in solving the mystery. I'd told him that if he ever mentioned its existence to anyone, it could mean his life, and sworn him to silence. But Morris, in his arrogance, had obviously told someone about it, in detail, before he died. And that someone was Delcona.

Delcona had believed Morris enough to send two thugs to retrieve it. And Delcona wanted it enough to kill to get it. He had to know by now his people were dead, but he couldn't know that Billy had grabbed the paper from Diz and flushed it down the toilet, so I fully expected him to send others. Even if he decided not to pursue the matter, I had no intention of forgetting he was ultimately responsible for the deaths of my friends. I vowed that once I got my life back on track, I wouldn't rest until Delcona paid for his actions— one way or another.

◆ ◆ ◆

Over the next six days I did little else except sit in the hotel room and plan retribution. I suspected Delcona was well protected and wasn't going to be an easy target. There was also the probability that he was under twenty-four seven surveillance by the Bureau and/or NYPD. I would have liked to use my computer to access the FBI system and view the file on him, but I had been ordered not to get involved in the case. If I accessed the FBI system, there'd be a trail to everything I'd accessed, so I had to find another way. I wished I could just slap the gizmo up against the wall and begin a surveillance that no one could ever detect.

I was having lunch when the call came from the mortuary. Billy's body had been released from the morgue, and they were preparing to transport it to Binghamton. The funeral home there had been alerted and was ready to receive it. I decided to wait until I was actually in Binghamton before notifying his folks.

◆ ◆ ◆

The roughly three-hour drive to the New York Southern Tier city would have been pleasant but for the purpose of the trip. The New York and Pennsylvania woodlands along the route were spectacular. It was especially beautiful in the autumn when the leaves were changing colors in response to the colder overnight temperatures.

The funeral home director was waiting for us, and the transport coffin was quickly unloaded onto a casket dolly and moved inside. I followed behind and then walked to the office with the director to complete the paperwork. When the formalities were wrapped up, I phoned Billy's parents to let them know Billy was home. Mr. Boyles wanted me to come over to their house right away, but I begged off, promising I'd come over the next day. I was a little tired from the drive and just wanted to get something to eat and go to bed. I had made reservations at a local motel, and I picked up a take-out meal on the drive there.

After checking in, I sat down at the small table in the kitchenette to eat but tossed the food in the trash after just two spoonfuls. I was expecting a Mexican Carne Asada burrito, because that's what I'd ordered, but the aluminum foil pan contained something that sort of resembled an Italian manicotti in a tortilla wrap drowning in Hungarian goulash. I should have realized that even the locals didn't like the food there because it was still the dinner hour and I was the only customer in the place when I'd placed the order. I'd have to ask Billy's folks to recommend a few restaurants in the city since I expected to be here at least a week.

◆ ◆ ◆

I met the Boyles at the funeral parlor the next day to finalize the arrangements. After selecting the coffin and liner, and taking care of all the small details such as the date and time of the wake and the printing of the remembrance cards, I accepted an invitation to come to the Boyles' home. They had already spoken to their parish priest and made arrangements for a funeral mass and graveside burial ritual. The cemetery had begun preparing for the burial and the plot would be excavated over the next few days. Relatives and family friends had been notified, and a few who lived in other states were making arrangements to fly in. Things would get progressively busier in the days ahead, but for now we had done everything we could.

As we sat down to have coffee, Mrs. Boyles said, "Colton, please tell us again what happened."

I had known this would be asked again and had prepared what I hoped would be an appropriate response.

"I gave Billy a key to my apartment some time ago because I was traveling so much. He would occasionally drop by to check on things in my absence. I was recently in Europe for an extended time while I worked an art theft investigation, and Billy had dropped by the day I returned, although I hadn't informed him I was returning and didn't know he was there when I arrived home. As I entered my darkened apartment, I was jumped by two thugs who were waiting for me. Billy was there, being held at gunpoint. One of the thugs spun me around and held a gun to my neck while he patted me down, looking for weapons. The other thug should have been watching Billy but apparently let his attention wander to me because I probably represented a far greater threat. When one of the thugs admitted to a recent murder in New Jersey, I knew they couldn't let us live. Billy must have realized the same thing. He suddenly jumped up and threw himself against the thug who was supposed to be watching him. Then he threw himself against the one patting me down. The second thug had already taken my service weapon, but he hadn't found my backup yet. Billy's action directed their attention away from me. I was able to get my backup and shoot both thugs, but not before they shot Billy. He died in my arms a few minutes later."

"Then Billy saved your life?"

"I would have to say yes. As I mentioned, by admitting to the murder in New Jersey, one of the thugs had incriminated himself in front of a law enforcement officer and a witness. At that point, the fate intended for us was obvious. By acting when he did, Billy saved my life. I only wish I could have saved his."

"Billy often talked about you when we spoke," Mr. Boyles said. "He had a lot of friends, but we know you were his best friend. He loved you like a brother. We're sure you did everything possible. God just decided to call Billy home. We're sure he's in heaven now."

Upon first entering the Boyles' home, I had immediately noticed that religious statuary and images were everywhere. I had never been very religious myself, and my faith all but disappeared when my folks were killed, but I nodded in silent agreement.

While staying with the Boyles over the next four hours, I recounted the story about how Billy and I had met when I'd gotten into his cab and we struck up a conversation about professional sports in New York. I also told them about the bar league and the YMCA teams where we had played, including anecdotal stories about various games.

At dinnertime, the Boyles invited me to stay and eat with them. I accepted, all the while hoping the food would be better than the takeout I'd had the previous evening.

I shouldn't have worried. It was, by a very wide measure.

◆　◆　◆

The Boyles' relatives began arriving the next day, so I stayed out of the way and remained secluded in my motel room for the next several days. I would have an opportunity to be introduced to everyone at the wake on Thursday evening.

◆　◆　◆

The family had arranged for a full funeral mass on Friday morning. Not everyone who had been at the wake came, but there were many I hadn't met yet. There were also a lot of folks from the City. Most were cab drivers, but there were a few guys from the bar league. Billy had been a great guy and had been very popular with everyone who knew him.

The biggest surprise for me came when I saw Kathy Marin arrive and step into a pew on the other side of the aisle. She was as lovely as always, and I felt a pang in my chest as I looked at her. I had an urge to join her in the pew, but propriety dictated that I wait until the service was over before saying hello because I didn't knew how she would react. The last time we'd talked, she had hung up on me.

◆ ◆

As Kathy exited the church following the service, I approached her. She spoke first.

"Hello, Colton. I'm so glad you weren't hurt."

"Thanks, but I'd really rather it be me in that coffin than Billy."

"I'd rather it wasn't either of you."

Following an awkward pause, I said, "How have you been?"

"I'm doing fine."

"I've missed you."

"And I've missed you. But you've changed. You're not the man I fell in love with."

"I'm still the same man you met at our friends' wedding. It's just that circumstances pulled me along an unexpected career path."

"You went willingly."

"Kathy, I was trying to build a life for us. One that had a bright future. It's not like I've done anything illegal. It's quite the opposite. I've been working *against* crime, not for it."

"I can't live with the danger you seem to have embraced. I can't help thinking it could be me in that coffin if I'd moved in with you or simply been waiting for you in your apartment."

"I haven't embraced danger, Kathy."

"Colton, I read the story about the Amsterdam case in *Art World Today Magazine*. You killed two men in Europe. And now you've killed two more here. I can't be a part of your life while you and everyone around you are in such danger.

- 25 -

Perhaps if you gave up your job with the FBI and went back to writing, we could start over. You once told me you were only trying to make enough money so you could write without having to worry about finances."

I looked down at the ground because I didn't want to see the look in her eyes as I said, "I can't stop yet. Not until the people responsible for Billy's death have been caught and punished."

"Then I guess there's nothing more to be said. I'll remember all the good times we had, and there will always be a special place in my heart for you. Goodbye, Colton."

I stood there and watched her as she walked away. She never looked back. I knew I also had a special place in my heart for her, but she was right that her life could be in danger if we were a couple again.

The cars were emptying from the church parking lot, and I had to get a move on in order to get to the graveside for the final service.

◆ ◆

As everyone gathered around the grave, I purposely moved to the opposite side from where Kathy was standing. I felt it was better to maintain my distance for now. And I was glad I did when I noticed two men who seemed out of place. They reminded me of Diz and his pudgy friend, the two men I had killed in my apartment, although their appearances were very different. I think it was their demeanor that made me associate them with the two dead thugs.

One was of average height with darting eyes and a narrow face. He seemed to be extremely nervous about being at the funeral. I nicknamed him Weasel.

The other was about six-two, like myself, but he was carrying at least fifty pounds more than I was, and it sure wasn't muscle. He looked like a kid I'd known in grade school who had a reputation for pulling the wings off flies before dropping them onto anthills. He had liked to kick every dog or cat that came within range of his leg. I nicknamed this one Ox.

I felt my heart rate and respiration increase as I watched them with my peripheral vision. It wasn't just their appearance that put me on edge. Every once in a while, I saw one or the other glance in my direction and stare at me for several seconds. I never looked directly at them after my first look, but I continued to watch them. The Glock 23 under my left arm and the Glock 27 in my ankle holster had never before given me such a comforting feeling. Perhaps Kathy was right. Maybe I was embracing danger.

CHAPTER THREE

Following the graveside ceremony, the Boyles invited everyone to come to their house for cake and coffee. Most declined because they had to get back to work, but some agreed to follow them back to the house. My attention was on Weasel and Ox, the two men I had spotted at the grave. They followed the procession but disappeared just before we reached the house. I hadn't gotten their license plate number, but I knew it was a New York plate. I would be watching for them, or anyone else, in case they were Delcona's people. Since I wasn't living at home and hadn't been moving around Manhattan, it made sense that they would try to follow me back to the city to learn where I was staying.

I couldn't refuse to return to the Boyles' home for a short stay, but I felt very awkward. Everyone must have learned by now who I was, and some might have even blamed me for Billy's death. Kathy was there, but she avoided me, and no one else seemed disposed to converse with me. When I saw several women staring at me and whispering among themselves, I decided it was time to leave. I made my way to where the Boyles were talking with two couples and informed them that I was leaving. They thanked me for helping with all the funeral arrangements and for having been such a good friend to Billy. I hadn't forgiven myself, but they weren't blaming me for his death.

An hour later I had checked out of my motel in Binghamton and was on my way back to Manhattan. I kept watching my rearview mirror but never caught sight of the car used by the two men who had stood out so prominently at the gravesite. At least they stood out to me— but I had become more and more attuned to spotting such types. It was unlikely that anyone other than a law enforcement officer would have given them a second glance. During the entire trip back to Manhattan, I never spotted any vehicle that appeared to be following me.

◆ ◆

Once I arrived in the city, I drove in a circuitous route that I believed would enable me to spot anyone tailing my car. I was sure there was no one back there. Of course, they could have placed a tracking device on my vehicle and been following from a distance. But I had no choice; I had to put my car back into my secure storage parking garage. By parking before I went to my hotel, a tracking device would be rendered ineffective for discovering where I was living.

When I called for a cab, I didn't give my correct destination. I changed the address with the driver after I was in the cab and we were headed cross-town. It was doubtful that giving an incorrect destination initially made any difference, but one never knew these days. I still kept my cell phone in a special case, one that blocked the built-in GPS signal until I needed to use it. I could have turned it off, but it was all too easy to accidently activate again while it was in my pocket. I had heard a news story about a felon who discussed a planned theft with an associate after accidently activating the cell phone in his pocket. The person who overheard the plan notified the police, who then interrupted the crime during its commission. And removing and replacing the battery frequently was too much trouble.

I paid the driver with cash when we reached my hotel, then carried my suitcase and garment bag inside. A bellhop rushed to greet me just inside the lobby and took my things upstairs while I followed along. I had already earned a reputation as a good tipper, so hotel employees were always anxious to assist me.

It had been a tense morning followed by a long drive, so I took a hot shower to relax and unwind. I was so glad the unpleasantness was over. I had been able to think about little else during the past few days. I would miss Billy terribly, but it was time to move on.

◆

After removing my cell phone from the signal-blocking case, I began dressing while it 'checked in' with the service provider. If anyone was tracking me, they might know I was at the hotel in mid-town Manhattan, but not precisely where. There were no messages, so I accessed the directory and called the real estate agent I had been working with before I left for Europe.

"Peggy MacDonald," I heard as the call went through.

"Hi, Peggy, it's Colton James."

"Hi, Colt. How are you? I was so sorry to hear that you and Kathy split up. I thought you were perfect for one another."

"So did I, but Kathy saw it differently— and I understand. She couldn't live with my being an FBI Special Agent."

"A shame."

"Yes," I said in agreement. "Peggy, I'm calling because I still need a condo or co-op. Owing to a recent tragedy, I've revised my requirements. I'm still not looking for Carnegie Hall or the Philharmonic, but I do want a bit of space. Most importantly, it must be very secure."

"I heard about the attack at your apartment."

"I want to make sure that can never happen again. Intruder access from the ground or the roof must be almost impossible, there must be a parking space where my car will be totally secure from tampering, limited elevator access would be helpful, and I must be able to enhance the security measures inside the co-op, such as adding a safe-room if it doesn't already have one."

"What you want comes with a stiff price tag, Colt."

"I have four million cash, and I'm reasonably sure I can get a mortgage."

"Can you afford nineteen million? If you can, I think I have the perfect place for you. It's thirty-five hundred square feet, plus a secure garage, twenty-four-hour high security, and a safe-room built to withstand an assault by a SWAT team. It has five bedrooms and was recently remodeled with all new cabinets, counters, and appliances in the kitchen. The co-op is vacant and in move-in condition. It shares an elevator with just three other apartments, all of which are owned and occupied by people who need the maximum in security. "

"Criminals?"

"No, of course not," she said with a chuckle. "One is a Wall Street banker, one is an actor, and the third is a pro basketball player."

"A Wall Street banker? I thought you said no criminals."

"Colton."

"Okay, I'm sorry. Just joking. Peggy, nineteen million is a lot of money."

"You're getting a lot of real estate, a fantastic view of the Central Park, and a lot of security. You certainly won't have to worry about coming home and finding murderers lying in wait for you in your apartment."

"Any chance the owner would take less?"

"Not much. They've turned down several previous offers."

"How high were the offers?"

"I don't know. I'm not the listing realtor so I haven't seen that information. All I know is that there have been other offers, and those offers were rejected. You're free to make whatever offer you feel is appropriate, and I'm required by law to give it to the listing realtor for presentation to the seller."

"Any other places that possibly meet my needs?"

"I know of a place over in Jersey. It would just be a ferry ride away, but that could mean an hour or more most days."

"No, I want a place here in Manhattan."

"I don't have anything else right now that would meet all of your requirements."

"Okay. When can I take a look?"

"How about tomorrow morning at nine?"

"Give me the address." As I wrote down the information, I was surprised to see that it was only about six blocks from the hotel. I could walk it in fifteen minutes or be there in a cab in less than five. "Okay, Peggy, I'll see you there at nine."

"Have a good night, Colt."

"You too."

◆　◆　◆

Peggy MacDonald was waiting for me when I arrived several minutes before nine the next morning.

"Good morning, Colton," she said as I entered the lobby.

"Hi, Peggy."

"What do you think of the location?"

"It's perfect. It's quite a bit different from the locations you were showing Kathy and me."

"Your price range has jumped up considerably. Back then you were looking for something under what— ten million?"

"Actually five— and I still don't know if I can afford this. I haven't checked with any banks to learn if they'll back a mortgage this high."

"How much did you earn for your last art theft case?"

"Five million."

"And your down payment is only four million?"

"Yes, and that represents my entire home purchase fund accumulated from several cases. Don't forget, the government takes half of everything I earn."

"If your bank doesn't go for it, I'll find someone who will happily extend a mortgage to the famous art recovery expert Colton James. Shall we go take a look before we start worrying about money?"

"Lead on."

"Let's start with the parking garage and end up in the co-op."

"Fine with me."

We walked past five elevators in the central bay before arriving at the one Peggy was looking for. There was no button, just a key lock. She inserted a key and twisted it, then twisted it back and retracted it. About twenty seconds later, the door slid open and we stepped in. Peggy used the same key inside the elevator.

"You said only four co-ops share this elevator?"

"Yes— and no," she replied as she pushed the key into one of five key slots. "Let me explain. What I meant is that there are only four co-ops on the eleventh floor. This elevator can stop at any of the floors from eleven to sixteen."

"So the elevator is shared with twenty-four co-ops?"

"Your key, like all of the others, will be authorized for just one floor. All keys only work for the one floor where their co-op is located, the lobby, and one of the garage levels. If you wish to travel to any of the other five floors, you have to use that phone," she said, pointing to a handset behind a glass door, "to speak to the security guard in the lobby. He'll verify your identity and then direct the elevator to go to the floor you want between eleven and sixteen. To visit any floor other than between eleven and sixteen, you must go to the lobby and take a different elevator, using the phone to have the guard direct your travel in the building."

"Sounds inconvenient."

"You always sacrifice a little convenience for heightened safety and security."

After pressing the B2 button, the elevator began to descend. When the door opened, we were at a garage level. I could see four rows of cars with two drive-through lanes. Peggy led the way out and through the garage. "The garage levels are served by an automobile elevator that takes you up to the street level and by the elevators in the central bay, so it's very secure. The security guard in the lobby can watch all movement through any one of a dozen cameras located down here."

"What about power failures?"

"The building has two enormous emergency power generators like you'd find in hospitals and government buildings, so power for the elevators and common areas such as the lobby and hallways will never be out for more than five seconds while the systems switch over. That means no getting stuck in an elevator unless there was physical damage to the shaft or cars, such as from an earthquake. Additionally, each co-op has from three to five emergency lights connected to that system, depending on the layout. The stoves, like the generators, are all natural gas, so as long as you have matches you still have basic cooking capability if the city suffers a power outage.

"Ah, here we are," she said, pointing to a parking location. "This is the spot owned by the co-op unit. The one next to it is also available for purchase from the same co-op owner."

"I was hoping for a spot with less access by others to eliminate the possibility of someone tampering with my vehicle."

"This garage level is only available to co-op owners whose cars are in here. But if you want more security, you can erect floor-to-ceiling gates around the parking spot, like that spot down at the end of this row. The only requirement is that the front be a roll-up or slide-up so as not to interfere with vehicles traveling in the drive-through passageways on the garage levels."

"I can live with that. Uh, how much is the second spot?"

"One hundred thousand dollars."

I grimaced and said, "Nineteen million and they can't throw that extra spot in?"

Peggy simply shrugged, then said, "This is New York City."

"How long has the co-op been on the market?"

"About four months now, I believe."

"Do you think the owner would cave a little and throw in the second spot? I mean, the co-op has been on the market for quite a while."

"We could try, if you want to submit an offer."

"Let's go look at the co-op."

When we exited the elevator on the eleventh floor, only five sets of double doors could be seen in the hallway.

"As you can see," Peggy said, "only four co-op doorways are accessible in this corridor. The fifth set of doors is a freight elevator. The doors are similar in design to the co-op doors so they don't look out of place. You must make arrangements with the guard station in the lobby to use that elevator, because a guard must operate the elevator for all deliveries or removals. There are two cameras in the hallway, in addition to the two cameras in each elevator. Each co-op can access those four feeds using the closed-circuit monitor inside the unit, in addition to the main camera over the security guard station in the lobby. And each co-op has a camera built into the left-side door instead of having one of the old peepholes.

"There's also a tiny mic and speaker so you can talk to someone at the door without opening it." Walking to the set of doors marked 1102, she stood in front of the left door and said her name. I heard a click, and the door opened automatically. "You get a real key for backup in case the computer fails."

The co-op was gorgeous. I knew that it should be for nineteen million, and it didn't disappoint. It had high ceilings and an open design for the main living room, kitchen, and dining room. Each of the five bedrooms had its own private bath, but the bath in the master bedroom rivaled the best I'd ever seen in hotels, private homes, or real estate listings. The master bedroom also contained two walk-in closets that were each as large as the entire bedroom in my former apartment.

The safe-room was about twelve by twelve, and the four-inch-thick steel entrance door looked like something out of a bank. It was motorized and slid almost noiselessly out of, or back into, its pocket in less than five seconds.

"I love it, Peggy. If I can get the mortgage, I'll take it— if the owner throws in the extra parking space. Unless there's something you haven't told me."

"Such as?"

"I don't know. Are there any liens on the property, or any reason why I can't move in as soon as we close? You know what I mean— those little bad news items that sometimes crop up just after the customer gets excited."

"Nope. No bad news, Colton. If you can get the financing, you can move in as soon as everything is settled and you've completed whatever remodeling construction you have in mind. Oh, wait a minute, there is one thing you have to know. Your purchase must be approved by the co-op association."

"Okay, Peggy. I'll sign the purchase agreement with the provision that the deal is subject to my securing the necessary financing, as well as co-op association approval."

"Wonderful. Let's go to my office and we can take care of all the paperwork."

When I returned to my hotel several hours later, I was nineteen million poorer, but happier, and excited about my new home. Now all I had to do was come up with an additional fifteen million dollars.

◆

"This is Colton James," I said into my phone. "Is Mr. Fodor available?"

"One moment, Mr. James. I'll see if he can be disturbed."

About twenty seconds later I heard, "Colton. Congratulations on recovering the artwork in Europe. How are you?"

"Good morning, Mr. Fodor."

"I think we know each other well enough to use first names, Colton. Call me Saul. What can I do for you today?"

"I need money, Saul. I was wondering if you might know of anyone seeking the services of a currently unemployed art recovery expert."

"You need money? Did the Europeans stiff you?"

"No, no, not at all. They paid me promptly. But I need a new place to live. My old apartment was trashed and was never very secure."

"I read about that attack. I'm glad you survived."

"Unfortunately, my best friend wasn't as lucky. Anyway, I've found a very secure apartment on the Upper East Side, but I don't have enough to buy it, and I haven't yet even given the government their half of the five million I just earned in Europe."

"So how much do you need?"

"Fifteen million."

"Are you free for lunch?"

"Uh, yes."

"Good, meet me at my club at noon."

"Okay."

"I'll see you then, Colton."

"Okay, Saul."

◆   ◆

When I told the person who greeted me at Fodor's club who I was there to see, he immediately led the way to Fodor's table. Saul was sipping from a brandy snifter as we arrived, but he put the glass down and stood up. As he extended his hand, he said, "Hello, Colton. You're looking very prosperous for someone who needs fifteen million dollars."

The first time we'd met I was wearing an inexpensive off-the-rack suit from a midtown men's store. I smiled and said, "You know what they say— you can't borrow fifteen million from a bank unless you don't *really* need money. But in this instance I do. I was hoping to wait until I had all the money I needed before I bought a home, but the attack proved I can't wait any longer. I guess I've made a few enemies."

As a waiter came to the table, Fodor said, "Let's sit down. The chef's special dish today is King Crab cakes. I recommend it. Do you want a drink?"

To the waiter I said, "I'd like a double Scotch on the rocks. And I'll have the King Crab cakes special."

The waiter bowed slightly and said, "Very good, sir," then turned and left.

"Tell me about the co-op you want to buy, Colton."

I gave him the address, then added, "It's highly secure and even has a safe-room. The parking spot is in a secure underground garage. The thirty-five-hundred-square-foot co-op has recently been remodeled and has five bedrooms with private baths. That's about it, except it makes my old place look like a mining-town hovel."

"It sounds nice. Is fifteen million enough? What about closing costs and furnishings?"

"I think I have that covered. It'll be close, but I'll get by until I earn some more recovery money."

"Don't cut yourself short. Go for sixteen million. It'll give you some breathing room until you get everything organized."

"I don't even know if a bank will loan me the fifteen million I *must* have."

"I doubt that's a problem. I have a proposition for you."

"A proposition?"

"Insurance companies have a lot of cash flow. We're always looking for solid investments. We don't usually get involved in the housing market on such a small scale, but we could make an exception for an employee."

"An employee? Me?"

"Well, not exactly an employee. I once offered to put you on retainer. You'll earn two hundred thousand annually, plus receive ten percent of insured value of any items you recover. However, you must be available immediately when I call. And in addition to the annual retainer fee, I'll see that you receive a mortgage of sixteen million on your new co-op, which will remain in effect for as long as you're on retainer."

I took a deep breath, exhaled, and then took a sip of the drink the waiter had just brought over. It could take me months to get an answer regarding the mortgage from a bank, and there was no guarantee I'd get an approval. Fodor was practically laying it in my lap.

"Okay, Saul, with one caveat."

"Which is?"

"I'll make myself available to you immediately no matter what private case I might be working. But— if I'm in the middle of something for the FBI, other than a cold case, the government case takes priority."

"How many active FBI investigations have you been involved with?"

"None to date. I was hired to help clear up their cold case files. Everything so far has been a case so cold it wouldn't suffer if I postponed it for a while. But they've reserved the right to call me into an active investigation. I'm speculating I might one day be called to do something that might involve national security."

Fodor nodded. "Done. You drop everything else and immediately take on our case *unless* the FBI has assigned you to an active case where your involvement can't be delayed."

Fodor extended his hand across the table and I shook it, sealing the deal informally. I was sure paperwork would follow— a lot of paperwork.

"Are you ready to go back to work while the co-op purchase moves towards closing?" Fodor asked.

"I have a few more things to wrap up, then I'll be ready to go to work. I need to arrange for an office in midtown and such. That will probably take about a week."

"I'll help spread the word for you. I'm sure a lot of companies will be anxious to hire someone of your remarkable recovery accomplishments, even though I don't know of anyone at the moment."

"I appreciate it, Saul. And I appreciate your holding the mortgage on my new home."

"We'll naturally have to inspect the property before final approval can be given, but considering the address I'm confident that's just a formality." Raising his glass, he said, "I'm delighted to have you on retainer."

As I raised my glass and nodded before taking a sip, our dinners were brought to the table. The crab cakes smelled heavenly.

◆ ◆

After leaving Fodor's club, I called Peggy MacDonald and informed her that I had secured tentative funding approval for the co-op, subject to an inspection of the property. She told me the list realtor had spoken to the owner and my offer had been accepted, including the extra parking space for the nineteen million, but it still had to be approved by the co-op association. With the attack on my apartment having been front page news, I hoped there wouldn't be a problem.

My next task was to organize my recovery business, and I expected that to take from several days to several weeks.

I had originally thought to rent a small office in midtown and hire a couple of part-time people to screen calls, but on reflection I decided against that. It wasn't that I had any reservations about using real people for screening calls. Although my background was as an IT specialist, I personally hated automated call-handling systems because by their very nature they were cold and impersonal. It was so much more satisfying for a caller to hear a real person on the other end of the line.

Most of the companies using automated systems for screening or routing were those that either had a virtual monopoly in their field, such as government or public utilities, or those that were so concerned with the bottom line on the spreadsheet that they unwisely chose to ignore maintaining good customer relations. However, it was different in my case. After the attack at my apartment, I felt that having real people screening calls might place them in potential danger from people who wanted to get at *me*. So, as much as I hated having my calls screened by a computer, I decided it was the best way to go.

I managed to find inexpensive office space in mid-town, a minor miracle in itself. Actually, it wasn't much more than a large closet and didn't even have a suite number on the door, but I never intended to spend any time there, and it did give me a mailing address in mid-town. Then I arranged for two telephone lines and an internet connection. I next made arrangements with a friend from my IT days to install a computer with a sophisticated call-answering system.

Once installed, the computer system could be reprogrammed remotely, further reducing my need to ever visit my 'office.' When calls came in, a message would inform the caller that I only accepted cases where the misplaced or stolen item had a value of one million dollars or greater. Hopefully, that would discourage recovery requests from people looking for lost pets or a date. After my first recovery, I had been so inundated with trivial calls that I'd had to change my phone number. If the caller hadn't terminated the call by the time the message completed, the system would invite the caller to leave a message for a callback. If the caller was a previous customer, such as Fodor, the call could be immediately routed to whatever number I established, such as to my cell phone or home phone if a special five-digit code was punched in after the answering machine message started.

It took eight workdays for the telephone company to install the lines and assign the numbers, but once that was done I visited a print shop and arranged for business cards. I went for quality all the way with the business cards because I wanted to impress anyone to whom I gave the card. I selected the finest card stock and told the printer that the cards had to be perfect in every way. On the front of the card it simply said 'Restorations and Recoveries' in fancy script. On the back it had my name and the phone number at my midtown office.

Although my background was IT, and I was certainly capable of creating a website, I went with a professional web designer I knew. She did an incredible job, and after seeing the site, I knew *I* would certainly hire me.

Now all I needed was a caseload and the ability to solve the cases.

CHAPTER FOUR

Despite having a conditional pre-approval from Fodor, it still took a month to get the official approval from the insurance company. There was the usual requisite property search to ensure the deed was free of any liens or encumbrances and a complete inspection of the premises so no structural problems or code violations would endanger the mortgage loan value.

To my surprise and genuine delight, the co-op association immediately and unanimously approved my purchase. I feared that one or more property owners might object to having a neighbor with a reputation for killing people, even if my 'kills' had been strictly limited to murderous criminals trying to take my life at the time. Peggy MacDonald, who had attended the meeting, said they understood why someone in my position needed a high-security home and would actually feel safer having an armed FBI Special Agent living on the premises.

The security guards were all required to wear loaded sidearms while on duty, but it was doubtful that anyone else in the building owned a handgun. People who could afford to spend nineteen million on a home often had armed body-guards for their own protection. They live on a different plane of reality than the 'little people,' unless someone had been lucky enough to win the lottery— or find a gizmo.

When all the approvals were set, I got a call from Fodor's office that the paperwork was ready and they would host the closing as soon as a mutually acceptable time could be arranged among all parties.

◆　◆　◆

Two days later we gathered at the insurance company offices downtown to oversee the property transfer. My personal attorney and I sat on one side of a long conference table, while Peggy MacDonald, representing both myself and the realtor who had listed the property, and an attorney representing the seller, sat across from us. Several attorneys from the insurance company sat towards the head of the table, while two insurance company clerks sat at the opposite end.

The first document to be signed was the agreement with Fodor that required me, throughout the life of the mortgage, to respond immediately when called to investigate any theft of property on which the company held the policy. I would receive the agreed upon annual retainer fee plus ten percent of the policy amount if I was instrumental in the successful recovery of the stolen property, and I could cancel the agreement at any time with ninety days' notice and payment in full of the outstanding mortgage balance.

The caveat I had insisted upon regarding a pressing FBI case was detailed in the document. I had previously informed my attorney as to the terms I expected and, while I read a copy, he examined the document to ensure it didn't exceed my understanding of what was required of me. He was satisfied, so I didn't let my confusion over some of the legal terminology stop me from signing.

Then there was a flurry of papers as I signed away my life. The clerks, who I learned were there in the capacity of notary publics, stamped and signed as witnesses wherever required. The exchanged checks were filled with enough zeros to make anyone's head spin.

When I left the insurance company offices, I was carrying a new set of keys— and the burden of sixteen million dollars in debt. I couldn't stop thinking that, in real terms, I had to earn at least thirty-two million dollars *before taxes* in order to pay off the loan.

◆　◆

The keys to the co-op and the elevator had been changed by building security as soon as the previous owner accepted my offer so that any keys in the possession of realtors or the previous owners or tenants were now useless.

As nice as my stay at the hotel had been with its room service and housekeeping services, I was anxious to once again sleep in my own place, so my first stop after heading uptown was the new co-op. As I entered the lobby, the guard at the desk looked at me curiously. I held up the new keys and said, "Colton James. Eleven-oh-two."

The guard punched the numbers into the computer and said, "Yes, sir. I need to see ID and take your photo."

When I showed him my FBI ID, his eyes widened a bit. I was sure there weren't very many FBI Special Agents buying nineteen million dollar co-ops in the building. He told me where I should stand so the mounted camera could capture my image, then snapped the photo.

"Okay, Special Agent James, you're all set. Once the guards on duty recognize you, you won't be bothered as you come and go. Until then, just tell them your co-op number and they'll be able to instantly confirm your residency by pulling up your photo from the computer. To initiate the voice recognition system, just insert the key into your door and turn it to the left, not the right. The system will ask you to identify yourself. Once it has an acceptable voice print, it will tell you to remove the key. When you do, the door will then open on your vocal command. Welcome to Cyprus Towers."

"Thank you."

I walked to the elevator Peggy and I had used and was soon at my new front door. After inserting the key and turning it to the left, it took three attempts before the system had an acceptable voice print. I didn't know if there was problem or if it simply required several attempts for verification. Anyway, when I removed the key and said my name, the door unlocked and popped opened about an inch.

After stepping inside and closing the door, I removed a small notebook from my pocket and began to detail the renovations I wanted to make. The first thing I intended to do was beef up the security at the front entrance. I was glad

Fodor had added the extra million to the mortgage amount because I wanted to expand and improve security within the co-op. My most important renovation would be to create a security vestibule just inside the front door. I intended that the second door could not be opened until the corridor door was closed. That would prevent more than two people from entering at a time, unless the control was temporarily over-ridden from inside the apartment. And once in the vestibule with the front door closed, no one was getting out unless they were authorized to be there. Next, I intended to have a contractor check the walls common to the hallway and other apartments. If they were just gypsum board, I would be adding materials that prevented anyone from breaking through with anything short of explosives.

I would also need to protect my two parking spots by installing fencing and a gate. It was okay if people could see my cars, but I intended to prevent any tampering with bugs or explosives. Lastly, I would have a security expert sweep the apartment for bugs, then install whatever security measures were necessary to help keep it secure. I also had to make sure that the safe-room didn't completely block electronic signals when the vault door was closed. A simple wired relay to outside could accomplish that.

I knew some people might think I was paranoid, but I had already experienced enough to know that adequate security measures, while seeming a bit too extreme to people whose lives were seldom in danger, were a real necessity. I might be in danger when I left the building, but I wanted to feel completely secure when I was at home.

◆ ◆ ◆

Just when it began to seem like the work would never be completed, it was. Everything seemed to come together all at once, and the workmen were finally gone. I had never let them start making noise before nine a.m., and they had to stop by six p.m., but I wondered how long it would be before my new neighbors forgave me. I don't know how much of the noise had carried to the other co-ops, but it had been excessively noisy in my place.

The co-op looked remarkably similar to the way it had looked before the work started except for the new vestibule, but it was far more secure than before. The vestibule required handprint verification to open the inner door, and the surrounding walls beneath the sheetrock were covered with two layers of three-eighths-inch-thick plates of steel welded together to provide a nearly impenetrable barrier, as were all interior walls common to the corridor and neighboring co-ops. My two parking areas were now protected from tampering by stainless-steel fencing and a similar roll-down gate. Between the steel bars were panes of bullet proof glass. People would be able to see my cars but find it difficult to slip even a sheet of paper into the area where they were parked. I'd had my security expert check my apartment for tracking and eavesdropping bugs after the workmen had finished the remodeling work, but he found nothing.

For the first time since returning from Europe, I felt completely confident that no one could attack me while I was home and that no one was spying on me. The newly installed eavesdropping safeguards in the co-op should alert me if anyone tried.

Entering the safe-room, I closed the two wooden doors that provided visual privacy when the vault door was open. So far, the only furniture in the room was a small table and an office chair.

Removing my lighter from my pocket, I flipped up the cover. With my thumb and forefinger, I gripped the perforated guard on top where the flame was normally produced, then pulled upward while slightly pressing on the raised icon of a Bald Eagle with outstretched wings on the front side.

As I pulled gently but firmly, the insides of the lighter came free. Attached beneath a small felt pad saturated with lighter fluid was a metal box with a protective cover. Setting the outside of the lighter down on the table, I used a fingernail to gently pry open the cover of the box so I could remove a tightly folded piece of paper that had a slight silver sheen. As I took it in my left hand and set the rest of the lighter down with my right, the paper started to open. And as I placed it against the wall, it assumed its full 8.5" by 11" shape, perfectly flat and without a hint of wrinkles.

Billy's selfless act of bravery to ensure the gizmo didn't fall into the wrong hands had saved my life. As he lay dying, I couldn't tell him that the piece of paper he'd flushed down the toilet was only a decoy. After arranging with the owner of the second hand shop to alter the lighter, I had visited a stationer's shop in Amsterdam and found some paper that appeared similar in appearance to the gizmo. The paper had originally been intended for use in a special copier released just before Xerox relinquished its hold on the dry, electrostatic toner process. The newly announced copier, a wet toner device invented by a small European firm, had suffered a speedy death, and the special ream of paper had been taking up space in the stationer's shop since the mid 1970s. He was delighted to at last find a customer for it.

He sold it cheap, but I would have paid a premium to get it. Naturally, creases didn't immediately disappear, but the distinctive silvery sheen was amazingly close to that of the gizmo. The package of paper was now in my suitcase. I had to remember to pick up some pocket stick matches so I would have another decoy if Delcona's men managed to jump me again.

Now that events in my life were settling down, it was time to get back to work. Following the violence at my old apartment I had decided not use the gizmo until I was absolutely sure no one could be watching. Although it was unlikely that my room at the hotel had been bugged in any way, I wanted to be virtually one hundred percent sure before I removed the gizmo from its special hiding place. While in Amsterdam, I had wondered what the owner of the secondhand shop thought I might be smuggling in the lighter. Since the drug problem was so acute there, he might have thought I intended to use the space for a private stash of narcotics.

I had considered taking a leave of absence from the FBI to deal with the Delcona issue but then decided against it. My association with the Bureau could prove invaluable as I turned my attention towards the mob boss. But if I didn't produce some results in the cold case investigations, my employment at the Bureau might be terminated. I had been given two new assignments before I accepted the art recovery job in Europe, and after doing some basic research into both, I had decided to concentrate on the serial killer investigation first. I hadn't begun efforts in earnest on the second case— a bank robbery with a kidnapping— before deciding to accept the extremely lucrative case in Amsterdam, so I refreshed my memory now while printing out the entire case file.

As the printer poured out a steady stream of paper, I activated the gizmo for the first time since leaving Amsterdam. Before I even started on the bank robbery case, I watched the ceremony at the graveside and tagged the two men who looked out of place. Then I moved to the cemetery parking lot and noted their car's license plate. I would run it later. I jumped ahead by six hours and found them lounging at a house as they enjoyed what appeared to be alcoholic beverages. Moving the gizmo image out of the house after recording the GPS address, I raised the image up one hundred feet. There was no mistaking the New York City skyline in the distance as seen from Staten Island. It confirmed my belief that Delcona was having me watched, but that things were still too hot for him to make another try for the gizmo at this time.

Billy's unexpected arrival at the apartment had probably confused the two thugs he'd sent for the first try and completely upset their plans as well as their belief they could jump me and hustle me out of the apartment with little trouble. If Delcona made another move now while the New Jersey State Police VOCC North, NYPD, the New York State Police BCI, and the FBI were watching him, he'd probably spend the next several years sitting in courtrooms, even if he wasn't eventually convicted. The question now had to be— how soon would he feel secure enough to come at me again?

After I had read through the entire cold case bank robbery file, I watched the theft and kidnapping firsthand, tagging the perpetrators in anticipation for tracking them to the present and learning their identities. The robbery was like so many others. Armed gunmen burst into the bank, corralled the customers and bank employees in one area, grabbed cash from the vault, and left. What was different in this case was that they took a hostage and warned the customers and employees that if the police were called during the next ten minutes they would never see the young female teller again. But they didn't strike anyone or threaten anyone else. The kidnapping victim was released unharmed and unmolested a few hours after the robbery, which had been my reason for working the serial killer case first.

The thieves had stormed in so fast and taken the employees by such complete surprise that no one had activated the silent alarm. The robbers wore full masks and clothing that completely concealed their identities, so none of the witnesses could even speculate on the race of the robbers. But all agreed they were male.

Because the thieves only took used bills, the haul was rather small. The total loss reported by the bank was just over thirty-six thousand dollars. The robbers must have known that the sequential serial numbers of new bills might be traced if any were spent, so they ignored the stacks of new bills.

The subsequent investigation revealed nothing that allowed the authorities to identify the thieves. No witnesses came forward who might have seen the robbers exit the bank, so the police couldn't put out an alert for a particular vehicle. The kidnapped teller later said they had a red getaway car parked on the side of the bank, but that they had pushed her into the trunk before leaving the scene. The driver drove sedately, ostensibly to avoid attracting attention, for about twenty minutes, then stopped. The teller said that when they opened the trunk, one of the robbers held a cloth against her face. She remembered blacking out but nothing after that until she awoke on the shoulder of a back road far outside of town. She said she had never seen any vehicle except the first one.

The police found the abandoned red car ten minutes from the bank, parked next to a large combine in a farmer's field. The local resident who owned the car hadn't even missed it until the police showed up at his house. Tire tracks found near the abandoned car provided some clues to the case. The FBI had been able to learn the brand of tires and estimate the second car's weight and wheelbase, which made them confident they knew the make and model, although not the year. They had also found several footprints, which gave them shoe size, shoe brand, and the approximate weight of the perpetrators.

Unfortunately, the thieves were long gone before the evidence was available to roadblocks checking cars containing three men and a woman hostage. While the information could help in building a case once the robbers were found, it didn't assist in learning their identities or whereabouts. I learned from watching the robbery that the robbers had two other cars stashed a few miles from where they'd left the teller. Once they split up, and without a description of any of the three cars, the roadblocks were totally ineffective.

Using the evidence they'd been able to accumulate, the FBI had tried to match the thieves to perpetrators of other bank robberies, but they hadn't come up with any hits. The investigation was eventually put on the back burner in the hope that better information would be available the next time the same team robbed another bank. But there had been no other robberies they could tie to the same three perps. Finally, the crime was added to the cold cases file.

Although I would be able to determine the identities of the three men who had committed the crime, I had the same problem as on previous cases—namely, explaining how I'd solved the case.

After reviewing the bank's video footage, watching the crime and escape from every angle on the gizmo, and reading the investigation file repeatedly, I could understand why the case was still unsolved. The perps could not be connected with any bank robbery before or since. They only took used bills, and there were no witnesses to their escape. It was well planned and well executed. And they'd had their share of incredible luck.

I finally turned off the gizmo, put it back into the secret compartment in the lighter, and headed for bed. Other than the office chair and small table in the safe-room, my bed was the only new piece of furniture in the co-op. I had gone all out and bought a beautiful new king-sized solid walnut frame and top-of-the-line mattress. It was like floating on a cloud compared to the lumpy old mattress in my former apartment. After spending nineteen million to buy the co-op, I wasn't going to move any of my old furniture, which had been third-hand when I'd gotten it. But I wanted to bring over some of my personal possessions and all of my memorabilia.

I was still paying the rent on my former place and had reimbursed my landlord for all expenses to repair the damage from the shooting. The bathroom was practically brand new since the door, tub, toilet, sink, floor and walls had all been damaged by gunfire. The lease would be up in three months and I had until then to clean out the apartment.

◆ ◆ ◆

Luckily, my new co-op came with all the major kitchen appliances, including a built-in microwave oven. I had purchased a new coffeemaker and toaster oven, or I would have been eating untoasted bread or dry cereal for breakfast while I only dreamed about a steaming cup of coffee. A refrigerator large enough to supply a catering service was filled with all of my favorite foods, so although I had to eat in the safe-room because it contained the only chair and table in the co-op, I was at least able to enjoy OJ, hot coffee, and cereal with real milk. I didn't have any glasses, dishes, pots and pans, or kitchenware yet, so I was getting by with plastic eating utensils, paper cups, and paper plates. The paper bowls, although coated, got soggy quickly so I had to eat fast.

I had finished my bran flakes and was sipping at my coffee while I thought about the bank robbery case when I had an inspiration. The thieves hadn't yet been associated with any similar crime, which would indicate they were first timers. But the escape seemed too well planned for amateurs. So either they or someone else must have cased the bank to determine the best time of day for the robbery and then planned the escape route. The file indicated that the FBI lab analysis of the bank's videos hadn't identified any visitors to the bank over the previous months that had the same basic build and movements as any of the three thieves. So either the teller they kidnapped had been part of the robbery, or a fourth person had been involved.

After I had removed my breakfast dishes, I took out the gizmo and went back to work. I had previously tagged the three thieves, so now I tagged the teller and performed a search to locate any time prior to the robbery where she'd had contact with any of the robbers. The search turned up nothing, which probably meant she wasn't involved. Of course, she could have had contact with a fourth as yet unknown robbery suspect, or perhaps the bank had been cased by a fourth person who didn't participate in any other way. There were no outside cameras, so the previous investigators couldn't look for suspicious people or vehicles watching the bank. But I could. However, it was going to be a time-consuming job, so I decided instead to jump to the present and see where the perps were now and if they still got together. By searching for the latest date where the three perps were together, I found them working on a car in an automotive garage.

The gizmo gave the garage's location coordinates, date, and time. Rather than turning on my laptop to determine the geographic area, I used the gizmo's features to maneuver around the garage. I found a current Charlotte newspaper on a workbench, so they were probably in North Carolina now. I'd verify the specific location coordinates later. As I watched, a fourth man joined the three working on an engine in a racecar. I immediately wondered if the fourth man could have been involved in the robbery. I tagged him, then jumped to the bank where the robbery had taken place.

When I performed a search to learn if the fourth man had ever been in the bank, the gizmo immediately jumped to a time three weeks before the robbery. I watched as the fourth man at the garage entered the bank and stood in line to exchange a ten-dollar bill for a roll of quarters. As he waited, he looked around, stopping his scan at each of the cameras, the location of the vault, and the layout of the desks outside the counter. The only connection the gizmo provided with the kidnapped teller was that she was in the bank while the fourth suspect was casing it. There was no guard on duty at the time and there hadn't been in any of the bank videos I'd viewed.

So I had four suspects for sure now. There might be more, but I would have to spend a lot more time viewing with the gizmo. Instead of starting that, I decided to learn who I was dealing with. Using tags on each of the suspects, I went back to the day each was born and read the names off their birth certificate. They all had the same last name and parents.

"So this was a family affair," I muttered. "I guess the family that does stickups together, sticks together."

Knowing who had committed the robbery was a good first step, but I knew I couldn't go to Brigman yet. The first thing he'd say in that unpleasantly gruff voice of his would be, "How did you come up with this completely asinine theory, James?"

I had no answer for that yet. In fact I didn't even have the remotest idea how I could respond to such an interrogative. Without the gizmo, I would have no more idea about the identity of the perps than the dozens of law enforcement personnel who had worked to solve the robbery case before it was assigned to me.

There was nothing to do except start with the brother who cased the bank and watch every movement until I found a link I could exploit to show that I had solved the case with good old-fashioned police work.

◆ ◆ ◆

After a week of searching for something I could use to wrap up the case, I was still no closer to a solution. I had spent hours reading and rereading every page of the FBI file until the sheets were dog-eared. When I finally headed for bed at night, my eyes were bloodshot from having spent so much of the day staring at gizmo images. There just wasn't anything I could use to explain how I had solved the case. It was easier with the insurance companies because their main interest was in recovering whatever had been stolen. If I managed to provide them with evidence that proved the identities and guilt of the thieves, it was a bonus.

But Brigman wouldn't simply accept that I had solved the FBI cold case without knowing how I had found what everyone else had missed. I was beginning to think I wouldn't be able to report this one as solved. The one good aspect was that by devoting all of my attention to the robbery, I was able to forget about Delcona for most of the day.

CHAPTER FIVE

After two more days of fruitless searching for the clue I needed, I decided a road trip was called for. So, before retiring for the evening I arranged for a limo to the airport, plane reservations to Texas, and a rental car when I arrived. I had expected all along that I would have to put in some time at the scene of the crime and interview the people involved, but I was hoping it would be in support of my crime resolution hypothesis rather than searching for the hypothesis itself.

♦ ♦ ♦

I checked into a national chain hotel immediately following my arrival. It was Sunday, so I watched a little TV as I thought about the case, then fell asleep thinking about Delcona.

♦ ♦

Before heading to the bank in the morning, I stopped at the local police headquarters to alert them I was in town and was looking into the cold case. I wanted to avoid any incidents like the confrontation with police at my last bank robbery investigation. I showed my ID and spoke to the lieutenant in charge because the police chief was not available.

"Welcome to our community, Special Agent James," Lieutenant Finn said. "Say, are you the FBI special agent who was attacked in his home a few months ago?"

"Uh, yeah. That was me. You heard about that down here?"

"Yeah. Congratulations on surviving the attack. After we heard about it, we scheduled another training session for our guys about home invasion by perps intent on revenge following an arrest."

"Yes, it's something every law enforcement officer has to keep uppermost in his or her mind. Criminals hold a grudge and are always anxious to *get even.*"

"Are there any new leads in the bank robbery case?"

"Not yet. I'm here to see if I can find something we can pursue. Do you have ideas as to who might have committed the robbery?"

Finn paused for a couple of seconds before saying, "A witness believes they might not be Texans."

"How did they arrive at that?"

"At a dance recently, I was talking with a couple of the bank employees. One— Samantha Hutton— mentioned that we should be looking in Kentucky. When I asked why, she said the leader had sort of a Kentucky accent."

"I never read that in the official report."

"She said she didn't realize it at the time. She went to the last Kentucky Derby and got into a conversation with a couple of ladies there who were talking about the entries. She engaged them in conversation because their accents were very similar to one she'd heard at the bank on the day of the robbery. Eventually she asked them where they were from, and they told her they had both grown up near Sparta, Kentucky. She has an incredible ear for accents and told me how close their accent was to that of the bank robber who'd done all the talking."

"There wasn't any audio on the bank's videos, so we can't confirm that," I said.

"Yeah, I know. According to Samantha, two of the robbers said almost nothing. They just grunted a couple of times. But the leader said enough for Sam to note his accent, although she didn't recognize it as being Kentuckian at the time. She naturally knew it was Southern but couldn't quite place it with a more definitive location because his accent seemed to have traces of numerous South-eastern states. But

when she heard those women talking at the Derby, she knew
he had to have come from that same area while he was
growing up."

"That's interesting. Any other ideas, Lieutenant Finn?"

"No, that's all." Shaking his head slightly, he said, "These
guys were pros."

"What makes you say that?"

"They were in and out and left no trace. No fingerprints,
no stray human hairs, no nothing."

"It's possible they're professional criminals. But they've
never pulled another bank job, as far as we know."

"Perhaps they were picked up for another crime and have
been incarcerated."

"That's always a possibility. If that's the case, we want to
find them before they get out and resume their life of crime.
Well, I guess I'd better get to work before the bank closes.
That's going to be my next stop. Thanks for your insights,
Lieutenant. I'll check back with you before I leave town. Nice
meeting you."

"Likewise, Special Agent James. I hope you can find
something that's been overlooked. Good luck."

"Thanks, Lieutenant."

As I drove towards the bank, I thought about the new
evidence. If I could spin it right, it might give me the opening
I needed to identify the perps. *No*, I thought, *it's still too slim.*

The bank, like so many these days, was located in an open
strip mall, but it was a standalone building near the edge of
the property. On one side was a teller's window for drive-up
convenience, while the other side was windowless and used
for parking.

It reminded me of the first bank robbery I'd investigated
because the street behind the bank was just open land. Not
that a few eyewitness neighbors here would necessarily have
been able to add anything that wasn't already known.

After scouting the area around the bank and matching the surroundings with what I'd seen in the gizmo, I entered the bank. Along the right side was a standard bank-style, chest-high counter with teller-access openings about five feet apart, so I headed to the left where four office-style desks were located. The woman at the first desk smiled and said, "Can I help you, sir?"

I took out my ID and showed it to her as I said, "I'd like to see the branch manager or whoever is in charge today."

"One moment, please." She picked up the phone, pressed a button, then said, "Mrs. Newberry, there's an FBI man here, and he'd like to see you."

The woman nodded and then put the receiver down. Looking up at me, she said, "Mrs. Newberry is with a depositor. If you'll have seat, she'll be with you in a few minutes." She gestured towards a small informal seating area with four comfortable chairs.

As I sat down to wait, I scanned the bank and checked out the staff and the customers waiting in line. The most dangerous-looking customer was a man of about sixty, wearing stained and worn bib-overall jeans and ankle high boots caked with something that looked like mud at first. I pegged him as a pig farmer.

"Are you the FBI man?" I heard from a few feet to my left. I looked up and saw an attractive woman of about forty-five. She was wearing a grey, two-piece business suit with slacks.

As I stood up and moved closer to her, I extended my hand and said, "Special Agent Colton James, Mrs. Newberry."

She took my hand and shook it lightly, then said "And how can I help the FBI today?"

"I'm investigating the robbery that you folks had awhile back."

"And how can I help?"

"I was wondering if you might have remembered any-thing you perhaps overlooked during your past interviews."

"No, nothing I'm aware of."

"And your staff?"

"No one's mentioned remembering anything that wasn't reported during their interviews."

"I see. Would it be possible to speak privately with Samantha Hutton?"

"Samantha? Why?"

"Just part of my follow-up investigation. Is she here today?"

"You don't know what she looks like?"

"I've never met her. Is there a reason why I shouldn't speak with her?"

"Uh, no. You just caught me off guard."

"Is she here?"

"Yes."

"Is there a place where we can speak in private?"

"We have a small conference room in the rear just past my office."

"That would be perfect. Would you send her in, please?" Without waiting further, I headed for the rear of the bank and turned into the room just past the one that said 'Mrs. Newberry – Branch Manger' on the door. I took a seat at the conference table and waited.

Several minutes later a woman of about twenty-six entered the room. She bore a striking resemblance to Mrs. Newberry but was dressed a little less formally in a brown skirt and thin beige sweater that left little to the imagination. I stood up and extended my hand. "Mrs. Hutton?"

"Miss Hutton."

"I'm Colton James of the FBI."

"Yes, I heard. I'm a bit surprised that you asked to see me. I wasn't the woman who was kidnapped."

"I know. That was Sherri Mondel. Shall we sit down?"

She nodded.

"The reason I wanted to speak with you," I said after we had taken our seats, "was because of a conversation I had with Lieutenant Finn. He told me you had new information that hadn't come out during your past interviews."

"You mean about the accent of one of the robbers?"

"Exactly."

"And you came all the way down here from New York to ask me about that?"

"Who says I came from New York?"

"You. Your accent gives you away."

"The FBI has offices all over the U.S., and special agents can be posted to any of them."

"So you're not from New York?"

"Can we get back to the robber's accent?"

"Of course. Sorry."

"Please tell me what you know about it."

"There's not very much, really. I mean, I don't *know* very much. It's really just something that occurred to me while I was at the recent Kentucky Derby. I overheard a couple of ladies speaking about the race and was intrigued by their accents because they reminded me of the way the robber spoke. So I joined their conversation, and, during a lull, I asked them where they came from. They said they were both from Sparta, Kentucky. That's all there is to it. I can't prove the robber was from Sparta, but the speech pattern of the women reminded me so much of his."

"I see. What was different about the way he talked? Was it unusual phrasing? Or was it just his pronunciations, emphasis, or drawl?"

"He didn't say anything unusual. He ordered us all into the center of the room, and everyone was in such shock that no one hit the silent alarm. I'm just as guilty as everyone else.

I don't think there's been a bank holdup around here during my lifetime."

"So he didn't say anything unusual, such as the kind of hyperbolic gangster talk we all hear in the movies?"

"No, they just grabbed all the used bills from the vault and prepared to leave. After they grabbed Sherri, the leader warned us not to call the police or hit the alarm for at least ten minutes. Then he said, 'Let's go,' to the others and they hurried out."

"Okay. Thank you, Miss Hutton."

"Wait a minute. Now that I think about it, he didn't say, 'Let's go.' He said, 'Let's draft.'"

"Let's *draft*? You're sure? Could it have been 'let's drift?'"

"No, I'm sure he said, 'Let's draft.' Until I began replaying it in my mind just now, I didn't realize it. I guess I was still pretty shaken up right after the robbery."

"That's common. It had to have been an emotionally draining experience. That's why we perform several follow-up investigations. Thank you, Miss Hutton. And for the record, I did come down here from New York, but it was as part of the continuing investigation. I just learned of your new information an hour ago when I spoke to Lieutenant Finn."

"I only told Bobby about that a couple of weeks ago. And I *knew* you were from New York. But I— don't think you were born there."

"Right again. I attended college there and stayed. It's my adopted hometown now."

"I knew it. But you *were* raised within— a hundred miles?"

"Yes, I was." I smiled and said, "You have a sharp ear that matches your sharp intellect. May I ask you a question about *your* heritage now?"

"Of course."

"Are you related to Mrs. Newberry?"

"She's my oldest sister."

"I see."

"We do look a lot alike."

"Yes, you do." Standing up, I said, "Thank you for your cooperation and information, Miss Hutton."

"Samantha. Or Sam," she said as she stood up and moved around to where I was standing.

I smiled and said, "Thank you, Sam."

"Um, are you going to be in town for a while?" she asked as she moved even closer.

"Not long. Maybe a couple of days."

"If you're still here on Friday and you like to dance, I recommend the Hitching Post."

"Uh, thank you. I'll remember."

"I hope to see you there, Colton."

"I can't promise anything. It depends on how my investigation goes."

"I hope it goes slow."

I smiled but didn't say anything. She smiled again, then turned and left the room, leaving the powerful scent of her perfume wafting in the air.

Mrs. Newberry was at the door before I could leave. "Is everything okay?" she asked.

"Fine, Mrs. Newberry. Thank you for your cooperation and for that of your staff."

"Was Samantha helpful?"

"She was very cooperative. Whether her information is helpful or not remains to be seen. But every small piece of data we collect helps us put the case together."

"What did she say?"

"She said you're her older sister."

"What's that got to do with the robbery?"

"Not a thing. Now, if you'll excuse me, I have other visits to make."

I understood Mrs. Newberry's interest. Perhaps she felt that her sister was under investigation and, as the older sister, was probably acting in a protective capacity. But it was up to Sam to tell her what we discussed, or not.

◆　◆

I visited each of the locations where the cars were swapped and where Sherri Mondel was left, asleep, in the grass on the side of the road. As expected, I saw nothing that would help me advance the investigation. The grass was still ripped up a bit from all the law enforcement vehicles that had converged on that spot, but the original tracks were long gone.

◆　◆

I picked up some takeout on the way back to my hotel and sat down to eat after cleaning up and taking a hot shower. The food was still warm but barely edible. I wondered if my taste buds were changing since I'd begun eating quality food, or if my palate was simply becoming too discriminating for takeout from a greasy spoon diner. Since my college days I'd been able to eat virtually anything served up as food. I ate as much as I could tolerate, then tossed the rest in the waste basket and lay down on the bed to think. If I spent much more time on the road I was going to lose weight.

The expression 'let's draft' was helpful. Drafting was a racing term that referred to the slipstreaming process where one or more cars followed directly behind another car to cut down wind resistance and used the slight vacuum created behind a lead vehicle, therefore improving fuel economy during a race and increasing the time between fueling stops. It was also used in bicycle racing, speed skating, and a few other such racing sports but was far more often associated with car racing.

Unfortunately, I still had no way to tie the four men to the bank robbery. I needed something else, and I didn't think I was going to get it here. I thought about Sam— her young, lovely body, and the subtle invitation. It was a shame I couldn't find an excuse to stay around town for a while and perhaps learn if she was as approachable as she appeared, but I had important things to take care of in New York, and I couldn't allow myself to get distracted. Perhaps after I had finished my business on Staten Island I could return for a follow-up visit.

Before turning in, I made reservations on a flight to Cincinnati and arranged for a rental car. This would be my first trip to Cinci, but I didn't have time for sightseeing or anything else right now.

◆　◆

I stopped at the police headquarters to say goodbye to Lieutenant Finn after checking out of the hotel in the morning.

"Leaving so soon?" he asked.

"Yes, I've completed my tasks here. Thanks for the tip about Samantha Hutton and the robber's accent. I'm going to Sparta, Kentucky next. It's a fairly small community, and I don't hold much hope I'll learn anything there, but you never know."

"Good luck, Special Agent James."

"Thanks, Lieutenant."

◆　◆

I turned in my rental car at the airport, then got in line at the metal detection/x-ray station. When it was my turn, I held up my FBI wallet and opened it. The TSA person came around the metal detector and looked at my ID, then at my face, then back at the ID.

"Just step around the metal detector, Special Agent James," he said.

I nodded, walked around the metal detector stall, and continued on to my gate where I sat down to wait for my flight.

◆　◆　◆

I exited the highway near Sparta when I saw the signs for the Kentucky Speedway. There was a Ramada Inn there by the intersection with the Sparta Pike, but I didn't check in because I didn't know how long I would be in the area.

My electronic road atlas instructed me to follow the signs for Highway 35, and a couple of minutes later I entered the town of Sparta. Then, about ten seconds later, I crossed over railroad tracks and saw only open country ahead. I assumed I had left Sparta, so I turned around and went back. I didn't mean to disparage the community. It looked like a nice place to live. It was just a lot smaller than I'd expected, and I hadn't begun with high expectations. The actual township boundaries might have included a large land mass, but my reference was to what would normally be considered the business district.

There was a small convenience store there, and I was feeling thirsty, so I stopped in to get a soft drink. The owner was apparently a racing fan, and he had a lot of images and memorabilia decorating the wall behind the counter. As I scanned the pictures, one of the images jumped out at me. It was one of the perps from the bank robbery.

"That fella there in the center picture looks familiar," I said in a sort of southern drawl. I knew Samantha Hutton would never be fooled for an instant, but I hoped the store manager didn't have as keen an ear.

"That there's Jimmy Cotton. He's our local hero. He's made it into the Sprint Cup top twenty-five drivers this year. We expect to see him go all the way over the next few years. Just a couple of years ago it looked like he was out of it forever."

"Really? What happened? Bad accident?"

"No. Money troubles. He hadn't been able to line up any decent sponsorships, and he blew his only two engines a couple of months before the qualifying rounds here. Racing engines are damn expensive, and he didn't have the money to buy replacements. He and his brothers disappeared, and we figured they were gone for good. Then a couple of days before the qualifying race, they showed up with two brand new engines. Said they went to Vegas and ran a hundred dollars into thirty-five thou. Anyway, he qualified, and then came in ninth. It was enough to get him some serious sponsor money, and he was on his way to the big time. He's one gutsy driver, and we know that one of these days he'll make it to the top."

"He still live around here?"

"His folks still live here, and the boys come to visit once in a while, but he and his brothers live down in Charlotte now. That is, when they're not on the road."

I finished off my soft drink and said, "Thanks. I hope they make it to the top." Then I turned and left the store.

Before starting the car and heading towards Interstate 71 and Cincinnati, I thought about what I had just learned and hoped I had the lead I needed. I could easily get the date of the qualifying race from the internet. If that tied in with the bank robbery, I had the motive. If I could learn where he had purchased the two engines, I might be able to prove they had paid cash. Once I spelled out all the connections, it should be enough of an evidence trail to suit Brigman.

It's true that without the gizmo, I never would have known what the perps looked like. And if I hadn't known what the driver looked like, I probably wouldn't have struck up the revealing conversation with the store manager. Knowing that the perps were in Charlotte also helped me confirm that I had the right people. But I believed I could convince everyone that I had done it all with brilliant deduction.

CHAPTER SIX

W hen I reached Cincinnati, I had to decide whether to stay in town for the night or head home. New York won out, so I drove straight to the airport and turned in my rental car.

◆ ◆ ◆

As I entered the lobby of my building, the guard on duty was one I didn't recognize. He looked legit, so I said, "Colton James eleven-oh-two."

He punched the apartment number into the computer, looked at the monitor, then looked up at me before saying, "Okay, Special Agent James. Welcome back."

I pulled up short and said, "What?"

"I said welcome back."

"How do you know I've been gone?"

Looking at his computer monitor, he said, "The computer has you using the elevator Sunday, and this is the first record of you being in the building again. And your key hasn't been used in the elevator system or your front door."

"I had no idea you recorded all that information. I thought the system was only to verify my identity."

"The system is really sophisticated and collects a lot of data. It's all intended to give our co-op owners the maximum in protection."

"I see. Thanks. Good night."

"Good night, sir."

As I rode up in the elevator, I was a bit dismayed by what I'd just heard. We all know it's getting increasingly difficult to maintain a low profile these days. Every retailer and online internet site was collecting, assembling, and storing as much information about us as possible, not to mention the social sites that also kept track of our relatives and friends. They knew what we bought, when and how often we bought it, how much we spent, where we shopped, what sites we visited on the internet, and what data we searched for. They could even track our every movement using the GPS feature in our cell phones. The government collected telephone conversations without our permission and could even listen to conversations when they were conducted within earshot of a cell phone that had been turned off. The only way to stop that was to remove the battery and wait until the internal power system lost its charge, or keep it in a secure metal container, as I do. And now, SMART TVs and cable system boxes could literally watch us and listen to conversations in our homes, all without our permission. The millions of video cameras that were mounted everywhere were being used to capture criminals in the act and identify perpetrators, but they could also be used for less legitimate purposes.

Of course, I have the near-ultimate snoop device. My gizmo can go anywhere and see anything, and the subject would never have a clue they were being observed. The ultimate would be if the gizmo could pick up conversations. But if it could, I hadn't figured out how to activate that feature. Even so, it really had become a world without secrets.

I had to admit it was nice coming home and knowing no one was lying in wait for me in the darkness of my co-op. All of the exterior regular glass in my unit had been swapped out as part of my renovations, so my home was now as bullet-proof as the White House. And the double-layer, welded, heavy-duty steel plating that completely covered the inside surfaces of the walls along the corridor, as well as the walls common to other co-ops, made them bulletproof as well.

But no visitor should ever realize that because sheetrock had been glued to the steel and then painted. The walls looked exactly like the wall construction seen in most homes, except my construction couldn't pass the knuckle test. Normally, a hollow sound was heard when a sheet-rocked wall was thumped, except when encountering a wall stud. Lastly, my safe-room could withstand a rocket barrage.

The lights came on in the vestibule as I opened my front door. Although the building security people could get into the vestibule, they'd never get beyond the inside door with less than an hour's effort and a whole lot of construction equipment. The steel door was sheathed in wood to make it appear like an ordinary, albeit highly decorative entrance door, but it was anything but. As the exterior door closed and locked, I pressed my hand against the palm-print sensor to unlock the inside door. For security reasons, I had chosen not to have the inside lights come on automatically. If someone did manage to get the interior door open and I was in the apartment, the invader would be backlit while I was in darkness.

As I reached over and waved my hand in front of the switch, the interior lights came on, highlighting the starkness of the bare rooms. It dismayed me a bit. I had to shop for some furniture now that I had wrapped up the bank robbery case.

I pulled my wheeled suitcase to my bedroom and emptied it, with my dirty laundry going into the hamper and my shaving kit going into the bathroom. After hanging up my suits, I put the now empty suitcase in my walk-in closet. The suitcase and clothes stood out prominently in the otherwise starkness of the enormous closet.

Although it was late I wanted a shower, so I stripped down and stood in the spray, savoring the steaming hot water until I felt weariness overtaking me. I'd read recently that some so-called experts were now suggesting that people not bathe or shower daily. Perhaps their advice was related to the severe drought currently being experienced on the West Coast and they were more interested in conserving water than out of any concern for health. I'd always been told that cleanliness was next to godliness. Regardless of their motives, I didn't shower as often as I did out of an obsessive desire to be clean as much as the sheer pleasure I derived from the simple act.

After quickly shampooing my hair, I lathered and washed my body. I was yawning practically non-stop as I stepped out and began drying myself off. The clean sheets felt wonderful against my bare skin. I'd intended to write my report tonight, but I just didn't have the energy.

"Oh, hell," I murmured. "I'll worry about finishing the report to Brigman in the morning."

With that, I closed my eyes and was lost in sleep almost immediately.

◆ ◆

After a quick breakfast and several cups of coffee in the morning, I headed to the temporary office in my safe-room. I didn't expect to use the gizmo, but the office would give me the visual privacy I wanted if I did. Despite all the security in the building, I had decided not to use the gizmo in my apartment following an absence until I had performed a full security sweep. This time I had only been gone for a couple of days, but it paid to play it safe.

The dates of the bank robbery and the qualifying NASCAR race matched up perfectly. I was sure the robbery had been perpetrated to get the money for the two racecar engines. Deciding I needed to use the gizmo after all, I got out my security equipment and performed a sweep of my office. When it proved to be clean, I used the gizmo to learn where the Cotton brothers had purchased the car engines.

Once I had that information, I searched the internet for the small company that had sold them the engines. They had a website, and they even mentioned on it that the Cotton brothers had been successful at the Kentucky Speedway after purchasing two of their engines. Knowing what little I did about NASCAR racing, I was surprised the Cotton brothers had been able to get two high-performance engines for the amount taken from the bank. Perhaps they had some other cash available, or perhaps someone owed them a favor.

"Well, not my affair," I said aloud as I began writing up the report.

An hour later I was finished. I had done my best to show the evidence trail I had followed and carefully documented the places where speculation and deductive reasoning replaced clear evidence. I then logged into the FBI via the secure system and filed the report.

I might be called downtown to waste another hour sitting outside Brigman's office, but I figured I should have plenty of time to devote to Delcona for a while. Even if Brigman immediately assigned me two more cases, I could delay starting work on those without worrying they were going to terminate my employment.

I was still wearing just a bathrobe, so I decided to shave, shower, and dress before I completed the security sweep and started work on my vendetta project.

◆ ◆

An hour later, I was back at my desk and ready to start work, but I was interrupted by the doorbell. My senses were instantly on full alert. No one should be able to get to the eleventh floor unless I authorized the security guard to send them up. Unless— it was someone from one of the three neighboring co-ops. I decided to play it safe and retrieved my service weapon from the bedroom.

As I activated the wall-mounted security monitor just outside the entrance to the kitchen that allowed me to view the entire eleventh floor hallway, the sight that filled the screen made my heart skip a beat and caused my throat to constrict, preventing me from breathing for a few seconds. I immediately felt dizzy and had the sensation I might be dreaming, but there on my monitor was Mia Kosarros, the most beautiful woman to ever share my bed, and probably the most beautiful woman I'd ever known. And she was here, standing just outside my door! Wearing a silky white blouse over a grey pencil skirt, she was, as always, a vision of loveliness.

She carried a coat over her right arm and held a designer handbag in her left. I had once told her I loved high heels on women, and since then I'd never seen her wear heels that added less than five inches to her substantial height. Standing five eleven in her stocking feet, her skyscraper heels had always let her win out over my six-foot-two height and added to the Greek goddess impression that left most men, including me, panting.

I could see the entire hallway, so I knew she was alone, unless there were others standing just inside the front doors of my 'neighbors' co-ops, ready to charge the door of my co-op when I opened it. Well, that was why I had built the vestibule, after all. I also checked the camera feeds from the elevator and saw it was empty.

It wasn't fear of an attack by Delcona's men that made me hesitate to open the door. It was because I had thought the chapter of my life that included Mia had been permanently closed. But I hadn't properly said goodbye when I left Amsterdam, so I guessed I owed her something. I took several deep breaths and tried to compose myself.

As I pushed the button that would unlock and open the door, I watched the hallway near my 'neighbors' doors. No one charged out any of those co-ops as the front door of my unit opened, and then it was too late because my front door was closed and locked.

I took a deep breath and opened the vestibule door, prepared for whatever came— I thought.

I was wrong.

As soon as the door opened, Mia dropped her purse and coat and leaped at me. She wrapped her arms around my neck, and before I was able to even open my mouth in surprise, she had planted at least three kisses on my cheeks.

"My darling," she uttered as she took a brief break, "I'm so happy you're okay. When I learned about those awful men attacking you as you arrived home, I took the next plane to America."

"That was many weeks ago," I managed to utter.

"You are a hard man to find. I've been looking for you ever since then. After you disappeared from Amsterdam so quickly, I told my uncle's investigators to find you. It was they who reported the attack on you. But then they couldn't find any trace of you. None of your former neighbors knew how to locate you, and the FBI wouldn't tell them where you'd gone. They finally located you when the deed to this apartment was recorded in your name and the information was available on the internet. Why did you leave Amsterdam without saying good-bye, my dearest?"

"I sent a note and flowers."

"Yes, but a note and flowers are hardly the same thing as a goodbye in person. And why did you even have to leave? I thought we would have some time together once you solved your case."

I took a deep breath. I was going to have to tell her, as much as I didn't want to. She would never let the issue drop if I didn't. "I left to give you privacy with that other man."

"Other man?"

"The one with the tiny moustache and the scar on his cheek."

Mia's mouth opened, but she didn't say anything right away. And she didn't relax her hold on my neck. Finally, she asked, in a slightly husky voice, "How do you know about him?" Then she got indignant, released me, and took a step backwards. "Were you spying on me?"

It was the kind of response I expected. Many people, when caught with their hand in the cookie jar, would instinctively go on the offensive.

I didn't answer right away. I couldn't tell her about the gizmo, so I decided to be ambiguous. "I'm a policeman, remember? I see things, hear things, and deduce things. Less than two days after telling me I was your one, true love, your Prince Charming, you went to bed with another man. How was I to feel? I decided the best thing to do was leave forever."

"Did one of my bodyguards tell you Marcus was there overnight? Is that how you learned?"

"Is that his name? Marcus? It doesn't matter. All that matters is that it happened."

"Do you know who he is?"

"You said his name is Marcus. What more do I need to know?"

"That he was my husband."

That shut me up, although my jaw dropped open slightly. All I could do was stare at her. Since meeting her, I had believed she was unmarried. The reason was simple— she had *told* me she was unmarried. This was reinforced by the fact that she wore no wedding ring.

"Don't look at me like that, darling. Haven't you ever made a mistake?"

When I found my voice again, I said, "I've made my share of mistakes, but I've never before slept with a married woman. And I've never had one tell me I was the love of her life."

"I'm not married."

"What? I don't understand. You just said Marcus is your husband. Are you trying to say you don't love him anymore?"

"It's complicated."

"Then perhaps it's best if you don't explain. I left quickly so we wouldn't have this awkward moment. I hoped to only have happy memories of our brief time together."

"I don't love Marcus. I'm not sure I ever did."

"Yet you married him?"

Mia looked downward, sighed, then said remorsefully, "I was young; a silly girl and very lonely. Fearing for my safety, my uncle had kept me almost totally isolated on Thasos after my parents died. I met Marcus while shopping in Athens and he seemed so exciting. He told me wonderful stories about all the places I had always wanted to visit but not been allowed to. So I disobeyed my uncle, snuck away from my body-guards, and began dating for the first time in my life.

"Marcus took me to parties and introduced me to people. We traveled together and enjoyed all the pleasures life has to offer. He seemed so smart, so strong, so worldly, and one day he told me he loved me. I thought I was in love too. I never suspected that he only wanted my money. Fortunately, my uncle wouldn't let me marry him without an ironclad pre-nuptial agreement. Marcus agreed, believing he could get my fortune some other way once we were wed."

"Why didn't you divorce him?"

"I did."

"But you said a couple of minutes ago that he was your husband. Did you remarry?"

"No, we're still divorced. I said he *was* my husband. He showed up at the hotel the day after you left to conclude your business. The bodyguard on my door called to say Marcus was in the corridor, on the floor, crying like a young school-boy who had been hurt. I said to let him in. When Marcus got to where I was standing, he fell to his knees in front of me. He told me he was deep in debt and begged me to give him some money or some very bad people were going to kill him. I felt so sorry for him. Even though I don't love him anymore, he managed to seduce me and we wound up in bed."

"Even though you don't *love* him?"

"I *don't* love him," she said angrily, then softened her voice and said, "but I don't hate him either. Is that so hard to understand? I once thought he was so worldly, but I've learn-ed he is like a little boy. And like Peter Pan, I don't think he'll ever grow up. I gave him the money he asked for, but I told him that was the end of it. I told him to never ask again, because all I would do next time was cover his funeral and burial expenses."

"When did you divorce?"

"Two years ago, next month. We met at a lawyer's office in Athens. I gave the lawyer a check for a million Euros to cover all the expenses of the divorce, with the remainder going to Marcus as a sort of settlement. Then we signed the papers and it was over. Since both parties were agreeing to it without contest, all the lawyer had to do was file the documents."

"Why don't you simply tell your security people to turn Marcus away and not contact you?"

"I have. But when the one on my door called to tell me Marcus was lying on the carpet, weeping, my heart overrode my good sense."

"And you're never going to see him again?"

"Never. I promise." Mia moved in close to me and put her arms around my neck again. I didn't try to stop her. I knew I didn't want to stop her. "I only want to see *you* every morning when I wake up for the rest of my life."

"And if I have to go away on business?"

"I will count the seconds until you return, but I will not share our bed with anyone else."

At that moment I felt a bit foolish. I was swallowing everything she said. I realized it was because I *wanted* to swallow it. I really *had* fallen in love with her the first day we met, and I'd been crushed when I saw her in bed with Marcus. But I wanted to believe now with all my heart that she was being truthful. She must have seen it in my eyes because she smiled and began kissing my face. I resisted as long as I could, then pushed her away slightly so I could align my lips with hers before leaning towards her for a kiss that lasted at least an hour. Okay, it didn't last an hour— but it lasted at least a full minute.

When we parted, I asked, "How did you get up here? Security isn't supposed to let anyone through unless the tenant authorizes it."

"I told the security man that I was your fiancée and that I had just arrived from Europe. I told him it was a surprise. He didn't want to let me through, but I begged him not to ruin the surprise. He finally said he would let me go up in the elevator, but he couldn't let me into the apartment. He also made me take off my coat, then checked it and my purse for weapons. He waved one of those airport wands all around me and finally let me go but made my security people stay in the lobby. I told them to return to their hotel if I didn't come back down within a half-hour. Your security man said he'd be watching me in the elevator and in the hallway when I got to the eleventh floor. Colton, the security here is very tight."

"That was one of the main reasons I chose this co-op. Uh, where are you staying?"

"Here— with you. But it looks like you're moving out. Where have you sent your furniture, my darling?"

"I just had a lot of remodeling done, so I haven't furnished the new apartment yet. All I have is some kitchen stuff and a bed."

"A bed and a little food is all we need," she said with a giggle. "Show me your home, darling."

I gave Mia a quick tour of the co-op— quick because there was nothing to see except empty rooms. I saved the master bedroom for last.

"I wasn't expecting company, so the bed isn't made," I said as we entered the room.

"Oh, Colton, it is all so wonderful. I love the view of the park, and there is so much potential for the apartment. I will help you furnish it and make it into a real home. But first, let me see how comfortable the bed is."

She took my hand and gently pulled me towards the bed. I didn't resist. We sat on the edge for a few seconds, then she giggled and lay back. As I looked down at her, memories of our lovemaking in Amsterdam came flooding back into my conscious mind. My existence had been pretty hollow of late, having lost my best friend. And I'd been so consumed with thoughts of vengeance against the people who killed Billy and Morris, I hadn't even accepted what I believed was an invitation for a sexual encounter with the lovely Samantha Hutton. I had only wanted to get the bank robbery case wrapped up so I could concentrate on Delcona.

I lay down next to Mia, expecting to talk, but she turned towards me and was suddenly on top of me. We didn't do much talking during the hour that followed.

◆　◆　◆

When I awoke, Mia was sleeping peacefully next to me. I managed to sidle out from under her arm without waking her so I could walk to the bathroom and take a hot shower. Mia always managed to arouse passions in me like no other woman ever had. I wasn't claiming to be a great lover, but a modestly handsome, six-foot-two college football player normally had quite a few opportunities to sample the pleasures found in the bedrooms of co-eds, and I'd never squandered my opportunities.

Since college, my love life had been a bit dismal. Working in IT meant that most of my work hours were scheduled for times when everyone else was out partying and enjoying life. Then, after the big corporate meltdown at my place of employment, I didn't have money to enjoy life. Lately, I'd had the money but not the opportunity. And now that the opportunity was presenting itself, I had a conflict between the mission I'd established for myself and enjoyment of the life I'd been working towards.

I stayed in the hot spray until my fingertips began to wrinkle, then dried off and headed to the kitchen to brew a fresh pot of coffee. When it was ready, I took two cups plus sugar and creamer to the bedroom. Mia was still in the position she'd been in when I'd gone to take a shower. I lifted her arm and moved it to her side, then put one of the cups near her nose to see if it would have any effect. When her eyes fluttered, I knew the aroma was working.

"That smells heavenly," she mumbled.

"You'll have to sit up if you want any."

"I don't know if I can. You wore me out."

"This was the first time I've had sex since Amsterdam. I had a lot of pent-up energy."

"It's my first time also— except for the times with things that run on batteries."

"I don't run on batteries, but I'm recharging as we speak."

She looked up at me and smiled. "Then I'd better have some coffee if I want to be ready."

◆ ◆

"Hungry?" I asked about six hours later.

"Starving."

"Let's get dressed and go out. I know a great little restaurant a few blocks from here. It's nothing like the club you took me to in Amsterdam, but the food is always good."

"I know of a few places here that serve only five-star meals."

"In New York City?"

"Is it so unexpected that you can get such food in New York?"

"No, not that. It's just unexpected that you know of them."

"I've traveled extensively in the United States, darling. I can take you to the best restaurants in New York, Chicago, Washington, D.C., Miami, New Orleans, and L.A."

"Okay. Let's go."

"I can't go like this. No shoes, no service is standard. But what do they say about totally naked women?"

"If they're smart, and the naked women look like you, they just sit back and admire the view."

"I think I would feel a little self conscious."

"Okay, I'll give you time to dress."

"I can't wear what I wore coming here."

"Why not? You looked lovely."

"I have to call my security team and have them bring some clothes over from my hotel."

"Okay. But I thought you were hungry."

"I am. But it won't take long." Looking over at the window and seeing that it was still hours from sundown, she said, "It's still early. We have plenty of time."

◆ ◆

About an hour later, the security guard at the desk in the lobby called. "Sir, there's a delivery here for you."

"It's expected. Send it to the eleventh floor, please."

"Yes, sir."

A few minutes later, the doorbell rang. When I checked the monitor, I saw six men in the hallway. All were burdened down with suitcases.

"Mia, were you expecting *six* security people with suitcases?" I hollered towards the master bath.

"Yes, darling. Have them put the cases in the bedroom."

I shrugged and opened the front door, then opened the inside vestibule door so they could just walk through.

As the men entered, they scrutinized my appearance as only security people do. I recognized one of them from Amsterdam. He had been outside the corridor door of Mia's suite in the NH Barbizon Palace the day I left to wrap up the art theft case.

I pointed towards the master suite and they carried the cases into the bedroom. When they reemerged, one asked, "Does Miss Kosarros require anything else?"

"I'll ask."

I walked to the bathroom and knocked gently. "Mia, your people want to know if you need anything else of them."

"Nothing tonight, darling. Tell them they can have the rest of the night off."

I relayed the message, then walked the men to the elevator. After they were inside, I removed my key and the doors closed. They would be taken to the lobby without any opportunity to alter where the car would stop unless they pulled the emergency knob. And if they did that, alarms would sound in the elevator and at the security desk.

◆ ◆

After taking my third shower of the day, I dressed and then spent the next two hours sitting at my safe-room table because it was the only chair in the co-op. The office chair was decidedly more comfortable than sitting on the throne in one of the spare bathrooms. Mia had taken over the master bedroom and bath, and I'd tried to stay out of her way as much as possible.

When Mia finally emerged from the bedroom, she took my breath away. She was beautiful naked, but when decked out in ten thousand dollars of designer clothes and jewelry, her beauty was incomparable. I just stood there staring at her as she walked towards me.

"Is it okay?" she asked.

"Aphrodite would be jealous. And with good reason."

Mia smiled and then pecked at my check when she was close enough. I reached for her and she pulled back.

"Darling, do you want to wait another fifteen minutes while I undo the damage to my makeup?"

"Uh, no. I'm too hungry."

"Then let's go eat." With a smile she added, "We'll play later."

CHAPTER SEVEN

The restaurant Mia had frequented since coming to New York was like the one she took me to in Amsterdam. A person had to be a member to even be aware of its existence. It was located below a high-rise office building in midtown. We walked past a bank of elevators and stopped at a plain wooden door bearing an embossed brass plaque that simply said 'Private.' Mia pressed a doorbell on the wall next to the door, and several seconds later the door opened inwards.

We stepped into an area similar to my vestibule but large enough to accommodate at least four people. Rather than a second door, we were facing an elevator door. Mia pressed her hand against a palm-print sensor and the elevator opened. There were several locks that someone with a key could use to access different levels, but only one button. When Mia depressed the button, the elevator began to sink.

It was impossible to say how far we traveled, but I'd have guessed at least three floors. When we emerged, my first thought was whether the restaurant was safe in the event of fire. I mean, how would we get out if we couldn't use the elevator? I figured I'd been spending too much time lately worrying about personal safety issues. I tried to put the thought out of my head so I could simply enjoy the evening.

Mia spoke to the maître d', who obviously recognized her from her recent visits, and we were escorted to our table.

Unlike the restaurant in Amsterdam, I recognized a number of patrons. There were politicians, sports stars, movie stars, CEOs, and of course, the so-called financial wizards of Wall Street. It was the sort of place where I would expect to find Saul Fodor having dinner with the mayor, governor, or perhaps a senator. I felt like a complete outsider, even if I *had* just purchased a nineteen-million-dollar co-op. At least I was appropriately dressed. My daily wardrobe might not equal that of Saul Fodor, but my eveningwear probably came close these days.

There were no prices anywhere on the menu, and no one seemed to mind, so I held my tongue. The fact that I had been afraid to stop at a fast-food hamburger joint for lunch just a couple of years ago from fear that I'd blow my monthly budget was never far from my mind. The difference between the food I'd struggled to swallow while I was on the road recently and the food in this restaurant was like the difference between a crack in the sidewalk and the Grand Canyon. I hardly had to chew. It just slid deliciously down my throat as it sent my taste buds into overdrive.

The restaurant I'd suggested to Mia served excellent food, but it was a poor cousin compared to this one. My only worry was that I couldn't afford to support Mia and provide for her in the custom to which she was obviously accustomed. I had never bothered to check her net worth because it wasn't important to me, but it had to be substantial from the way she talked about traveling around and patronizing only the finest hotels and restaurants. And her clothing bills alone would probably exceed the gross domestic product of some small countries.

We started off with a bottle of '97 Mascarello Barolo and then launched ourselves into a veal steak dish with caramelized onions that was almost as great as sex with Mia. We followed that with a traditional tiramisu. Chefs had been offering variations of tiramisu for years by substituting one or more ingredients, but the original dessert that had captured everyone's imaginations and taste buds was still the best when prepared by someone who knew what they were doing. And the pastry chef in this private club certainly knew what he or she was doing. I decided I would find out what I had to do to join the elites now that I could probably afford it. As yet, I didn't even know the name of the club.

Following dinner, we talked and danced for a while. The club reminded me of those lavishly elegant clubs always seen in the early musicals from the 1930s where the 'little people' were never in evidence, except as waiters, bartenders, or bouncers. I have to admit it was an experience to be one of the elite for a change.

When we were ready to leave, Mia signaled to one of the waiters. He brought the bill and she started to sign it.

"My treat tonight, dear," I said as I reached for my wallet.

"Not tonight, darling. They don't accept cash or credit cards."

"What forms of payment do they accept?"

"At the end of the month, a statement is sent to the member or their representative. Mine go to my attorneys, who pay all my bills. That way I never have to carry large amounts of cash or even credit cards, and I'm less of a target for thieves."

"I see."

After she had signed the bill and the waiter had left, she said, "Shall we go, darling? I'm ready to let you mess up my makeup."

◆　◆　◆

"We need some furniture," Mia said the following morning as we enjoyed our coffee. "I'd like to have a place to sit other than in bed."

"I've kinda been enjoying sitting in bed since you arrived."

"That's only because we spend so little time actually *sitting*."

I chuckled and said, "Yeah, you're right."

"I'm going to redecorate the entire apartment. We'll start today."

"Today?"

"The sooner we begin, the sooner the apartment will be a home instead of just an empty shell where you come to sleep."

"How long do you think it'll take?"

"Weeks. Maybe even months. Of course, we never really finish decorating our homes. We must always add or change as time passes and styles and tastes change."

"Months? I can't spend months decorating the apartment. I have to work."

"Just leave it to me, darling. I'll take care of everything."

"New York is too dangerous. I can't let you run around alone."

"I won't be alone. I'll have my security people to protect me when you're not around. You just concentrate on doing whatever you have to do, and I'll take care of everything else."

"Uh, okay. Just one thing. The small room I'm using as an office is off-limits. I don't want anybody coming in to measure or plan or anything else. My work involves reading and preparing highly confidential materials. I'm going to lock the doors to that room."

"Of course, darling. Your office is strictly off-limits. I promise."

◆ ◆ ◆

I had been ecstatic when my remodeling was finished and the workmen were gone, but as Mia began decorating the co-op, the place was once again alive with workers making a mess throughout the day. There were decorators, painters, furniture salespeople, accessories salespeople, movers, and numerous others in the apartment throughout the day. I had taken Mia down to the security desk so she could have her picture taken and be listed as an occupant of the co-op. Then I helped her set up the voice recognition so the front door would open on her verbal command and registered her handprint so she could open the inside door. Lastly, I showed her how to operate all of the video systems so she could check on visitors before they were inside the apartment. Mia's security people were always there to protect her during the day, so I stayed locked in my office so I could accomplish as much as possible.

Just after the work began, Brigman sent me a note to report to the office.

◆ ◆

For the first time I didn't regret sitting outside Brigman's office for an hour. It was wonderful to get away from all the noise and commotion for a while.

"How did you come up with this lame-brain idea, James?" Brigman asked when I was finally called into his office and I approached his desk. He always called my ideas foolish, absurd, or crazy, but every one of them had closed an open case. The same three people who had been present every time I visited Brigman's office were there today.

"I documented everything, sir. The facts fit my theory perfectly when you take the hard evidence and throw in my speculation. The filed reports speculate that the thieves were pros because the robbery seemed so practiced, the actions so well coordinated, and there was absolutely no dissention or even discussion among the thieves. I submit that it went so smoothly because the thieves were brothers, used to working together as a close knit group on a daily basis."

"You're saying these four brothers perpetrated the bank robbery to buy a couple of *car engines*?" the lone woman asked.

"High-performance racecar engines are extremely expensive, and you don't have a chance of winning a major NASCAR event if you don't have one under the hood. And you always need a backup."

"And you got onto this path simply because a teller said the leader of the robbery had a unique accent?" one of the men asked.

"It was all I had to work with, so I performed a follow-up. Then I learned about the four brothers when I visited their hometown and spent some time talking to a clerk in a small local convenience store."

"It's thin," the other man said.

"It's imaginative," the woman said.

"It's all we've got," the first man said. "Does anyone feel we should forget this theory?"

No one suggested they not investigate the four brothers.

"Okay," Brigman said. "I'll assign a couple of *real* special agents to look into it. Here're your next two assignments, James. That's all."

I slipped the paper containing the two case numbers into my wallet and left.

As I headed uptown, I smiled. I would now have months before I had to produce another case solution. I could begin my work on the Delcona problem without worrying about being terminated by the Bureau.

◆ ◆

The co-op was a frenzy of activity when I arrived. Entering from the inner vestibule door, the view was an open-concept panorama of the main living room, kitchen, and formal dining area. There were people in each area, painting, measuring, or holding fabrics up for Mia and her decorator to approve or disapprove. Two of her security people were there as well.

As I walked in, Mia hurried over and kissed me, then pulled me into the main living room to look at some fabric. I nodded and said 'nice' or 'very nice' several times if it seemed like something she liked. When I was allowed to leave, she kissed me and turned back to discuss something with her decorator. I headed immediately for my office before I was subjected to a new round of opinions.

When I bought the co-op, the steel door of the safe-room could only be activated from inside. I'd had it changed so I could open or close it from outside with a tiny controller like the fobs used for car alarm activation or deactivation. If the door was closed using the switch inside, the fob wouldn't operate it. Since Mia had arrived, the steel door was always closed when I wasn't in the room. When I was using the room, I only closed the two wooden doors for privacy, but I locked the doors to make sure no one entered while I was using the gizmo. I knew the safe-room was secure from snooping, but once the workpeople were all finished and gone, I would perform a full security sweep of the apartment.

Since leaving FBI Headquarters, the only thing on my mind had been Delcona. I was finally free to implement my plan for revenge. But as I sat down, I saw the message light blinking on my answering machine.

The machine recorded messages forwarded by the computer system in my downtown office. Although my website was operational, no one had yet attempted to hire me to recover anything. And the only other way someone would have my number was if they were given it by Fodor. Of course, the call could be from one of those damned annoying telemarketer systems that simply dialed every number in sequence. I had long ago instituted a personal policy with telemarketers, to wit, I would never buy anything, ever, from a telemarketer, because it only encouraged them to keep calling people at random. If everyone, everywhere, stopped buying from telemarketers, we might finally be able to enjoy our dinnertimes in peace.

I pressed the button on the machine and sat back to listen to the message. The call was from an insurance executive who identified himself as Charles Schiller. He said he'd been referred by Saul. It wasn't an art theft this time but an automobile theft. A collector had arrived home from a business trip ten months ago to find his most prized antique car missing from the special building he'd built to house his collection next to his home in Maryland.

The 1957 Ferrari 250 Testa Rossa, of which only twenty-two had been produced, was insured for thirty-two million dollars. My jaw dropped when I heard the amount. The insurance company had just six weeks left before they had to pay the claim. The caller had left both his office number and his cell number.

I really wanted to begin work on my special project because I knew it was only going to be a matter of time before Delcona made an attempt to acquire the gizmo again. I was surprised he hadn't tried already, but I supposed the investigations into Morris's death and the attack at my apartment were still forcing him to keep his head down.

His home was no doubt still under twenty-four seven surveillance by either the New York State Police or the FBI. I knew I was going to have to be extra careful to avoid detection when I made my first move. But I also needed to start paying down the mortgage on the new co-op, and a million six after taxes for recovering the Ferrari would sure sweeten my depleted bank account. I sighed and went online to pick up some quick information about the vehicle.

A Ferrari from that year and series had reportedly been sold in the U.K. for an estimated thirty-nine million dollars. It was a private deal, so the amount hadn't been publicly released but reportedly came from well-placed sources. I decided to put my private project on the back burner and called the Hartford, Connecticut number left by the caller.

A receptionist answered the phone, and when I identified myself, she asked me to hold while she put the call through. A couple of seconds later, Charles Schiller answered the phone with, "Mr. James. Thank you for returning my call. I doubt there's an insurance executive in the industry who hasn't heard of your successes, but you're a hard man to locate. I was fortunate that Saul Fodor had your phone number. Do you think you can help us?"

"Mr. Schiller, it's been more than ten months since the theft. That car is probably overseas, sitting in some Russian oil tycoon's collection. These days, stolen cars that aren't chopped up for parts are usually out of the country within days."

"We realize that. But if it's been shipped overseas and we can learn who has it, we can begin to put international pressure on them to return it. But we won't know what we can do until we know who has it."

"Okay. What's the recovery fee?"

"We're offering the standard ten percent."

"That would have been acceptable nine months ago, but now you're asking me to drop everything else and work this case because you have to pay off on the policy in six weeks. The international implication means this could be a lot more complex and a lot messier than domestic theft cases."

"Saul said you'd probably require more than the standard recovery fee. He mentioned they paid you two million for the recovery of the Merchendes Collection, which had an insured value of eleven million dollars, because they were just thirty days away from having to pay the claim. The Ferrari was insured for almost three times the artwork, so my Board of Directors has approved six million *if* you can recover the car before we have to pay the insured."

"And if I locate the car in a foreign country that ignores international laws pertaining to stolen vehicles?"

"We'll still pay the original ten-percent fee of three point two million dollars if you can provide irrefutable proof that the car is where you say it is. There's a clause in the policy that allows us to postpone paying the insured for an additional six months if we can prove we know where the vehicle is. The six months is to allow us time to recover it."

"Okay, Mr. Schiller. I'll need a complete copy of everything in your files regarding the investigation to date. I'll also need a letter from you detailing our recovery fee agreement. If the perpetrators are out of the country, I can't promise they'll ever be arrested. And even if they're still here, I can't promise arrests, but I'll identify them for you."

I gave Schiller my address so he could send the files and required letter and told him I'd get back to him as soon as I had something.

"I forgot to mention that the Board requires weekly reports," he said.

"Then give them weekly reports."

"No, I mean they require weekly reports from you."

"I'm sorry, but the only report I make is when the case is solved. I'm an independent businessman, not an employee of your company, and I don't take orders from your Board of Directors. If such a requirement is included in the letter you'll be sending, you can spare yourself the effort because I won't be taking on the case. I don't do progress reports, but I'll notify you as soon as I have something to report."

"I'm afraid the Board was insistent. They're concerned because of the limited time remaining before the claim has to be paid."

"If I take on this case, you'll know exactly where the vehicle is before the claim has to be paid. That's the best I can promise."

Schiller hesitated for a few seconds. He was over a barrel but knew I had the best reputation in the business for solving cold cases. "Okay, Mr. James. I'll take care of the Board— somehow. And I'll have the materials and the letter on the way in an hour."

"I should also have a letter of introduction to the insured party so I can examine the crime scene."

"I'll include that as well."

"I look forward to receiving everything. This case will get my immediate and full attention until it's solved."

◆ ◆

Three hours later I received a call from the guard in the lobby that there was a delivery for me. The delivery person wouldn't leave it unless it had been signed for by me.

I put on my jacket to hide my service weapon and went down to the lobby. A young woman was standing at the desk.

"Are you delivering a package from Charles Schiller?" I asked.

"Yes, sir, Mr. James. He sent me down by helicopter so you'd have it as soon as possible. It was my first helicopter ride."

I smiled, signed for the box, and thanked the young woman.

"It's my pleasure, Mr. James," she said with a smile. "We flipped a coin to see who would get to deliver the box. I won."

I didn't know what to say, so I simply smiled at her again.

"Uh, could I get your signature?"

"I just signed for the package."

"No, I mean as an autograph."

"An autograph?"

"You're famous in Hartford— at least among people in the insurance industry. We started a pool today for how long it will take you to find the missing car. Do you have any idea yet?"

I signed the small notepad she extended towards me as I said, "Not yet, but I'll do my best."

"We're rooting for you, Mr. James."

"Thanks. Uh, what's your name?"

"O'Neil. Susan O'Neil."

"Have a safe trip back to Hartford, Susan."

As I rode the elevator back to the eleventh floor I had to smile. I had my first groupie. A recovery expert groupie?"

◆ ◆

The previous investigators had done their best, and I couldn't spot any holes in their efforts. The crooks were just too good. They had disabled two very sophisticated alarm systems and made a clean getaway without hurting anyone. And without even having the crime discovered until the owner returned home from his business trip.

After reading through all the materials sent to me and verifying that the recovery fee letter agreed with our telephone conversation, I set up the gizmo and solved the case. If only it was that easy with the FBI cases, but they were focused more on prosecuting the criminals than recovering stolen goods.

Time was short, so I made reservations for the following morning to fly to Maryland. It was a brief flight lasting less than an hour, and I would pick up a rental car when I arrived. I didn't make hotel reservations because I would only be there for a few hours. With my plans made, I contacted the car owner and told him who I was and when I'd be there.

He agreed to meet with me. If he hadn't, I would just have walked around the storage garage and left. I only wanted to get a better feel for the layout and kill a day as well. My biggest problem each time was making it look like I was as smart as— or smarter than— all the great fictional detectives in literature or the movies. And that was always a stretch.

Mia was already in bed when I entered the bedroom. She was looking through magazines, seeking inspiration for decorating the co-op.

"All finished for the night, darling?" she asked as I stripped off my clothes and slipped into bed.

"Yep. I have to go out of town tomorrow. I should only be gone for one day. I might even be back tomorrow night. I don't know yet."

She dropped the magazines onto the floor and rolled over to me. "You're going to leave me all alone?" she said as she rubbed my chest with her hand while rubbing my left leg with hers.

"Not for long. It's for the new case I mentioned."

"The stolen car?"

"That's the one."

"Just one day?"

"That's what I expect. And I don't want you sneaking away from your security people while I'm gone. And whenever there are workpeople in the co-op, I want you to always have at least two of your people here."

"Okay, darling."

"Promise?"

"I promise, darling."

"I'm serious. The people who attacked me at my last apartment might try again."

"I promise, darling. My security people may not be as good as you, but they are all professionals. My uncle would not have hired them if they weren't among the best."

CHAPTER EIGHT

The special garage constructed to house the antique car collection looked more like a museum than a garage. I found it more impressive than a similarly sized segment of the Smithsonian. The car's owner, Jeffrey Thaddeus Bolimer by name, was waiting with another man when I arrived. After shaking hands, he asked to see my ID, so I showed him my FBI ID and badge.

"FBI? I thought you were a private investigator."

"I'm an independent property recovery expert. In between private cases, I help the FBI solve and close their cold cases. I'm sort of a consultant, but they required me to become a Special Agent as part of our work agreement."

"I see— I think. So you're getting paid by the government when you're working for yourself?"

"No, I only get paid by the government for each case I actually solve and close, according to a sliding scale. If I don't solve a case they assign to me, I don't get paid for any of the time spent investigating it. And I'm working this case purely as a private citizen."

"Okay, I see." Pointing to the other man, Bolimer said, "This is Peter Hollingshead. He's my security expert. He set up the two alarm systems."

"Hello, Mr. Hollingshead," I said as I extended my hand.

"Hello, Mr. James. I've heard of you. I sort of expected to see you with a deerstalker hat and one of those fancy pipes with a curved stem and large bowl."

"What?" I said with a smile. "No magnifying glass?"

"I thought we'd see that once we were inside."

"I'm sorry. I'm just an ordinary man."

"Not to hear Charles Schiller talk," Bolimer said. "He told me my car is as good as recovered now."

"I'll do my best. Would you care to give me a tour of the museum, pointing out all of the security measures as we walk?"

"This way, Sherlock," Hollingshead said.

I accepted his remark as a compliment.

◆ ◆

Hollingshead showed how the thieves had bypassed his alarms and praised their ingenuity. He promised that the shortcomings had been corrected and could never be exploited again. The investigative reports I'd read praised his system and expressed genuine surprise anyone had been able to disable it. But that's the way it always seemed to be. Every time someone invented a better mousetrap, the mice got smarter.

"Thank you, gentlemen," I said as we wrapped up the tour. "I see no fault with the alarm system or theft-prevention measures. We just have a slightly more intelligent class of crooks this time around. I'll find your car, Mr. Bolimer."

"I hope so. It's not like I can just run out and buy a replacement. The last one sold allegedly went for over thirty-nine million. If I have to settle for the insurance, I can't afford to get a replacement. I know where there's one available, but the owner wants forty-eight million."

"Incredible," was all I could say in response.

"Yeah. I don't think he'll get it though. At least not for a couple of years. But the way the prices have been climbing, who knows?"

"Thank you for your time, gentlemen. I'm going to do my absolute best to recover the car, Mr. Bolimer, so don't put any nonrefundable deposits down on another car just yet."

◆ ◆

I made it back to the airport in plenty of time to catch my flight. When the announcement came that we were descending into Hartford, I put my tray table up and prepared for the landing.

After picking up my bag and arranging for a rental car, I called Schiller.

"Hello, James," he said when the connection went through. "Any problem with the agreement?"

"None at all, Mr. Schiller. Can you spare me a few minutes for a face to face?"

"Sure. When?"

"Now."

"Now? Like in today?"

"Like in an hour or so. I'm at Bradley International Airport."

"Uh, sure. Whenever you can get here."

"I'll see you within the hour."

◆

When I arrived at Schiller's outer office, I was immediately escorted into his office. Schiller stood up and extended his hand, and I shook it as we exchanged the usual greeting pleasantries. I then sat in the chair he indicated.

"So, to what do I owe this visit?" Schiller asked. "You said the recovery fee agreement is acceptable."

I took a deep breath and said, "Normally, I take my time and wrap up *all* the little details before contacting the insurance company, but we're in a time-imperative situation."

"Yes, we only have six weeks. Less than six weeks now, actually."

"I wasn't referring to the date you're obligated to pay the claim but rather to the opportunity we still have to prevent the car from being shipped overseas. But we must act quickly. I'd much rather receive the six million than the ten percent, and I'm sure you'd rather avoid all the international entanglements involved with trying to get the car returned."

"What are you saying? That you know where the car is? That's impossible. You've only been working the case since yesterday."

I took an envelope from my inside vest pocket and held it out towards Schiller. He looked at me with some skepticism but took it, then opened it and read the brief report.

"Is this a joke?" he asked as he looked up.

"I never joke when there's six million dollars involved."

"But you couldn't *possibly* have located the car since yesterday."

"Why not?"

"Because— because— it's impossible."

"Then, what I think you should do is— call my bluff."

"What do you mean?" Schiller asked.

"Hop over to the airport and fly down to the Port of Savannah in the company jet. Give the shipping-container information I recorded in the letter to the customs people. Ask them to examine that container for illicit cargo. If you leave today, you can have them do that before the container is loaded aboard ship tomorrow."

"You're sure about this?"

"I wouldn't be here now if I wasn't."

"How did you possibly track down the missing car in one day."

"Computers."

"Computers?"

"Once upon a time, I was an IT guru. I lived and breathed computers. Anyway, these days most containers are weighed when they arrive at the shipping terminal. I simply estimated a weight range using the minimum weight of the car and the minimum weight of the shipping container as the base, and then searched all available shipping records in the U.S. looking for containers that fell within a certain range.

"Since it's too late to stop containers that have already completed their journey, I started with the latest recorded shipments and worked backwards to the date of the theft. If a check of the shipper credentials showed the company to be reliable, I skipped them and concentrated on the unknowns. Then I examined the manifests they had filed and their destinations. Anyway, to make a long, boring story short, I came up with a list of possible illegal transports. The weight of the container I identified in the letter is almost precisely what that container should weigh if it had the Ferrari inside. And with all of the other dynamics and requirements factored in, the odds that this container houses the stolen vehicle are ninety-nine-point-nine-nine percent. So, it's the one most likely to contain the car."

"Most likely? You want me to fly down to Georgia on a hunch?"

"A hunch? Why did you come to me, Mr. Schiller?"

"Because— you're reputed to be the best."

"And yet suddenly you doubt me, and call my painstakingly careful and accurate investigative analysis a hunch?"

"You've only been working on this case for one day, James."

"And you feel that no one could possibly solve the case in one day because your people couldn't do it in ten months?"

"No. I mean— yes. You couldn't possibly accomplish in one day what they failed to accomplish in almost a year."

"Very well. I've just put the stolen car into your hands. If you refuse to follow up and recover the car while it's easily within your grasp, I won't be held responsible. I've had customers who were skeptical of my findings, but this is the first time anyone has refused to follow up when I've told them I found the stolen item. I guess there has to be a first time for everything." Standing up, I said, "Well, I'm headed back to New York. Good luck recovering the car once it arrives in China."

"China?"

"That's its destination. Just another one of those dynamics and factors I used in my analysis that you're calling a hunch.

There are a great many nouveau-riche comrades in that country. And the Chinese government has been *remarkably* uncooperative in matters of international law so it's doubtful you'll be able to recover the stolen car within the six month policy payment exception."

"Wait a minute." Schiller stood up and took a turn around his office before saying, "If I go to Savannah and the car isn't in that shipping container, you owe me dinner at the best restaurant in New York City."

"I'll go you one better. Just for going to Savannah and examining the shipping container I've named in the letter, I'll buy you dinner at the best restaurant in New York City."

"Whether I find the car or not?"

"It's the least I can do for someone who is going to be giving me six million dollars this week."

◆ ◆ ◆

The following afternoon I received a call from Schiller. I was working in my safe-room and had shut the vault door in an attempt to block out the noise of the decorating people. It worked, and it was so quiet that I half jumped out of my chair when the phone rang.

"You owe me dinner at the best restaurant in New York City," Schiller said.

"The car wasn't in that container?" I said in complete surprise.

"Yes, it was. You owe me a dinner because I'm the man who is going to be handing over six million dollars."

"A promise is a promise."

"What about the perps?"

"I still have a bit of work to do there, but we've done the most important part by recovering the stolen car. I bet Mr. Bolimer is going to be happy."

"Happy? I naturally couldn't see him through the phone, but I suspect he was dancing on the ceiling of his museum as we talked."

"So everyone is happy. Except the thieves who lost their loot."

"I hope you can identify them before *they* get out of the country."

"I'll do my best."

"Colton, I apologize for doubting you. You *are* the best in the business."

"Thank you, Charles."

"Call me Charlie. Can I call you Colt?"

"Of course."

◆　◆　◆

I had really hated to turn over the car to the insurance company so quickly, but it was absolutely necessary if I was to get the entire six-million-dollar recovery fee. The problem was that people would either start to get suspicious or perhaps expect me to do it every time. And I was sure that when Delcona heard, it would confirm to him that I really did have the gizmo. Of course, any crime I solved would probably have that result, but solving a crime like the car theft in one day would leave no doubt in his mind. And it might provide greater impetus for him to come after the gizmo again, even if he was being watched by law enforcement people.

I spent the next several days matching names to the perps who had stolen the Ferrari and the names of the people with whom they'd had contact just before and just after the theft if I thought they might have some possible connection to the robbery. My final report was complete, as it should be for six million dollars. I couldn't provide any proof the perps had stolen the car, so they couldn't be arrested, but simply identifying them as suspects might make practicing their chosen profession more difficult for them in the future if the police named them as suspects.

The insurance company wired the recovery fee directly to my bank, and it swelled my depleted bank account tremendously. It would look impressive until the next quarterly income tax filing date. Using my bank's on-line account access, I moved three million dollars into the account where I stored the government's half-share of my earnings until it was time to send it to Washington and Albany.

When I had been a virtual pauper, I'd always chuckled when I heard political hacks say the wealthy had to pay their fair share. I knew even then, as I struggled to pay my rent each month, the wealthy paid at a much higher rate than the little people, many of whom paid no income taxes at all. During the 2012 presidential elections, a video of candidate Mitt Romney stating that forty-seven percent of Americans in the bottom tier of households paid no income taxes at all was used as part of the usual mudslinging. The clip was later credited with significantly damaging his chances of becoming President. One of the current presidential hopefuls had proposed that fifteen million people at the lower range of the employment scale be totally exempt from all payroll taxes. His idea of *them* paying *their* fair share was to give them a completely free ride. I'd often wondered if there'd ever been a politician who hadn't promised to lower taxes while increasing government services and benefits. Now that I was no longer a pauper, I grimaced as I turned over millions of dollars to the government because I imagined I could hear hacks spouting the party line that I still wasn't paying my fair share.

My mortgage with Fodor's company permitted me to make advance payments on the principal without penalty, and that naturally reduced the monthly interest payments, so I used two million to start paying down the balance. *Two million down and fourteen million to go*, I thought. Judging from the richness of the new furnishings, courtesy of Mia's wonderful taste, the million I held back might not even cover the co-op decoration efforts. It might soon be time to get another recovery job.

My name was once again splashed across newspapers and television news programs for a couple of days as car enthusiasts across the country cheered the recovery of the Ferrari, even though few of them would ever see it. A number of news people called in an effort to get an interview, but I had no interest in publicity and didn't return the calls. The people in the insurance industry who needed my services would find a way to contact me without any help from the media.

After sending the final report off to Schiller, I debated about what to do next. I needed to get going on my private investigation, now more than ever, but I decided to take a preliminary look at the two cases Brigman had assigned me. I suppose I was being driven by a sense of guilt. I had gone from near poverty and obscurity to wealth and some degree of celebrity. I had established a multimillion dollar business from a piece of street trash and had just made a major score. I was closing cold cases for the FBI when I could have been using the gizmo for making more money while depriving criminals of the fruits of their illegal behavior and contributing fully half of everything I earned to the government in taxes. But I still felt an unshakable obligation to 'give back' more.

The first case file I read was a missing child investigation. Three-year-old Amanda Matthews, last seen playing in her home's fenced backyard, had simply disappeared. When the local police failed to find any sign of the girl in the immediate area around her home, they ruled it a probable kidnapping.

I had to choose between starting work on the Delcona surveillance and working the missing child case, so I flipped a coin. The missing child case won. I loaded up my printer with paper and it began spitting out pages from the case file.

Using the gizmo, I tagged the young Matthews girl playing in her yard on the day of her disappearance. Then I jumped ahead to the present. I half expected to see an unmarked grave but instead was greeted by the sight of the now seven-year-old girl sitting in a classroom full of similarly aged kids. I was happy to see that the girl hadn't been killed by the kidnapper.

Since I hadn't read through the file yet, I was unaware of the facts. Perhaps the kidnapping had been perpetrated by a family member who had lost custody rights, or someone who desperately wanted a child of their own. Whichever, the case was suddenly less imperative. I still intended to solve it and hopefully return the young girl to her legal guardians as soon as possible, but this case wasn't like the serial killer case where I'd feared he might start up again.

After debating the issue with myself for a while, I decided to go against the coin flip. I would start working the Delcona issue, and work on the child abduction case when I needed a break from watching mob thugs brutalize innocents or even lower echelon criminals.

I hadn't yet formulated a plan for how I was going to deal with Delcona, but whichever path I chose, I still needed to perform a lot of background investigation. I had to know his habits as well as I knew my own before I took any action. I had to know how he would react in the face of personal danger. If he learned I was coming, would he ignore the danger to his person and rely on his bodyguards? Or would he, as in the 'The Godfather' story, 'go to the mattresses?'

I began by tagging Delcona during his last time in a courtroom and traveled back to his birth. After verifying that the man known as Damiano Orsino Delcona was the same person as the baby of the same name, I began watching him as he grew up. I knew my 'stakeout from home' was going to be a time-consuming effort, and I intended to skip as much 'dead air' time as I could by using the simple jump-ahead tricks I had learned. But I knew of no tricks that would give me what I needed in mere days.

◆ ◆ ◆

I watched enough of Delcona's early life to see that he was frequently abused by a father who had been in and out of prison since he was himself a minor. By the time Delcona was eight, he was following in his father's criminal footsteps. He began by running simple errands for the local mobsters and eventually graduated to running numbers and delivering drugs. At night, his gang of future prison fodder broke into cars, stores, and homes, stealing anything they could carry away.

It would be easy to feel sorry for a young boy dragged into a life of crime, but Delcona went willingly. Perhaps it was the brutal treatment at the hands of his father that made him receptive to a life of crime himself, but that was immaterial. I knew him to be a criminal and murderer, and I had no intention of forgiving his crimes because he'd had a hard life when he was young.

◆　◆　◆

Once Delcona reached his teens, I had trouble skipping over any part of his life where he wasn't sleeping. It seemed like every minute was devoted to crime. He was a lot smarter than his father. As he rose through the ranks he was always able to avoid arrest and incarceration. Sometimes he had others handle the crimes while he supervised from a distance, and other times witnesses simply disappeared without a trace. As I watched his life of crime, I made copious notes.

After a week of watching Delcona's life, my eyes were bloodshot and I was using eye drops several times a day. While applying the drops one day, I had a sudden inspiration. I had never been able to find a way to hear what was going on during the scenes I watched, and I also hadn't been able to hook the gizmo to a video recorder. But I had never tried to take a picture of the gizmo display. I suddenly felt like such an idiot. If *I* could see what was going on, a camera should be able to see as well.

After I finished berating myself, I realized that I could never show the images to anyone because they would prove the existence of my gizmo. So even if I could video the event, I could never use it effectively. Still, I wanted to try to record the images.

Using my smartphone, I aimed it at the gizmo and started recording. After about twenty seconds I stopped and played it back. The image was perfect. I still couldn't hear anything from the event, but I could see everything. And because the gizmo could be manipulated to record anything from any angle, the pictures provided the ultimate in unusable 'evidence.' But I would have the images for my own records without using the gizmo to refresh my memory while preparing my final reports.

Although the smartphone image was good, I wanted the best, so I sealed my office and headed to an electronics shop in midtown that sold professional recording equipment.

When I arrived back home, I set up the new wall-mount arm that would hold the camera. I could leave the camera right on the arm, then swing it out of the way when I wasn't using it. It would be a lot more convenient than a standard camera tripod. Using the log of Delcona's crimes, I returned to several that I wanted to record. After reviewing the crime from a number of angles, I selected the best shot, checked the camera for alignment and focus, and started filming. It took me a full day to record everything important I had witnessed so far since I'd begun the investigation, but I had some of the most damning evidence anyone could ask for. And as they do at football games, I could shoot the scene from different angles and have my own version of instant replay so there was no question about the call.

From that point on, whenever Delcona took a personal hand in anything, I recorded it. I was sure he would have convicted himself a dozen times over by what he said in meetings with other mobsters, but visual imagery was all I could get.

◆　◆

As I crawled into bed after a long day of filming criminals at work, Mia awoke and smiled dreamily up at me. "Finished at last, darling?" she asked.

"For tonight. I couldn't keep my eyes open any longer."

"I don't understand how you can do so much work from your home. I thought policemen had to be out watching for crime or something."

"I do most of my work on the computer. It's more effective and more comfortable."

"We haven't made love in three days. When do you make time for that?"

I thought for a minute before saying, "I'm declaring tomorrow a work holiday. We'll do something together during the day and then spend the evening in bed."

"Oh, darling, I wish I could. I have an appointment to look at some antique chairs with the decorator tomorrow."

"Okay. How about the day after?"

"I can cancel my two appointments."

"Okay, you cancel your appointments and we'll spend the entire day together."

"Where will we go?"

"Anywhere you want."

CHAPTER NINE

The weather for my impromptu holiday with Mia was perfect. Mild temperatures beneath a clear blue sky set the stage as we started with a ride north, crossing into the Bronx, then north on the Bronx River Parkway to the Sprain Brook Parkway, which became the Taconic State Parkway up by Yonkers. We exited at Route 202 and drove west through Peekskill, then crossed the Hudson River on the Bear Mountain Bridge. Turning north again, we drove up Route 9W until Old State Road in Fort Montgomery and turned off for Highland Falls.

We entered the West Point Military Academy grounds through the South Gate. I'd heard that at one time a person could just drive onto the Academy grounds after slowing down, but these days people had to stop and explain their visit. As always at official government checkpoints, my FBI ID helped get us through without any delay. We parked and then walked around the beautiful post as cadets hurried about their business.

The Hudson Valley was alive with history. It was difficult to travel anywhere without seeing references to the American Revolution. There were preserved battlefields, important crossroads, river crossing locations, and various homesteads once used for military headquarters.

After touring West Point, we headed north along Old Storm King highway. I stopped the car at a rest area that overlooked the Hudson from a cliff wall with an almost vertical drop. As we stood there, a private plane following the river south passed our promontory position. The plane had significant elevation above the river but was lower than where we stood at a low stone wall intended to keep visitors from venturing too close to the edge of the precipice or cars from driving over the cliff.

Turning south again after driving through the Village of Cornwall-on-Hudson and then the Village of Cornwall, I drove south on Route 9W. We used the Tappen Zee Bridge to traverse the Hudson River. An hour later we were back home. It had been a wonderful and incredibly relaxing day, and our next big decision was whether to go out for dinner or spend the evening in other activities. The 'other' activities won out.

By the time we fell asleep, we were both physically exhausted. It had been a day to remember, and I promised Mia that from then on I wouldn't work on Saturdays or Sundays unless I was out of town. She promised she wouldn't schedule any time with decorators or workmen on weekends, but the apartment was nearing completion anyway. She had done an incredible job, and it was no longer the empty shell of my pre-Mia days. Thanks to her efforts, it had taken on a look of elegance while maintaining the warmth of a home.

Over the following weeks, I continued recording Delcona's criminal past. It was difficult to imagine that one man could be responsible for so much pain, misery, and death and not be a Third World dictator. I finally reached the time when Morris was interrogated in one of Delcona's warehouses. His hands were tied behind the wooden chair where he sat and his ankles were tied to the legs of the chair. His face was masked in fear. Gone was the smug I-am-a-scientist-and-better-than-you look that had always annoyed me so much. Morris was filled with fear, and rightly so. He may have still held some hope he would survive, but I couldn't fairly judge that. I already knew his fate.

It was impossible to know for sure since I had no audio, but it appeared that Morris hadn't contacted Delcona personally. Rather, I believed that someone Morris called had passed the information on to the mob boss. Whatever information was passed along, it was persuasive enough for Delcona to have Morris kidnapped and brought to the warehouse. If Morris had been in touch with Delcona, a kidnapping and brutal assault to gain information would not have been necessary.

I knew lip-reading wasn't a hundred percent accurate, but I wished I was at least modestly proficient in that skill at the moment. I'd heard that back in 2007 someone had produced a computer system able to transcribe a silent movie of Adolf Hitler by using advanced facial movement techniques, but I hadn't heard anything about it since. I knew the FBI used all sorts of facial recognition systems but relied on professional lip-readers for the most accurate speech translation results. I decided to look into it now that I could film events. It was complicated because people moved their heads while they talked, but as evidenced by my gizmo, computers were getting more sophisticated every day.

Over the course of several hours, I watched as Morris's face was slowly and methodically beaten to a bloody pulp by the thug named Diz. Between blows, Delcona would ask questions. If he got an answer he approved of, he'd ask another. If he didn't get an answer he approved of, he nodded to Diz, who then grinned and punished Morris's face.

I would have preferred not to watch the pummeling, but I had no choice. I had to see everything. Perhaps knowing that Morris was going to die made it a little easier on me, because I knew his pain was a thing of the past. It was a bit like the days when I had first starting using the gizmo. I had managed to watch the death, mutilation, and suffering on ancient battlefields and during natural events only by telling myself that the people involved were long dead, and their suffering was in the past.

When the grilling was apparently over, Diz stepped behind Morris's chair and used a piece of thick nylon rope to strangle the helpless man. Diz grinned manically with a kind of light in his eyes as Morris fought with a sudden burst of energy to fill his lungs one last time. When he finally stopped struggling and slumped over, Diz tied the rope tightly about Morris's neck. The other three thugs and Diz's pudgy pal just stood about watching, smiling, or laughing at the death struggle. I knew my fate would have been the same if Billy hadn't acted when he did.

My recording equipment captured every second of the event, with high-resolution images of all participants. Since justice had already been dispensed for two of the participants in the deaths of Morris and Billy, a criminal justice system that had repeatedly failed to protect the public from these two animals wouldn't get another chance to err on the side of caution and possible doubt about their guilt. And I wouldn't make the same mistake either when it came time for the others to pay the piper.

◆　◆　◆

I'd heard so many times how easy it was to get a handgun if you needed, but it wasn't so easy if a person didn't travel in the right circles. I couldn't use either my service weapon or my backup for what I was planning. I needed a 'clean' handgun. By that, I meant one that had never been used in the commission of a crime, was not stolen, and was not traceable back to me. Preferably, it would be one that had never even been registered. I didn't want to involve an innocent party in my private little war.

I couldn't access the FBI information system to search for illegal gun traffickers because there would be a record of my search. So I did what billions of other people do every single day and searched the internet using a standard search engine. The search for recent arrests in gun trafficking in New York City turned up what I needed in a second. A large bust had recently occurred of a gang that was bringing weapons from a state that didn't have the ultra stringent handguns laws of New York.

In NYC, only law enforcement personnel and criminals generally carried handguns. The few exceptions were private security forces personnel or people who had been able to justify their need to be armed after undergoing a tedious and expensive process. And of course, diplomats. NYC was home to the United Nations Headquarters, and there were literally no restrictions on what diplomats could do.

Unless an armed criminal was unfortunate enough to try robbing a cop, another criminal, or a diplomat, the pickings were generally pretty easy. It had been estimated that perhaps only one civilian in ten thousand had made the decision to ignore the politicians and carry a concealed handgun they could use to protect themselves. The rest were more afraid of being caught with a weapon than they were of being robbed, because the imposed penalties for having the nerve to protect oneself and one's loved ones with a handgun could be stiffer than drug possession or committing robbery. Criminals like Diz and Pudgy rarely worried with the odds that much in their favor. They'd just gotten careless when they attacked me.

Once I had the names and arrest information of the gun traffickers as provided by the news article, I tagged them and then hopped back a few weeks so I could watch everyone they'd had contact with. It took a few days of hopping around, but I eventually found three people to whom they had sold weapons in the past and who were buying them to stock their own small armory from which they resold the weapons and ammunition. I watched the three individuals carefully for several days and decided which one I would approach. The decision was based both on the assortment of weapons the gun seller had available for sale and the ease of access to the gun seller himself.

◆ ◆ ◆

"Freeze," I shouted, from behind the safety of a large steel garbage dumpster. The seller of illegal guns was walking through a front lot that led to a dilapidated garage with large wooden doors hanging drunkenly on ancient hinges. Over the doorway was a sign that advertised car repair services, but a large, rusty hasp and lock holding the doors closed indicated the garage might no longer be performing repairs to vehicles. It was after midnight and almost black as pitch in the shadows created by the three-story buildings that bordered the lot. If the gun dealer hadn't been wearing a light tan-colored leather jacket and hat, I might not have been able to see him.

The seller froze for a second, then started to turn his head to see who was behind him.

"I said freeze," I shouted. "You looking to get shot?"

"Waz this bout?"

"Raise your hands above your head— slowly. I know you're armed, so there'd better not be anything in your hands as you raise them."

The gun seller, Malcolm by name, hesitated for a second, then complied. I knew he could tell from my voice that I wasn't a street punk looking for an easy score. I was hoping he'd think I was a local cop. I stepped out from behind the dumpster and walked up to Malcolm. Pressing my Glock 27 lightly against his neck, I retrieved an envelope from my pocket and slipped it between the thumb and forefinger of his upright left hand. At first, he was slightly startled by the envelope, then realized it was only a piece of paper.

"Waz up?"

"I need a handgun for a special job. I've been told you can supply it."

"By who?"

"Doesn't matter. I never name names, but the source is reliable."

"You a cop, man?"

"No, I'm not NYPD, this isn't a sting, and I'm not looking to rip you off. I just didn't want to get shot before the introductions were complete. My business credentials are in the envelope. Check them out."

"I gotta put ma hans down."

"Just don't reach for anything in your clothes and you won't get shot. I'm just hoping for a nice friendly business arrangement. You supply my needs and I'll be gone."

"And if I don't have what you want?"

"Then I leave and take my business credentials with me."

Malcolm lowered his hands, opened the unsealed envelope, and peered in. "Just how many guns you lookin fo, man?"

"I want a new, never fired, 9mm black-finish automatic. A quality weapon such as a Walther, Sig, Glock, or Browning with a high-capacity clip and four *spare* high-capacity clips. No Saturday night specials crap. Plus a hundred rounds of quality 147 grain 9mm hollow point or jacketed HP. No reused brass."

"An what else?"

"That's it."

"Man, there's about four grand in this envelope."

"Call it a tip for a forgetful memory. And— it would be best if the piece had never been registered and couldn't be traced back to you."

"Nuttin I sell can ever be traced back to me."

"Do you have what I need?"

"I thin we can do bizness— but not out here."

"Then take me to where you conduct business."

Malcolm relaxed slightly and turned his head to look at me. He didn't appear surprised by my height, but I think the nylon stocking I was wearing over my head earned a double take. "What do I call you?"

"Never call me."

"Okay, uh— Mista Neva. Folla me."

Malcolm led the way to a door on the side of the automotive repair garage. Once inside, he pulled on a dirty shelving unit filled with greasy, used automotive parts. The shelving unit must have had concealed wheels because it moved easily once he'd unlocked it somehow. A set of stairs going downward led to a tunnel, and over the next several minutes we followed a twisting route, winding up in a basement beneath one of the local apartment houses.

Malcolm immediately walked to a solid-looking cabinet and produced a key to unlock it. As he opened the doors, a wide assortment of handguns lying on shelves was revealed. He reached up and took a box down from an upper shelf and carried it to a workbench. The box appeared to be brand new, and the printing indicated that it was a Sig Saur P229. Malcolm opened the cardboard box to reveal a black, hard plastic case. When he flipped the two snap clips and raised the cover, I saw a brand new Sig P229. He handed me the pistol and a bore light.

I could tell immediately that the handgun hadn't been fired since leaving the factory. There was an empty thirteen-round Sig clip in the case. While I was checking the pistol, Malcolm retrieved four Ram-Line fifteen-round clips and five boxes of 9mm ammo from another cabinet.

"You plan'en on statting a small war?" Malcolm asked.

"Ending one."

"Thas a good, dependable piece for it, man."

"Yes, it is. Okay, you've got a deal. Got a bag or sack or something to carry it?"

"Sure. Need a holster?"

"No."

Five minutes later Malcolm was letting me out the side door of the garage. "Come back again, Mista Neva. But next time don't make me shit ma pants."

As I passed the dumpster, I pulled the nylon stocking off my head. Mia wouldn't miss it because it had a run in it, and I had found it in the trash bin. Still, I didn't discard it. I would leave it where I'd found it in the apartment.

I didn't have any problems as I walked the block to where I'd parked the rental car. I hadn't dared bring my own car to this neighborhood in the Bronx.

◆　◆

In the morning, I pulled on a pair of cotton gloves and disassembled the Sig to clean and lubricate it. I really liked the feel of the handgun grips and the balance, and wished I could use it instead of my Glock service weapon. The 229 was available in 40 caliber, and I'd heard it was used by the Department of Homeland Security, but I had to carry the officially approved weapon. The Glock 23 had a reputation for never jamming, but I'd heard that disputed by some users.

When I was done, I sat back in the chair to think about my next move. I had the weapon I intended to use and sufficient ammo to take on a small army. If I survived the fight, the Sig, wiped clean of any fingerprints, would end up in the Hudson River or the East River like so many weapons before it that had been used for other than lawful purposes.

But I had two major problems to overcome. I had sketched floor plans for both Delcona's house and the warehouse where he conducted most of his business, and I knew where his sentries were posted at both locations and generally how many I would encounter when it was time to do the deed. But I didn't have a solid plan of attack. I didn't know how I was going to overcome a dozen armed men and reach Delcona before police arrived in response to reports of gunfire. And if I didn't take out Delcona, I'd have to consider the mission a failure, assuming I even survived the battle with the sentries.

If Delcona's home had been in the Bronx, the police might not be in any great hurry to arrive before they had plenty of backup, but a nice, quiet residential neighborhood on Staten Island was another matter. Another problem was that the house had more video cameras than a television studio. That probably meant I should forget about an assault on the house and concentrate on a plan for the warehouse where not a single video camera could be seen. It wasn't surprising that Delcona wouldn't want a record of the activities that occurred there.

Both Delcona's home and his main warehouse were under constant observation by NYPD. I had located the stakeout teams and verified they were watching twenty-four hours a day. Until they removed the teams or at least cut back the hours of observation, I had no chance of getting to Delcona and then getting away afterwards. It was one thing to take on a dozen armed men but quite another to do it and live to fight another day.

◆ ◆ ◆

I sat around for several days, occasionally checking on the stakeout teams watching the warehouse location and wishing they'd end their surveillance while I studied every square inch of the warehouse and tried to formulate a plan of attack that would allow me to reach Delcona and escape unscathed. There seemed little chance that Delcona would come at me or that I'd be able to get at him while the surveillance teams were in place, so I finally decided to spend some time on the child abduction case assigned during my last trip down to FBI Headquarters.

According to the file, the child was playing in her backyard while her mother washed dishes in the kitchen. The woman had an unobstructed view of the backyard and her daughter but left the sink temporarily when the doorbell rang. A door-to-door vacuum cleaner salesman engaged her in conversation for about five minutes, and when she returned to the kitchen, she couldn't see the child from the window, so she walked outside. When she saw no sign of the girl she became frantic and ran around the yard screaming her name as she looked behind every bush and in every possible hiding spot. Determining that the girl was not in the yard, she ran inside and phoned the police.

A patrol car arrived at the house about twenty minutes later. By then the woman was 'practically a basket case,' according to the responding officer who called for an ambulance after failing to get a coherent statement about the missing child. The officer was able to learn the husband's phone number at work and had Dispatch contact him. He arrived home as the still hysterical woman was being cared for by the EMTs.

The police put out an alert on the missing child, but it was hours before the woman was calm enough to give them all the details. They managed to locate the vacuum cleaner salesman a few blocks away from the site of the abduction as he was just finishing an in-home demonstration. A neighbor had called the station to inform police of his location after another neighbor had mentioned they wanted to question the man.

The police, and later the FBI, determined that the salesman most likely had nothing whatsoever to do with the disappearance. He had been working the area for weeks, giving demonstrations of his product and writing orders. He was married, had two kids of his own, and had no police record. Everything he said checked out.

Once I had the background information down, I watched the snatch. A woman approached the rear fence using a footpath that ran behind all the houses. There were only houses on one side of the footpath. Beyond that the terrain sloped steeply downward, dropping some thirty feet into a ravine before rising again to a flat area that appeared to be part of a farm or ranch.

I naturally couldn't hear what the woman said, but she called out something that got the attention of the girl, then held out a red lollipop. The three-year-old girl seemed to know the woman and hurried gleefully over to accept the proffered sweet, then tried to remove the cellophane covering. While the young child struggled to access the candy, the woman reached over the unusually low three-foot-high chain-link fence and lifted the child up and over. It was obviously there only to contain small children or pets. The little girl never cried out or resisted as the woman whisked her away to a car parked on a rutted section of road where the footpath ended. In ten minutes the car was far from the little girl's home. The woman drove calmly and at a sedate pace that would never attract attention. The small girl sat in a child seat in the rear, securely belted in while she enjoyed her lollipop.

It took me just a few minutes to track the kidnapper back to her birth and learn her real name, but I spent an hour trying to determine the name she was using on the date of the kidnapping. I finally got it from a piece of mail in her apartment. The given name remained the same, but the last name had changed. Perhaps she had married. I needed to find out how she was able to get the small girl to trust her so completely, so I tagged both her and the mother of the girl and then let the gizmo take me to a time they were together. It appeared that the kidnapper had been the child's nanny at one time, and I wondered how that could possibly have escaped the attention of the investigators working the case.

Once I knew where the girl was, how the crime had been committed, and the identity of the perpetrator, I really only needed one more thing. It was my usual problem. How was I going to explain how I'd solved the case?

CHAPTER TEN

I t would have saved so much time and effort if I could have revealed the truth behind my amazing ability to solve cold cases. But once revealed, I knew I wouldn't retain ownership of the gizmo for very long. Most likely, the government would seize it in the national interest, which meant that the politicians in charge would put it to their own use.

If the government didn't take it, some quasi-official organization or a major government contractor privy to government secrets would confiscate it by force. And their affiliation with the government, a.k.a. powerful and corrupt politicians, would protect them completely from prosecution. It was obvious that the gizmo's existence would have to remain secret for as long as possible, but I couldn't help wondering what the world would be like if everyone could go down to the local computer store and pick one up.

I knew I would have to take a trip to visit the kidnapping location and try to find something that would let me close the case, but I didn't want to go. By day, I worked my cases or surveillance of the Delcona mob, and by night I devoted myself fully to Mia. We travelled around the city, attending shows or events after dining, or made love. Most nights we did both. When it came to making love, Mia was insatiable. But I did my absolute best to keep up. Don't get me wrong. The effort certainly wasn't a chore— it was pure pleasure. Since our first outing, Mia and I had spent all our time together on weekends.

I expected that at some point, Mia would leave. I didn't think she'd leave permanently, but she was used to jet-setting around the globe, following the wealthy and famous to whatever destination had mutually been decided as the flavor of the month. Several times she had wondered wistfully what the weather was like in New Zealand, Fiji, or the Canary Islands. That she'd stayed with me as long as she had was amazing.

It had taken months to decorate the apartment, but that task was largely done now. Mia continued to pick up small items while she shopped for clothes, and the apartment had taken on the appearance of a home with a lifetime of occupancy rather than the Spartan look it would certainly have had if Mia hadn't come to New York. It was wonderful.

The clothes Mia had brought with her and the new clothes she had purchased since arriving completely filled one of the two enormous walk-in closets in the master bedroom, and Mia was now filling up the closet where I had my clothes. If she continued to stay with me, I would have to convert one of the spare bedrooms into a clothes closet for her. I didn't complain, of course. She always looked beautiful, and as long as she took her bodyguards when she shopped, I knew she was just as safe as if she had been with me.

I procrastinated for days, then scheduled a trip to Missouri so I could make it appear as if I had solved the kidnapping case with proper investigation. I also hoped the visit would reveal an evidence trail I could use to satisfy Brigman. In order not to interfere with my weekend with Mia, I made my reservations for early Tuesday morning. I was on the first flight out to the Springfield-Branson National Airport in Springfield, Missouri.

◆　◆　◆

I arrived in Springfield just after ten a.m. local time, and after picking up a rental car and wolfing down a couple of burgers from a chain burger place, I checked in with the local PD. I wanted to circumvent any possible problems with neighbors reporting a stranger walking around in the neighborhood. I'd learned that following any major crime, even one that had occurred years earlier, people became much more attuned to the presence of strangers. But I was hardly prepared for my reception at the police department.

"Special Agent Colton James," the desk sergeant read from my ID as I held it up. Looking at my face, he added, "We've been wondering when you'd show up."

"Uh, you have? Are you saying you were expecting me?"

"Well, yes. Sort of. Of course we didn't know exactly when you'd arrive."

"I don't understand. How could you be expecting me?"

"The chief started following your cases after you solved that old serial killer case in California. He has a file on everything he could find. There was the bank robbery committed by those three teenagers, then the kidnapping case of that executive. And there were the art robberies in Boston, Philadelphia, and The Netherlands. Recently there was the bank robbery by those NASCAR racing people, but it was the case of the stolen Ferrari that you solved in one day that made the mayor contact the governor and request that he ask the FBI to send you to solve this case. He's a friend of the family that lost their little girl."

"Oh. I wasn't told that my services had been requested. The kidnapping was simply added to my caseload."

"We never developed a single solid lead, and the state police investigators never made any progress either. The family never received a ransom note or call, and there were no witnesses. We've had two FBI teams here, and they were never able to find a single reliable clue. You're our last chance to find the missing kid— or her body."

"I've read the case file. The previous investigators all did a great job. I may not be able to find anything either."

"Well, at least we'll know the best was here and tried."

"Uh, okay. I'm going to visit the alleged crime scene now. I just wanted to stop by and let you know I was working in the area."

"The chief will be sorry he missed you. He's at a city council meeting."

"Give him my regards, and tell him I'll stop back when I have a chance."

"Will do, Special Agent James. Good luck."

I nodded and turned to leave, only then noticing that several nearby police officers were watching me and hanging on every word. I nodded to them as well, then moved towards the front door.

◆ ◆

I parked the rental car in almost the same spot where the kidnapper had parked, on a side street that dead-ended at what seemed like open farmland. It appeared as if there had once been plans to continue building homes on the other side of the ravine. Where the pavement ended, the road continued another thirty or forty feet.

Grabbing my overcoat from the rear seat, I walked along the street that ran in front of the houses. The houses didn't present an appearance of great affluence but did seem to be upper-middleclass.

It was a quiet neighborhood, and there were few people in evidence on this chilly day. That would probably change in a couple of hours when school let out and the school buses began disgorging their cargoes of children.

When I reached the end of the street and came to another short street to nowhere that ran towards the supposed farmland, I followed it until I reached the footpath that ran along the rear of the houses. It hadn't changed very much from the images I'd seen during the kidnapping four years earlier. I then followed the path until I reached the home of the kidnap victim. The backyard fence still looked the same, except that it had recently been painted. The home was well maintained as well. A young child's swing set, made from some sort of plastic, sat unused off to the side of the yard. It was slightly faded from the sun but would probably last forever, unlike the steel sets of generations past that began to rust in a few years.

As I stared at the house and yard, a woman emerged and strode purposefully towards me. She was carrying a small child of about four. As she reached me, she said, "Are you Mr. James?"

I took out my ID wallet and opened it so she could see it as I said, "Special Agent James of the FBI."

"I'm Mrs. Matthews. Could you come into the house so we can talk?" she asked tentatively.

"Of course. I had intended to speak with you after I'd had a look around. Should I go around to the front?"

"No, this is fine with me— if it's okay with you. There's a gate down by the corner of the yard." She pointed towards the gate, and I never let on that I already knew it was there.

The house was spotless. I imagined the woman didn't work outside the house and took great pride in her home.

"Would you care for a cup of coffee?" she asked.

"Thank you. That would be great."

"It'll just take a few minutes to brew," she said as she sat the child down on a small throw rug by some toys and moved towards a coffeemaker on the counter.

As the coffee began to drip, the woman turned towards me and said, "Please have a seat, Agent James."

It was warm in the house, so I removed my overcoat and sat at the table where she had pointed. She took a seat opposite.

"When I saw you out back, I phoned the police. I always report strangers now. They told me it was okay and that you were with the FBI. They said that if anyone could find my baby, it would be you. They said you're the best there is."

"I'll certainly try my hardest to find your child."

"Do you think she's st— still alive?"

"In most kidnapping cases where the child is as young as your daughter was, no harm is intended. Beyond that, I can't speculate. I've read the reports prepared by all of the previous investigators, but perhaps you can tell me everything you remember from that day."

"Of course. I remember everything. I've relived that day over and over in my nightmares."

I listened without interrupting as she related the story of how the young girl was playing in the rear yard while she washed dishes at the sink. She could see her daughter the whole time. But then the doorbell rang and she went to answer the front door. It was the vacuum salesman, and he was persistent. It took her about five minutes to get rid of him without being rude, and when she returned to the kitchen, she couldn't see her daughter. She imagined the child was somewhere not visible from the window so she went outside to check on her, but her daughter was nowhere to be found. Frantic, she hurried into the house and called the police. She was in tears by the time she finished telling me her story.

I gave her a few minutes to compose herself, and she took advantage of the break to pour two cups of coffee. After adding milk and sugar to my cup, I said, "That corresponds to everything I've read in the official reports. Tell me, do you know of anyone who would steal your child?"

"My God, no. I mean, I know a few women who envy me and the wonderful life I have, but I don't know anyone who would kidnap my little girl."

"The previous investigators were very thorough, but I saw a name on the list of people who'd had contact with your daughter but for which there was no follow-up report. I'd like to close that gap. Do you know the current whereabouts of Helen Williams?"

"Oh, poor Helen. I haven't even thought of her in several years."

"Why *poor* Helen?"

"Because she's dead."

"Deceased? Do you know that with absolute certainty?"

"Do you remember that really bad industrial explosion in Oklahoma about four to five years ago? The one where part of a small town was destroyed by the explosion and fire?"

"Yes. I recall hearing about the incident on the news."

"Well, Helen died in that explosion. She had been our nanny until a few weeks before that. That's probably why her name is mentioned in the reports. One day she got a letter from an attorney saying that an aunt had died and left her some money. Somehow, her ex-husband heard about it and demanded she give him half of her inheritance. She reminded him that they were divorced and that she owed him nothing. Helen said he told her he had spoken with an attorney, and he could tie up the money in court cases for years. He told her she would have to spend every penny on lawyers if he didn't get half. Helen told him she'd give him part of it if he promised to leave her alone after that and never bother her again.

She then left to meet her sister in Oklahoma so they could go to the attorney's office together. She and her sister were the only two surviving relatives of her aunt. Well, her sister's home was one of the houses destroyed in the explosion. They found what was left of poor Helen's car, but the explosion and fire destroyed the house completely. It was such a tragedy. Poor, poor Helen. And just when she'd have a little money to enjoy life."

"So as far as you know, she died in the explosion?"

"She, her sister, her sister's husband, and her husband's mother were all officially declared dead by the fire investigators."

"I see. Did you hire another nanny after that?"

"I interviewed a dozen women over a six-month period, but I didn't get a warm sense from any of them. I was already pregnant with Dora by then, so I decided to raise my daughters by myself. I quit my job as a real estate salesperson and became a full-time mother."

"Dora was in the home when Amanda went missing?"

"Yes, she was only two months old at that time. She was asleep in her crib when Amanda disappeared. I was an absolute wreck for several days, but one of my neighbors had seen the police cars out front and came over to see what was going on. She helped take care of Dora— and me— until I was able to take over again. If I hadn't had the responsibility of caring for my baby, I might not have recovered."

"I see. Well, I think that's all for today."

"Please be honest with me. Is there any hope you'll find Amanda?"

"There's always hope, Mrs. Matthews. I'm going to do everything in my power to find your child."

◆ ◆

After checking into a local motel and settling in, I took out the gizmo and activated it. I set the device to the date and time of the kidnapping and set the location to the area behind the house. When I saw the woman who I knew to be Helen Carter because I had traveled back to her date of birth and gotten the name from the birth certificate, I jumped ahead to the present. Williams must have been her married name, but I needed to know what name she was using now.

As I moved the gizmo's window through the house, I finally found a utility bill sitting on the counter in the kitchen. The envelope was addressed to a Mrs. Gloria Wilson. I roam-ed around the house but found no sign of a Mr. Wilson. However, I did find plenty of indications that a seven-year-old girl was living there.

I sat back in the desk chair and took a deep breath. I was glad my job would end when I filed my report. I imagined there was going to be a lot of crying and heartbreak when the authorities arrived to collect the child and return her to her rightful family. I wondered if the child was even aware that Helen wasn't her real mother. Who knew what lies she had been told during the past few years?

Although I knew all the facts and where the child was, I still couldn't file my report because I couldn't show how I had learned that Helen Williams was now Gloria Wilson, living in Tacoma Washington with Amanda as her daughter.

I laid on the bed thinking about it until about six, then went to find something to eat.

I pulled into three restaurant parking lots in my search for food. It was the dinner hour, but the first two were only marginally busy. The third was practically 'standing room only,' so I parked and went in. As soon as I began eating I knew why the place was packed. The prices were fair, and the food was delicious.

◆ ◆ ◆

After visiting the local PD on Wednesday morning and again missing the chief, I headed the rental car towards Oklahoma.

It was well after business hours when I arrived in the Sooner State, so I got a room and grabbed a meal at a diner right next to the motel. The food was decent. Then I passed the hours until bedtime by watching a couple of movies.

On Thursday morning, I spent a few hours scanning through the official reports filed after the explosion and studying the list of recorded deaths. Only about half of the filed death certificates had been supported through actual identification of the bodies. Numerous bone remnants found in the ashes and rubble still remained unidentified, so the deaths of many were assumed after careful investigation and testimony by eyewitnesses that the people had been home that day. Death certificates were needed so survivors could file life insurance claims. I ordered a full set of photocopies made of everything I had viewed, even though I was only interested in two of the names listed as victims of the carnage. If the previous investigator who had included Helen Williams' name in his report had checked, he would have found that Helen Williams had been legally declared dead. He simply hadn't included that additional information in his report.

I next looked into the reported inheritance. I found the obituary notice of the aunt and followed the trail to learn the name of the aunt's attorney. I followed up with a visit to his office and spent ten minutes learning about the inheritance.

With my business in Oklahoma concluded, I had a decision to make. Should I fly home to New York, travel to Tacoma, or remain here while I considered my next move? I decided to remain in Oklahoma for at least one more night. I still had to find a way to show how I had made the connection between Helen Carter Williams and Gloria Wilson.

◆ ◆ ◆

A good night's rest cleared my mind. I awoke with a plan and headed back to Missouri after grabbing a quick breakfast at a place where the parking lot was filled with pickup trucks and small vans. The food, when it arrived, was hot, plentiful, and delicious. Even the coffee was delicious. And while money wasn't a problem, it was nice to get a great meal for not much more than a large coffee at one of those designer coffee places that offered eighty-six flavors of coffee, and nothing but coffee.

The interstate highway system in the U.S. was great, but I'd always wondered what birdbrain had decided the roads should run through large cities. It would have been smart to ensure that no main highway came within twenty miles of a city. The highway could then have been accessed with a dedicated section of road that gave fast highway access to and from the city. By routing the interstate highways *through* cities, the cities were able to adopt the highway as part of their urban traffic network. Trying to pass through a busy city without any intention of stopping there could be a nightmare during rush hour. The highway folks had tried to remedy the situation by constructing sections of road that circle around a city, just outside the city, but those highways always ended up also being co-opted into the urban sprawl. When normal road maintenance functions were factored in, it was easy to see why interstate highway traffic slowed to a crawl at times.

Once I'd managed to stop-and-go my way through Tulsa, traffic volume dropped significantly and I made good time. The next major traffic snarl would be St. Louis, and thankfully I wasn't going that far.

It was late afternoon when I reached Springfield, so I checked into the motel where I'd previously stayed and decided to get some work done before going out for dinner.

Using the gizmo, I concentrated on watching the activities of Helen Carter Williams just prior to the explosion that supposedly claimed her life, as well as the lives of her sister's family. Then I watched her in the weeks before the snatch and her activity just after grabbing the child. She had spent a full week casing the neighborhood, paying particular attention to the activities of the door-to-door vacuum cleaner salesman. She always wore a wig and dark glasses, and never left her car. She also never parked. She just drove slowly through the neighborhood at different hours, never hanging around long enough to be noticed. It was obvious that the vacuum salesman was not involved in her activities but that he figured into her plan.

It made no sense to go back to New York for the weekend, so I decided to stay where I was. I called Mia to tell her I wouldn't be home for a few more days.

"But darling," she said, "you promised we would always have the weekends for ourselves."

"I'm sorry, sweetheart. This trip is more complicated and taking longer than expected, but I have to find the little girl who was kidnapped, and I think I've found a good lead. Tell you what— when I get back I'll take some time off from work and we'll travel to someplace where it's warm for a getaway vacation. You pick the destination."

"Anywhere?"

"As long as it's on the planet Earth."

"You promise?"

"I promise."

◆ ◆ ◆

I spent about half the weekend watching the Delcona mob and more closely examining some of their activities. Every time I saw Delcona, my blood began to boil. I kept seeing a mental image of Billy's bullet-riddled body and began to picture Delcona lying on the floor, bleeding profusely from multiple bullet holes in his body as I stood over him with a smoking gun. I tried my best to stop thinking about it so much, but I couldn't help myself. I wanted Delcona dead more than I'd ever wanted anything in my life. There's an old saying that before you leave to seek vengeance, dig two graves. I certainly didn't have a death wish, but even my death would be worth it if I was able to end the life of the crime lord and murderer responsible for so much misery. The law enforcement surveillance teams were still watching the warehouse and the private residence of Delcona, and it seemed as though they intended to be there for a while, so neither he nor I could proceed with our plans. I wondered if he regretted sending those two thugs after me, or if he regretted not sending a dozen.

◆ ◆ ◆

On Monday morning, I pretended to be a real investigator. I first visited the real estate office where Williams had leased an apartment when she was still nanny to the Matthews family. I was greeted by a Mrs. Helmar.

"FBI?" she said. "What does the FBI want with us? We pay our taxes promptly."

"The IRS has its own people who investigate tax issues, Mrs. Helmar. The FBI investigates other forms of dishonesty. And this company is not the focus of any investigation that I'm aware of. I'm only seeking information about one of your previous tenants."

"Oh, I see. That's a relief. I'm scared to death of the IRS. I've heard so many terrible stories about them and how they operate. I understand that with them, you're guilty until proven innocent instead of the other way around."

"I've heard that as well. And, like yourself, I always pay my taxes on time. Today, I'd like any information you can share about a tenant named Helen Williams."

"Williams? Helen Williams? I'm afraid I don't have any listing for a Helen Williams."

"I'm investigating what we call a *cold* case. Ms. Williams rented an apartment through this agency four to five years ago."

"Let me check the files. This will take a few minutes. We only computerized current and new listings about three years ago."

Mrs. Helmar turned and walked to a door that opened into a very large closet, or perhaps a small office that had been converted to a file room. I watched as she pulled open a drawer and began riffling through file folders. Finally, she stopped and pulled one out, then returned to where I was standing.

"Please sit down, agent, while I review the contents of this folder."

I joined her at her desk and sat in the side chair.

"Yes," she said after a few moments, "a Mrs. Helen Williams, who was separated from her husband, did rent a place through us. I remember this tenant now." Reading from the file, she said, "After about two years, she suddenly stopped making her monthly payments. Up until then she had been very prompt. Our efforts to contact her were ineffective. We had just begun legal proceedings to evict when we were contacted by her husband. He told us that she had been killed in Oklahoma and that he would be collecting her personal possessions from the apartment.

"He wanted a key. We told him the monthly rent was three months in arrears and he would have to pay that, prove his identity, provide us with a copy of a death certificate, and show us a court order that granted him ownership of her possessions before we could give him anything. He stormed out of the office after a bit of cursing and yelling that he would see us in court. We get so many empty threats that we've become used to them."

"So what happened?"

"We never saw him again, and he certainly never began legal proceedings. If he'd contacted a lawyer, he would have been informed that everything we'd told him was according to the mandates of state law."

"What happened to Ms. Williams' personal possessions?"

"When we received the right to evict, we contacted a firm that performs cleaning services. They cleared the apartment and cleaned it so it could be rented again."

"What happens to the tenant's possessions?"

"They're crated up and taken to a storage location owned by the cleaning firm. They're under contract to us to hold the tenant's possessions for six months. If the tenant tries to claim them, they must pay the past due rent, cleaning service charges if they exceed the damage deposit, and the storage charges. If they refuse or never try to claim them, the cleaning firm acquires ownership and sells them. They keep whatever proceeds they collect."

"And you get nothing?"

"Correct. Once the possessions are removed from the apartment, we're completely out of it unless the tenant claims their property and pays all charges. We don't even want to know the final disposition of the property. We'd only get involved if a tenant came to us with a complaint that the cleaning firm sold the possessions before the six months were up. But that's never happened."

"I see. Can you provide me with the name and address of the cleaning firm and any document numbers related to their activities on your behalf?"

"Of course," Mrs. Helmar said and began writing that information on a sheet of letter paper. "Here you go, Agent James. Uh, what is this about? Did Mr. Williams file a complaint against us?"

"No. As I said, the focus of this investigation doesn't involve your firm at all. I can't tell you any more than that."

"I see."

As I stood up, I said, "Thank you very much for the information and for your cooperation, Mrs. Helmar."

"You're most welcome, Agent James. Please keep us in mind if you ever need to rent an apartment in this area."

"I will. Good day."

◆ ◆

My next stop was the cleaning service. I stood at the front counter until it was my turn and then, after showing my ID, explained that I wanted to speak with someone about a cleaning that had been performed more than four years ago. The clerk picked up a phone and spoke to a manager, who hurried out.

"I'm Mr. Ambrossa. How can I help you, Agent James?"

I handed him the sheet of paper that Mrs. Helmar had given me.

"This invoice number is about four years old."

"Yes. I'd like to hear anything you can tell me about it."

"Please come into my office."

I followed the short, heavyset man down a corridor and into a smallish office.

"Please have a seat, Agent. I'll pull the file."

Several minutes later, the man reappeared, this time holding a thin file folder. He took his seat and opened the file, then began to read. "The personal possessions we removed from the apartment remained with us for just over six months. They were sold as one lot in the next monthly auction. The buyer returned the same day with one of those rental trucks and two local odd-jobs people. They removed everything that was in the storage unit. That's all we know."

"Do you have his or her name?"

"Yes," he said, looking at the file again. "It was a Mrs. Sheila Smith."

"Did she pay by check or credit card?"

"Nope. According to the paperwork, she paid cash."

"Do you require identification?"

"Not when folks pay with cash."

"Do you remember the name on the rental truck?"

"No. Sorry. The file doesn't say. It just says a rental truck and two local odd-jobs guys came back to pick up everything the same day."

"I see. Okay, Mr. Ambrossa, thank you very much for your cooperation. Could I get a copy of that page you were reading from?"

"Certainly. There's no confidential information on it." He swung his chair around and placed the page on a small copier behind him. A couple of seconds later he handed me the photo copy.

"Thanks again, Mr. Ambrossa," I said as I rose and left his office.

"I'm always happy to cooperate with the authorities."

◆ ◆

I groaned slightly as I thought about canvassing all of the places that rented trucks while seeking information about a rental that was four years old. So instead I returned to my motel and used the gizmo. I watched the auction and saw Mrs. Helen Williams, aka Mrs. Sheila Smith, win the contents of the storage locker. She was pretty lively for a dead woman. I tagged her, jumped ahead a half hour, then performed a search for the next time she came to the storage location. When I saw her get out of the truck, I recorded the license plate info and all other markings on the vehicle, including the VIN.

The truck rental company was a national chain, so I called the headquarters and got passed around for five minutes before I found someone who would assist me. I gave her the license number and VIN of the truck, and the date it was rented. In seconds she was able to pull up the name of the renter and where the truck was turned in after use, but she wouldn't give me the information until I emailed her an image of my ID.

Once she had received that, she confirmed that the driver had provided a photo ID driver's license, but she still wouldn't send me a copy of anything until she verified that I was really

FBI and got an approval from her supervisor. I gave her the telephone number at the New York office so they could confirm my identity and asked that they call right away and then send me the requested information.

About an hour later, after receiving papers from the truck rental company, I made plane reservations, packed my things, and headed for the airport.

CHAPTER ELEVEN

I t was late when I arrived at Seattle-Tacoma International. I picked up a rental car and headed to the national chain hotel I had decided on after a quick computer search. It had been an exhausting eight days, and I was anxious to wrap things up and head home.

◆ ◆ ◆

The next day when the school where Amanda Matthews attended first grade recessed for the day, I was waiting outside near the parents waiting to pick up their children. I had learned through use of the gizmo that the girl was now named Samantha Wilson, and I used my smartphone to surreptitiously take the girl's picture when she emerged from the school. I also got an image of her 'mother' when the girl reached her. I pretended that I was trying to place a call by repeating my own phone number over and over out loud as I snapped the pictures. I didn't interfere with them, and as soon as they walked past me, I ignored them completely. I pretended I was waiting for my own child and kept looking anxiously towards the front entrance.

It was obvious the child was being well cared for, so I had no intention of interceding. That would be a task for others. Possibly child welfare workers would take care of the girl until she could be reunited with her real parents. I was glad I wouldn't have to be part of the heartbreaking scenes I expected would occur.

My work in Tacoma was done, and after the SUV driven by Mrs. Wilson pulled out of the parking lot, I ended my fake vigil and headed for the airport. I had everything I needed to wrap up my report and would complete the assembly after I arrived home. I could now turn my attention back to Delcona without any feelings of guilt over not working the child kidnapping case.

◆ ◆ ◆

Mia welcomed me home as if I'd been gone for months rather than just over a week and a half. I had to drop my suitcase and computer case as I entered the apartment and she wrapped her arms around my neck and began kissing every square inch of my face from ear to ear. I smiled like a fool as I picked Mia up instead of my luggage and carried her to the master suite, where I set her gently down on the bed. Having become accustomed to nightly lovemaking, ten days of celibacy seemed like a year. We never got dinner as we made up for the separation, but we raided the kitchen around midnight for snacks and wine.

◆ ◆ ◆

As wonderful as the first night back was, the following morning was the opposite. I discovered that the surveillance teams were still camped at Delcona's doors twenty-four seven and tailing his car whenever he went out. His operations never ceased— he simply stopped taking an active part in anything illegal where his involvement could be proven by the surveillance teams.

What was said in meetings behind closed doors where no audio was available could never be proven. It was all the more frustrating to me because I could see everything that was going on but was unable to hear even a single word. At least his personal involvement in physical mayhem had been curbed for the time being. I was sure the surveillance teams were as frustrated as I was.

I had promised Mia we would go away as soon as I wrapped up the kidnapping case, and she wanted to leave right away. She was a little disappointed that we weren't already on our way to the airport, but I explained that my role in the case wasn't complete until my report was filed and I was called downtown to discuss my finding with the gruff, stone-faced Brigman. I completed organizing my notes and filed my report before three in the afternoon. Then it was simply a matter of waiting until I heard back.

Mia had decided she wanted to go to Fiji for our getaway because she hadn't been there in several years. She said she knew of a great place to stay, and I never doubted her knowledge for a second. But because of the air travel required, I suggested that Hawaii might be a better destination.

"But you said I could pick the destination for our vacation getaway," she said with a pouty expression that matched the timbre of her voice.

"And I meant it. I only suggested the Hawaiian Islands because the travel time will involve substantially fewer hours in the air. If you don't mind the extra travel time and want to go to Fiji, then we're going to Fiji."

Mia squealed in delight and wrapped her arms around my neck before treating my face to a virtual assault from her lips that made my arrival home seem lukewarm.

Never one to squander my chances, I swept her legs up with my left arm and carried her to the bedroom.

◆

When I hadn't heard back from Brigman by the next day, I sent him an email informing him that I was going out of the country on personal business for a month. I figured the message would generate a response, and I received a call within an hour from his secretary. She told me to be at his office at nine a.m. the following day.

◆ ◆

I arrived a few minutes early and took a seat to await Brigman's summons to enter his inner office. This was just my second visit downtown since the night I was attacked at my apartment, but the security people in the lobby apparently remembered my appearance that night and looked me over from head to toe each time I arrived, seemingly expecting to see blood dripping from somewhere on my body.

My waiting time was minimal on this occasion and I was called into Brigman's office after no more than five minutes. The same three still-unidentified individuals occupied chairs in front of Brigman's desk. They looked up at me dispassionately while Brigman glared at me from his office chair.

"Okay, James," Brigman said, "you think you've solved another cold case? Tell us about it and explain how you arrived at your conclusions."

"Yes, sir," I said as I planted myself in an empty chair even though I hadn't been invited to sit down. "After a full review of the previously filed reports, I knew those investigators had all done a very credible job. I did…"

Brigman interrupted with, "We knew the *real* agents had done a good job. We want to hear how *you* arrived at *your* conclusions."

I stared at Brigman in silence for several seconds, then resumed my statement from where I had been interrupted. "As I started to say, I did find one thing that didn't add up, so I queried Mrs. Matthews on that point. There was a reference in one report to a Helen Williams, but there was no associated report of a follow-up investigation. Mrs. Matthews informed me that Williams had been the child's nanny before the kidnapping. Since the child had never cried out during the abduction, as far as we know, it appeared as if she knew her abductor and trusted him or her.

"The parents were then, and still are now, together, so it seemed obvious it wasn't a child custody situation. Williams was the only possible lead I had, so I pursued it. But Mrs. Matthews informed me that Williams was dead, having been killed in an industrial accident in Oklahoma.

"With nothing else to go on at that point, I went to Oklahoma. I learned that, in fact, Mrs. Williams had apparently been a victim of a devastating explosion and fire there. She had been legally declared as deceased, but there had never been a formal identification of her body because they found no body. However, a good number of people known to be in the area on the day of the explosion were also declared dead without any proof of death simply because the horrific destruction at the accident scene reportedly obliterated bodies.

"It's a situation similar to when an airliner goes down and minimal human remains are located. If the passengers were checked in at the boarding gate, they're assumed to have been on the plane when it crashed. The burned-out and melted hulk of the auto that Williams drove to Oklahoma was found very near to what was identified as the foundation pad of her sister's destroyed house. The concrete base was the only identifiable remnant of the house. Neighbors who survived the disaster attested that Williams had been staying there and had been seen there as recently as several hours before the explosion at the industrial plant.

"I had learned that Williams and her sister had been the sole surviving heirs in a sizable inheritance and that Williams was being pressured by her ex-husband for half of her share. It made sense that she could have taken advantage of an opportunity to disappear and start life anew. So I set about trying to prove she was dead."

"What about the inheritance?" one of the nameless three asked. "If she had been declared dead, she shouldn't have been able to claim it."

"She and her sister had already claimed the inheritance. At least most of it. The deceased aunt had inherited a significant portfolio of oil stocks when *her* grandfather died, and the portfolio had increased appreciably as the result of stock splits and dividends. A couple of decades ago, whenever the aunt received a dividend, she began purchasing gold rather than using the dividend for purchasing additional stock. Mostly she acquired gold coins, but some of it was in bullion. She had leased a small vault at a private precious-metals depository in Tulsa and kept her gold there.

"The attorney estimated, from information in purchase records, that the vault contained as much as a hundred pounds, or sixteen hundred ounces if you prefer. Most of the purchases had taken place before 2004 when gold was about four hundred dollars an ounce. At the time of the aunt's death, gold was trading at about eighteen hundred dollars an ounce. A hundred pounds of gold would therefore have been worth almost three million dollars.

"The portfolio of oil stock shares had been immediately liquidated by the sisters, who purchased more gold with the money. In total, I estimate that the sisters found themselves with almost two hundred fifty pounds of gold. That translates to over four thousand ounces, which in turn means more than seven million dollars. Even dividing it between the two women, that's enough to provide a very comfortable lifestyle.

"I also learned that the aunt's house was put up for sale, and the lawyer had the power of attorney to complete the sale. When the house sold, the proceeds were put into a trust fund for the heirs of Helen Williams and Ilene Tallago, but so far no one has come forward to claim it."

"So you believe her sister is also alive?" Brigman asked.

"I've found no proof of that, but it's entirely possible. Let's speculate that the sisters went for a long walk just before the explosion. Or perhaps Helen had purchased a new car, and they went for a test drive. There could be any number of reasons why they weren't in the home at the time of the explosion."

"When the sister's family was killed," one of the nameless men asked, "would she just leave? I mean, without grieving the loss?"

"If the sister was as unhappy in her family relationship as Williams appears to have been in hers, why not? It was a chance for a new life— a new beginning. We know the sister had no children. There was just her husband and her mother-in-law living at the house with her."

"You're not suggesting that Williams or her sister was responsible for the explosion, are you?" the lone woman in the unidentified group asked.

"I have no reason to believe they were involved in any way. The investigative reports state that it was a horrible accident caused by excessively hot weather and inadequate industrial safeguards."

"Where's the gold now?" one of the nameless men asked.

"I learned that the gold vault was emptied prior to the explosion. Where the gold is would be pure speculation."

"Two hundred fifty pounds of gold is a bit much to carry around," the other nameless man said.

"If Williams *had* purchased a new— or at least newer— car after she learned the size of her inheritance and hadn't registered it yet, she had transportation. She probably drove away with the gold in the trunk. There was no report of finding it— melted or otherwise— at the scene of the explosion. Two hundred fifty pounds isn't all that much to transport when you have a car available."

"Your report says that Williams is in Tacoma with the child," Brigman said. "You're absolutely sure of that?"

I removed several pictures from my briefcase and handed them to him. I had printed them on my computer at home. "I took the first two images using my smartphone earlier this week. The third image is a computerized age-progression image of the missing child to account for the four years since the last image of her was taken. If that's not Amanda Matthews with Williams, then the likeness is *uncanny*."

Brigman looked at the photos closely, then passed them to the nearest of the unidentified trio. After each member of the trio looked at them, one of the two men said, "I'm convinced we have enough to proceed. A DNA analysis will prove or disprove the child's familial association with the Matthews family. Let's send a team to pick up the child and the woman."

"That's all, James," Brigman said.

I stood and turned to leave the office, then stopped and turned back to face Brigman. "I understand that the serial killer case in California has been officially closed. I was wondering if the drain pipe at the location on Magorim Street yielded any evidence."

Brigman scowled and gritted his teeth. When it became clear he wasn't going to respond, the nameless woman said, "Yes. We found an earring that was positively identified by the husband of one of the victims and a tooth that was positively identified by dental records and DNA as having belonged to another of the women. A few other small personal items were retrieved but nothing that could be proven as having belonged to the any of the victims."

I nodded to the woman and left the office. It seemed to me that the nameless trio had treated me a little more respectfully than in past case review sessions. I wondered if they were beginning to respect my abilities as an investigator. Each of the cold cases I had worked prior to today had been successfully closed as a result of my investigations.

Of course, Brigman hadn't changed. His comment at the start of the session about knowing 'that the *real* agents had done a good job' was like a slap across my face. If I turned in my badge and gun, Brigman would probably celebrate for a week. I decided I wasn't going to give him the satisfaction. The Bureau might terminate my employment if they weren't satisfied with my work, but I wasn't going to resign because of Brigman. I could have learned the answer to my last question by accessing the computer file on the serial killer case and reading any updates. The question was posed only to annoy Brigman and retaliate for his *real* agents comments. He'd choke before he'd ever compliment me on my success with the cold cases.

◆ ◆

Mia wasn't in the apartment when I arrived home, so I made myself a tuna sandwich on toasted rye with tomato, lettuce and mayo, and took it to my office to munch on while I worked. Now that I had wrapped up the kidnapping case, I was free to make the vacation trip reservations. Mia had written down the name of the resort where she wanted to stay and even specified which of the cottages she wanted, so I called the resort reservations number. I knew it was late there, but I figured they probably handled reservation calls twenty-four seven.

I learned that the cottage Mia wanted was already booked for the first two weeks of our planned month in the sun, so I had to choose between delaying the vacation until I could get the booking Mia wanted or taking another cottage for the first two weeks. I put the reservation people on hold while I called Mia's cell phone, but she didn't answer. I didn't want to lose the four-week window currently available, so I booked the available weeks. It would mean a two-week delay on the start of our holiday, but it wasn't possible to accommodate her wishes sooner. I knew she was going to be disappointed either way, but at least she'd get the vacation she wanted once we arrived in Fiji.

I was concerned that Mia hadn't picked up her phone when I called. It wasn't like her. She usually responded before the third ringtone. I got out the gizmo, placed it on the wall, and activated it. It took me just seconds to tag Mia from before I had left to go downtown, then jump to the present time. She was seated in a restaurant, and I could see one of her bodyguards standing near a wall in the far background. I breathed a sigh of relief that she was safe. I'd had a momentary concern that Delcona's men might have grabbed her. I swung the window around to see who she was dining with, expecting it to be one of the designers Mia had worked with when decorating the apartment or perhaps a new girlfriend. The sight that greeted my eyes ruined what had so far been a pretty decent day.

◆ ◆

I was sitting on the sofa in the main living room when Mia arrived home. As she noticed me, I took a long pull on my beer bottle and drained it. Mia came over and leaned in to kiss me. I didn't respond.

"What's the matter, sweetheart? Did you get bad news?"

"You might say that."

"What happened?"

"I tried to make the reservations for the cottage you wanted in Fiji, but it's already booked for the first two weeks of our planned vacation."

"Oh! Well, I suppose we could take another unit. It's just that I liked the view from that cottage."

"The cottage you wanted *is* available for four straight weeks two weeks into our planned vacation period, so I booked that."

"You mean we won't be leaving for another two weeks?"

"I tried to contact you to ask what you wanted to do, but you didn't answer your phone."

"Oh. Yes. I was occupied. I was having lunch, so I let it take a message. But you didn't leave one, so I figured it wasn't important."

"Well, that's why I did what I did. I wanted you to have the cottage you wanted, and it's only a short delay."

Mia smiled. "You're so thoughtful. That's one of the reasons I love you so much."

"But not enough. Right?"

"What do you mean?"

"Why didn't you tell me your luncheon date was with Marcus?"

Mia didn't respond right away, but the smile disappeared from her face.

"You told me you were never going to see him again. That promise didn't last very long, did it?"

The expression on Mia's face turned to anger. "You're spying on me, aren't you?"

"Don't go there."

"Don't go where?"

"Into the realm of righteous indignation. I'm not spying on you. You always pick up by the third ring, so when you didn't, I was concerned that something might have happened to you. I traced the GPS signal from your cell phone and learned where you were. Then I called the restaurant to ask if you were there and confirm you were okay. A waiter confirmed you were safe and having lunch with a gentleman. I asked him to send me an image of the guy, and he did, using his smartphone."

I held up my cell phone, showing her sitting at a table with Marcus. The image had clearly been taken by someone in the restaurant because the heads of other patrons were visible in the foreground. If I had been in the restaurant, she, or one of her bodyguards, would have spotted me. Actually, I *had* taken the picture, but it was taken from my office using the gizmo. I could never tell her that though. Following Billy's death, I'd made a silent vow that I would never again tell anyone about the gizmo. That included Mia most of all. I wanted her to be able to truthfully deny any knowledge of the device if it ever became an issue for any reason.

Her mouth opened for a few seconds, but she didn't say anything. I was having trouble reading her mood, but she appeared genuinely pained. Finally, she said, "It wasn't a lunch date. I was already seated in the restaurant, waiting for service, when Marcus sat down at the table. I didn't invite him. I didn't even know he was in New York."

"What does he want this time?"

"The same old thing— money. He said that if I didn't give it to him, he would tell you we'd been carrying on an affair whenever you've been away."

"And this is the first time you've seen him since Amsterdam?"

"Yes. It was the very first time since then."

"And what did you tell him?"

"That you know all about him. That you know he and I were married once. And— that I've been giving him money."

"And he said?"

"That he would make you believe everything he decides to tell you. He can be very convincing. I was frightened that you might."

"How much does he want?"

"A million Euros."

I took a deep breath and said, "I believe you."

She looked surprised. "You do? Really?"

"When you love someone, really love them, you trust them and believe what they say unless you have proof to the contrary."

"You love me?"

"Of course I love you. I've told you that."

"No, you haven't. I think I've known all along how you felt, and I've been waiting for you to say it, but you never have. We've talked about lovemaking, and the foods and drink we love, and you even told me once how much you love the look of high heels on a woman. But you've never told me you love *me*."

I was momentarily speechless as I realized she was right. Perhaps I feared our relationship wouldn't really last, and I was trying to minimize the pain I would feel when it ended. "I'm sorry, darling. I should have said it before today. I do love you. Far more than I've loved anyone ever before."

Mia wrapped her arms around my neck and kissed me deeply and passionately. As she pulled back, she said, "And I've never felt like this about anyone before. I love you more than life itself. I don't know what I'd do if I lost you because of some stupid lies Marcus tells to get more money from me."

"It's time to say goodbye to Marcus."

"Then I shouldn't give him the money he wants?"

"No. And don't worry about him anymore. I'll take care of him and ensure that he never bothers you, or us, again."

She stared at me for a few seconds, studying my face. "You have a look like I saw on my papa's face sometimes when he was having trouble with someone. That person usually disappeared and was never seen again. Are you— are you going to— kill Marcus?"

"I'm just going to make sure he never bothers you, or us, again. Don't worry about Marcus. From this point forward he's out of your life."

CHAPTER TWELVE

Our lovemaking that evening seemed better than ever. Perhaps it was my open admission that I loved Mia, or perhaps it was my assertion that I would ensure that Marcus never bothered her again. Or perhaps it was all in my mind. But there did seem to be a higher level of vitality than in past weeks. All I know for sure is that when we were done, I fell into a deep sleep and didn't stir again until after sunrise.

Following a hot shower and breakfast, I retreated to my office. Mia wasn't up yet and even the offer of hot coffee had failed to rouse her. I locked the wooden doors so she couldn't walk in on me, then set up the gizmo. I tagged Marcus in the restaurant meeting of yesterday and a quick check showed it was as she had said. She was as genuinely surprised to see him as I was.

I tracked Marcus back to his entry into the U.S. and learned that he had flown coach from the U.K. From what little I knew of him, I suspected that wasn't his usual style of travel. I continued to follow his movements and learned where he was staying. It was an inexpensive hotel a few blocks from Times Square. Then I studied his daily habits. He was spending a lot of time watching my building, probably hoping to see Mia leave so he could follow her. If she hadn't gone out by two o'clock, he'd walk to E. 57th Street and grab a cross-town bus to the West Side. At 9th Ave, he'd walk south until he was in the heart of Hell's Kitchen. I jumped to two-thirty on several days and saw that he patronized the same restaurant every day. He must really have been on the ropes financially to eat at the greasy spoon he'd chosen.

Mia still wasn't up when I left the co-op at one-thirty. I knew Marcus was watching the building, but he'd never get past security. I also knew he wouldn't follow me. I grabbed a cab and headed downtown, then had the cabbie head over to the West Side after we were a few blocks south. After I had the cab drop me near Marcus's preferred dining establishment, it was simply a matter of concealing myself where I could watch for his arrival at the eatery.

◆

Marcus arrived right on schedule. I watched as he appeared just north of my observation point and entered the restaurant. I waited ten minutes, giving him time to get seated, and then followed him in. He was seated at a booth near the rear of the place. I walked sedately towards him, but he never looked up from the menu he was studying. I would have thought he'd have it memorized by now.

As I slid into the seat across from him, his face mirrored the surprise he must have been feeling. Then he smiled.

"I wondered when you'd approach me," he said. "I guess today is the day."

I said nothing. I simply stared into his brown eyes. I had to admit that he was handsome, in a boyish sort of way, and he had an infectious and innocent smile.

"Nothing to say?" he asked after a full minute of silence between us.

"I'm a man of action, not words. I'd like to show you something."

I had removed my service weapon from its underarm holster and placed it in my right jacket pocket before entering the restaurant in preparation for this moment. I took the Glock out and rested just the front of the barrel on the top of the table. When he looked down and saw it, fear filled his eyes. I then covered it with the cheap, frayed cloth napkin from the customer setup where I was seated so no one else would see it.

The action hadn't been wasted on Marcus. He'd seen the barrel aimed at his chest and believed he might be about to die. All color seemed to drain from his face. There was something about a loaded weapon being pointed at a person that made them take you seriously. I knew I'd never use it in the crowded restaurant, but he didn't. The press about the people I'd killed in protection of my life should be enough to make him believe I'd shoot.

"I want you to stay away from Mia forever."

"You can't kill me," he said nervously. "I'm unarmed."

I knew that was true because I'd watched him dress before he left his hotel room. If he was carrying, I wanted to know about it.

"I always carry a cheap, unregistered 9mm handgun as an untraceable throwaway. If I have to shoot an unarmed perp, I can just drop it on the floor. The perp would be dead, so he couldn't deny it was his."

I had worked on my expression before leaving the co-op today. I wanted Marcus to believe he was staring death in the face, and it seemed to be working.

"Ready to order, hon?" a waitress said as she appeared next to the table.

"Give us a few more minutes, please," I said.

After she had walked away, I said to Marcus, "What's it to be?"

His mouth opened slightly but nothing came out.

"Well? Are you going to leave her alone, or do we settle this here, right now?"

"I don't have to leave her alone. She's my wife, and you're sleeping with her. You'll never get away with killing me."

"I'm sorry, your honor," I said in a calm, very subdued voice. "I tried to reason with the blackmailer, but he pulled a gun. I had no choice but to shoot." I smiled evilly and added, "You're not a citizen of this country, and I can build a great case for blackmail. You followed your ex-wife here to extort money, and things got out of hand."

"She's not my ex-wife— she's my wife."

I was silent for a minute as I tried to figure out his angle. "Won't work. Mia told me she gave a lawyer a million Euros two years ago as settlement for the final divorce."

"There was no divorce. We're still legally married according to the laws of Greece. There was a prominent lawyer who was away on an extended vacation and the office was closed. I knew his law clerk and knew he had a key to the office. I convinced him to play the role of his boss. After Mia left, I tore up the papers. If you shoot me, you'll be shooting the husband of the married woman you're having an affair with. How will that play out in court?"

"I don't believe you."

"Check it out. I'm sure you have the resources to do that. Mia is a child in many ways— so trusting and innocent. She believed me when I told her I would follow-up on the process until the divorce decree was final. That was the supposed reason for fully half of the money. I told her we'd have to buy a few judges off to have the decree granted quickly. But, as I said, I never filed the papers."

As I looked into his frightened eyes, I believed him. And it fit with everything else I knew about him. He was a swindler, liar, and con man. But he was also a coward. He might be lying now, but I didn't think so.

"I'll check it out. If you're lying, it would be better if you're long gone before I learn the truth."

"I'm not lying."

"We'll see. And I'll be seeing you again."

The Glock was back in the holster before I slid out of the booth and stood up.

"You'll have nothing more to do with Mia. If you approach her again, I'll know and I'll find you. When I've learned the truth about the divorce, I'll be in touch."

I didn't look back, but from the corner of my right eye I watched his reflection in the mirrors behind the lunch counter. If he had so much as twitched, I would have hit the floor and pulled out the Glock. He didn't, and I didn't.

◆

After leaving the restaurant, I didn't grab a cab. I wanted to think, so I began walking north, turning east on 58th street, walking until I reached Columbus Circle. After crossing the street, I entered Central Park and walked aimlessly along the pathways for perhaps three hours before heading home.

As I entered the apartment, Mia stuck her head out of the bedroom, then came out to greet me. "Sweetheart, I didn't know you were going out to today," she said as she reached me and then kissed me on the cheek.

"I went to see Marcus."

"Marcus? Is he…?"

"Darling, do you remember when you first arrived here? You told me you paid Marcus a million Euros for a divorce."

"Yes."

"Marcus says he never filed the divorce papers."

"What? But he promised to follow through."

"I don't think promises mean very much to Marcus. His failure to file the papers isn't the worst of it. According to Marcus, the lawyer you went to visit wasn't a lawyer at all. He was the lawyer's clerk whose boss was out of town for an extended time. Marcus said he convinced the clerk to play the role of the lawyer, but I suspect Marcus blackmailed the clerk because the legal penalties for that kind of impersonation are stiff. So the divorce process wouldn't have been legal anyway."

"That bastard," she said with venom in her voice. "I trusted him. I once told you I didn't love Marcus anymore but that I didn't hate him. That's changed. I never want to even see him again."

"Marcus insists you're still his wife, and we need to know for sure. Can you verify the status of your marriage through your contacts in Greece? Your uncle, or perhaps your attorneys?"

"I'm sure my uncle can check to see if Marcus filed divorce papers and learn the current status of our marriage."

"Good. Why don't you call your uncle today. Now in fact."

"It's very late there, darling. There's a ten-hour difference. It has to be about four in the morning."

"Then call tonight once they're up."

"I will. I'll call around eleven p.m. That will be about nine a.m. there. Thank you, darling."

"For what?"

"For believing me. For believing *in* me."

"When you love someone, really love them, you trust them and believe what they say. I know I haven't said it enough, but I do love you with all my heart. And I'm going to say it often."

Mia smiled widely and took my hand. "Come with me," she said, then pulled me towards the bedroom. I went willingly— as always.

◆　◆　◆

I didn't know how the bombshell about Mia's divorce was going to play out or if we'd have to cancel our vacation plans, but in any event I had two weeks of time on my hands before we were scheduled to leave. There was probably little I could do about Delcona before then, although it would be highly satisfying to know the matter was settled as we lay on the beach in Fiji.

And another matter was plaguing my thoughts these days. I had long ago decided that I would see Delcona pay the ultimate price for his crimes even if it meant my death. But now I had Mia to think about. She had whirled back into my life at a time when I was at one of my lowest points and lifted my spirits to the heavens.

I still intended to see that Delcona paid for his sins against humanity and his crimes against my friends, but I was no longer so willing to walk into a gunfight where I might be outgunned twenty to one. However, no matter what I chose to do, I could do nothing while he was under maximum twenty-four seven surveillance. If only there was some way I could use the evidence I had filmed on the gizmo. There was no statute of limitations on murder. Morris's murder alone could be enough to put Delcona away permanently.

I had solved one of the two most recently assigned cases, so I decided to begin work on the other. I logged into the FBI system with the intent of getting a hard copy of the files. As the printer began spitting out the first sheets about the case, which promised to consume a full ream of paper, I pulled off the top few and began reading.

The case was four years old, and the last two reviews had turned up nothing new. It was another abduction case, but this time it involved an adult. A young woman of twenty-two failed to return home after work one day, and a ransom demand was received in the mail the next day with orders not to call the police. The woman's father immediately called the police and they set up shop in the victim's home.

No further contact from the kidnappers was ever received, and the ransom note, printed on a computer printer using an inexpensive brand of copier paper available everywhere, provided no significant clues. There were no fingerprints on the note or the envelope, except for those of the mail carrier. The woman's home was in Pittsburg, but the note had been mailed in Baltimore.

When no further contact had been made by the kidnappers in two weeks, the investigation team moved out of the woman's home. The Pittsburg PD and the FBI kept the case open until it was obvious that no further contact from the kidnappers was forthcoming. The last time anyone had seen the woman was when she'd pulled out of the parking lot at the company where she'd worked. But for the note, the case would have been treated as a simple missing persons case.

I powered up the gizmo and tagged the woman at her home the morning of the abduction. Then I jumped ahead to the present time. The woman was now living in Denver, Colorado. She had changed her hair color and style, and her eyes looked different. I guessed she was wearing colored contacts. But there was little doubt that it was the woman who had allegedly been abducted. It appeared to be another one of those cases where I found it so difficult to explain how I arrived at a solution.

I let the printer run, but knowing there was really no victim caused me to lose interest in solving it quickly. I was just sitting there, waiting for the printer to finish its task, when a call came through on my business line. I sat back and listened as the prospective client left a message.

The caller identified himself as Edward Harris, and I was instantly alert. It was a name from my past. Harris ran a bail bond operation downtown, and I had sought work there locating skips after first finding the gizmo. Harris was the first one to use my services, but he had tried to cheat me after I located his skip. When I refused to locate another skip for him, he paid me the full amount we had agreed on initially for the first job. There was no problem with payment for the second.

"Colt," the answering machine recorded, "I know you're a big, hotshot recovery expert earning million of dollars for every job these days, but I'm desperate. I have a skip that failed to appear in court. His phone has been disconnected and no one has seen him since before the court date. I stand to lose five hundred G's if I can't get him back. I'm begging you. I need your help. If anyone can find my skip in time, it's you. Please call me back."

Harris had given me my first job and then vouched for me when I went after my first artwork recovery job. Since I wasn't really occupied at present, it couldn't hurt to do this for him. I didn't actually have to pick up the skip since he had guys for the muscle work. I'd only have to find the guy and then run support from home using the gizmo when they grabbed him. I dialed the number Harris had left as I glanced up at the clock. It was one-oh-eight p.m.

"Ed, Colt James," I said when he answered.

"Colt buddy, thanks for calling me back. Can you help me out?"

"I'll see what I can do. Give me the particulars." After Harris had given me the skip's name, description, date and location of his original court appearance, and the crimes he was accused of, I told him I'd get back to him soon.

I set up the gizmo and located the perp at his arraignment hearing. Then I tagged him and jumped to the present. With a bond of five hundred thousand I expected he'd be in Venezuela or some other remote place where extraditions are difficult at best. Instead, I located him hiding out in Cleveland.

I debated how long I should wait before calling Harris back. It was like the case with the Ferrari— if I called too soon, he'd expect me to always call within that timeframe. But if I waited too long, he wouldn't have enough time to get his people in place. After putting the gizmo away, I sighed and reached for the business phone to call him, but before I could pick up the receiver, the phone rang. I stopped and then listened to the message as it was recorded. It was Saul Fodor, and he needed to speak with me right away. I picked up the phone before he finished leaving the message.

"Hi, Saul. It's Colt. I'm at home. What's up?"

"Hi, Colt. I'm glad I caught you in. One of our clients in Memphis was burglarized overnight. He just got home and discovered it. The police are there now. How quickly can you get to Teterboro? The company jet is being prepped now. Uh, you're not tied up on an active FBI investigation, are you?"

"No. I just took on a small case for an old friend, but it should only take me a day to wrap up."

"I hate to pull rank, but you remember our deal. Normally I wouldn't worry about one day, but this is a very important client. I promised him that the best recovery expert in the world would be at his estate before midnight."

"What was stolen?"

"Irreplaceable country music awards and memorabilia."

"What was robbed? Graceland?"

"No, but in country-music circles he's as recognizable as Elvis. I don't even want to say his name over the telephone because we have to keep this quiet. A car will meet the company jet at the Memphis airport and take you to the estate."

"Okay, Saul. I'll get ready immediately. I should be at Teterboro in about an hour, or maybe three, depending on traffic. This time of day the tunnels and bridges get really bogged down with outbound traffic."

"This time of day it will probably take you the three hours to get to Teterboro. Head over to the W 30th Street heliport as soon as you can. I'll arrange to have a chopper hop you over to Teterboro."

"Okay, Saul. I just have to shave and take a quick shower. Then I'll be on my way."

"Call my secretary when you leave your building. She'll coordinate all your travel arrangements."

"Okay. Anything else?"

"Just that *anything* this client wants, this client gets, okay?"

"Got it."

As I hung up the receiver, I knew the decision about Harris had been taken from my hands. I would be too preoccupied to be playing timing games with his guys. I would have to squeeze them in as best I could.

"Hello, Ed, your guy is in Cleveland," I said as he answered the phone.

"Cleveland? What the hell is he doing in Cleveland?"

"Ask him when you see him. Get Vinny and his guys on the road as quickly as possible. Tell him to call me when he gets to Cleveland. If I don't pick up, tell him I'll call him back as soon as I can. I'm heading to the airport now."

"You're going to spot for him and the other guys?"

"Yes, just like before."

"What's the address in Cleveland?"

"I don't have that yet, but I'm sure your guy is there."

"You're amazing, Colt. We've been looking for this guy for a month and you find him in less than an hour. I wish you could teach us how you do it."

"It's magic, Ed. Smoke and mirrors."

"I don't believe that. You're just the best there ever was."

"Don't lay it on too thick or I'll have to raise my price."

"Uh, it's the same as before, right? Ten percent with half going to you and half to be split between Vinny and his pickup team?"

"Yeah, same as before. I gotta go, Ed. I have a plane to catch."

"Okay. Thanks, Colt. I appreciate you doing this for me."

"You're welcome, Ed. Nice talking to you again. I'll call you after the skip is in the van and give you the account number at my bank so you can deposit my half of the recovery fee."

"Okay, Colt. I'll talk to you tomorrow."

As soon as I was off the phone, I locked up my office and ran for the shower.

Mia had gone out shopping, so I called her cell phone. She picked up on the third ring.

"Darling, are you through working?"

"No, sweetheart. In fact I have to go to Tennessee on a recovery case for Saul Fodor. I'll call you tonight once I know what's what. Have you instructed your bodyguards that Marcus isn't to be allowed anywhere near you?"

"Yes, dear."

"Okay. I'll talk with you tomorrow. I love you."

"And I love you. Have a safe trip."

◆ ◆

I flagged down a cab as I stepped from the building and gave him the heliport address. As he pulled back into traffic, I called Fodor's secretary. She told me the chopper was already waiting at the pad and the jet was doing its preflight procedures.

Then I sat back, took a deep breath, and looked out the window as the cab driver wove his way through car, bus, and truck traffic, narrowly missing a bike messenger at one point.

CHAPTER THIRTEEN

W hen the chopper touched down at Teterboro, one of those golf-style carts they use at airports for a variety of purposes was waiting for me. It whisked me to the company's corporate jet, which started to move within seconds of my fastening my seatbelt. It was great getting the deluxe treatment. It beat first-class service on an airline by a city mile and coach class by ten miles.

After we were in the air, the flight attendant asked me what I'd like to drink and handed me a wine and beverage list. I told her coffee was fine. Then she gave me a small menu and asked what I'd like for lunch. I had a choice between chicken alfredo, teriyaki salmon, or a vegetable plate. The meals were naturally pre-prepared and refrigerated, and would be heated in a microwave when I chose which dish I preferred. I selected the teriyaki salmon and endless coffee during the eighty-minute trip.

◆ ◆

The jet touched down at Memphis International on schedule and taxied to a parking ramp area at the north end where a limousine was waiting. The driver took my suitcase and placed it in the trunk, then held the rear door so I could get in. I was loving the star treatment. It probably wouldn't have impressed Mia, who had grown up with wealth and privilege, but it was unique treatment for me.

When we reached the estate, the gate was open and the guard waved us through without even checking to see who the occupants were. Perhaps he knew the driver. Or perhaps the driver had phoned as we neared the estate. The darkened window between the front of the limo and the rear seats was closed, so I wouldn't have heard the conversation. Perhaps the driver was even part of the estate staff. I had assumed the transportation connections were all legit and had been made by Fodor's secretary, so I hadn't bothered to check any credentials.

As we neared the front portico, I saw why it wasn't necessary to check the identity of the limo's occupants. There were six police cars parked in the driveway and an officer standing in front of the main door. What surprised me was that there were no media people in evidence. I surmised that news of the robbery had been totally suppressed. That was unusual where high-profile folks were involved. I'd expected to find paparazzi trying to storm the front gate while helicopters and drones with mounted cameras buzzed overhead.

The limo driver jumped out after parking behind the line of police cars and opened the left-side door for me because the other door was blocked by bushes. As I walked to the main entrance, the officer held up his hand and said, "The family isn't receiving any visitors today, sir."

I reached into my jacket and pulled out my FBI credentials, flipping open the wallet as I said, "I have a special invitation."

The officer looked at the ID, lowered his hand, and stepped out of the way. "Of course, Special Agent James. You're expected."

Even though I was expected, I didn't want to barge in, so I rang the bell. The door was answered by a young woman wearing an apron but not a maid's uniform; however, I assumed her to be part of the housekeeping staff. She opened the door wide before asking who I was, then stepped aside to allow me to enter when I identified myself.

"Wait here, please," was all she said before disappearing towards the rear of the house.

About thirty seconds later the owner of the estate came out to greet me personally. Although I'm not a country music fan, I recognized him instantly. "What, no deerstalker cap?" was all he said at first, then smiled wide enough to light up the room. "Betcha never heard that one before," he said jokingly as he extended his hand.

"Maybe once or twice," I said as I smiled and shook his hand.

"That's the problem with being identified with the most famous detective in literature. And Saul says you're even better than old Sherlock on his best day. He says you have a one hundred percent recovery record."

"So far, that's true. But the odds in favor of a failure get larger with every case. However, that's not going to happen on this investigation."

"That's what I like to hear."

"Have the police concluded their investigation, Mist..."

I stopped talking when he held up his hand. "Just Georgie to my friends. No Mister."

I smiled and said, "I'm Colt to my friends."

"Welcome to my home, Colt. Let's go into the front room."

Georgie led the way to the front room and gestured towards a couple of comfortable-looking chairs. "Have a seat, Colt, and we can talk. Normally I take guests into my study when I want to talk, but the police have temporarily taken over that room."

After we sat, he continued, "The cops are still here in force, but they can't seem to find much to go on from what I've overheard. Don't let the cop in charge, a lieutenant named Danners, annoy you. His shorts are in a twist because Saul called you in so soon. The insurance policy allows the police and insurance company investigators a full year to recover the stolen items before the payout is required, but in a year's time my stuff could be spread across the globe, making it impossible to recover.

"Music fans are like sports fans. They want so bad to own something that once belonged to an idol that they'll pay exorbitant prices to get it even knowing they can never show it to anyone else. The actual value of the items from a materials standpoint is low. They can't be melted down and sold in a different form. It's like an old baseball. By itself, it's probably not worth much, but with Babe Ruth's autograph on it, it can be worth plenty. And if you have a provenance that proves it was the winning homerun in an important game, the value can skyrocket. Without the celebrity status associated with it, it's just a dirty old baseball."

"Since you believe the lead cop may not be cooperative, perhaps you can tell me what *you* know, Georgie."

"I was at a party up in Nashville and arrived home this morning. We found the gate wide open and the security guard asleep in the booth. At least I thought he was sleeping. But my bodyguard shook him and couldn't wake him up, so I had my driver call an ambulance and then stay with the guard while my bodyguard and I walked up to the house. The front door was *wide* open and the lights were all on.

"I called out, but no one answered. There should have been a second security guard, the one who patrols the grounds, but he was nowhere in sight. My bodyguard told me to wait outside while he looked around inside. A few minutes later he returned. He had found the missing guard and the house staff— my cook and a housekeeper— in the kitchen. All appeared to be asleep, but like the gate guard we couldn't wake them. I immediately called the police and told them what we'd found. And I told them we were probably going to need more medical people. There wasn't much to do then except wait for them to arrive. I didn't want to touch anything and possibly ruin fingerprints, but I looked around. The crooks really cleaned me out. Every award I ever received and had here at the house is missing, along with autographed photos of me with other famous people and a ton of memorabilia."

"What's the value of the missing items?"

"To me, they're priceless. It's difficult to put a price on a lifetime of memories, ya know. I still have my personal memories, of course, but looking at the things that were stolen never failed to help me remember little details I might otherwise not have thought about. The policy with Saul's company is for thirty million, assuming all of the insured items were stolen. I looked around, and that appears to be the case, but I'll have to get a copy of the list from my attorney before I can say for sure. I called his office, but he's in court today. His secretary said she'd messenger it over as soon as she could."

Georgie must have seen my eyes open a little wider when he said the policy amount because he immediately defended it by saying, "It's a reflection of my life's work, Colt. Hell, it *is* my life. It's actually beyond any monetary value. And the premiums aren't that bad. I still bring in a lot of money."

"I understand, Georgie. I was just a little surprised given what you said about the material's value. What about your family, Georgie? Are they okay?"

"My wife and daughter are in Paris for a brief shopping trip, and my son is on a concert tour in Colorado. I haven't told any of them yet. My wife might be happy some of it's gone. She's complained more than once that I attach too much significance to some *old trophies*."

"Any ideas on who might be responsible for the theft?"

"No. None. After the medical people arrived, we learned that the gate guard was tasered, then drugged. Last time I checked, he was still out, as are the others, but they're all expected to fully recover. Perhaps they can shed some light on this when they wake up. The people who did this knew what they were doing because they found the secret security room where the recording devices are located. They took the DVDs with the day's recordings and then shut the equipment off."

"You don't send a feed to an external monitoring site?"

"No way. I'm just a country boy who got lucky and made it big. I like to walk around the house in my tee-shirt and boxers when I don't have company. My cook and housekeeper are okay with that, and I trust them to keep that information private, but I certainly don't want some unknown person at a remote monitoring site to see me. The pictures would be all over the news and internet in a day. For privacy's sake, I mostly use the indoor pool and spa to avoid the planes, helicopters, and now drones that are always flying around. Whenever I appear outside the house, I'm fully clothed."

I smiled and said, "I prefer to walk around my house in my tee-shirt and shorts too. My girlfriend doesn't seem to mind. At least she's never said anything."

"What's to mind? Really. You can see advertisements of half-naked men and women in almost every newspaper, magazine, and TV ad these days. And premiers and award ceremonies seem to have become an opportunity for women to wear as little as possible. I expect that one day we'll see a starlet show up in just pasties, g-string, and heels. But to the general public, or the media at least, it's a scandal if a male celebrity isn't wearing a tux or at least a suit. I swear they'd make more of it if a male celeb wore tennis shoes with his suit than if a female celeb wore pasties as the only thing above her navel."

I laughed. "You may be right, Georgie."

"Right about what?" we heard from the hallway. A man in an inexpensive, off-the-rack suit entered the room. His face had 'cop' written all over it. I wondered if I was getting *that* look. I probably was.

"Colt," Georgie said, "this is Lieutenant Danners. He's heading up the robbery investigation."

I stood up and extended my hand as Danners reached us, but he ignored it. *Another Brigman,* I thought as I dropped my arm.

"So this is the great Colton James. What, no deerstalker cap and pipe?"

I smiled and said, "I guess I left them in the car, along with my magnifying glass." I looked over at Georgie and saw he was grinning. "Well, have you solved the case, Lieutenant, and recovered the stolen items?"

"We believe we know who pulled the job and my people are out looking for them now. We should have all the items back by tomorrow. So you can head back to Washington, or wherever you came from."

"That's great news, Lieutenant. I'm preparing to go on vacation to Fiji. I have all my reservations in place, but this has to be wrapped up before I leave. So it's wonderful that you've identified the perps and now it's only a matter of hours before the items are all recovered and the perps are apprehended. What do you figure? An hour? Two?"

Danners looked at Georgie before saying, "It may be a little longer than that. We won't know until we bring in our suspects."

"Oh. Well. I'll stay out of your hair if you'll share your findings with me. Deal?"

"Sure, call me in six months and I'll send you a copy of my final report."

I looked Danners in the eyes before I said, "So that's the way it's going to be, eh? Okay, I can handle that."

"What do you mean by 'handle that?'"

"You conduct your investigation and I'll conduct mine. After I've learned who committed the crime and forwarded my report to the insurance company, they'll be in touch with your captain so he can send you and your boys out to round up the thieves and get the stolen items back. I always prefer to work *with* the local authorities in a spirit of full co-operation, but when they won't have any part of it, I'm fine with going it alone."

Danners grimaced, looked at Georgie, then turned and left the room.

"I don't think he'll be adding your name to his Christmas card list, Colt," Georgie said.

"I guess not. It's a shame. I really do prefer to work with the local authorities in a cooperative sense, and I'm happy to let them take the public credit. Can I see the secret security room where the recordings were wiped?"

"Not right now. The police have declared it off limits to anyone except their people. Perhaps tomorrow."

"Okay. Well, I can't view the crime scene, can't view the security room, and can't interview the witnesses. Not a real productive first hour." I smiled. "But no worry. I'll get your precious memories back to you Georgie, in spite of Danners lack of cooperation. Since there's not much I can do here, I might as well go to my hotel and start working the case with what I know."

"That's not much to start with."

"On the contrary. What you've told me gives me a tremendous amount to start with. I'll begin by writing every-thing out and then start assembling a profile of the robbery and the perps. Criminals are creatures of habit, as are most humans. I'll start scanning the histories of past crimes to see if anything matches up. If it does, I'll begin checking to see where the perps are now, or where their children, relatives, or former cellmates are.

"It appears to have been a professional job. It may not have been committed by professionals, but whoever planned it knew what he, or she, was doing— unless it was plain dumb luck. The thieves struck when the entire family was away, in addition to your bodyguard and driver. They in-capacitated the gate guard before he could give a warning, and they had some kind of advance notice about your security room. Find the planner and we're on our way to recovering everything that was stolen."

"Do you think Danners is onto anything?"

"In all honesty— no. He sorta reminds of the Chief of Police in the movie Casablanca. What was the character's name— Captain Louis Renault? Remember when, in the final minutes of the movie, Renault orders his men to 'round up the usual suspects,' all the while knowing that none of them was guilty?"

Georgie chuckled. "Yes, I remember that scene."

"It was just a cover story for Renault to hide behind so it would appear he was doing something productive in the investigation should anyone later ask. Uh, is the driver who picked me up at the airport one of your people?"

"Yes. Maximilian has been with me for— six years. Do you suspect him?"

"No, not at all. I was just wondering if he was one of your employees. When we arrived, the guard at the gate waved us through without checking to see who was in the car."

"He already knew that Max went to pick you up."

"I see. Do you happen to know if Saul's secretary made hotel reservations for me?"

"No, I don't."

"Okay, I'll call her. Can Max drop me off at a car rental place?"

"Sure. Just tell him where you want to go."

"Great. One last thing. Is there a direct number where I can usually reach you?"

"Sure, it's…"

Georgie stopped when I held up my hand. I took out my cell, activated an app, held the phone towards his mouth, and nodded. He gave me the number. I checked to make sure the phone had recorded it correctly and said, "File phone number as Georgie," then nodded when it completed the storage request.

"Okay, Georgie. Thanks for your hospitality. I'll be in touch."

We shook hands and I left. Max was standing by the limo, buffing the hood where a bird had just dropped its signature in white, with a little green and black mixed in. Even the rich and famous got shit on occasionally.

I reached Saul's secretary and learned where reservations had been made, then asked Max to drop me at the car rental agency nearest the hotel.

◆ ◆ ◆

Every time I checked into a motel or hotel in the U.S. these days, I thought wistfully about the wonderful hotels in

Europe. Don't misunderstand me— I didn't mean to say the U.S. hotels weren't pristine. And the hotel staffs here were great. It was just that the rooms and buildings in Europe had a certain charm missing in many U.S. hotels. Here, everything seemed to be glass, plastic, or vinyl. But the beds were always great, and that was what I was mostly interested in when I traveled on business.

My departure from New York had been with such urgency that I'd never had a chance to view the robbery. So as soon as I was settled into my room, I took out my lighter and extracted the gizmo. As I placed it against the wall over the small desk and touched the corner, the crease lines disappeared and it illuminated.

I used a new app on my smartphone to learn the latitude and longitude of Georgie's house, set the date for last evening and the time for six p.m. Nothing was happening at that hour so I kept jumping ahead an hour at a time until the guard at the gate was not visible through the window because he was lying on the floor.

I then kept pushing the time backward in five-minute intervals until the guard was upright. I watched as the time passed and made a note of the time when the perps attacked. I tagged the driver and then backed up the time by ten minutes and located the small van where it had been parked about a mile from the house until the perps were ready to move in.

The art theft case where I'd first met Saul Fodor involved a smash-and-grab team that didn't harm anyone because no one resisted. But I could tell just by looking at them that they wouldn't have hesitated to pound someone into the ground if that person had given them an excuse. This new team made that other group look like a bunch of little leaguers. I hoped I never had to come up against any of them because there was no doubt in my mind that it would end in gunfire.

There were seven men in all, and I got a good look at them before they rubbed some kind of black makeup all over their faces and pulled their ski masks down. Only the van driver refrained from using the blackface. It seemed as if someone had cleared out death row at the nearest Tennessee prison to pull this job. I watched as the van pulled up at the estate gate.

The guard came out of his booth and walked to the driver's window as it rolled down. Without uttering a word, the driver raised a taser pistol above the bottom edge of the open window and fired it into the chest of the guard. I was surprised they chose to electroshock the guard, but they probably wanted a silent approach to the house. Once the guard was down, and while he was still shaking convulsively from the electroshock, one of the team jumped from the van and jabbed a needle into the neck of the incapacitated man. In seconds the guard stopped moving and appeared to be unconscious. Meanwhile, the driver had applied black makeup to his face.

As the van then moved sedately towards the house, the robbery team prepared to jump out and head for prearranged positions. I followed each man until I happened upon two who went around to the kitchen door. The guard who was supposed to be patrolling was sitting at a table drinking what I assumed to be coffee or tea while he joked with two women who were also seated at the table. I watched as the thugs barged in, guns at the ready. They waved their guns in a threatening manner as they shouted orders at the frightened trio.

One of them went around behind the three employees and stuck a needle into the neck of the guard. Almost instantly he began to go limp. I was surprised that rather than simply letting the man fall, the robber with the needle grabbed him and lowered him to the floor. Perhaps that was to help calm the women, but they began screaming anyway. Their voices were quickly silenced as they too were drugged.

With the staff taken care of, the second robber in the kitchen gave some sort of "all clear" signal. The other robbers left their outside posts and raced to either the front door or the kitchen door. A large cargo van, which I hadn't seen until then, entered the grounds and approached the house.

All of the robbers were dressed alike in black clothing. They wore driving-style gloves to cover their hands and knit caps that covered their heads completely but for their eyes, nose and mouth. It was obvious their faces were blackened beneath the ski masks so even their race couldn't be surmised.

Once the house was determined to be clear, one of the team hurried to the secret security room. The entrance was through a hall closet, and he had to have had inside information to know its location, how to open the entrance, and even how to turn on the lights without performing any kind of a search. I watched as he expertly typed commands into a keyboard. One by one, the monitors went black. Once the recording was ended, he issued commands to clear the cache memory and open the four DVD recorder trays. As he removed the discs, he slipped them into a zippered pocket of his pant leg, closed the zipper, and left the room.

Meanwhile, the other robbers had carried large chests into the house from the cargo van and were busy packing them with memorabilia. Each man had a list of the memorabilia he was responsible for removing. I was surprised at the delicacy they exhibited as they carefully wrapped each item and stored it in one of the chests. They had to know they had all night to do the packing. I watched the activity at a number of points around the house. The lists made them aware of everything they were after, and they worked methodically to get every last precious item.

When the last chest was packed into the cargo van, the house was cleaned out of awards and memorabilia. Little evidence remained that the house was occupied by an icon in the country music industry. The walls in Georgie's study were virtually bare, and the desk and tables were empty. The robbers piled into the small van and the two vehicles left the premises.

As my stomach began reminding me I hadn't eaten anything since lunch on the plane, I glanced at the clock on the nightstand. I was surprised to see how long I'd been at it. I knew this hotel didn't offer room service, so I would have to go out.

At the front desk I asked the clerk if he could recommend a good restaurant in the area. Reaching below the counter, he produced a printed page that listed nearby facilities. He said the hotel forbid recommendations by hotel employees, but I noticed his right index finger was pointing to a nearby steak house. I nodded and thanked him for the list as I slipped him a ten dollar bill.

An hour later I was enjoying one of the best prime rib dinners I'd had in a long time. I washed it down with a couple of bottles of my favorite beer, skipped dessert, and paid the bill. There was nothing like a great meal to make it seem like all was right with the world.

When I returned to the hotel I wanted to identify the team members, but I had another priority to take care of. I had to locate the skip for Ed Harris.

I reset the gizmo and located the skip, then began putting together a plan for his capture. I first identified a location for the capture team to assemble, then tried to see what weapons the skip had available. I was surprised to find none. The skip was charged with narcotics possession, and those guys were usually well armed, but there were no weapons in evidence. That didn't mean there were none. I was unable to see inside closed drawers, cabinets, and dark closets, or beneath seat and couch cushions.

I completed the plan for the skip recovery and then just had to wait until I heard from Vinny.

CHAPTER FOURTEEN

When I returned to work on Georgie's case, my first task was to identify the members of the robbery team. I'd become somewhat adept at tagging people and then zipping back to their births and getting their names from the hospital records. Then it was a matter of observing them when they were congregated to determine the leader or leaders. Once I had that information about the group, I followed them when they left the estate to see where they stored the loot from the job.

I watched as the cargo truck driver parked the truck near a storage business and then got into the small van with the other members of the team. Except for the driver, the guys in the van had all changed their clothes. The driver then took the van to an untended parking area across the road from a factory that worked around the clock. As the small truck emptied, each of the robbers headed for a separate car. They didn't appear to have a common destination as they drove out of the parking area.

I stayed with the person I believed to be the team's leader, and recorded his address, then returned to the time where the team left the parking lot and followed each one to learn where they were going. In an hour I knew where each one was currently residing. Of the eight robbers, six were living in cheap motels. The leader and the cargo van driver were living in what appeared to be furnished apartments. At least that was the impression I received when first seeing their lodging because there didn't seem to be any personal items in their apartments. Without the cheap furniture, the apartments would have had the austere appearance of my apartment before Mia arrived.

Having compiled a complete list of the thieves' names and addresses, I decided I needed a break. A nice hot shower always relaxed me more than anything else, so I stripped down and spent the next ten minutes under the hot spray. As I slipped between the sheets, I felt great.

◆　◆

I was awakened from a deep slumber by the ringtone emanating from my phone. Although I usually put the phone into the special protective case that blocked all signals, I had left it out in case Vinny called.

"Hello?" I mumbled as I tried to wake up.

"Colt, it's Vinny. Sorry to call you so late, but we just got into Cleveland. The van broke down and it took half a day to get it fixed. But we're all ready to go whenever you are."

"Hi, Vinny. Get some rest if you can. It's better if we do this in the daylight. Got something to write with?"

"Yeah, Colt."

"Okay, be at this address around ten a.m." I gave Vinny an address a few blocks from where the skip was living, then said, "I'll fill you in at that time. Keep your guys out of sight in the van, and try to look innocuous until you're ready to move in."

"Innocu what?"

"Try to blend in with the community and not appear threatening."

Vinny chuckled. "No problem. We've got magnetic signs for the sides of the van now and a ladder on the roof, so it looks like a painting contractor's van. We even wear coveralls splattered with paint until it's time to move in."

"Great Vinny. Call me at ten. I'll verify the skip's location and tell you the best place to park the van for the pickup."

"You're going to assist, right? I mean you're going to watch the action and advise?"

"Of course, Vinny."

"Okay, Colt. Thanks. I'll call you at ten. It's nice to be working with you again."

"Same here, Vinny. Talk to you in about— eight hours."

◆ ◆ ◆

When I awoke at seven, I immediately used the gizmo to verify that the skip was home. He was, and he was still sleeping. I performed another video sweep of the apartment and still failed to see any firearms, but I didn't believe he had none available. It just didn't fit with the profile of a narcotics dealer. They weren't only concerned with the police. They were also always worried about being ripped off by competitors— and even underlings looking to move up. After carrying a gun long enough, a person begins to feel undressed when they don't have one on them, and positively defenseless if they don't have one handy.

When Vinny called I used the gizmo to verify he was parked where I had told him to wait. He was. And there was no indication that there was anyone with him. His guys were completely out of sight in the van. I gave him a new address and instructed him on where he should park the van to be close to the skip's home. I watched as he drove the van and parked exactly where I said.

"Okay, Vinny. The skip is in his apartment. It looks like he's getting ready to eat a late breakfast. No, wait. He's pulling on a jacket. I think he's getting ready to leave. Stand by."

I watched as the skip finished dressing by opening a drawer and removing a 9mm automatic, sticking it in the waistband at the small of his back. Then he removed a small-caliber revolver and stuck it in his right calf-length boot. A straight-edge went into the left boot. Fully dressed and armed, he headed for the door.

I filled Vinny in on the weapons he would be facing and their locations. Then it was simply a matter of seeing where the skip went.

Sometimes you get lucky, and sometimes you're unlucky. This time Vinny got lucky. The van was parked on the same side of the street as the skip's residence, just three houses down, and the skip headed in that direction. Vinny, with his painter's cap pulled down, was bent over two gallon-sized paint cans on the sidewalk, ostensibly trying to open them. The skip walked right past him without paying him the slightest notice. Vinny stood and spun, then leapt onto the skip's back while the other guys opened the van door and piled out. Vinny had the guy down on the sidewalk with his two-hundred-plus pounds of muscle preventing the skip from getting to his feet. He had his arms wrapped around the skip, which prevented him from reaching any of his hidden weapons. The other guys were on the skip in seconds as well. If this had been a game of football, they might have been penalized for piling on. But using their weight to squash the target to the ground was an effective technique when dealing with an armed drug-pusher because it quickly ended all resistance.

In under a minute the skip was disarmed and handcuffed. The guys locked him in the small cell in the back of the van and the excitement was over for another day. They stripped off their disguises so their uniforms would be clearly visible to local residents who might have seen the activity and called the police. One of them also removed the phony magnetic signs so their law enforcement team logo showed everyone that they were just performing a legal recovery of a wanted and dangerous felon. Most of the recovery team was white, and the narcotics dealer was black, so it was expected that the recovery might make the news if anyone had recorded it with their cell phone.

Vinny wanted to get out of the area before the local activists and protestors showed up, so he had his guys pile into the van. As they started to pull away from the curb, one young guy who had observed the arrest did jump in front of the van in an effort to stop it. But Vinny's driver faked him out by turning the wheel to the right, and then quickly drove around him on the left. The young man was left shaking his fist at the van after throwing a rock he found in the gutter at the quickly disappearing vehicle.

"Thanks, Colt," Vinny said as they headed for the freeway. "You made that about the easiest grab of a narcotics felon we've had in a long time. I wish we had you available for every recovery. By the way, just where the hell *are* you?"

"Not all that far, Vinny. Tell Harris I'll call him later. I've got to get back to work on the insurance case I'm working. Good luck to you and the guys. I'm glad no one was hurt."

"You and me both, pal. Take care."

After the call ended, I sat back and took a deep breath. It had been an exciting few minutes. Even though I was never in any danger myself, I knew my heart had been racing. The guys who actually did the collecting felt like an extension of my body when I was watching the action and warning them about the dangers. It was like watching an exciting movie that had successfully drawn me into the action. There was no personal danger, but I felt a part of it just the same.

With the excitement over, it was time to get back to the mundane tasks. I checked on the cargo van left by the storage facility and discovered it was now gone. Backtracking through time, I learned that it had been moved as soon as the facility opened. The leader of the operation and the driver of the van had offloaded their booty into a formerly empty storage locker. Before Vinny and the guys had even tackled the skip, the storage locker had been sealed and the cargo van had disappeared into the growing traffic as local residents began their work day.

I knew who had committed the theft and where the stolen items were. All I needed now was to identify the mastermind behind the theft and the person who provided the information about the security room and schedule of the family. They might even be the same person. And who better to plan a robbery than a family member who would be far away during the robbery? Someone may have had more to gain than the value of the awards and memorabilia.

It was almost noon, so I decided to have lunch before wrapping up my investigation. A full stomach would make it easier to think up a pretense for how I had solved the case.

There was a Chinese restaurant listed on the page the desk clerk had given me, so I checked it out. It was busy, which was always a good recommendation, so I sat down and ordered a dinner of shrimp with lobster sauce over white rice. There were a few too many bamboo shoots in the lobster sauce to suit me, but I pushed them aside and ate the rest. It was good, and if I stayed in town, I would return at some point for another meal.

Back at the hotel I had just sat down to work again when I suddenly had a thought. I quickly checked the accommodations of the eight robbers. Every one of them appeared to be gone. The rooms and the closets, where I could see inside, were empty of all personal possessions. They had skipped town. But had they really left all their loot behind? I reset the gizmo to the time when the thieves were cleaning out the houses and tagged four of the larger items. Then I jumped ahead to the present time. All four of the tagged items were inside the storage locker, even though it was too dark inside for me to see them. So the robbery team was gone but had left at least some of their loot behind. Perhaps they feared police roadblocks or something where all vans would be searched. Or perhaps they had been hired just to pull the job and store the loot for a third party. They might have been paid off and were now enjoying the fruits of their one night's work.

Well, it wasn't a tragedy. I knew who they were, and with the gizmo I could locate them at any time. I decided to write up my report for Saul Fodor. The insurance company was more interested in getting the stolen items returned quickly than in knowing who had committed the crime, but I gave him the names of the thieves as a bonus.

When I finished the report I sent a copy to the business email address of Saul's secretary. As always, I didn't like 'solving' cases this quickly, but I wanted to make sure all of the stolen items were accounted for before I left for home.

Plus I had a definite personal interest in stealing any possible thunder from Danners. I suspected he would fly into a rage when he learned I had found the missing items and named the robbers, but perhaps that would be a good lesson to him that cooperating with other professionals could be beneficial. If he had, I wouldn't have cut him out of the picture so completely in my report.

As much as I wanted to head back to New York, I also had to wait until I heard from Saul. He might want me to notify Georgie personally or represent the insurance company in seeking a search warrant of the storage locker. So, with nothing presently left to do in Memphis for the moment, I called Mia.

"Darling, where are you? New York?"

"Still in Memphis, sweetheart."

"Are you coming home today? I miss you."

"It doesn't look good for today, but I should be home tomorrow. Any trouble?"

"It can wait until you get home."

"What is it? Marcus?"

"Um, sort of."

"What's that mean? Come on, tell me."

"My uncle called. He had his investigators look into the marriage. Officially, I'm still married to Marcus. When I explained what happened at the lawyer's office, Uncle Yannis went wild and started cursing. He said he was going to track Marcus down and kill him."

"His anger is understandable. What Marcus did was despicable. He apparently felt that as long as he remained married to you, he'd be able to siphon money out of you. And if you passed away before he did, he might inherit your fortune."

"No, that last part couldn't happen. The prenuptial agreement covered that. If I pass on before Marcus, he doesn't get a single Euro. Uncle Yannis wanted to make sure Marcus had no reason to kill me, and, in fact, he wanted Marcus to make sure nothing ever happened to me. Uncle never trusted Marcus."

"I applaud his instincts. So what's the next step?"

"Uncle Yannis is filing a petition on my behalf for a divorce. He's going to name the law clerk who participated in the scheme as a conspirator in preventing me from already having gotten a divorce. Uncle Yannis said I should come home so I can testify if necessary."

"When?"

"He wants me to come right away. Today."

"What about our vacation?"

"I'm sorry, darling."

"No, baby, it's okay. We want to get this settled once and for all. We can vacation after it's over. It'll be like both a vacation and a celebration. Do you want me to go with you?"

"I'd love for you to come with me and meet my whole family. I know Uncle Yannis will love you. Everyone will love you as much as I do."

"I'd love to meet your family, and I'm ready to leave here now, but— I have to wait until I hear back from Saul. Has Marcus tried to contact you?"

"No, not since that day in the restaurant. I told my bodyguards I don't want them to let him get anywhere near me."

"Good. Listen, why don't you make your reservations for a flight to Greece? I'll wrap up things here and try to catch a late flight up to New York tonight, or early tomorrow if I get delayed."

"Reservations for two?"

"Don't forget your bodyguards. We may need them if things are as tumultuous in Greece as the media is reporting."

"Okay. I'll make the reservations as soon as we're through talking."

We were on the phone for about another half hour, but it was mostly small talk about inconsequential things that had happened during the time I was in Tennessee and her shopping trip where she purchased a small painting that was perfect for the co-op.

The call was a pleasant interruption to a boring day, but I still had work to do, so following the call I activated the gizmo again and began my search for the person who planned the robbery and the individuals who provided the insider information about the security room and the family's absence on that night. I might be looking for just one person, but I felt there were two or more individuals still unnamed.

I was still working an hour later when my phone announced that Saul was calling.

"Hi, Saul."

"Colt, do I understand you've solved the case already?"

"I was anxious to wrap it up. I was supposed to go to Fiji in a couple of weeks."

"And now you're not going?"

"I'm probably going to Greece instead."

"I'd go to Fiji. This isn't a good time to vacation in Greece. The economy there is on the verge of possible collapse."

"I can't avoid it. My girl believed she was divorced from her husband two years ago. We learned this week that the papers were never filed. She has to go there to try to get the divorce pushed through."

"You're talking about the lovely Mia Kosarros?"

"Yes. Things have been getting serious between us. Her not being divorced came as quite a shock to both of us."

"I can imagine. Does this mean you'll be retiring to become a member of the jet set?"

"I don't think that's likely to happen."

"With a wife worth more than thirty billion, you certainly wouldn't have to work ever again."

"Thirty billion? I knew she was wealthy, but that's more than I expected. However, if the Greek economy collapses, we may have to rely on my ability to provide for us."

"Her fortune isn't dependent on the stability of the Greek economy. The parent company of the conglomerate is actually a Swiss corporation headquartered in Bern. Her father began distributing the family assets to closely held corporations all over the globe soon after he gained control from his father. He was a brilliant entrepreneur. He took a very good business and made it into an operation that's the envy of the shipping world. It's too bad he died so young. It would have been interesting to see how far he could have gone. I imagine by now he would own airline companies, trucking companies, and who knows what else. Perhaps you should take over the reins of the company when you're married. Yannis Kosarros is getting on in years."

"Saul, we haven't even discussed marriage."

"Really? From what I've heard, it's all set except for the date."

"Oh? And where have you heard that?"

"Colt, whenever you're out and about town, the beautiful Miss Kosarros is on your arm. You two seem to be inseparable. Everyone is waiting for the wedding announcement."

"Well, that won't be coming any time soon. Bigamy is still against the law in much of the civilized world."

"Your lovely lady won't have any trouble getting a divorce in Greece. They'll be tripping over themselves to keep the family happy. The company may not be reliant on the Greek economy, but the Greek economy is reliant on the Kosarros conglomerate. When a country's economy is teetering on the brink, the loss of a major corporation can send it into a nosedive. If Yannis Kosarros closed down the company's docks and warehouses, the ripple effect could cause the Greek unemployment rate to rise from the present twenty-five percent to fifty percent practically overnight.

Trust me, your young lady will have no trouble getting a divorce decree."

"If you don't need me down here any longer, I'd like to head home."

"Perhaps you should stick around until the arrests are made."

"Too late. The thieves have already cleared out."

"But the insured items are still there?"

"As far as I know. We can't be sure until we get a search warrant for the storage facility locker and open it up. But I'm reasonably certain everything is intact."

"And how can you be so confident about that?"

"I have my sources."

"Which means you're not going to tell me."

"If I tell you, and you tell somebody else, and he tells somebody else— well, pretty soon I wouldn't be the world's greatest recovery expert any longer."

I tried to say it in an amusing way, and I heard Fodor laugh, so I assumed he wasn't insulted that I wouldn't take him into my confidence.

"Okay, Colt. I'll just trust you. I'm going to get our lawyers in on the act and have them contact the DA down there about getting a search warrant. Hang around until we know what's going on. I'll send the company jet to pick you up when the police confirm they have the insured items. Perhaps you could drive over to the estate and tell the insured individual that recovery is imminent?"

"If that's what you want."

"I do."

"Okay, I'll take care of that as soon as we're through talking."

"Good. I'm done. Give him my best."

"I will Saul. Talk to you later."

Knowing Saul was aware I was the one who had identified where the stolen awards and memorabilia were located meant that nothing Danners could say would matter. He could sputter and trip over his tongue trying to say how he knew where the loot was hidden all the time and was waiting until the thieves returned to check on it before his people pounced. I really didn't care who got the credit as long as I got the ten percent of the policy amount.

After turning over fifty percent to the government, I would be able to pay another million dollars off my mortgage and still have enough to party with Mia for at least a few months. I'd say that life was good if I'd concluded my business with Delcona. I had tried to stop plotting my revenge and put him temporarily out of my mind so I could concentrate on other tasks, but he was never very far from my thoughts. The government surveillance was keeping him in check for the time being, but I knew he'd come after me again at some point. I just had to be ready to turn the tables on him and plant him six feet under when he made his move.

But right now I had other matters to attend to. I called Mia and told her I couldn't come with her but that I'd join her on Thasos as soon as I could. She was disappointed but accepted that I had to finish my work in Tennessee before I could leave the U.S. Then I called the resort in Fiji and cancelled the reservations. They issued me a credit for half the reservation fee that would be applied if I made new reservations within sixty days. I thought that was very generous of them because I had expected to lose the entire fee.

CHAPTER FIFTEEN

I didn't recognize the guard at the gated entrance to Georgie's estate. He wasn't the one on duty last time I was here, and it wasn't either of the pair who had been drugged the night of the robbery. I stopped the car and held out my FBI ID as he stepped out of the booth and leaned over to look into the car.

"FBI?"

"Just tell your boss that Colton James is here to see him."

The guard nodded and walked into the booth. I saw him make the call and waited until he was given his orders. The gate started to open as the guard came out of the booth and said, "Go ahead up to the house, Special Agent James."

"Thank you," I said as I put the car in drive. I held my foot on the brake until the gate was open wide enough to accommodate the car, then drove slowly up to the house. It was late afternoon, but the sun was still shining. It had been a great day in many ways.

Georgie was standing in the doorway as I walked up onto the portico. "Colt, welcome back."

"Thanks, Georgie. How are you doing?"

"Still feeling a little low. I've had to hire temporary staff to stand in for my employees who were drugged. They're going to be okay, but I gave them a month off with pay to recuperate."

"Is Danners still around?"

"Nope. He and his people left yesterday."

"I assume he hasn't called to tell you he's found either your precious possessions or the thieves."

"Nope. I haven't heard a word. Have you made any progress?"

"As a matter of fact I have. I sent a copy of my final report to Saul Fodor a few hours ago. He asked me to stop out here and fill you in."

"Your *final* report?"

"I've located all the stolen items."

Georgie, who had been looking a bit depressed, lit up with excitement. "You're serious. You got my stuff back?"

"I know where it is and reported that to Saul. He has his people working with the local authorities to get a search warrant from a magistrate so the police can move in and recover the stash."

"And it's all there?"

"We can't know if everything is there until an inventory can be done. But I know most of it's there, and I have no reason to believe it's not all there."

"That's great news, Colt. You've made my day. How soon can I get it back?"

"That'll be up to the police and the D.A. Sometimes they like to hang onto stolen merchandise until the court case is settled."

"Well, just knowing I'm going to get it all back at some point is enough for now," he said with a huge grin. "It's the cocktail hour. Come on inside and have a drink. I feel like celebrating."

◆

"Name your poison," Georgie said as he led the way into his study and opened up a wall to reveal enough alcoholic beverages to stock a bar. "I've got whiskey, wine, and beer."

"I enjoy wine with my dinner when I'm out with my girl, but most of the time I'm just a beer man."

Georgie looked at me and smiled. "That's why I like you so much, Colt. You're a lot like me. I don't enjoy playing the role of upper crust sophisticate. And fortunately I don't have to most of the time because most country western singers and songwriters are just plain folks." Georgie turned and opened a door that turned out to be a refrigerator. "Bud okay?" he asked as he reached into the box.

"My favorite, if it's in a bottle."

"I only drink bottled beer," he said as he returned to where I was standing, handed me a bottle, and gestured towards a couple of comfortable-looking chairs. As we sat down, he said, "Some guys tell me they can't tell the difference. And that might be true when the beer is just out of the fridge and icy cold. But if you're not swilling it down in under a minute, the beer is going to warm a bit. And when it does, that's when you can taste the difference between the same brand in a bottle and a can."

Georgie stopped talking long enough to open his beer and take a sip while I did the same.

"So tell me, Colt. How did you, working alone, beat the cops at finding the crooks and my stuff?"

"Technology. I used to be a computer guru, Georgie. While the local PD guys are out searching for clues, I'm on the computer searching for clues."

"So you're saying you solved this case simply by using your computer?"

"There's nothing simple about it. The crooks are getting smarter every year, but technology is advancing even faster. Look at the terrorist bombing at the Boston Marathon. Within hours they had identified the suspects by using technology. They had actual video images of the bombers walking along the streets with heavy backpacks and then later images where the bombers had already passed the spots where the bombs were planted. But they no longer had the backpacks in the later images.

"The cops were able to identify the perps and begin the manhunt before the bombers could disappear back home to Chechnya. I'm not saying we don't need the crime investigation folks. They collect the evidence that frequently help us computer geeks find the bad guys, and they provide the evidence needed in court for a conviction. It's a partnership between legwork and computer work."

"Does Danners know you solved the case?"

"If he doesn't, he will soon."

"I'd like to see his face when he learns. He was pretty rude to you."

"I'd like to see that as well."

"Uh, tell me, Colt. What happens if something is missing from the stuff that's recovered?"

"Then I go back to work and find it. The insurance company is responsible to recover everything you insured."

"And what happens if the missing item isn't on the list of insured items?"

"Then the insurance company isn't obligated to find it. But I make every effort to recover everything."

"I know you also work for the FBI part time. Do you have to tell them everything you learn?"

I hesitated before answering. It seemed like Georgie wanted to ask me something that might be illegal, or borderline legal, without getting his ass caught in a wringer.

"I don't lie to the Bureau. If they ask a question, I answer it. But if they don't ask, I'm not obligated to offer anything about my private life. I won't cover up a crime though, and since I'm not a licensed private investigator, a priest, or a lawyer, I can't claim something was privileged information."

"But you don't have to report everything you learn?"

"No. What are you getting at Georgie?"

"Uh, there's something missing that isn't on the list of insured items. I didn't realize it until the police had finished in here and left."

"A personal item?"

"Uh, yeah."

"Not an award or memorabilia?"

"No."

"Something you don't want to report to the police as being missing?"

"Uh, that could have— complications."

"It's not drugs, is it?"

"Drugs? No way. Only dopes use dope."

I stopped probing and stared at him. Either he was going to tell me or he wasn't.

Finally, Georgie sighed and said, "I guess I should wait until the police pick up my stuff and I'm able to check through it for the item."

As if that was its cue, the phone on his desk rang. Georgie looked at it for second, then picked it up. He answered, listened for a second, then asked the caller to hold on while he pressed the speaker button.

"Would you repeat that please?"

"This is Lt. Danners. I'm happy to report that through the hard work of my team and the Memphis PD, we've recovered all of the stolen items."

"That's wonderful, Lieutenant. How soon can I get them back?"

"That will be up to the captain and the DA. It's evidence in the continuing investigation."

"Did you catch the thieves?"

"I'm sorry to say they've eluded us so far. But we've identified all of them, and it's only a matter of time before they're caught."

"I'm delighted by your fast work, Lieutenant. Can I at least see the recovered items?"

"Of course, sir. But it appears the thieves took special care not to damage anything."

"How soon can I see for myself?"

"If you'll come to the station in an hour, everything will be in the recovered-property room. My people are loading it into a truck now."

"Thank you, Lieutenant. I'll be there in an hour."

After he hung up, Georgie looked at me. "Well, I guess I'll know in an hour if the item I'm concerned about is there."

"I don't know what it is, but I'd be willing to wager it won't be."

"Why do you say that?"

"This robbery just doesn't feel right. The crooks clean out your house, store the stuff in a storage locker in town, and then bug out? Something isn't right."

"They probably just wanted time for things to cool down so they could transport it without worry about roadblocks."

"If they intended to transport the stolen goods, they could have done that last night. They got away clean. Your people were all down for the count, and they had hours before you returned. In that time they could have been five hundred miles away, well beyond any roadblocks for a simple robbery where no one was injured or killed. Something isn't right. Or as some would say up in New York— something isn't kosher. This item that you're missing— was it hidden from view?"

"Yes."

"Very well hidden?"

"I believed so."

"How many people knew you kept it here?"

"I hadn't told anyone I had it here."

"But people knew you had it?"

"Just a couple— two."

I took a long pull on my beer and drained the bottle. "And do you trust them?"

"I'd trust them with my life."

"But would you trust them with your wallet?"

Georgie stared at me for a few seconds before answering. "That's a strange question to ask, Colt."

"Money does strange things to people. Especially if it's a lot of money. I've known people I would trust with my life and every penny I have. But I've also known people I would trust with my life only if they had nothing to gain by my death. And I sure wouldn't ask the latter group to hold ten grand for me. Are we talking about that much?"

"More. A lot more. But I would trust either of these people with my wallet."

"Well, until I know what we're talking about, I can't speculate further."

"Let's wait until I have a chance to see what they recovered. Do you want to go with me?"

"No, I imagine Danners is pretty upset with me right now. But it's okay with me if you mention I had notified you earlier that I'd tracked down the stolen items but that we'd have to wait until a search warrant was issued and served before entry to the storage locker was possible."

Georgie smiled. "I think I'll just play along if he wants to take credit for finding my stuff. I still have to live here after you return to New York."

"I understand, and that's probably a wise position." Standing up I said, "Georgie, thanks for your hospitality. I'm glad I was able to find your insured items so quickly, and I hope it's all there, but if any of the insured items are missing, give me a call right away. I'm planning to head home tonight."

"But what about the, uh, extra item?"

"We don't even know for sure that's not with the recovered items, although I'm reasonably certain it isn't. Give me a call if you want me to assist in its recovery, should it be missing."

"I will, Colt. I definitely want you to find it if it's not with my other stuff."

"Okay, I'll hang around until you know for sure whether it's with the recovered items or not. But if it is still missing, be prepared to be completely open with me. I'll have to know exactly what I'm looking for."

"You got it, buddy."

As I drove back to my hotel, I thought about the missing item that hadn't been insured. Two people whom Georgie would trust with his life knew of it. If it was as well hidden as he suggested, then perhaps he shouldn't be trusting both of them. The known facts indicated that someone with intimate knowledge of the memorabilia, security, and staff had been involved in planning the robbery. Was the robbery of the memorabilia only intended to mask the theft of the uninsured item? It seemed likely at this point.

I really wanted to head home, but Saul wanted me here for as long as Georgie needed me around, and I owed Saul a lot. It was dinnertime, so after parking the rental car I walked the two blocks to the same restaurant where I'd gotten the great prime rib dinner the night before. I wasn't disappointed as I ate my way through the most tender and flavorful New York Strip steak I'd enjoyed in some time and washed it down with a couple of bottles of my favorite beer.

I'd intended to work on tracking down the mastermind behind the robbery when I got back to the hotel, but I just didn't have the energy. It had been a long day, so I took a hot shower and went to bed.

◆ ◆ ◆

I awoke early the next morning and, after dressing, walked to the breakfast buffet where I was able to enjoy a large blueberry muffin and two cups of coffee before returning to my room to work.

I was curious to learn what Georgie was so reluctant to talk about, so I activated the gizmo and began watching the perps as they cleaned out his study. I zoomed in on every article removed from the room, but I never saw anything taken that appeared not to be memorabilia or an award, nor did I see anyone open any special hiding places such as a hidden drawer or door. I figured I must have missed it, so I went back and started over. But again I failed to see anything out of the ordinary taken during the robbery. And by saying ordinary, I didn't mean to disparage Georgie's awards or memorabilia. I simply meant that items I would have expected to be removed seemed to have been the only things stolen.

I had been so thorough that I figured a third pass would be a waste of time. It was already coming up on ten o'clock, and I hadn't yet tried to backtrack with the robbery team's leader to see if I could identify any clandestine meetings with someone who might be from Georgie's present or past.

I had just begun my search when my cell rang and announced I was receiving a call from Georgie. I had been expecting to hear from him.

"Hi, Georgie."

"Morning, Colt. Uh, could you swing by the house this morning— if you're not too busy, that is."

"Sure. I'm at my hotel. Is now a good time?"

"Yeah, that would be great."

"Is this in reference to what we discussed yesterday?"

"Uh, yeah. But I don't want to talk about it on the phone."

"Okay, Georgie. I should be there in about thirty minutes."

"Thanks, Colt."

The guard at the gate waved me through without my having to stop, and the temporary housekeeper was standing with the front door open when I pulled up. She escorted me to Georgie's study, knocked once, then opened the door without waiting for a response. She pulled the door closed behind me after I entered the large room.

Georgie looked terrible. It appeared that he hadn't slept all night. His agitation seemed ten times higher than when he thought just his awards and memorabilia had been stolen. He came out from behind his desk and grabbed my hand to shake it.

"Thanks for coming, Colt. The item we discussed yesterday wasn't among the other items at the police property room."

"Was everything else there?"

"It seemed to be."

"So the robbery might simply have been to cover up the theft of the still missing item?"

"Maybe."

"And you want me to find it without telling anyone what I'm searching for?"

"Uh, yeah."

"So this is outside my arrangement with Saul and the insurance company?"

"Uh, yeah. They can't know a thing about it. Nobody but us can know anything about it."

"Okay. My fee is a standard ten percent for recoveries."

"Ten percent?"

"That's the industry standard percentage."

"Uh, okay."

"So, what is it exactly that I'm to look for?"

"It's a journal. It looks sort of like a standard day planner. It's about six inches wide by nine inches high with a rich, brown leather cover, and the edges of the pages have like a gold look when the book is closed."

"Okay. And where was it kept?"

"I'll show you," he said as he moved towards his large desk. "From behind the desk, you open the center drawer at least two inches but not more than four, like this, then open the bottom right drawer at least three inches but not more than five, like this, then push this little brown circle here." He had opened the drawers as a demonstration, then pointed to something that looked like it was only part of the right-hand edge of the desk. "It looks like it's just part of the fancy woodcarving, but it's actually a release button. But the door won't open if the drawers aren't in position." When he pressed it, a panel popped open on the side of the desk.

"That's a pretty fancy arrangement, Georgie."

"I had it custom built in Germany to my specs by an old woodcarver who used to build custom clocks. I'm not talking about little cuckoo clocks, but *big* clocks, like you see in people's hallways."

"Okay. Did you have it built just to hide the book?"

"Yeah."

"So you never told anyone about the secret panel that opens?"

"Just my wife, my son, and my daughter. They had to know about it in case something happened to me. But they don't know about the book. The only ones who know about the book are my accountant and my show manager."

"I understand. So the book is missing, and you want it back."

"I need it back. It has information vital to my future."

"In what way?"

"It contains information regarding my financial holdings that represent my retirement funds."

"And this book is the only way to reference those holdings?"

"Uh, yeah."

"And if someone else were to get their hands on the information, could they steal your funds?"

"It's possible, but it would be difficult. First of all, it's written in my own private encryption code. Second, they'd have difficulty moving the funds and investments without my signature."

"So can't you just work up a new book?"

"No, that would be impossible. There are a lot of number-ed accounts, special pass codes, and even identity cards that are needed to access the funds."

"So what's the value of the investments recorded in this book, Georgie?"

"Roughly seven hundred fifty million dollars."

I couldn't stop myself from coughing, but it was only one cough as I said, "Did you mean to say seven hundred fifty *million* dollars? As in three quarters of a *billion* dollars?"

CHAPTER SIXTEEN

" **U** h, yeah. So you can see why I'm so distraught."

"I can certainly understand that. At my usual rate, my fee for the recovery would be seventy-five million, but that's excessive. Let's say that if I recover your secret book, a special rate of one percent would be adequate."

"Uh, that's more than generous, but— I can't pay you the seven and a half million."

"It would only be owed if I recover your book."

"Even if you recover the book, I can't pay you."

"But you'll have your three quarters of a billion dollars back."

"You don't understand. The government doesn't know about the money."

"Hmmm, that does complicate things. How did you amass three quarters of a billion dollars without the government knowing about it?"

"You said you don't have to tell the FBI about everything you learn unless they specifically ask, right?"

I nodded.

"The money is from a lifetime of overseas tours and sales of my music. Using a variety of methods, I was able to funnel it through legitimate foreign corporations in countries where the tax rates are far more favorable than here, and it was deposited into special accounts that aren't in my name. A lot of the money is in cash and gold in special deposit boxes but most is invested in blue chip companies. I intended to retire overseas one day and renounce my American citizenship so I wouldn't have to pay taxes on the money I earned outside the

U.S. once I started accessing it in my retirement. You're not going to tell anyone, right?"

"Not a soul. I promise."

"So getting the money to you is impossible until I can access it without Uncle Sammy grabbing half of it. The government had nothing to do with my earning it. I paid taxes in the country where it *was* earned, so I don't feel the IRS should be entitled to take half of what's left simply because I reside in this country most of the year. They already get half of everything I earn here, and that's considerable."

"So you want me to recover your millions— gratis."

"Not at all. What I'd like to propose is payment in land."

"Land?"

"Yeah. Many years ago, when I first hit it big, I bought some property in Wyoming. Back then I had some idea of retiring there when my popularity waned. A lot of music and showbiz folks fall out of popularity after a while, and I never expected mine to last this long. Anyway, I got the property cheap when compared against today's prices, and I've been paying property taxes all these years and never stayed even one night on the land. If you can recover my retirement package, I'll sell you the entire parcel for one dollar."

"Georgie, I live in a high-rise co-op in New York City. I'm not a country boy. What am I going to do with a ranch in Wyoming?"

"You don't have to live there. You could sell it. I *can't* pay you in cash right now, but you won't lose on this deal. If I were to give you cash, you'd have to give half to the government, right?"

"Yeah."

"Well, what you do is hang onto this land for a year, and then sell it and pay the long-term capital gains tax rate of twenty percent, which is the current rate for someone in your tax bracket. You instantly save thirty percent, and it's completely legal. I benefit because I get my retirement package back. I know I'll never use the land once I buy my own island in the Mediterranean. See, this way everyone is happy."

It sounded great, but I'd have to check with my accountant to make sure it was legal. "Uh, how large is this piece of property?"

"Somewhere around eighteen thousand acres."

"Eighteen *thousand* acres?"

"Yeah. It's not big compared to some ranches out there. I understand there's a ranch in Wyoming that consists of five hundred forty thousand acres. So my ranch is just a little bitty place compared to that."

"And what's its estimated value on today's market?"

"If you're in a hurry to sell and dump it quick, you won't get less than the seven point five million that represents your one percent offer. But if you can take your time and find the right buyer, you might be able to get six or seven times that amount. It's a real pretty piece of land, Colt. It's God's country. Lots of streams and brooks, and a thirty-acre lake. There's a particular spot I really like. It's right on the shore of the lake where you get the most magnificent view of the distant mountains. And there's a flat area within a stone's throw that's large enough to land a corporate jet."

"Georgie, I can't take your ranch just for finding your retirement package. It's too much."

"Colt, the ranch is not even worth your usual ten percent fee. And you don't get the ranch unless you deliver. Believe me, getting my package back is worth it. I liked you from the first few minutes after we met. You're the type of man I'd trust with my life and my wallet. I know you'll never tell a soul what's in the book."

I sighed. I felt like I was taking advantage, and that's something I never do. But Georgie was insistent, and the recovery of his book was worth it to him. "Okay, Georgie. I'll start working on the recovery of your missing book today. When was the last time you actually laid eyes on it, and where were you?"

"Uh, right here, and it was about a month ago. I made a couple of new entries, put the book away, and burned the notes I had worked from because they hinted at the encryption scheme I use."

"Can you be more precise about the date?"

"Uh, let me check something?"

Georgie opened a file drawer in his desk and pulled out a folder. After a few seconds of scanning papers in the folder, he gave me a date.

"You're pretty sure that's the last time you saw the book?"

"It's the best I can come up with. I never thought I'd have to know exactly, so I didn't make any specific notes."

"Well, it gives me a starting place. When I find your book, do you want to know who stole it?"

"You're damn right I do."

"It's most likely someone you'd trust with your wallet."

"I have to know, Colt. If for no other reason than to never trust them with my wallet again."

I nodded and said, "I'll be in touch."

◆　◆

I called Mia as soon as I arrived back at the hotel.

"Sweetheart, things down here have suddenly become a bit complicated. I can't return home right away."

"Oh, no. The reservations for the flights are for tomorrow morning. Uncle Yannis called. He used his influence to get the hearing scheduled for Monday. He says I have to be there."

"Okay. You go with your bodyguards. And be careful."

"Oh, darling, I wanted so much for you to meet my family."

"I still will. Just as soon as I can get away, I'll join you on Thasos. I'm looking forward to meeting Uncle Yannis. He sounds like someone I'll like. I'm looking forward to meeting your whole family, but I have to wrap up this investigation before I go."

"I'm disappointed, a little, but I understand."

"You'll be so busy between the hearing and renewing old acquaintances that you won't even know I'm not there."

"Darling, don't say that. I miss you every minute we're apart."

"And I miss you as well. Give my love to your family and tell them I'll be there soon."

As soon as our call ended, I took out the gizmo and went to work. First I used the gizmo's tagging feature to mark Georgie, then I tagged the desk in his study. Starting on the morning of the day he identified as the most likely date he had last seen his book, I watched every time he was in proximity of the desk. He had said he liked to walk around the house in his tee-shirt and shorts, and I could certainly confirm that. But I never once saw him open the secret panel in the desk. Even viewing in a slightly fast forward mode, I never saw any hint that he had opened the panel even once during that entire day. I was afraid to go too fast because it would only take a second to stash the book, so I had to watch boring hour after boring hour while he either worked at his desk or simply sat there drinking beer and watching television.

It was mid-afternoon when I finished watching Georgie in his office. He hadn't opened the secret panel once. So I went out to get something to eat. I found a Greek restaurant that looked inviting and was about to enter when I remembered that I would soon be in Greece. I was sure I would have plenty of Greek food in my diet over the next few weeks, so I passed the restaurant by and stopped into a Thai restaurant instead. The food was a bit dissimilar to the Thai food I got in New York, but it was tasty.

After I had halted the rumblings in my stomach, I headed back to the hotel and resumed watching Georgie in his underwear. The gizmo was great, and I owed everything to having found it that fateful day in New York, but I knew of no way I could set it to search for what I wanted to view this time. So I would just have to sit there like a cop on a stakeout and try to watch without falling asleep.

Over the next few days I did have some much appreciated interruptions. Saul called to congratulate on me on finding all of Georgie's missing possessions. I told him to take a third of my recovery fee and apply it to my mortgage, then deposit the rest in my bank account. I also spoke to Ed Harris, who was delighted with recovering the skip, and I told him to deposit that recovery fee in my bank. He asked if he could call on me again. I told him I'd be happy to help out if the recovery fee was decent, but I probably would refuse if it was less than ten grand. I knew that if I made the amount too low, he'd be calling me for every skip he had to find.

I spoke to Mia every day once she arrived in Greece. She said things appeared calm, but the economic situation was terrible with so many people out of work. I continued to promise her I'd join her just as soon as I could.

◆　◆　◆

It was eight agonizingly boring days before I witnessed Georgie opening the secret panel in the desk and removing the book. I immediately tagged the book and was ecstatic to see it was large enough for the gizmo to get a lock on it. I'd been afraid all of the surveillance might be wasted effort if the gizmo couldn't track the book. To my dismay, I had learned during the Amsterdam case that some objects are just too small to tag.

With the book tagged, I could tag the robbery team members one by one, starting with the leader, and then search for a time when they were in proximity of the book.

My attempts to mate the book to any of the gang members didn't yield a single hit. Obviously, none of them had ever touched it. Even worse was the realization that the book could not have been in the desk the night of the robbery. If it had been, I would have had a match with every team member who entered the study.

Knowing the book wasn't in the study on the night of the robbery meant that someone had removed it earlier. It could have been an employee, a trusted visitor, or a family member. If it was any of the latter, it was going to be difficult breaking the news to Georgie.

I started with the person who probably had the most opportunity to take the book and who also was most likely to know of the book. Georgie's wife was presently in France, but I went back a year and found her at home. I tagged her, and then attempted a match. She had been in the study a number of times prior to it being stolen, but in none of the matchups had she ever handled the book. It was not even out of the desk on those occasions.

Next, I located and tagged Georgie's daughter. Again, there were no matchups where she touched the book.

My next suspect, and my last, was Georgie's son Jimmy. I hit the jackpot. I witnessed Jimmy's theft of the book and discovered that it was still in his possession. Georgie was going to be shattered. He had done everything in his power to promote the kid's career. Jimmy didn't have half the musical talent of his dad, but Georgie kept trying to make him a star.

It was still before noon, so I used my laptop to make a flight reservation to Colorado, then showered, shaved, and headed to the airport. I didn't even have a carry-on because I didn't intend to be there more than a few hours.

The gizmo had shown me where Jimmy was staying, his room number, and that he liked to sleep in the raw. I figured he might be up by now, and I knew the room number, so I went directly to the elevators. When I knocked on the door, a young woman wearing only bikini panties opened it. She smiled at me and showed no embarrassment that her chest was entirely and beautifully exposed for me and anyone else in the hallway to see.

"Jimmy up yet?" I asked.

"Who are you?"

"My name's James. That's my last name."

"What's your first name, honey?"

"Colton."

"Or Colt?" She added in a provocative voice, "Like a young stud horse?"

"More like the gun," I said as I held up my FBI ID.

She suddenly seemed embarrassed by her nakedness.

"We're not doing anything wrong, officer. I'm twenty-one, and I can prove it."

"Is Jimmy up yet?"

"No, not yet. He likes to sleep until five once the party ends."

"Wake him and tell him I'm here."

"Yes, sir."

The girl hurried away, allowing the door to swing open. I walked in and stood in the middle of the sitting room.

I heard some excited talk coming from the bedroom and then some commotion like drawers slamming and closet doors closing.

A few seconds later, Jimmy came out of the bedroom, wrapping a robe around him as he walked. He looked at me, then looked around to see if anyone was with me.

"Who are you?"

"Colton James. I'm a friend of your dad's."

"Geez, what's he want now? I'm doing everything he told me to do."

"What he wants is his book. You have it. He wants it back. *Now.*"

"Geez, I don't know what you're talking about. What book?"

"The one you took out of his desk in the study."

"I don't know what you're talking about."

I held up my ID. "Would you prefer I called the local PD and have them come with a search warrant? You'd be arrested and booked for grand theft robbery. That would probably end any chance for a music career you might have unless you get as lucky as Johnny Cash and build your career inside prison."

The kid went white. He had been bluffing while he tried to think of what he should do. If he could call his father, Georgie would usually straighten out any mess. But this time it was his father who'd sent the cops.

"When I said now, I meant *now*."

"Uh, I'll get it. Just give me a minute."

He turned towards the bedroom and I followed along. He stopped, turned, and said, "I said I'll get it."

"Great. And I'll watch you until you do."

He grimaced, then turned towards the bedroom and resumed walking, mumbling or grumbling under his breath.

As we entered the bedroom, I saw two girls lying on the bed. The one who had answered the door was leaning against a dresser. I wasn't surprised. When I'd verified his location, I had seen him in bed with all three.

Jimmy walked to a guitar case, laid it down on the carpet, and opened it. Taking out the book, he closed the case.

"Here you are, officer. What now?"

I flipped through the pages and saw that everything was encrypted, just as Georgie had said.

"You can't read anything. It's all in some sort of code."

"So I see. Okay, Jimmy. I don't know what your dad is going to do with you for taking his book, but I'd start practicing my apologies and pleas for forgiveness."

All he did was shrug and grimace, so I shrugged and grimaced back and then left.

I got to the airport just in time to catch a flight back to Memphis. As the plane leveled out somewhat after reaching altitude and the flight attendants began dispensing drinks, I pulled out the book and glanced through the pages. All entries were in code, but it didn't look like a financial journal. After quickly glancing through the entire book, I put it away. What the book contained was unimportant. All that really mattered was that I had recovered it. Or was it?

I thought about the book all the way back to Memphis. I couldn't get it out of my head. Things just didn't add up. Why didn't a supposed financial journal resemble a financial journal in form? Even if the page data couldn't be interpreted, it should still be laid out like a financial journal. And why did Georgie's son steal something he couldn't possibly use? Was he simply trying to keep his father from using it? That didn't make sense if it was a financial journal of Georgie's retirement funds, unless he wanted to keep his dad from leaving the country and renouncing his American citizenship.

When the plane touched down in Memphis at 8:47 p.m. I had decided on a course of action that would hopefully answer my questions. I took a cab to my hotel and set up my computer as soon as I entered my room. Using my handheld scanner, I copied every page of the journal onto my computer's hard drive. Then I used an optical character-recognition program to convert the handwritten text to digital text. Occasionally the program would stop and highlight something it was unsure of. I'd enter the text using the keyboard and the program would continue until it found more confusing data. In just over an hour I had a fairly faithful version of the original printed document on my hard drive.

Working with the digital copy, I opened a decipher program I had in my laptop. It wasn't the most sophisticated on the market, but then this wasn't a foreign government encryption. The program was having some success but stated that the probability of accuracy was only forty-two percent. So I halted the operation and used the gizmo to return to a time when Georgie was making a new entry. I positioned the gizmo's view so it was hovering over Georgie's desk as he wrote, and I had a perfect view of what he was transcribing. I stopped the time progression when his hands were out of the way and copied the original document. I immediately knew my first assessment of the book had been correct. It wasn't a financial journal.

I associated the page I copied with the page in the digital copy and reactivated the decryption program. In twenty minutes I was able to read the entire journal. It was a bit of a shock. I then encrypted the revealed document with my *own* encryption algorithm and uploaded a copy to a cloud account I had set up recently. I didn't like cloud storage because it meant someone else had easy access to my private data, but once it was encrypted, the danger of someone stealing it and understanding it was lessened considerably, assuming they didn't have a gizmo like mine.

The entire process took just three hours. I hadn't eaten anything all day, so I went out to grab some dinner, then returned and spent a couple more hours on the computer and one with the gizmo, preparing for a morning encounter with Georgie.

CHAPTER SEVENTEEN

"**C**olt, do you have good news for me?" Georgie asked with a smile as soon as I was admitted to his home by his housekeeper.

"I have news, Georgie. Whether it's good is something you'll have to decide."

The smile disappeared. "That sounds ominous."

"I think we should talk in private," I said, turning my head slightly towards the housekeeper for a second. He got the hint.

"Yeah, of course. Come on into my study."

As soon as the doors were closed, he asked, "Did you recover the book?"

"Yes."

"Great. Let me have it. I want to see if it's been tampered with."

I opened the case I normally used to protect my computer while traveling and removed the book. Georgie reached for it, but I pulled it away. "First things first, Georgie." Reaching into the computer case again I removed a document and handed it to him.

"What's this?"

"A Quitclaim Deed for the property in Wyoming. I accessed the computer records on the property and filled in all the required details from the deed on file in Wyoming. All you have to do is sign it."

"Now?"

"Yes, right now, before you get the book."

"Don't you trust me?"

"Where millions of dollars are concerned, I tread carefully until I know the man and would trust him to hold my wallet. When I first met Saul Fodor, I made him give me a signed letter outlining our deal before I'd give him my report on an art recovery. It's nothing personal."

Georgie grimaced and looked at the book in my hand, then took the Quitclaim Deed and walked around behind his desk. He read the simple document, then leaned over his desk to pick up a pen so he could sign it. He was surprised by the flash from my cell phone as he penned his signature and looked up quickly. "What's that for?"

"Just one more bit of documentation in case there's ever a legal challenge."

"So you *don't* trust me."

"Trust has to be earned, Georgie. I've known you for just a very short time."

He handed me the Quitclaim Deed, and I turned over the book. He immediately began flipping through the pages, stopping here and there, then took a deep breath and smiled.

"It doesn't appear to have been tampered with," he said.

"So you have your book, and I have my payment, even though it isn't exactly as you said."

"What do you mean?"

"You told me you bought the property years ago and that if I wanted to sell it quickly, I would easily get the seven point five that would have been my payment in cash at the special price I extended. The first part of that was true, but you never mentioned that you took out a loan for seven million dollars using the property as collateral. And naturally you didn't mention that you're well behind on your payments and the creditors are preparing to declare you in default and go to court to get possession of the property."

Georgie didn't say anything, but he had an angry expression on his face.

"I spoke to them this morning," I said, "and promised to wire transfer the delinquent payments within ten days, as well as the current payment if you signed the Quitclaim Deed today. They agreed to wait."

"You know that as soon as you file that deed, you assume responsibility for all outstanding debts on the property."

"Are there any others? Such as loans for which the paperwork hasn't been filed with the county clerk?"

"No. No one else would extend a second loan on the property once the first lien was filed."

"I'll have to take your word on that, even though your word hasn't proven very reliable so far."

"I was desperate, Colt. I needed my retirement package back."

"It may be your retirement package, but it's not a financial record of hidden overseas assets. I know what it is."

With a shocked look, he said, "You couldn't. No one can read this except me."

"No?" I said as I handed him a copy of the most recent entry from the book.

When he realized what it was, his shocked look turned to one of horror. He had really thought he had an unbreakable cipher. And perhaps he did have a cipher unbreakable for anyone other than the experts. Without the gizmo, I knew I wouldn't have had an accurate translation."

"How did you get this?"

"When I discovered you'd told me a web of lies, I decrypted your journal. If that's your retirement package, I'd have to guess you were intending to do a little blackmailing. Perhaps a lot of blackmailing. I think your son realized that also, and that's probably why he took the book."

"Jimmy stole the book?"

"Even though he couldn't read it, he must have known what you were up to. He loves his dad, and I imagine he was only trying to protect you from yourself. Goodbye, Georgie."

Georgie followed me to the front door. As I opened the door and stepped out onto the portico, he said, "You don't think Jimmy had anything to do with the robbery here, do you?"

I stopped, turned halfway around, and looked Georgie in the eyes. "No. He had nothing to do with the robbery of your awards and memorabilia." I turned back around, walked several steps, then stopped and turned back again. "But then— *you* already knew that, didn't you?" I turned again and walked down the stairs and out to my rental car.

As I drove back to my hotel so I could pack and go home, I thought about Georgie's financial condition. What little I knew appeared to be a bit bleak. Perhaps those shopping trips to Europe by his wife and daughter were the problem. Or perhaps they only exacerbated the losses from a series of bad investments. It wasn't the first time crushing debt had driven someone to commit insurance fraud.

My dilemma now was whether or not to tell Saul Fodor. The insurance company was not out the policy amount. Their only loss was my fee for the recovery. I would have to decide if I should tell Saul about the fraud I'd discovered. If Saul and the insurance company pressed charges, it would end Georgie's career, outside of prison. I really had no proof, and I had named all of the thieves. Perhaps I should just let fate take its course. If the leader of the team was apprehended and turned on Georgie to get a lighter sentence, justice would be served.

Before I could head home, I had to go to Wyoming and record the Quitclaim Deed for the property, so I stayed one more night in Memphis and grabbed an early flight to Denver. From there I took a flight up to Wyoming in a small commuter plane. Once the deed was recorded, I sent a check to the company holding the only recorded lien on the property.

I wanted to see the property up close, so I hired the owner of a local flight school to fly me up there in a small four-seater. Before we climbed aboard I showed him where the property was on a map, and he overflew it at a thousand feet so I could get a good look, then dropped lower over the area by the lake. It was as beautiful as Georgie had said. Once Mia's divorce was settled and we returned to the States, we'd have to come out and drive to the property so we could get a good look.

With that taken care of, I headed back to Denver and a connecting flight to Newark. It would have been nice if I'd had use of the insurance company's jet for the trip, but I settled for a first-class ticket aboard a major carrier.

It was great to get home. Mia was anxiously awaiting my arrival in Greece and during our daily phone conversations, naturally kept asking when I was coming.

But I needed a day of rest since I was beat from the hectic pace of the past few days. I called her and said I had concluded my business in Memphis and was at the apartment. I had made reservations for my trip to Greece before calling her and told her I'd be on my way in two days. She wanted me to leave the next day, but I told her how exhausted I was and how much I needed a rest. She was disappointed, but I think she understood, and she was happy I was coming at last.

I went to bed early and slept in the next day, not getting out of bed until after two in the afternoon. As I drank my first coffee of the day, I couldn't help but think of Delcona. I was amazed that I'd been able to put him so much out of my mind since I'd arrived in Memphis. But I was back in New York now where the specter of Delcona's criminal influence loomed large over the city.

Still sipping my coffee, I walked into my office, took out the gizmo and activated it. First up was a look-see at the stakeout positions of the government investigators keeping a twenty-four seven watch when I left. The faces were different from the last time I'd looked, but the new group seemed just as vigilant. I knew Delcona hadn't reformed, and trying to link him with crimes that constantly occurred all over the city was a herculean— if not impossible— feat.

As for Delcona himself, he was sitting at home reading a newspaper and enjoying life. I couldn't bear to replay the events that had occurred in my apartment the night my best friend died, but if I ever needed to refresh my loathing for Delcona, all I had to do was view the scene in the warehouse where Delcona had directed Diz to beat and then murder Morris as he, Delcona, looked on dispassionately. Just thinking about it caused my blood pressure to spike. I took a deep breath, turned off the gizmo, and tried to calm down as I finished the last of my coffee.

◆　◆　◆

I'd rested pretty well with my R and R the day before, so I awoke early the next morning, showered, shaved and dressed, then packed my bags for an extended stay on Thasos Island. I didn't know how long I'd be in Greece, or even if Mia and I would be returning directly or going on to Fiji from there, but I'd booked my nonstop overnight flight as a round trip fare because the round trip ticket was actually less expensive than a one-way. If I didn't need the return trip ticket, I would just toss it away. Although I had a healthy bank account, I still couldn't help being a little frugal at times, especially when the big airlines were playing their silly games with pricing. I was scheduled to leave JFK at 4:46 p.m., arriving at ATH at 9:35 a.m., so I had several hours to kill.

I was relaxing and reading a book while I enjoyed a cup of freshly brewed coffee when the house phone rang. Only a very few people had that number.

"Special Agent James?" the caller asked. "This is security officer Williams at the lobby station. There are two other Special Agents requesting to see you. They've identified themselves as Special Agents Osborne and Snow."

The security system monitor usually showed a quad image from the two cameras in the hallway in front of my front door and the two cameras inside the elevator used to access the floor, but I could change the picture to see the front lobby or the parking garage if I pushed the right buttons. I verified that it really was Osborne and Snow before speaking to the security officer again.

"Yes, they're legit. You can send them up. Thanks."

"Yes, sir."

I watched as Snow and Osborne walked out of the camera's view on their way to the elevator before switching the monitor to show the usual quad view. I saw them enter the elevator and wait until the security officer instructed the computer to close the doors and send the car up. There was a slight lurch as the elevator began to rise. When it reached my floor, the doors opened and the two men got out and got their bearings by looking at the sign that directed people towards the co-op unit they were seeking.

Snow and Osborne walked down the hall and stopped in front of my door. Snow pushed the doorbell, but it hadn't been necessary. I had watched them every foot of the way since they left the lobby security desk. I pressed the button that would unlock both doors at once, then pulled open the inside vestibule door as they entered through the hallway door.

"Come in, gents," I said. "Welcome to my new digs."

They entered the co-op without saying anything, then stopped and took a good look around as I closed the inner door. The outer door had already closed and locked.

"Wow. You've sure come up in the world since that dump over on the West side," Osborne said.

"The Amsterdam art recovery made the down payment possible. Then all I had to do was put myself in hock for sixteen million."

"Jeez," Snow said. "Sixteen million? After a major down payment?"

"Yeah, the co-op wasn't cheap. But after what happened at my third-floor walk-up on the West Side, I wanted an apartment as secure as Fort Knox."

"You certainly got it," Osborne said. "This building seems almost as secure as the downtown office. And your apartment looks like a real home. That last place you had looked like a man cave."

"I owe the homey appearance to my girlfriend's talents, aided by professional interior decorators."

"Nice," Snow said.

"Is this a social visit or business?" I asked.

"Business," Osborne said. "A guy in the Bronx had your name and this address on a piece of paper in his pocket."

"Really? My name and address? Was it someone I tagged when I was mainly doing skip recovery?"

"Not this guy. He had no criminal record in the U.S. He was here on an Italian passport."

"Someone from the Amsterdam case then? Looking for revenge over losing the haul of a lifetime?"

"We don't know yet. We were just sent to ask if you knew him, or of him."

"Why you and not NYPD?"

"When they ran the name, they ID'd you as a Special Agent. You know how the Bureau is. Anytime a Special Agent is involved with any crime, or supposed crime, they want in right away."

"So what was the crime?"

"Murder. And someone tried to make it look like an accident. The interesting thing about the guy is that he has a genuine connection to you."

I waited for Osborne to let the shoe drop. Snow hadn't taken his eyes off me as he tried to gauge my reaction to everything Osborne was saying.

"And that connection is what?"

"He was the husband of your mistress."

"Marcus?" I said in genuine surprise.

"Yeah. Marcus Antonio Fabrizzi. Does Mrs. Fabrizzi happen to be here?"

"No, she's out of the country."

"We've learned that you two have been quite the topic of conversation among the hoity-toity in the city," Snow said.

"The society types are saying they expect you to announce your marriage plans any day. I imagine her current marriage to Fabrizzi would create a bit of a problem though. His death seems to pave the way. How long has Mrs. Fabrizzi been out of the country?"

"A week and a half. She believed her divorce from Marcus had been finalized two years ago. They had gone to a lawyer in Athens and signed the no-contest paperwork back then. She also gave Marcus a sizable settlement, even though she had a pre-nup which guaranteed him nothing. We only learned two weeks ago that the divorce papers had never been filed. Marcus came here looking for more money."

"How big a settlement did he get?" Osborne asked.

"A million Euros."

Snow whistled, then said, "Nice. Now that's a settlement."

"And he came here looking for more."

"So when you learned that your mistress and Fabrizzi were still married, you decided to make the divorce final by yourself?" Osborne asked. "You send her out of the country so she can't be implicated and then you do the deed?"

"Come on, Osborne. She's in Greece to have the divorce filed and finalized. She doesn't need his participation because it seems the lawyer Fabrizzi took her to wasn't really a lawyer. The guy has admitted in court, under oath, that Fabrizzi blackmailed him to pose as one and that Fabrizzi had agreed to a no-contest divorce in his presence at that time. The guy was only a law clerk in the office of a lawyer who was on vacation.

"The court over there has issued an arrest warrant for Fabrizzi if he ever returns to Greece, and the divorce is as good as finalized. Things just usually move slowly in Greece justice courts. I'm amazed that Mrs. Fabrizzi's case was heard so quickly, but a sizable donation to the right— causes— can do wonders."

"So it was simple revenge for the extra grief he put you through?" Snow asked.

"Guys, it's been fun, but I'm getting ready to join Mia in Greece, and then we're going on vacation. So if you have anything *reasonable* to say, say it now, or I'll see you when I get back."

"Where were you three days ago?" Osborne asked.

"Let's see," I said, pointing to each of my fingers as I ticked off the travel I'd done over the past three days. "I was in Memphis on the morning of the third day, then out to Denver in the afternoon, then back to Memphis in the evening. The next day, two days ago, I flew back to Denver again from Memphis, then up to Wyoming, then back to Denver, and then here. I slept in yesterday because I was beat from all the traveling. And today I'm heading for Greece."

Osborne looked at Snow and shrugged.

"Okay, Sherlock," Osborne said, "I'm sure you can prove all that travel. Right?"

"That's up to you to do, and you'll probably need official paperwork because, while the airlines will probably all verify in a simple phone call that someone with my name was on all those flights, you'll have to go examine the video surveillance records at all the airports to verify it was actually me. So knock yourselves out, guys, if you don't believe me. Of course you could simply send someone to view the video records at the hotel where I was staying in Memphis. They'll show I was there in the morning and again in the evening three days ago. Is that when Marcus was killed?"

"Yeah," Osborne said. "Around ten p.m."

"I arrived back at the hotel about nine p.m. Central time, which is ten p.m. Eastern time. That will be easy to verify from the lobby video records at the hotel. I can't be in two places at the same time, so I couldn't have done the deed. How was he killed?"

"His head was crushed in by something like a hammer," Snow said, "Then he was run over by a car."

"Yuck," I said. "Messy."

"Yeah," Osborne said, "And it makes it difficult to find the murder weapon."

"What was he doing in the Bronx?"

"Who knows?" Snow said. "Maybe looking to score some drugs for resale to the rich and famous he knew. His wallet was empty, so whoever clocked him probably helped themselves to whatever coin he had."

"Yeah," I said. "Well, whatever. He's one less headache for the people who had to share this planet with him. I doubt anyone will mourn his passing. One less scumbag in the world is always a good thing." Changing my tone to a more jovial one, I said, "Well, guys, it's been fun, but I have some packing to do, and then I have to go catch my flight."

"Where to after Greece?" Osborne asked.

"Fiji."

"Nice," Snow said.

"I hope so. I've never been there— but Mia has. She picked the destination."

"We'll see you when you get back," Osborne said as he turned towards the door. "Take it easy on the Mai Tai's."

As soon as they were gone, I hurried to my safe room and took out the gizmo. I had plenty of time before I had to leave to catch my flight. Going back to the time in the restaurant where I spoke to Marcus, I tagged him, then moved ahead to three days ago at ten p.m. Marcus was already dead on the pavement with a crowd around him.

I backed up an hour and saw him riding in a car with someone I didn't recognize. I watched, jumping ahead five minutes at a time, to see what happened. When the car stopped in front of a low-income housing unit, Marcus and the other man got out and walked towards the building. They never actually entered; they just walked towards the shadows at the entrance where another man was standing.

Marcus said something to the new man in response to something the man had said. The new man then pulled out what looked like a 32 caliber automatic, judging solely by its size, and handed it to Marcus. Marcus accepted it and pulled the slide back. The slide remained open, indicating the clip was empty. The new man then nodded at the first man while Marcus examined the handgun.

All of a sudden, I saw the man who had accompanied Marcus in the car bring something down on Marcus's head, and Marcus collapsed to the ground. The new man picked up his handgun, while the first man went through Marcus's pockets and came up with his wallet. He pulled out the cash, counted it, then gave half to the new man. The new man then appeared to whistle, and two other men came rushing over. The new man gave some orders and the two men dragged Marcus away.

I assumed he was already dead or soon would be after seeing the viciousness of the assault. I knew where the two men were taking him, so I didn't need to see the rest. As I'd said, the world was better off without Marcus. I had an intense dislike for the man, first because of the way he had treated Mia while they were still together, but mostly because of what he had done after she finally left him by making her think they were divorced.

I took the gizmo down, secreted it in my lighter, and then walked out to grab my bags and head to the airport.

CHAPTER EIGHTEEN

Overseas flights had become even more maddening than transcontinental flights in the U.S. because the airlines kept making the seats smaller and smaller, and the passengers were required to remain in their seats for a much longer time. It probably wasn't nearly as bad for the average five-foot-tall woman, but for a six-foot-two man like myself, it had become all but impossible to be comfortable on a flight unless I traveled first class.

I always traveled first class at this point when it was available, not for the significantly better food and complimentary alcohol, but simply for the larger seats. And I had booked a direct flight from New York to Athens so I wouldn't have to sit for hours on end in an airport at London, Paris, Rome, or some other hub while waiting for a connecting flight to Greece. For a time, most direct flights from the U.S. to Athens had been cancelled, so it was wonderful they had been reinstated.

Traveling to Memphis aboard the insurance company's jet, with its spacious cabin, extremely comfortable seating, and a flight attendant who was there just to cater to my needs, had been like a dream. But a person would have to travel often enough to justify the great expense of not only the original cost of the plane but also the salaries of the pilots and crew, plus the constant aircraft maintenance.

Once we were airborne and had climbed to altitude, I enjoyed a couple of glasses of wine and stayed alert long enough to enjoy the meal they were serving. Then I put the seat back down and closed my eyes. The air over the Atlantic was bumpy, and I was awakened several times by the turbulence, but I managed to get enough sleep overnight to feel pretty good when the cabin attendants came around with the simple breakfast fare they were offering to first class passengers on the flight.

The economic situation in Greece had become so bad that there had been protests and work stoppages everywhere. The Athens airport had even been shut down at various times by workers protesting wage and pension cuts as Greece struggled to repay bailout loans so they could remain part of the EU. I was happy we were able to land without incident on this day.

When it was my turn to be checked by customs officials, I produced my passport, FBI credentials, European Firearms Pass (EFP), and the license issued by the DNR to carry my weapons in the Netherlands. The eyebrows of the official raised as he looked at each document and then me before returning his eyes to the next document.

"Are you armed, sir?" he asked, when he had looked at everything.

"Yes, I am. I'm carrying the weapons listed on the EFP."

"And are you here on an investigation?"

"No, I'm here on holiday."

"Then why have you brought your weapons with you?"

"I've made a great many enemies in criminal circles because of my law enforcement efforts. I must remain armed at all times in case they decide I'm an easy target because I'm not working a case."

"I see. And where will you be staying?"

"I'm to be the guest of Yannis Kosarros and family at their home on Thasos."

"Do you know Mr. Kosarros?"

"I've never met the gentleman yet, but I'm a close, personal friend of Mia Kosarros."

The official's eyebrows rose again before he said, "One moment, please." He walked over to a small counter where another official was looking at a computer monitor and said something, then handed him my documents. The second official, perhaps a supervisor, looked at everything, then at me, then said something to the first official, who returned to me. He stamped my passport and said, "My supervisor has heard of your law enforcement efforts in the EU and approved your carrying the licensed weapons for personal protection. Enjoy your holiday, Special Agent James."

"Thank you, sir."

As I passed beyond the customs area I saw a man holding a makeshift sign on which was written 'Mr. James.' Mia had told me that someone would meet me at the airport and that I would be brought to the house on Thasos Island, so I said to him, "I'm Colton James. Are you waiting for me?"

"Yes, sir. I'm to take you to the helipad. May I take your bags?"

The guy was only about five-three and couldn't weigh more than a hundred-ten pounds, so I said, "Let's each take one. These suitcases with wheels can be tricky when you have more than one because they sometimes decide they want to go in different directions." It was a slight exaggeration, but my cases were the large ones, and when trying to pull two of them I had to hold my arms out a bit and be extra careful not to trip someone else going in the opposite direction, or even myself. What the manufacturers needed to do was make a way to hook the suitcases together so I could pull them with one hand and the cases were in alignment behind me like a train on a track.

The little guy led me to one of those golf-cart-style electric vehicles and put my suitcases in the back. I climbed aboard and he was off like a taxi driver in Manhattan. He could weave and jog with the best of them and used his horn with abandon.

When we exited the terminal I discovered what a beautiful day it was. I breathed deeply and enjoyed the fresh air after breathing recycled air all night. The Athens airport was huge and spread out, so I was glad I didn't have to walk to where the helicopter was parked. The little guy removed my suitcases from the cart one at a time and took them to another man who put them aboard the air-taxi while I watched. I assumed the little guy wasn't going along, so when he was done I gave him a twenty. He smiled and nodded, then climbed into the cart and zipped back towards the terminal. The baggage guy gestured towards the air-taxi, so I climbed in.

It turned out that the baggage guy was also the pilot. I guess employment attrition in the country had people performing multiple roles, or perhaps that's the way it had always been for air-taxi pilots here.

I knew from having checked an atlas that Thasos Island, or Thassos Island, depending on the source, was in the northern Aegean Sea about four miles off the shore of northern Greece, so I estimated the flight would take about an hour. I supposed it wasn't a popular destination right then because I was the only passenger. The flight was mostly over water, so there wasn't much to see. I just sat back and relaxed as the pilot competently flew us to Thasos.

As we approached Thasos, I could see the beautiful white sand beaches that ringed the island and made it a popular resort destination. I imagined the local population was probably small, limited to those who worked as part of the tourist trade and those fortunate folks well-heeled enough to actually reside there. While the major industry was definitely tourism, the island was also known for its beautiful white marble. Agricultural products of the island included honey, almonds, olives, olive oil, and wine, and there were residents who earned their living through sheep and goat herding, or fishing.

The air-taxi pilot knew exactly where he was going, and the helicopter began to slow as we approached a large compound surrounded by high walls. What appeared to be the main house sat in the center of the compound, and there were several smaller buildings towards what I assumed was the rear of the compound. The main house appeared smaller than I'd been expecting. I suppose I thought I'd see something like the U.S. White House from the way Mia had talked about it.

The pilot expertly set the craft down onto a helipad outside the walls of the compound and wasted no time removing my bags and getting aloft again. Using a helicopter definitely saved many hours of time driving up from Athens and taking the car ferry from the mainland to the northern port city on the island, then driving to the house.

As I stood on the perimeter of the helipad looking at the surrounding landscape, Mia appeared from around a corner of one of the high walls. She raced at me with a huge smile and then jumped into my arms as she always did whenever we'd been separated for any amount of time, kissing my face a dozen times before I had a chance to catch my breath.

"Oh, darling, you're here at last," she said happily. "I was beginning to think you weren't coming."

"Now, sweetheart, you know I would have been here sooner if I could. But I had to wrap up that investigation in Memphis."

"I know," she said with a slightly repentant voice and matching expression. "And I know I'm being a silly little girl. I just missed you so much."

"You keep right on being silly. I love it, even if I do defend my absences just a little."

She smiled widely and started kissing my face again. I imagined it was going to take me several minutes to clean all the lipstick off.

"Come inside, darling. Leave your bags here. Someone will bring them in. I want you to meet my family."

Mia took my hand and led me to the gated entrance and then to the house. I supposed the house had looked small from the air because of the size of the compound, but as we entered, I saw it was anything *but* small. It was a three-story Mediterranean villa in the Italian Renaissance style. I estimated that each floor was perhaps five thousand square feet, making it a sizable house.

At that time I didn't know there were also two floors below ground that were used for storage and for safety in the event someone attacked the compound. It wasn't only law enforcement folks who had to always be concerned with safety. Anybody with a little money, or a lot, had to be aware that there were always people who would use any opportunity to take what others had worked for and accumulated.

I assumed the entire household had gathered to meet me because all of the chairs in the main salon were occupied. Mia took me around and introduced me to each individual. I met her grandmother first, then all of her cousins— at least the ones who lived at the estate—then an aunt and, lastly, Uncle Yannis. Yannis appeared to be in his sixties but still had the virile appearance of a much younger man. I had several inches on him, so he was about the same height as Mia when she wasn't wearing shoes.

"Welcome to our home, Mr. James," Yannis said in excellent English.

"Thank you, sir. But please call me Colt."

"And you must call me Uncle," he said with a huge smile. "Everyone does, even mother, whom everyone calls Grandmama."

"Thank you, Uncle."

"Mia has told us much about you. And I have done a bit of— research— on my own. I think I shall like you."

"I'm glad to hear that. From what I've heard from Mia, I believe I shall like you as well, and the entire family."

I was pleased that everyone smiled.

"It was an unpleasant business that brought Mia home, but we were delighted to have her back with us. And now the unpleasant business is all behind us."

"Really?"

"Yes. I just learned a short time ago that the divorce decree will become final thirty days from now. Marcus has that long to protest it in person. And if he appears in person, he'll be arrested on charges for the fraud he committed, as well as blackmail charges for his threats against the law clerk. So I don't ever expect to see him in Greece again."

"Uh, that's a certainty, Uncle."

"Why do you say it like *that*."

I turned to Mia before I said, "Marcus is dead."

"Dead?" she said with a slightly pained expression.

I nodded.

"Colt, you didn't…"

"No. It happened while I was in Memphis. I just learned about it yesterday. I had a little time so I looked into it. He was murdered while trying to purchase a handgun in the Bronx."

"A handgun?"

"Yes. I don't know why, but perhaps he was so fearful of me that he wanted protection. I had told him to stay away from you, *or else*. I assume the act of acquiring a handgun meant he had no intention of staying away from you and wanted to be ready when I showed up again. Or perhaps he intended to use the gun to force you to give him more money. I really don't know what was on his mind. But I know he will never bother you again."

Mia tried to mask it, but I knew she was pained from the news.

"So that means Mia has been widowed?" Uncle Yannis asked.

"Uh, yes sir, unless the official date of the divorce decree predates his death."

"It won't. It hasn't become final yet. So it isn't official." A smile lit up his face. "Well, this is wonderful news, Colt."

"Pardon me?"

"The church frowns on divorce, and Mia could have been excommunicated. But I'm sure I can cancel the divorce decree before it becomes part of the public record. Uh, you're *absolutely* sure Marcus is dead?"

"Absolutely, Uncle. There's no question that the individual I knew as Marcus Antonio Fabrizzi was murdered four days ago in the Bronx borough of New York City."

"Then we have cause for celebration. I never liked that fool. All he ever wanted was Mia's fortune, and he was so— how do you say in English— like glass?"

"Transparent?"

"Yes. He was so transparent about his motives."

Mia looked even more pained, so I pulled her to me and held her. I expected her to start weeping, but she held back the tears.

"Mia, why so miserable?" Uncle Yannis asked.

"I wanted to get away from Marcus, Uncle, but I didn't want him to be killed. I didn't believe Colt would do it unless he was forced to, so I was only a little worried."

"The world is better off without that scoundrel," Yannis said. "He was— as the Americans say— a waste of skin. He never earned a cent in his life. He only cheated people and stole whatever he could get his hands on. And now, because of his actions, he hasn't lived long enough to get his inheritance."

"Inheritance?" I said.

"Yes," Mia said. "He was to receive his grandfather's estate when he reached forty years of age. His grandfather knew what he was like, so he put his estate into the hands of a trust until Marcus was forty. Marcus used to curse his grandfather and sometimes laugh about the trust in a scornful way. His grandfather thought that if Marcus had to earn his own way until then, he would be more mature when he got his hands on the estate and then not blow it all in a few years."

A sizable inheritance could be viewed as a powerful motive for murder. I hoped we had heard the last of Marcus and his inheritance. Mia certainly didn't need the money.

"Marcus was a fool, sweetheart," I said, "Don't be sad about his passing. He had enormous treasure all along and didn't appreciate it."

"What treasure?"

"You."

Mia smiled. "Thank you, darling." She wrapped her arms around my neck and we kissed.

I didn't know how the family would react to such a public display of affection, but they apparently approved because when we parted, they were all smiling. Even Uncle Yannis.

"Colt, I understand you have quite a bit of wealth," Yannis said.

"Not so much when compared to Mia, Uncle, but I'm comfortable, and I don't need her money."

"I read that you made five million for that art recovery in Amsterdam, and then six million more for recovering a very expensive automobile recently."

"I've done well, sir. I just earned three million for recovering memorabilia in Memphis and acquired eighteen thousand acres in Wyoming from a related deal."

"Eighteen thousand acres? Let's see, that's about twenty-eight square miles?"

"Uh, yes, plus a little bit."

"That's about one-fifth the size of this entire island."

"Yes, sir. It's a large ranch."

"Ranch? Like in cowboy movies?"

"Yes, Uncle, but there are no cowboys on it. It isn't a *working* ranch. No cows."

"You didn't tell me about that, darling," Mia said. "Is that why you were delayed?"

"Yes. It was for the same individual, even though it wasn't part of the insured property. But the owner made it worth my while to stay on for an extra week after I recovered the other things so I could find something else that was stolen but not insured. I wanted the ranch to be a surprise. After we get back from Fiji, we'll take a trip out there and look it over."

"You haven't seen it?"

"Only from the air. But it looks beautiful."

Looking at Yannis, Mia said, "Colton has an enormous co-op apartment in a beautiful high-rise building in New York City. We have five large bedrooms. You must come and visit us there, Uncle."

"Perhaps one day. Right now all my attention must be on the company. These are difficult days in Europe, Colt, as you know, and Greece is the worst off of all the EU nations. We're a bit isolated here on Thasos from the worst of the problems— unemployment— because tourism is the major industry here.

"But it will reach even us, eventually, as transportation into and out of the country becomes undependable for tourists and then people stop coming here. Spain and France are in bad shape also, and the rest of Europe is not all that far behind. I fear what lies ahead for us here in the EU. I sympathize with the people who are most vulnerable in Greece, but they have to understand that an austerity program is not an *option* but a necessity.

"A person cannot live beyond their income, and neither can a government. If our company tried to do that, we'd be out of business in no time. Yet the politicians strove to do exactly that as they recklessly exhausted the country's treasury in order to get reelected rather than working to manage the country's finances prudently, following a sound financial plan. I understand the difficulty of their situation. There are so many people on social programs that it's impossible to get elected if you try to convince people a little belt-tightening is necessary.

"The most recent Prime Minister was elected because he promised to end the austerity cuts his predecessor tried to implement to get Greece back on a solid financial footing. Alexis Tsipras has been forced to do what he promised the voters he would *never* do. It was a foolish promise, but it got him elected."

"Yes, Uncle. We have the same problem in the U.S. There's a term we have for what our politicians do. We call it 'kicking the can down the road.' When they don't want to do something that might be unpopular with the voters, such as cutting a social program that will reduce benefits to one group or another, they delay taking any immediate action and allow a bad situation to worsen with each passing day. Then they raise the debt ceiling so they can borrow more money and plunge the country further and further into debt. I fear we're headed down the same road as Greece."

"You men can talk about boring politics later," Mia said after rolling her eyes. "Right now I want to talk with Colton, so I'm taking him for a walk around the grounds. Come along, darling," Mia said as she took my hand and pulled.

"The boss has spoken," I said with a smile to Yannis. "We can talk later."

He smiled knowingly.

Once we were outside, Mia said, "I knew I had to get you away or Uncle would have bent your ear for an hour."

"I like him."

"I knew you would. And I know he likes you. They all like you."

"How can you tell?"

"They're my family. You know, when Marcus would come here, they never smiled once. They all disliked him. I couldn't understand it. I guess I was blind to his faults. I thought I was in love and he was also. They recognized that *I* was in love, but that *he* wasn't. They tried to tell me but I didn't listen. I guess I thought they were jealous of my happiness."

"When someone is in love, they're often blind to a lot of things. Uh, you've never told me. Do they all speak English as well as Uncle?"

"No, not quite, but they'll understand almost everything you're likely to say, unless it's a saying that you have in America that isn't common here, like 'kicking the can down the road' or something similar. But you explained that very well."

"I'll try to limit my use of expressions like that."

"You don't have to, if you explain them. It's good for them to hear such things. That's how we learn, right?"

"When you talk to them, tell them I'll be happy to explain anything they don't understand, as long as they don't need me to explain it in Greek."

"I'm going to have to start teaching you some Greek."

"Great. How do you say 'make love' in Greek?"

She grinned and said, "Some things are better shown than talked about, but let's *discuss* that one later."

CHAPTER NINETEEN

One never knows what to expect from the relatives of a lover, and I anticipated that when I arrived at the Kosarros estate I might be put into a separate bedroom. But I soon discovered that it had already been accepted that Mia and I would share a bedroom as if we were a married couple. It appeared that everyone knew we were living together in New York, so it made things a lot easier on everyone to simply *pretend* we were married.

Mia and I hadn't even talked about marriage yet, although I hoped it might be a topic we'd seriously discuss at some point. I still feared she would one day tire of living in New York on a semi-permanent basis. To keep her, I would move anywhere in the world she wanted to live, unless that included her return to the days of jet-setting with the 'beautiful people' and following the sun around the globe most of the year.

But the more we had talked about life, the more comfortable she seemed to become with the idea of settling down. Jet-setting with Marcus had been a horrible experience for her because he was always trying to make new conquests while ignoring his wife. I learned how miserable Mia had been when Marcus would disappear from a party and not return to their hotel suite until after the sun was up, then give some phony excuse about talking sports all night with a few of the men after Mia had seen him sneak out with a woman.

I couldn't understand the man. He had this most incredibly beautiful, sexy, and intelligent woman as a wife, and he wanted to fool around with the bed-hopping bimbos at a party and risk everything. Well, he'd paid the price for his stupidity, as fools usually did. But I shouldn't complain. If not for his inexplicable behavior, I might never have met Mia.

The Kosarros family was wonderful. I hadn't had any kind of a family life since my folks were killed in a car accident while I was in college. My parents had both been only children, so there were no aunts or uncles, and both sets of grandparents, who had waited until late in life to begin their families, had passed on while I was still small. Even though I couldn't understand most of the discussion around the table at meal time, I could see that everyone else enjoyed the talk immensely.

And I was slowly picking up a few Greek words here and there as Mia explained what they were saying. If I stayed for any significant amount of time, I might be able to put enough of the basics together to at least understand the topic under discussion. It's said that the best way to learn a language is to become completely immersed in a culture and live where it's the only language spoken.

During the days, Mia took me on tours of the island, taking me to all of her favorite spots. Rather than having the principal population centered in one location, as it is on many islands, most of the population on Thasos Island was spread all along the shore wherever there were sandy beaches for tourism. The largest concentration of residents was located on the northern part of the island in a town also named Thasos.

While Mia and I were sitting on a beach one day staring out at the Aegean Sea, I asked her, "How could you ever stand to leave here? It's so beautiful."

"I wanted to see the world and experience life. Yes, it's beautiful here, and I did miss it, but the circumstances under which I left made it difficult for me to return. I'm glad I was finally forced to come back. I had to face up to the things I had said in anger before I left and make peace with Uncle. I know he loves me and that he was only thinking about my welfare, but you don't see things the same way when you're a teenager. You see your guardians as stifling you and holding you back. You think you are far worldlier than you actually are. I guess you just have to get away and make your own mistakes to learn that your relatives knew best all along."

"Well, perhaps they don't always know best, but they are more experienced, usually because they rebelled and got away from their parents and guardians and then made *their* mistakes. It's occurred to me many times that people don't really learn from the mistakes made by others. They have to make their own. Hopefully, the mistakes are not so damaging that you can't easily recover from them. As we mature, most of us become wiser."

"Some, like Marcus, never learn," she said as she put her hand on my shoulder in a sad caress. "My mistake with Marcus was almost one of those that you can't easily recover from. Thankfully, Uncle Yannis forced him to sign that pre-nuptial agreement. Without it, Marcus would probably have gone through most of my inheritance and then gotten half of everything that was left when I finally saw him for what he was."

"Let's talk about something more pleasant, Mia. Do you still want to go to Fiji?"

"Yes, I think I do. I love it here, and I love my family, but I want us to have some time together alone, away from family, the FBI, and recovery investigations."

"Okay. When do you want to go?"

"Are we in a hurry?"

"Uh, no, not at all. But I have to call and make reservations if you want to stay at the resort you requested. I cancelled the others because you had to return here to settle matters with the divorce."

"Then let's stay here for a while."

"How long a while? I don't mind, but I need a date for the reservations."

"Can we stay here for about a month and then go to Fiji?"

"Anything you want, sweetheart."

"Colton, you're so good to me. I love you more than life itself."

"And I love you, baby."

◆　◆　◆

I used my cell phone to make the reservations at the resort in Fiji. It was the first time I'd had it out of the protective case that blocks anyone from getting the GPS data but also blocks all calls. I saw that I'd had several calls from Saul Fodor while I'd been out of communication for several days. I really wanted to ignore his calls, but I owed him too much for helping me get the co-op by having his insurance company hold the mortgage. I was afraid he wanted me to come immediately, but a promise was a promise with me.

It was too late, or too early— depending on your point of view— to call Saul when I listened to the messages, but I would call as soon as the business day began in New York.

◆　◆

I didn't mention the messages to Mia. I wanted to wait until I was sure of the reason for the calls before I said anything to her.

Fodor's secretary put me right through when I called his New York office. Although it was four p.m. on Thasos when I placed the call, I calculated it was nine a.m. in the Eastern Time Zone.

"Colt, where have you been? I've been trying to reach you for two days."

"I'm in Europe, Saul. I'm on Thasos Island in the Aegean Sea. I hadn't used my phone in several days so I just heard the messages last night. I told you I was headed this way when I wrapped up the Memphis matter."

"Ah, yes, you did." Changing his voice to sound a little less angry but more desperate, he said, "I need you here. We have a major problem. There's been a robbery. Some of the world's finest works of art are missing."

"I'll be back long before you have to pay off the insured, Saul, and we'll recover the art then, okay?"

"I need you now, Colt. I'm sorry to intrude on your vacation, but I need you working on this. The police don't have any leads or suspects and don't know where to turn next. Our own investigation teams are bewildered as well. We need the best art recovery expert in the world working on this one."

"When did the robbery occur?"

"The same day you left for Memphis."

"So you knew about this long before I headed for Europe?"

"Yes, but I didn't think we'd need you on this one at the time because the police were saying they knew who committed the theft and were looking for the suspect."

"And?"

"They found him— or at least his grave. He died two months ago of pneumonia after having minor surgery on his right foot in a local hospital. His death has been confirmed."

"Why did they suspect *him*?"

"Because the theft was consistent with his M.O. Everything pointed to him."

"So he must have had an apprentice who learned his techniques. Find the apprentice and you've probably got your thief."

"The cops say he never had an apprentice. He never trusted anyone except himself to run an operation."

"Then perhaps a cellmate picked it up from him while they talked."

"He was released two years ago. His cellmate during that incarceration is still in prison and will be for at least six more years. Colt, we're afraid the art will wind up in Russia or China. Once there, it will be almost impossible to recover."

"What are we talking about for value?"

"The twelve pieces were appraised for two hundred seventy million."

"Was that the policy amount?"

"We've put out the word that we'll pay a two-million-dollar recovery fee for the artwork, no questions asked, but no one's responded."

"What was the policy amount?"

"It's crucial we recover the artwork as soon as possible, Colt."

"Saul, what's the policy amount?"

"Uh— three hundred one million, one hundred ninety-three thousand, two hundred seven dollars and seventy-two cents."

"That's a strange policy amount. Don't you usually just round the numbers with artwork because the value is so subjective?"

"That's the current currency conversion from two hundred seventy million Euros."

"Euros?"

"The artwork is on loan from a museum in Milan."

"Where was it on display?"

"It wasn't on display— yet. The exhibit is set to open in San Francisco three weeks from tomorrow. We have to get it back before then so the exhibit can open on time."

"I take it the theft hasn't been announced to the press yet?"

"No, it hasn't. And the museum is insisting that it not be announced until we're absolutely certain the artwork cannot be recovered before the exhibition date. A theft like this could damage their good name and they might have trouble getting such loans from other museums in the future."

"Okay, Saul. I'll take the next available flight back to the states. Have your secretary book me into a hotel in San Francisco, and overnight everything you have on the robbery to me, care of the hotel. Then have your secretary alert the museum that I'm on my way and that you expect them to give me their complete cooperation."

"Okay, Colt. And Colt— thanks."

"Sure thing, Saul."

As soon as we ended the call, I began making plans to leave. I contacted the air-taxi service and arranged to be picked up and brought to Athens, then contacted the airline I'd arrived on and booked a flight back to the U.S. The first-class round-trip ticket I'd purchased allowed me to change the return date for up to ninety days from the date of arrival, so for just a small charge I was able to use it after all.

◆

I knew Mia was going to be upset, but what could I do? I'd always heard people weren't supposed to go to bed when angry with a lover or spouse, so I told her about it before dinner. That way she'd time to get over it before bedtime.

"What? You're leaving?"

"Just for a short time. I'll be back as soon as I can. I'll be here in time to go to Fiji with you."

"But this is supposed to be our vacation."

"I know, and I'm sorry, but I signed an agreement with Saul Fodor that I would drop everything else to investigate any case he needed me for. It was one of the conditions for his company extending the mortgage on the co-op. The museum hasn't announced the theft yet because Saul told them they'd have the artwork back before the opening of the exhibition."

"You don't need his mortgage. I'll give you the money to pay off the mortgage."

"I can't take your money. That would make me no better than Marcus."

"Oh, darling, don't be silly. This is not the same thing at all. I'm living in the co-op also. It would be for both of us. Especially if it frees you from the instant demands of the insurance company while you're on vacation. Besides— I've been thinking about *us* a lot. Perhaps we should be talking about— merging our assets."

I could have been wrong, but the inference sure seemed to be marriage. "I love you, but this isn't the right time to be talking about such things. You're a little worked up right now because I have to leave on business, and a subject like this should be discussed when we're both unaffected by outside demands."

"But this isn't the first time I've thought about it, my darling. I've thought about it a lot. I had to stop thinking about it when I learned I was still married to Marcus, but I've begun thinking about it again since the court approved the divorce. And Uncle actually brought it up yesterday while you were swimming and I came inside to get some cool drinks."

"He did?"

"Yes. He said that if I was serious about you and you were serious about me, he approved. He said he had no reservations about you and he wouldn't require anything like the pre-nuptial agreement contract he required of Marcus. He likes you and approves of you."

"And I like him. I like your entire family. They've made me feel so welcome here. But, sweetheart, I have to go do this job. We can talk about— merging assets— at a different time. Even if I agreed to take the money you're offering, I would still have to go because this is part of a previous agreement that requires a ninety day notice for cancellation. Besides, I wouldn't feel right about dropping out without some advance warning to Saul."

"Uncle says you're a person of integrity, and I can't fault you for being honorable about your agreement with the insurance company. I'm just disappointed. I thought we were going to have all this time together."

"Believe me, I'm just as disappointed. But we'll have a lot of time together when I get back. And if you want to return here for another month after the vacation in Fiji, we can come back before going on to New York."

"Really?"

"Really. I know you love it here. It's so beautiful here, how could anyone not love it?"

"I love my family, and I was away from them for such a long time because of our disagreements over Marcus. I love you, darling."

"And I love you and your family. So— are you okay with me leaving to take care of this important business?"

"Yes, darling, I'm okay with it, but don't be upset with me if I act a little disappointed."

"I don't like to disappoint you, but I'd be a lot more upset if you *weren't* disappointed I was leaving."

Mia smiled at that.

◆

During dinner, Mia broke the news, in Greek, that I was leaving on business. I couldn't follow the discussion because my usual interpreter was in the center of the heated exchanges, but I got the impression that everyone was upset. I think they might have blamed Mia for having a spat with me or something and driving me away, which she seemed to strongly deny. By the end of the discussion, everyone had calmed down and smiles started returning.

"They thought I was chasing you away," Mia whispered to me as the meal continued. "I told them that you had to go solve an international art theft and that you would return. They said they hadn't heard about any big art theft and it was just an excuse I was making up. They wanted to know what I said that's driving you away. I told them that sometimes the police and insurance companies don't announce big thefts right away, or at all, because they hope that keeping it quiet will allow them to recover the artwork faster and that the museums hate publicity like that anyway."

"That's very true. So they're okay with it also?"

"Yes, I think so. I told them you would be back as soon as you could come back and I was staying here until then, and then we'd be going to Fiji before returning here. Right?"

"Right."

◆

When the air-taxi arrived in the morning, I was all packed and ready. The entire family came out to the pad to see me off, and there was a great deal of hugging and kissing. It was a very touching moment for me, mostly because I'd had no family to see me off on a trip for a very long time.

As the air-taxi lifted off the pad, everyone was waving. It made me want to hurry back as soon as I could.

The flight to Athens was a bit boring because it was predominantly over water, so I sat back and planned my trip. Mostly my plans revolved around trying to find a place where I could use the gizmo with no danger of anyone learning of its existence. I hadn't used it at the Kosarros residence because there was no place I was sure was totally secure. I couldn't afford to have Mia come in while I was viewing the robbery, so it would have to wait until I was in the hotel in San Francisco.

◆

The air-taxi folks had arranged for a golf-cart ride to the main terminal, and then it was simply a matter of waiting two hours for the plane to begin boarding. While sitting near the gate I heard an announcement that two days hence there would be no flights into and out of the airport for twenty-four hours. One of the unions had called for the one-day strike to protest reductions from what they said were necessary staffing levels. The country was in a hell of mess, and the unions weren't making the situation any better by having such an impact on tourism.

Nobody wanted to go to a place where they could suddenly discover that virtually the entire staff of a hotel was on strike, where the tourist destinations were all closed, or where their travel plans had suddenly been cancelled without notice. Local violence certainly didn't help either. I'd heard that Egypt used to be one of the 'must-see' destinations in the Middle East, with the country's economic stability coming mostly from tourist dollars, but few people reportedly went there anymore. Greece might be heading down that same path. I had hoped to view the famous sights such as the

Parthenon on the Acropolis of Athens when I came to Greece, but Mia advised against it. She said too many tourists were being attacked and robbed in the city. The economic situation was reportedly worsening by the day.

◆

When the announcement came that my flight would begin boarding, I stood and walked to the gate. Another of the advantages for paying three times the ticket price paid by the customers in steerage was boarding first. While the coach-class folks were trying to squeeze their bags into the overhead bins and dropping things on the heads of unlucky passengers sitting in the too-small seats below, I was relaxing in comfort with a pre-departure complimentary glass of wine. Traveling with the sun, we would arrive in New York at about four p.m. local time.

Once the plane had climbed to altitude and mostly leveled off, I put my head back and closed my eyes. I wasn't sleeping. I was merely thinking about the robbery in San Francisco. The lack of a secure place to view the event at the Kosarros estate meant that all I currently knew was the little info I'd gotten from Saul. I didn't even know where the robbery had occurred.

The actual theft could have happened anywhere from Milan, Italy, to the City by the Bay. I hoped it hadn't happened in Milan after I'd traveled all the way back to the U.S. because I'd have to turn around and head back to Europe again. I should have quizzed Saul a bit more, but I'd already begun worrying about breaking the news to Mia that I was leaving. However, I was fairly confident he wouldn't have asked me to rush back to the U.S. if the robbery had occurred in Europe.

Saul had told me the police had an M.O., which usually meant they knew how the theft had been accomplished even if they didn't know who had committed it. But he'd also said everyone was bewildered, which seemed to indicate they didn't know how it had been accomplished. They both couldn't be true. Could they? Well, I'd find out soon enough.

It would be late by the time I arrived in San Francisco because I would have to wait for a connecting flight at JFK, then travel for six more hours. It would still be the same day, local time, only because I was traveling west. Saul's secretary had emailed the particulars about the hotel, so all I had to do was check in when I got there.

CHAPTER TWENTY

A s curious as I was to learn the known facts of the art theft, I was just too weary to begin reading the reports when I finally reached my hotel in San Francisco and settled in. The suite was spacious and well appointed. I was certain I would appreciate it more in the morning because the only thing on my mind at that point was a good night's rest. Still, I took a hot shower to relax the tenseness in my muscles before slip-ping into bed.

I didn't request a wakeup call because I wanted to sleep for as long as my body needed it so I'd be alert when it mattered. I'd always had more of a problem getting my internal clock re-synched when traveling east to west. The bed was comfortable and the room was ultra-quiet, so I remembered nothing after laying my head down on the pillow.

◆ ◆

It was after eleven in the morning when I awoke. I felt well rested and ready to start the day, but my first order of business was to order a pot of coffee and a steak-and-eggs breakfast. I took a shower and was just finishing dressing when the breakfast was delivered. I signed the check after adding a tip that made the waiter smile, then sat at the table to eat and read.

The food was excellent, and I felt sated when I was done. I took my coffee over to the sofa and continued to read through the reports from the police and the insurance company investigators. Mostly there was boilerplate-type stuff used to bulk up the report, but from reading between the lines the situation appeared to be that all parties were bewildered. They didn't know who had committed the theft or even how. So to hide their confusion, the police had shadowboxed with the truth by saying they recognized the M.O.

I decided to start from the beginning and evaluate each step along the way where the paintings traveled from the Milan museum to the San Francisco museum, creating an image in my mind from the information in the reports written by the insurance company investigators.

According to the reports, the museum in Milan had had an independent, fine arts evaluation expert verify the paintings were genuine just before they were loaded into cases for their transportation to San Francisco. The cases were the standard cases designed for transporting valuable paintings and artwork. They were made of plywood sheathed by aluminum on the inside and stainless steel on the outside, with a stainless steel framework. Offered in a variety of sizes by the company that manufactured them, the insides were designed to be completely removable and could be adjusted to accommodate whatever size and shape painting or picture was being transported. The adjustable wood internal frames and foam padding would protect the artwork from anything short of having the outside case completely crushed, and it would probably take a plane crash to do that.

Once verified by the expert, each painting was sealed inside a separate case and the air evacuated using a small vacuum pump. Each case had an RF unit built into it, which could be set to a different code so the movement of the case could be constantly monitored and instantly located if it went astray. A piece of braided steel wire was passed through the hasp, and a flat lead seal with a special design prepared especially for this shipment was clamped onto the wire, sealing each case. They wouldn't stop anyone from breaking in, but any tampering would be immediately obvious.

Officials from the museum and the insurance company watched every movement of the verification expert and the packers. When the twelve cases were ready for shipment, each case was weighed and the precise weight recorded. A squad of museum guards and two representatives of the insurance company then remained with the cases until the armored truck arrived. The cases had also been under constant video surveillance by museum cameras from four angles.

When the armored truck arrived, one museum guard and one insurance official rode to the airport inside the rear compartment, while the others rode along in vehicles ahead of and behind the armored truck. All three vehicles were in constant radio contact.

At the airport, the three vehicles entered the airport area near the freight hanger. One of those large cargo containers that were preloaded and then put inside the body of a plane had been set aside for just the painting cases. After being placed inside and secured, the cargo container door was closed. The cargo container received the same steel wire and lead seal treatment as each individual artwork container.

The armored truck was allowed to leave, but the museum security and the insurance people stayed until the container was loaded into the plane and the cargo doors closed and sealed. The museum guards actually stayed at the airport, never taking their eyes off the plane until it rose into the sky. The cargo area wasn't heated, so no one could remain there, but there was a passenger area up near the cockpit capable of seating about a dozen people. That's where the insurance people had gone after the cargo container was loaded. They would fly to Newark airport with the cargo.

At Newark, the cargo container was removed from the plane and examined by the insurance people. The lead seals were intact and the RF signals were strong. A customs official checked the paperwork and approved the container's entry into the country. From that point on it was the insurance officials and a new team of security guards watching over the container until it was time to load it into a freight plane bound for San Francisco.

Hours later, the container was loaded aboard the new plane and the insurance people took their seats in the small passenger section for the six-plus-hour trip to San Francisco.

Once the plane landed, the cargo container was checked for tampering, then opened. The twelve cases were removed and put into an armored truck for transport to the museum. The small convoy made its way through the city without incident, arriving at the museum a little after eleven p.m.

When the containers were off-loaded at the museum and the seals had been checked for tampering, the containers were transported to the museum's work and storage area by museum personnel. Once the cases were inside the secure area and they had been weighed to ensure their precise weight was consistent with the weight recorded in Milan, the museum curator signed for the delivery and the insurance officials left.

The cases wouldn't be opened until the next day when a fine arts evaluation expert was on hand to verify the authenticity of the paintings. In the meantime, the cases were left in full view of several video cameras and museum security would be watching them all night.

At nine the following morning, the evaluation expert arrived and was escorted to the high security area where the cases had sat all night. A museum person opened the air valve slowly on the first case to allow air to flow back in. When the pressure had been neutralized, the wire seal was cut off. The case was lifted onto a table and opened so the adjustable wood frame inside could slide out. As the first priceless masterpiece was revealed, the museum officials and the expert were aghast. The precious painting had been substituted with a cheap piece of virgin canvas mounted in a coarse wood frame. Without waiting to verify the others, the museum curator immediately phoned the insurance company and the police, in that order.

The remainder of the cases had not been opened until the police detectives arrived. Then, one by one, it was revealed that each of the other original paintings had been removed and replaced with a blank canvas in a rough, unfinished wood frame. Since the evaluation was taking place in a secure area of the museum, the original discovery had been captured by no less than three cameras. The police immediately requested copies of the security system video discs for every minute of time since twenty-four hours prior to the arrival of the art-work.

The packet of papers sent to me even included the initial police report filed by the first officers to respond. It only included the date and time, their names, and the facts as related by the museum curator. The subsequent reports, filed by the detectives assigned to the case, indicated that the police were unable to determine when and where the theft had occurred. They had determined that there were no fingerprints on any of the replacement canvases or support framework. The outside cases were covered with fingerprints, but most could be associated with the people who had responsibility for handling the cases. An unidentified thumb print was later attributed to the customs official at Newark airport. The curator and fine arts expert had worn white cotton gloves when handling the cases and phony artwork.

There was still some coffee in the pot, so I refilled my cup and sat down at the desk to think about the robbery. I had to admit to having a small admiration for the people who could commit a robbery such as this one without hurting anyone. The smash-and-grab crooks were a dime a dozen, but this robbery took someone with intelligence and imagination. I was still going to do my best to find them and see that they were punished for their misdeeds, but I didn't have the feelings of animosity I had towards people who hurt other people. Of course, the people who committed the art theft in The Netherlands that I'd solved didn't hurt anyone during the robbery either. But that hadn't stopped them from trying to kill me— repeatedly.

The first thing to do was find out where the theft actually occurred, and how, so I took out the gizmo and stuck it to the wall over the desk. I went to the museum in Milan first and tagged four of the art pieces. Then I jumped to Newark when the customs official was checking the shipment. The paintings were still in the cargo container. Next I jumped to the San Francisco airport at the time when the twelve cases were being loaded into the armored truck. The four paintings were not in the cases being loaded.

"Okay," I said to myself, "So now I know the paintings were taken while the plane was en route from Newark to San Francisco. But that's a bit difficult to do while twenty to thirty thousand feet up. So how did they do it? And who did it?'"

Since I had tagged four of the paintings, it was easy to jump to where they were located after the plane had landed. They were inside a different container. So the switch was made in the air. At this point I didn't know if the entire shipping container had been switched simply by changing the outside identifications on the containers, or if the artwork had simply been moved to a different container. And question number two: why didn't the RF units in each individual art-work transport case alert everyone to the swap?

Setting the time on the gizmo to three hours into the six-hour flight, I jumped to where the paintings were. The light was a bit dim in the plane's cargo hold, but I could make out two men working to transfer the art cases from one container to another. I backed up the gizmo to where the men first appeared, zoomed in to see better, then sat back to observe the theft.

As I watched, the entire top of a cargo container rose on hinges and a man climbed out. Most air cargo containers were built to be accessed only from the side. All of the containers in this plane were constructed that way. That is, all except one. When a container was loaded aboard a plane, it was pushed into position and locked down to the deck so it didn't move around in rough air. That would make it impossible for anyone hiding in a container to escape unless there was no other container blocking their access point. By hinging the top, they could get out easily no matter where they were loaded, as long as there was room overhead. There was actually quite a bit of overhead space left in this plane while the cargo deck was fully loaded with containers.

The man who climbed out was wearing a rebreather mask and special clothing to protect him from the cold. A second man appeared almost immediately, and they began searching among the containers for something, which I assumed was the cargo container with the artwork.

When they located it, they began moving all of the containers, blocking access to the side door of the one with the artwork. Beginning at one end, they 'unlocked' a container from the deck, slid it to a new position, then locked it down again. They seemed very well practiced at doing it, and it took them just a short time to gain access to the container holding the cases with the paintings.

While one of them cut the wire seal and opened the side of the cargo container, the other man had returned to his original container and carefully began pulling out art transport cases identical to the ones used in Milan. Each of them had a yellow tag on the handle.

The first man removed all twelve cases from the genuine container and put a red tag on each handle. Then it was simply a matter of matching up the cases by size. Where there were multiple cases of identical sizes, the thieves used a small, electronic, kitchen-style scale to determine the weight of each. When twelve pairs of cases sat on the deck, one of the men produced a piece of electronic equipment and read the RF frequency from a box with a red tag on the handle by pressing a red button on the device and holding it for several seconds. He then placed his electronic box next to the same-sized case with a yellow tag and pressed a yellow button, which he also held for several seconds. I assumed he was encoding the frequency of an RF unit inside the replacement case to match the original. Then he returned the device to the original transport case and depressed a black button for several seconds. I assumed this either deactivated the original signal, or changed it to one no one would recognize or be monitoring.

Lastly, the yellow tag was removed from the phony transport case and it was placed into the museum's cargo container. They used a picture the first man had taken with his cell phone to place the box in the correct location within the container. The case with the red tag, the original, was then put into the cargo container with the hinged top. It took them just half an hour to swap all of the cases.

When they were done, they methodically checked to make sure they were leaving no evidence behind. They even counted the yellow tags they had removed after setting the frequencies to make sure they accounted for all of them. Those guys were thorough. Since the replacement cases were already all sealed with a braided steel wire through the hasp and a flat lead seal matching the original, all the thieves had to do was replace the wire seal on the cargo container and crimp a flat lead seal onto the wire. They then slid all the containers back to their original positions and locked them down to the deck.

As they finished up, they climbed back into the phony container and sealed themselves in. No one would ever know the robbery had taken place at thirty thousand feet over Kansas, or wherever.

I loved how the gizmo always made me look like a genius, but this one was going to be hard to explain. Even though I wouldn't have to explain to Brigman how I solved this case, I knew the value and importance of the artwork in this robbery was going to make headlines around the world, and people would constantly be asking me how I solved it. At least the robbery wouldn't reflect badly on the museum. Since the robbery hadn't occurred at the museum, they couldn't be blamed for a lack of security that would harm their chances of getting future loans of artwork.

I next jumped to the present time to learn where the four paintings were now. They were all together, and I hoped all twelve were still together. I had to move the window outside the building to get my bearings and then raise it up above the roof line. The skyline told me the paintings were still in San

Francisco, but since I wasn't familiar with the city, I had to use the GPS coordinates the gizmo provided. It turned out the four paintings were in a one-car garage just off Golden Gate Avenue in the Fillmore District.

I jumped back to Milan and tagged four more, then jumped to the present time and saw that they were also in the same warehouse. When I did the last four, I only detected three at the garage. I located the fourth in an upscale private home in Oakland, so this might have been a 'steal to order' where the purpose of the entire robbery was just to get one piece. The others might have been taken on the chance the thieves might be able to sell one or two someday, or just to cover up the real target in the theft.

The first robbery I had solved for Saul Fodor involved a 'steal to order' piece of art. The crooks had taken everything to cover the fact that they had only wanted the one piece. It was extremely difficult to sell major works of art because they were usually 'one of a kind,' well-known, and easy to identify. The thieves had to find a collector willing to possess stolen merchandise that he or she could never show to anyone else or brag about owning. Sometimes the thieves wound up selling the artwork back to the insurance company for a pittance of its value because a million-dollar work of art might be worthless to them otherwise. I'm sure that was the idea behind Saul offering just two million, with no questions asked, for return of three hundred million in stolen artwork.

So knowing now where all the artwork was, all I had to do was identify the two crooks, all the support people who provided help and information, and the person who had bought the one painting and probably instigated the robbery. I had become quite expert at identifying people since my first faltering steps using the gizmo.

Then, of course, I'd have to decide how long to sit on the information before giving it to Saul. If I waited too long, the thieves might decide to ship the 'extra' art out of the country. And if I solved the case too quickly, Saul would expect me to solve all the cases as quickly. I feared I was already reaching that point, which might be why he hadn't brought me into the case earlier. I was like his relief pitcher and would normally only be brought into the game in the ninth inning.

I was just about to start the identification process when my cell phone rang. Picking it up, I saw the call was from Saul Fodor.

"Good morning, Saul," I said when I made the connection.

"Morning? It's nighttime here in New York. Colt, the museum folks said you haven't visited them yet."

"That's correct, Saul."

"Colt, you have to get busy on this. We stand to lose three hundred million. My Board of Directors is all over my ass."

"Saul, I am working on it. I've spent every minute since I awoke today reading over all the reports to gain an understanding of the robbery and piece together how I think it happened. Meanwhile, my internal clock is still trying to get used to the time difference between San Francisco and Greece."

"Have you learned anything new?"

"I can't say for sure, yet, but I don't believe the theft occurred at the museum. I believe the paintings were taken while en route."

"That's impossible. The tamper-proof seals were never tampered with."

"Perhaps."

"Perhaps? Are you telling me it was an inside job?"

"No, Saul. I'm only speculating at this point based on what I've read. But I'm hard at work on the case even if I haven't visited the museum yet. When I do visit them, I believe it will just be to confirm that the theft did not occur there. That should make them feel better because their reputation for proper security won't be affected by the theft."

"That is, if you can prove it."

"Don't I always?"

"Uh, yes."

"Then calm down and trust that you have the best recovery person in the world working on the case full-time. Even though it may appear to you like I'm not working, I assure you I am hard at work. I'm anxious to wrap this case up quickly and get back to Greece, Mia, and my vacation."

"Okay, Colt. I'm sorry. I know you're the best. I'm just not used to having Board members calling me every hour to get a progress report."

"I understand, Saul. And I assure you I'll brief you as soon as I have anything concrete."

"Okay, Colt. Thanks."

"Goodnight, Saul."

As I ended the call, I knew Saul was going to be on my back until I wrapped up the case. I decided to 'find' the eleven pieces of art quickly. That would solve the potential problem of having them disappear to other parts of the world while also getting a little relief from the Board for Saul.

But for now, my task was to identify the perps and their immediate accomplices, if any.

Learning the identities of the two thieves was as easy as I had expected. I just tagged them and went back to the date of their births to get their names off their birth certificates as the doctors, nurses, or administration staff completed the documents. I was surprised to learn that one was a female and, later, that they had been a husband-and-wife robbery team for more than two decades.

◆

The following morning my internal clock was comfortably back on local time and I arose before seven. I enjoyed a good breakfast in my suite and then prepared for a busy day. The museum didn't open for a few hours, so I did a little sightseeing. It was my first trip to San Francisco, and I'm sure I gawked like a typical tourist. Even though I was a New York City resident and used to big cities, the sights were unique. At one point I realized I had seen the same two faces at several different tourist locations. They were trying to fit in, but they certainly weren't tourists. I decided to see how serious they were about following me, so I hailed a cab and had the driver take me to the San Francisco Zoo.

Ten minutes after entering the park, I spotted one of my shadows. He had one eye on the giraffes and one on me. There was an earphone in his right ear, but I doubted he had a hearing problem. I casually walked over and stopped immediately next to him as I stared at the giraffes. After a few seconds I said, "Seems like such a waste of taxpayer dollars to have an SFPD team following me around town. I'll save you some effort. I'm headed to the museum next. I was just killing time until they opened, and I decided to enjoy the sights." To his credit, he never tried to deny his role and, in fact, never responded in the slightest, so I wandered away.

◆

Rather than approach the museum staff immediately, I bought a ticket and wandered around looking at the exhibits. They had some wonderful artwork as part of their permanent collection, and I could have stayed there for hours studying the exhibits if I'd had the time, but I had work to do.

Approaching a security guard, I asked, "Where do I find Mr. Hewitt?"

Pointing, he said, "They can tell you at the administration office, sir."

"Thank you."

I repeated my question to a clerk at the administration office counter.

"What is this in reference to, sir?" she asked as she continued to sort though some papers.

"Three hundred million dollars in stolen paintings," I said in a lowered voice as I leaned in towards her.

She stopped looking through the papers and raised her eyes to stare at me.

"I'm afraid I don't understand."

"Just tell him Colton James is here. He'll understand."

"Mr. James? Yes, sir. He's been expecting you. One moment, sir."

She picked up a phone and entered several numbers, then said, "Mr. James to see Mr. Hewitt." She listened for a few seconds, then hung up the phone and said, "Mr. Patrice will be right with you. He'll take you to where Mr. Hewitt is working presently."

"Thank you."

The woman returned to her paperwork, and I stood near the counter looking around until a young man who looked like he might be an intern approached me. "Mr. James?"

"Yes."

My assumption that he was an intern was based on my assessment of his age. He didn't look much more than twenty-one, and he was wearing a suit.

"I'm Robert Patrice. If you'll follow me, I'll take you to Mr. Hewitt. He's been anxiously awaiting your arrival."

I followed the young man through the museum and then through a door that had required him to enter a security code before he could open it. After a few more minutes of traversing corridors, we came to a work area where half a dozen people were hard at work cleaning canvases, pottery, and whatever.

"Ah, Mr. James. Welcome to our work area. I'm Benjamin Hewitt."

"Hello, Mr. Hewitt. You have a very nice museum here, and your permanent collection is superb."

"Thank you, Mr. James. It's a lot of work to keep it clean and in top condition, but our staff is a dedicated group of professionals."

"I see that."

"And now, Mr. James, have you learned anything new about the robbery?"

"I only arrived in town yesterday, Mr. Hewitt, and I had just flown in from Greece. But I've read through the entire file of investigator reports, and I can say with certainty that the theft didn't occur here in the museum, so your security is not in question and you shouldn't fear being tarnished in any way by the crime."

"And what leads you to that conclusion, Mr. James?"

"The simplest of deductive reasoning, Mr. Hewitt. If the thieves had taken the paintings from here, there would have been no reason to replace them with phony canvases. The phony canvases were only needed so the cases matched the original weight and feel during handling. That delayed the time that the theft was discovered. It also served to keep investigators from determining exactly where the theft occurred."

"You said the feel of the cases during handling?"

"Yes. If they had simply replaced the paintings with a piece of lead matching the weight of the original painting, the case would have felt off balance and different."

"I see. One of the policemen said they probably replaced the canvases to make the investigators *think* the theft occurred somewhere else."

"No, the thieves wouldn't have bothered doing that. It would have required too much effort to get those phony canvases and frames into the museum. And if they had been stealing the paintings from here, they would simply have cut them from the frames to get out as quickly as possible."

"Yes, that makes perfect sense. So where do you believe the theft took place?"

"That's the big question. It naturally had to have happened while the paintings were en route. When I learn how they accomplished it, I should be able to pinpoint where it happened. As each part of the puzzle is revealed, we move one step closer to the thieves and the paintings. But since it didn't happen here, you won't be seeing much of me as I investigate. I'll be concentrating my investigations on the transportation part of the puzzle."

"Do you think you can recover the artwork before the exhibit is set to open in three weeks?

"I'd better, or my fiancée will have my head. We're supposed to go on vacation around that time."

CHAPTER TWENTY-ONE

After leaving the museum, I hailed a cab and headed for the local offices of the airfreight operation that had arranged for the cargo container transportation from Milan to San Francisco. I already knew how the theft had been accomplished, thanks to the gizmo, but I had to put in appearances here and there so everyone would think I was actually conducting an investigation.

I knew people were watching me. The SFPD had been easy to spot, but there were most likely others watching as well. The people behind the theft would want to know what I was doing and who I was talking to— not the husband-and-wife team that had actually committed the theft, but rather the brains behind the operation. According to their past history, the two who pulled off the heist weren't capable of organizing something on this scale on their own.

Someone with intelligence and a large bankroll had been pulling the strings from the beginning. The replacement cases had been prepared to weigh precisely what the originals weighed. Only someone with detailed inside information could have known the exact weights and managed to have them ready in time. And that same person had managed to get a copy of the lead seal image and make a die in time to get it aboard the plane at Newark.

That's the person I wanted to identify, even if I might never be able to prove his or her involvement in the crime. The really smart operators, like Delcona, had layers of people between themselves and the minions who actually pulled off the jobs and ditched or buried the bodies. The only way to bring them down was to find someone close to them who could be squeezed until their eyes bled and they agreed to testify against the top people in return for reduced charges and sentences, or complete immunity from prosecution.

At the airfreight office, I asked to speak to whoever the top manager was. When the counter person asked what it was in reference to, I opened my ID wallet and said I was investigating a theft. He asked what had been stolen, and I told him he wasn't high enough up the management chain to receive that information. He looked at me with disdain, then picked up the phone.

"Mrs. Weinwright, there's an FBI agent here and he's asking to see you."

After listening for a moment, the clerk said, "She wants to know what it's in reference to."

"I told you. It's in reference to a theft."

"Hs says it's in reference to a theft."

After a few more seconds, he said, "She wants to know what's been stolen."

I held out my hand for the phone receiver, and the clerk handed it to me.

"Mrs. Weinwright, this is Special Agent Colton James. The information I have is not to be shared with office clerks. Are you the senior manager here or not?"

"Yes, Mr. James, I am the Director for Terminal Operations in San Francisco."

"Then my information is for your ears only."

"I'm very busy today, Mr. James."

"Very well, Mrs. Weinwright, I shall make a note of your complete lack of cooperation in this very serious investigation. Good day."

I put the receiver down and turned towards the door, noting the looks of shock on the faces of the other clerks behind the counter. I hadn't reached the exit when the first clerk called out to me.

"Agent James. Mrs. Weinwright will see you in five minutes, if you can wait."

I turned back and nodded. The clerk told Mrs. Weinwright that I would wait.

It was actually twelve minutes before a young woman approached me and offered to take me to Mrs. Weinwright's office. I followed along and was guided through a hallway to a door where the lettering announced it was the office of the Director for Terminal Operations in San Francisco. The young woman gestured towards the door and said, "Go on in, sir."

I thanked her and entered the office. A secretary gestured towards another door and said, "She's expecting you, Mr. James. Go ahead in."

I entered the inner office and saw a woman of about fifty in an expensive business suit standing behind a desk. There was also a man in the office. Also impeccably dressed, he stared at me when I entered the office.

"I'm Colton James."

"I'm Mrs. Weinwright, Agent James." Gesturing towards the man she said, "This is Mr. Mangini. He's the Regional Head of Operations."

Mangini extended his hand and smiled. I took it, and smiled back as I shook it.

"May I see some ID please, Agent James?"

I took out my ID wallet and flipped it open. Mangini studied the ID for a couple of seconds then nodded.

"Mr. Mangini and I were discussing some very important matters. I apologize if I appeared abrupt."

"I won't take up very much of your time, Mrs. Weinwright. Please understand that the matter I'm going to discuss has not yet been made public and must remain that way for the present. Your company recently transported a collection of paintings valued at three hundred million dollars from Milan to San Francisco. Somewhere from the time the artwork was turned over to your company or its representatives at the Milan airport for transport to this terminus, and it arrived here, the artwork was removed from the cargo container. All twelve pieces were stolen."

"Do you have the shipment data?"

I removed a paper from my inside jacket pocket, opened it, and handed it to her. She took it and keyed something into the computer on her desk, then read from the screen.

"That shipment arrived at the Milan airport in an armored truck under heavy guard and the cargo was transferred to a cargo container and sealed. The container was then loaded aboard a flight intended for the U.S. The container was passed by customs at Newark and then loaded with others aboard a non-stop flight to San Francisco. The flight was met here by an armored truck and the shipment was checked and signed for. That's everything I can tell you about it."

"Somewhere between Milan and San Francisco, the twelve artwork transportation cases containing the paintings were opened, the paintings removed, and dummy substitutes inserted." I knew that the entire cases had actually been substituted, but I didn't want to share that information with anyone yet.

"That's impossible. The only place the cases would have been accessible would have been at the customs station at Newark. And nothing of that sort could have taken place there."

"And yet, the paintings were indeed stolen somewhere between Milan and San Francisco while in the care of your company."

"Are you making a formal accusation, Agent James?" Mangini asked.

"Not at this time, Mr. Mangini. And when I make a charge, there's never any ambiguity about it. Thank you both for your time. Good day."

As I rode back to my hotel in a cab, I thought about the discussion. I didn't know if either of them was involved, but it never hurt to stir the pot just a little to see what floated to the top.

◆

Once back in my room I ordered two pots of coffee. I expected it to be a marathon session as I tried to identify all the players in this heist. It might be impossible if they had never met face to face, but I had to try. At the very least I needed to identify who was in possession of the one painting in Oakland, so I worked on that first.

It didn't take long to learn who had possession of the painting that had been separated from the others. I didn't even try to suppress a laugh. The individual was a quite famous congressman, having retired and moved from his home state to California. I laughed because who was more likely to buy a stolen painting or commission its theft than someone used to believing they were always above the law?

I'd read that in at least one state in the Midwest, the police can't even arrest a sitting politician for other than a capital offense. As long as they continue to get reelected, they have the ultimate in immunity. Judging from the number of politicians at the federal level who have been tried and sentenced to jail terms, no such protections were afforded to them, except for the President and Vice-President, who could only be impeached.

Learning who had the twelfth painting concluded the easy part of the investigation. Trying to associate the dynamic duo who actually committed the crime with the person pulling the strings seemed an impossible task. I did learn that the woman was the brains of the duo. But watching her day and night by skipping ahead five minutes every few seconds for the weeks before the theft produced nothing but bloodshot eyes. She spent a lot of time on the phone, but almost all calls were incoming on one of the old style landline phones without a display. The outgoing calls were not to any one person or business.

After several days of making no progress with the thieves, I changed tactics. I went back to the robbery and wrote down all the information I could see on the phony cargo container outfitted as the hiding and storage place of the two thieves. It was too dark in the plane, so I jumped back to before it was loaded and examined it from every angle.

The information necessitated another trip to see Mrs. Weinwright. She was a little more cordial this time, perhaps because her supervisor wasn't there. She took the container information and ran the numbers through her desk computer.

"This container record is confusing. According to the file, the container had been damaged and removed from service at the Newark terminal. But then it was scheduled to be sent here, where it was to be put into storage."

"And was it?"

"Yes, according to the records it traveled on the same plane as the art shipment, and after being unloaded it was taken to our rehabilitation area where we fix containers and put them back into service."

"And has it been returned to service?"

"No, not yet."

"Would it be possible to see it?"

"Of course. Come with me."

Fifteen minutes later we were at the reclamation area and the supervisor was conducting a search for the container. After having a clerk check the computer and a member of his staff perform a physical check in the yard, he accessed the computer personally.

"It doesn't seem to be here, Mrs. Weinwright," he said finally. "And there's no record of it ever coming in or going out."

"Come on, Pete. The computer inventory says it was sent here for evaluation and rehabilitation."

"Your information comes from the transportation files, and that database does, in fact, state that it was sent here. But the rehab file is a separate database, and there's no record of it ever being logged in here."

Mrs. Weinwright turned to me and said, "I'm sorry Agent James. It appears we have a missing container. Perhaps it will turn up at some point. I'll have IT put a flag on that number in the transportation database, and if it is ever used again, I'll let you know."

"Okay, Mrs. Weinwright. Thank you for your efforts today."

"May I ask how you came to focus on that container number?"

"I'm sorry, but I can't discuss the details of my investigation at this time."

"I simply thought that if I knew more, I might be of more assistance."

"I wish I could share, but I can't. I'll continue to investigate the matter, and when I find your missing container, I'll let you know. Good day."

I was trying to make it appear that I was solving the case through real investigative work, so I was following the procedures I believed other investigators would employ. If the SFPD was still following up on my investigation, they'd learn what I just had. They wouldn't know how I'd learned about the missing container, but they would now know about it being missing and put two and two together. If they found it and were able to associate it with the two thieves, they might also learn about the private garage where the eleven paintings were stored. If the thieves had been smart, they would have rented the garage under an alias, but dumb crooks were what allow the police to stay in the game, considering all the rules that handicapped their ability to solve crimes. In any event, it was time to tell Saul about the garage.

◆

Before I called Saul, I verified that the eleven paintings were still in the garage in the Fillmore District. They were, so I placed the call. It was after company hours, but I had his private number so I could reach him at any time, just as he had mine.

"Hi, Saul," I said as he answered.

"Colt, tell me you have good news."

"I have good news."

"You've recovered all of the artwork?"

"No. I have to leave the recovery to you. But I can tell you where you'll find it. At least most of it."

"How much is most of it?"

"I believe you'll find eleven of the twelve pieces."

"And do you know where the twelfth painting is?"

"Not yet, Saul, but I thought this information might get the Board off your back. They'll see that you're making real progress."

"Yes, yes, thank you. They've been driving me crazy."

"I think this was a 'steal to order' case like the one in Boston, so the missing painting has been sent on to the person who ordered it."

"What about the thieves?"

"I've just sent you an email that contains the names of the two thieves who actually performed the heist, the address where they live here in San Francisco, and the address of the garage where the eleven paintings are currently located. I'd have the police pick the thieves up before recovering the paintings so they don't hear about the recovery and take off."

"Yes, definitely. So you know how the theft was accomplished?"

"I believe so, but I'm still trying to fit some pieces into the puzzle. I'll keep working on it and keep you updated as I learn more."

"Great. Thanks Colt. I'm going to get our legal staff here involved and working with the San Francisco Police unit that's investigating the crime so they can round up your two suspects and get a search warrant for the garage."

"Okay, Saul. Good night."

I decided it was time to track the phony cargo container from the time the plane landed to learn when the paintings were actually removed for transportation to the storage location and to learn what had happened to the container. The ability to jump around in time had meant that I didn't have to watch everything in chronological order as I used the gizmo, and I had gotten used to taking shortcuts so I had the most important information as soon as possible.

When the phony container had been removed from the plane, it was temporarily placed with all the others. I saw the armored truck arrive and collect the substituted cases from the genuine container, then leave. The phony container just sat there as activity in the area slowed to almost nothing in the hours following. I would have expected the other containers to be emptied and their contents sorted and stored away somewhere, but I guessed that would be done when the first shift arrived in the morning.

It was almost five a.m. when a forklift came and picked up the phony container. The operator took it around the side of the building and placed it onto a waiting flatbed truck. I used my smart phone to take a picture of the forklift operator. I also tagged him and would learn later who he was. I then photographed and tagged the security guard who opened the gate so the truck could leave the area and tagged the truck driver after making a note of the license plate number.

Many times the minions had no idea what was really going down. They only knew that somebody had given them a week's pay for doing five minutes' work they could later deny knowing anything about. Sometimes they got away with such behavior for years but then got caught and wound up with a criminal record that ensured they were never able to get a position of trust again.

It was the part of law enforcement I hated— prosecuting the little fish while the big fish just hired more guppies. Of course, sometimes the guppies knew more than the big fish was aware they knew and were able to help bring down the kingfish in exchange for a get-out-of-jail card, and sometimes they simply disappeared, never to be heard from again unless their body floated to the surface.

The truck driver took the phony container to a small warehouse with a garage door large enough to accommodate the truck and its load. As soon as the truck came to a stop inside the building and the door was closed, a forklift lifted the container off the truck and lowered it to the floor.

As the forklift backed away, a man walked to the container and rapped his knuckles on the top in a sequence that suggested a pre-arranged code. I zoomed in to catch the signal, but I missed it. I would have to back up at some point to learn the code.

As the man stepped back out of the gizmo image, the top rose and the smiling face of the male half of the robbery team appeared. I pulled back and watched as the duo passed the cases and all of their equipment out of the container. They used a flashlight to make sure they had everything, then hopped out and closed the top lid. After smiles and congratulations all around, eleven of the cases were put into the back of small van. One of the cases was put into the trunk of a car. I knew exactly where that was going.

The forklift driver then picked up the container and put it back on the flatbed truck.

As the truck driver backed the truck out of the warehouse, I decided to stay with the truck and come back to the warehouse later. The sun was up and people were heading to work, so traffic was getting heavy.

After crossing over the San Mateo Bridge, the driver dropped the phony container off at a recycling center in Union City. I jumped ahead and learned that the container was still there, although it was half buried under a growing pile of recycled stuff. I wondered if the driver had been told to dispose of it where it would never be found but had then decided he could get a few more dollars by recycling it. It didn't really matter as long as the container was still there when the police arrived to retrieve it.

I spent the next several hours learning the identities of all the people I had witnessed playing a role, however small, in the robbery. I was glad it wasn't my job to decide on the charges that would be pressed or on the innocence or guilt of the people involved.

◆

It was after two a.m. when I finished typing up my complete report on my laptop. I was beat and glad to be finished with this case. I sent a copy to Saul's email address at the insurance company and went to bed. Since it was after five a.m. in New York City, he'd be reading it in a few hours.

◆   ◆

I usually got up early unless Mia and I had partied too much the previous night, but I slept in the next morning because I had worked so late. I was awakened by someone pounding on the door.

I pulled on a robe, grabbed my Glock 23 from the holster, and opened the door a crack. It was the cop from the zoo that I had briefly spoken to at the giraffe pen.

"Yeah, what is it?"

"Special Agent James, my captain would like to see you."

"Sure. Send him in."

"He'd prefer you came to him."

"What time is it?"

"Nine twelve."

"Okay, tell him I'll see him at eleven."

"He's waiting to see you *now*."

"Are you placing me under arrest?"

"I hope I won't have to do that."

"What would you charge me with? Oversleeping while you had to be at work?"

"Look, will you *please* come with me."

"Yes, but first I have to shower and shave."

"How long."

"Half-hour."

"I'll be back."

"I'm sure."

I didn't hurry, but I didn't dawdle either, so I was dressed and ready when the detective came back. When I opened the door part way, I said, "May I see your ID, please?"

After looking at it, I opened the door the rest of the way and let him see me slip my Glock 23 into the shoulder holster under my left arm.

"Were you expecting someone else?"

"I always expect the unexpected. It keeps me breathing. People have tried to punch my ticket a few times."

"Yeah, we don't make many friends in this business, other than our brother and sister officers."

"For sure. Okay, Detective Lt. Hooper. Shall we go?"

"For sure, Special Agent James."

♦

"Good morning, Special Agent James," Captain Fasko said. "Thank you for coming in."

"My pleasure, Captain. How can I help you?"

"We received a request overnight to detain two of our citizens as suspects in the theft of priceless paintings. According to the request, you identified them as the people who actually committed the theft. Can you tell me how you know that?"

"Did you also get a request to search a one-car garage in the Fillmore District?"

"Yes, we did."

"And did you search the garage?"

"Not yet. We just received the search warrant this morning. We had to wait until a judge was available."

"That's too bad. The evidence you seek was there."

"Was?"

"Since it's taken you so long to get the search warrant, it may be long gone. Did you arrest the suspects? Or at least bring them in for questioning?"

"Not yet."

"Hmm. I wonder if they're still in the city."

"Why do you believe the art is gone and the suspects have fled?"

"Simple. This robbery has shown us that the thieves had access to the inner circle of people involved in the transportation of the paintings. In other words, they're connected."

"Connected to what?"

"It's connected to whom. And I'm simply saying that they've had access to highly confidential information. They may have already received orders to get out of town as fast as possible, or at least to go into hiding."

"You're saying that someone in my department would have warned them?"

"Would it be the first time someone on a police force, or at least someone with access to such information, was in the employ of criminals?"

"I don't like your inference, Special Agent James."

"I don't much care for it myself. But that doesn't mean it isn't accurate. It's easy to prove or disprove. Simply send someone to bring them in for questioning. If they're gone, their apartment will probably show signs of a hasty departure."

"Getting back to my initial question, why do you suspect these two individuals were involved?"

"Did you check their criminal history records?"

"Yes."

"Then why is it *you* don't suspect them of being involved? Their arrest records clearly show them as decidedly recidivistic and both capable of pulling off this theft."

"In San Francisco we must have probable cause. So far you haven't provided any."

"Your probable cause is, or at least was, in that garage."

"How do you know that?"

"I'm not prepared to name my sources."

"Then I'm not prepared to waste the time of my officers."

"What kind of a department are you running here, Captain? You can have your officers waste their time following me around the city hoping to learn how I solve crimes, or coming to my hotel to wake me up and bring me here so you can learn how I know what I know, but not arrest repeat felons and bring them in for questioning after I've identified them as the thieves who committed a major crime?"

"The two people you identified are citizens of this community. You're an outsider." With a slight sneer he added, "From New York City."

"Fine. If enforcing the law doesn't interest you, I'm wasting my time here."

CHAPTER TWENTY-TWO

I turned and left Fasko's office, then walked briskly to the building exit. I hailed a cab on the street and fumed all the way back to my hotel. But there was nothing I could do. If the police captain wouldn't detain suspects because he was afraid someone else would be credited with solving the case, *especially* someone from New York City, I was wasting my time talking to them.

When I reached my floor and walked to my room, I found Hooper standing in the hall outside.

"You made good time, Detective," I said.

"It's the flashing lights and siren. They make all the difference."

"You could have saved me the cab fare. Would you like to come in?"

"I was hoping you would ask. I thought you might slam the door in my face."

"Only if you agree with your captain," I said as I unlocked the door, pushed it open and stepped inside.

"I can never say I disagree with him," Detective Hooper said as he followed me in. "He's my captain. I still have two years before I can retire. I want those two years."

I picked up the phone and ordered a pot of coffee, a half dozen doughnuts, and service for two.

"I trust you like coffee and doughnuts?"

"What cop doesn't? You get used to it in the early years, and it becomes a lifelong habit. Of course, after work, I like to toss down a few beers."

"Do you want a beer now?"

"No, never while I'm on duty. Clear head, steady hand, and all that."

"Yeah." Gesturing towards the sofa and chairs, I said, "Have a seat."

"So why won't you tell the captain where you got your information?"

"My sources must remain *my* sources. I gave your department everything on a silver platter. I gave you the perps and the evidence. All your captain had to do was follow through. Well, it's his problem now. I'm sure the insurance company execs aren't going to be pleased. Did you get the information about the phony cargo container?"

"The one reportedly at the recycling center in Union City?"

"That's the one."

"I made a call. It's still there. I told the person I spoke to that if that container disappears before we can retrieve it, he better book some time aboard the space station because there's no place here on Earth where I won't find him."

I chuckled. "You didn't really say that, did you?"

"Hell yes. I wanted to impress upon him how important that container is. You have to be firm at times. How did you locate that by the way?"

"My sources must remain…"

"*My* sources. Yeah, I gotcha."

"I'm sure you don't share the identity of your snitches with all of your fellow detectives."

"No way."

"Exactly. Your sources must remain *your* sources."

A knock at the door drew my attention. "That was much, much faster than usual." As I approached the door, I pulled my Glock out and held it by my side.

"Who is it?"

"Uh— Room Service."

"Just a second."

The door was the two-inch-thick solid wood variety always found in quality modern hotels. It probably wouldn't stop a bullet, but it could slow one and ruin the trajectory. There was no peep-hole in the door, which was good and bad. I couldn't see out, but whoever was outside couldn't tell where I was in relation to the door. I wished I had a monitor that surveyed the hallway with cameras like I had at home.

I gestured to Hooper using a downward motion of my open hand, palm down, to indicate he should get down, or at least make himself a smaller target. He took me seriously, pulled his gun from his holster, and assumed a kneeling position on the carpet where he would be mostly hidden by one of the overstuffed chairs. When he was set, I unlocked the door and started to open it.

Suddenly, someone on the other side kicked it, putting everything they had behind it. I had planted my foot so it couldn't be pushed open, but the tremendous force took me by surprise and my foot was swept aside. As I started to fall backwards, I disregarded everything except bringing my Glock to bear on the large, heavy-set man standing in the hallway with an automatic in his right hand.

The attacker got a quick shot off as I was falling but the slug went over my head because I was halfway to the floor. My falling backward threw him for an instant. He probably expected I would simply be knocked backward, off balance, and struggling to remain standing.

His second shot went just slightly wide. I thought I heard the whine of the bullet as it passed my ear, but the sounds from my own weapon as I pulled the trigger had already begun to drown out all other noises.

I managed to fire three times before I hit the floor, and all three slugs caught the attacker center chest. From just seven feet away it's kind of hard to miss a target as large as the one he presented, even when falling. My three forty-caliber slugs completely halted his forward momentum just one foot into the suite, but he didn't fall down immediately. The expression on his face seemed to show surprise that he had been shot.

The sound of my gunfire hadn't even ended before I heard more gunfire. At first I thought there might be a second attacker in the hallway, but then I realized it was coming from behind me. The sound was from Hooper's gun firing.

It the attacker hadn't been dead when he fell backward into the hallway and started bleeding all over the carpet, he died within minutes. There were five large holes in his chest.

I immediately rolled one full revolution to my left just in case there was another attacker in the hallway, but no one else appeared in the open doorway, and I heard no other sounds coming from there until I heard a woman start to scream.

I looked over in Hooper's direction and asked, "You okay?"

He nodded, so I got up and moved to the doorway. I quickly peered out to the left and pulled back. I hadn't seen anything. Then I did the same to the right. Again I saw nothing.

"Seems clear," I said.

Hooper joined me over by the door and looked down at the attacker.

"Look familiar?" I asked.

"No. I've never seen him before. I better call this in. Ya know, we're going to need a lot more coffee and doughnuts. Those homicide detectives live on the stuff."

◆

"I've been told this isn't exactly unusual for you," Hooper said as the morgue folks were rolling the body out on a gurney. "One of the homicide guys filled me in with what happened at your apartment in New York. I understand now why you greet people at the door with your gun drawn. And your reaction time shows why you're still breathing."

"Yeah, I'm five-and-oh now. I'm glad you were here. Glad for the assist and glad I had a witness to what happened. I'd hate to spend the next two weeks in Fasko's interrogation room while he tried to pin a murder rap on me."

"If Fasko had his way, he'd lock you up and lose the key."

"He's not number one on my list of favorite people either. I thought I'd be heading out of town in the next couple of days. I'd concluded my investigation and wrapped up everything into a nice little package, but Fasko wouldn't accept it. I can imagine what the directors at the insurance company are saying right now. They'll have to pay three hundred million if Fasko blows this investigation. They won't look too favorably on him. He could wind up walking the two a.m. beat on Alcatraz Island."

"Nah. That's a federal property. The National Park Service patrols that. Well, I guess I'd better be going. I have to get back to the office and write up a report on this. So you have no idea who this guy was or what he was after?"

"When you enter a room firing a handgun, you aren't leaving much doubt about your intentions. I have no idea who he was or who he was working for. But I'll find out. I take attacks on my life and those of my friends personally."

"He had no ID on him, but they've already printed him, and we should know who he is pretty quick unless he's never been arrested."

"I wouldn't lay any bets on that being the case. He didn't just get up this morning and decide he was going to assassinate an FBI Special Agent and an SFPD Detective Lieutenant."

"I think he was just after you."

"I can't argue that point, Hooper. I guess somebody's pissed because I rained on their art-theft parade by solving the case. Maybe they figured that by terminating me, they'd halt the investigation before it reached them and took them down."

"Maybe. Well, gotta go."

"Come back any time, Hooper."

"It's Ron to my buds."

"I'm Colt."

"So long, Colt."

"So long, Ron."

It was another hour before everyone investigating the shooting had left the room. They had dug one of the perp's slugs out of the wall where it hit and another out of the floor, then photographed every square inch of the room. Then it was another half hour before the hotel staff completed their best efforts to remove the blood splatter in the suite entranceway and the heavy stains in the hallway from where the blood had pooled. They actually did a great job. The area looked wet, but it didn't look discolored with red. The final verdict would be how it looked after it dried. The manager offered to move me to another room, but I chose to remain in this one. I thought there might be some luck in this one since both Hooper and I had survived unscathed.

Once I was alone I got out my cleaning kit, cleaned the Glock, and reloaded the magazine. I was about to get out the gizmo and begin an effort to find out who had sent the gunman when my cell rang. I looked at the display and saw it was Saul, so I completed the connection.

"Hi, Saul."

"Colt, what the hell's going on out there?"

"There's a lot of— stuff— coming down, Saul."

"I just heard someone tried to kill you in your hotel."

"Yeah, he tried. He's at the morgue now. I wasn't hit."

"I'm glad for that."

"I feel the same way."

"So have the police recovered the artwork and the suspects?"

"No idea, Saul. The top cop out here isn't sharing any information with me. All I know so far is that one of the detectives has confirmed the location of the phony cargo container in Union City."

"That's all?"

"That's all I know so far. Fasko sent a detective to pick me up this morning and bring me to his office. According to his statements at that time, he hadn't dispatched anyone to pick up the suspects because he doesn't arrest San Francisco citizens without probable cause."

"Probable cause? Doesn't the recovery of the eleven paintings provide enough probable cause for questioning them?"

"At the time I was at his office they apparently hadn't moved to execute the search warrant at the garage in the Fillmore district, so he doesn't have the paintings."

"What?"

"My reaction exactly. Saul, I'm sorry, but I'm not empowered to invade private property and confiscate anything I find there, even if it is stolen artwork. Perhaps you can get further than I have with Captain Fasko."

"Dammit. It sounds like we have a cop with a bug up his ass because his people didn't solve the case."

"Seems that way."

"Okay, Colt. It's time to play hardball. I'll take it from here."

"Saul, I'm pretty sure there's someone inside the loop feeding information to the people who pulled off the theft. If the SFPD hasn't moved yet, the suspects may be long gone and the paintings in the garage may be gone as well."

"I'll find out, Colt. I'll talk to you later."

"Okay, Saul."

As soon as I finished talking with Saul, I put the gizmo up on the wall over the desk and went to the garage to check on the paintings. They were gone. I went back and tagged one of them, then jumped ahead to the present. The eleven cases were in the back of an SUV. I checked the GPS information and discovered they were on Route I-505 just north of Vacaville. If they continued on their route, they would be in Oregon in another four hours.

Then I went back and tagged the two thieves. Jumping ahead to the present, I saw they were together in a car headed east on Route 80. Presently they were near Davis, so in less than two hours they could cross into Nevada.

If Fasko executed the search warrant now he would find nothing. With the suspects and the evidence gone, he could claim they were never there and that the 'great' Colton James had concocted the entire story. His failure to act when he received the information put everything back to square one. I wondered how anyone in such a position of responsibility could be so dumb.

Then I realized that perhaps he wasn't just being dumb. He might be one of the inside sources feeding information to the people who committed the crime. If they had been arrested, someone in the know might implicate him. It might be better for him that they all escape. If I hadn't had the gizmo, I might have been unable to pick up the trail again. Of course, if I hadn't had the gizmo, I would never have solved the crime in the first place.

I put the gizmo away and moved to the sofa to think about the situation. The only plus side was that wherever the artwork wound up, there would be a different police captain in charge. Explaining how I tracked it was my biggest problem. I would just have to wait and see where it wound up.

I would have liked to go out for a walk, but I knew the press would be waiting for me to appear in public so they could harass me for information about the shooting while I repeated "no comment" over and over.

◆

I was still sitting on the sofa an hour later as I thought about the situation here and where I wished I was instead when the hotel phone rang. I walked to the desk and picked up the receiver.

"James," was all I said.

"Colt, it's Ron. I'm down in Union City at the recycle center where the container was brought. It's gone."

"Gone?"

"Yeah. The manager here says two guys who said they were from SFPD came with a truck and picked it up about a half hour ago. He didn't get a license number and they didn't show any ID, but they paid him in cash, double what he had paid to the guy who dropped it off."

"And he fell for that? Cops never pay cash. They give receipts for what they're taking and it's up to the person to file a claim to get paid."

"Yeah. Well, this guy isn't the brightest bulb in the lamp. It was probably the cash that convinced him not to ask for ID. But— there's good news as well."

"Give it to me. I could use some good news right now."

"The guy here dragged the container out of the pile after I called and hosed it off. Then he took pictures of it from every angle with the top open and closed. He figured he might be able to sell the photos to the media if the container was part of a big case. I got his camera and removed the memory chip with the images and confirmed they were on it before giving him a receipt for the chip."

"That's great, Ron. At least we'll be able to prove there *was* a container which *might have been* altered to commit the crime and which *might* have actually been used for that purpose."

I heard him chuckle before saying, "Yeah, well, it's the best I could do. And we've got an ID on the guy we took down in your hotel. His name was Carlos Rodriquez. He's an illegal alien, oops, I mean undocumented immigrant, who's been deported back to Mexico four times after committing violent crimes here, but he kept showing up back in San Francisco a few weeks later. Until now he's been a leg-breaker for a small time loan shark."

"I guess he was trying to move up in the world. Uh, I thought San Francisco was a Sanctuary City and you folks refuse to turn over illegal immigrants who have committed crimes to the immigration authorities for deportation."

"Those deportations occurred back before our city fathers enacted that law. Since then the police department has been required to release him back onto the streets if he was ever arrested. America, the land of opportunity. Give me your tired, your poor, your violent criminals yearning to be free to do whatever they damn well please— with the blessings of our enlightened politicians."

"How about the paintings and the perps? Did Fasko ever act on the search warrant?"

"There were no paintings in the garage and the two suspects are gone. They cleaned out their apartment and left in a hurry. We put out an APB for them and their vehicle. Their car was found in a parking lot near the airport. We figure they grabbed the first flight out."

"That'd be the logical thing to do for someone who wasn't a professional criminal. But these folks are pros. If you don't have much of a head start, being on a plane means you have no chance for escape if the police learn which flight you're on."

"So where do *you* think they are?"

"Probably headed for Nevada in a car. Possibly a car they borrowed. Do you happen to have any friends in the California Highway Patrol who might be patrolling I-80 East between Colfax and the Nevada border?"

"I might. Why?"

"Well, I thought perhaps you might ask them to watch out for a 2012 Ford passenger vehicle headed east."

"And why would they be watching for that car?"

"A little birdie whispered in my ear that the car might just contain a husband and wife robbery team suspected of committing a recent major crime involving priceless works of art."

"A little birdie?"

"Yeah. He also said the car might be a Ford Focus SEL in excellent condition, grey or silver in color, with California plates ending in 472."

"That little birdie has a lot of specific information, doesn't he? I'd like to have a little birdie like that for a friend."

"Perhaps having a friend of one is almost as good. And you know what they say?"

"What do they say?"

"Tweet tweet."

"Did your little birdie happen to mention where the paintings are?"

"He wasn't sure where they are— precisely, but if he had to guess, he'd say they were in a dark blue 2006 Ford E150 XL Passenger Van with California tags ending with 913."

"And does he know where the van is headed?"

"He believed it might be headed north on I-5 above Sacramento. It might even be somewhere between Redding and the Oregon border right now."

"Does this little bird usually have reliable information?"

"Always has until now."

"Okay, Colt. Well, I've got to go. I've been meaning to call a buddy in the Highway Patrol."

"Okay, Ron. Oh, by the way, while you're talking to your friend, if you happen to mention what the little birdie told me, you should tell him or her to consider these people armed and extremely dangerous."

"Yeah, I kinda got that message this morning at your hotel."

"Nice talking to you Ron. You be careful out there."

"Yeah. You too, Colt."

CHAPTER TWENTY-THREE

Although I'd known Fasko hadn't moved on the search warrant in time to stop the paintings from disappearing again, I appreciated that Hooper had filled me in on the situation at the garage and with the two perps. It was too bad the air cargo container had disappeared. I didn't know who had hired Rodriquez to hit me, but I was glad the former strong-arm had been such a rank amateur at assassination with a handgun.

I could perhaps follow the trail back to the person who had paid to have me killed, but it would be extremely time-consuming, and I wasn't in the mood just then. It was a job for later. I wondered if Saul was having any luck putting pressure on the SFPD to put someone in charge of the case who would cooperate, and I was also hoping that Hooper's contacts in the Highway Patrol could produce some results.

I needed to do something, so I decided to track down the missing air cargo container. I took out the gizmo, tagged the container when it was first brought to the recycle center, and jumped to the present time. I located the container at an auto wrecking yard. It was now part of a cube of crushed metal and totally unrecognizable as a cargo container.

I again felt angry and frustrated. I should be on a plane heading for Greece and Mia, and instead I was sitting on my ass in San Francisco, feeling totally impotent because of Fasko.

◆ ◆

As I drank my first coffee the following morning, I turned on the news. The lead story was the recovery of hundreds of millions of dollars in stolen masterpieces. My day was instantly brightened as I turned up the volume and listened to the announcer talk about the recovery by California Highway Patrol officers near the Oregon border. They had tried to stop a van, but the driver refused to pull over, so they set up a roadblock ahead. The driver of the van blasted through the roadblock but lost control of the truck when the spike strips laid down by the officers blew out all four of his tires and the van plunged over an embankment. When the officers got down to the van they found the driver unconscious and seriously injured. He was taken to a hospital for treatment and would be arraigned when he had recovered well enough to appear in court. The CHP officers found eleven cases of the type used to transport valuable artwork in the rear of the van. The cases appeared to be undamaged, except for minor cosmetic marks on the exterior surfaces. The lead seals were still in place and the cases were taken, unopened, to a museum in San Francisco where the condition of their contents would be evaluated. The CHP spokesman had credited the SFPD, working in cooperation with the world famous art recovery expert Colton James, with providing information about the van and its cargo.

After feeling miserable most of yesterday, I suddenly felt great today. I poured myself another cup of coffee and dug into my eggs and sausages. Eleven down, one to go.

◆

I had finished breakfast and was listening to a cable news channel when my cell phone rang. I had begun leaving it out of its protective case when I was in the hotel so I could be contacted more easily. This time the caller was Mia.

"Hi, babe," I said, as I answered.

"My darling, are you okay? We just heard on the news that someone tried to kill you in your hotel."

"I'm fine, hon. He missed. I didn't."

"The news report said you killed him."

"I had no choice. He broke into my room and started shooting."

"I'm always so frightened when you go away on a case. And you haven't called me since the night before that happened."

"I'm sorry, babe. I haven't been able to get a lot of cooperation from the police department here. If I had, we'd have recovered all of the paintings by now, and I'd already be on my way to you."

"How much longer will you be there?"

"I don't know. You might have heard that we've recovered eleven of the twelve paintings, but I can't leave until we get them all. I don't think it will be too much longer."

"I miss you. And my whole family misses you. At least the news report finally showed them you left because of work."

"They didn't believe us?"

"They did, but I think there was a small question in the back of their minds about whether there was a problem between us."

"There's no problem. I love you."

"And I love you, darling and I want you *here*."

"I'll be there soon."

We talked for another twenty minutes or so, mostly about our travel plans after I got back to Greece. Then for the rest of the morning I couldn't get thoughts of Mia and the beautiful island of Thasos out of my head.

◆

It was noon in New York when Saul called and brought me out of my reverie.

"Hello, Saul. Good news today, eh?"

"Fantastic news, Colt. I was beginning to think that fool Fasko at SFPD had cost our company three hundred million dollars. We still haven't gotten a straight answer from the department about why he didn't act on the search warrant as soon as it was issued."

"Well, it doesn't matter now. We've got everything back except the one piece that's in the possession of the former congressman."

"Yes, but I haven't been able to find anyone willing to take him on. I think they believe him to be too powerful and are afraid of him because we might be wrong about the painting being in his possession. Are you sure about your facts?"

"I was— yesterday. It's possible that the painting has been removed from his home if he feared we'd get a search warrant. I told you I believe there's at least one inside man, or woman, feeding the thieves information. From what I've seen, I now believe there could be a number of inside people involved."

"Is there any way to verify that the congressman still has the painting?"

"Well, I'll see what I can find out today."

"Thanks, Colt. Keep me informed."

"Will do, Saul."

Removing the gizmo from its storage location in my lighter, I put it up against the wall above the desk, then sat down to work. I quickly returned to Milan and tagged the still missing painting, then returned to a time two days ago and let the gizmo take me to the painting. It was still hanging on the wall in the 'congressman's luxurious basement back then. There weren't any windows down there, so there was no chance that anyone could see it unless they were in the room or they had a gizmo.

Then I jumped ahead to the present. The painting was in a new location. And wherever it was, it was pitch black. I raised the gizmo's window up until it was outside and panned around. It was still in Oakland and appeared to be in a commercial building on Adeline Street. That meant the connection to the congressman was probably gone. If he was smart enough to remove the painting from his house, he was probably smart enough to ensure it wasn't still on any property he owned or was connected with.

I wondered when it had been removed from the congressman's home, so I entered the coordinates of the house and went there with the intention of jumping backward in time until I saw the painting again. The image that appeared on the gizmo was a view of the surrounding area from above the house, so I lowered it down until it showed the room where the painting had hung.

The congressman was at home, and he was engaged in a very animated conversation on the phone as he walked around the room, waving his free hand with purpose. You could tell he was screaming at someone. I guessed he was tearing someone a new one for screwing up the robbery. I wished I could hear, but that wasn't meant to be.

In addition to the congressman, I could see two other men in the room. From their appearance, I'd have to say they were his private muscle. On demand, they could probably produce IDs that showed they were part of a private security company. But I wasn't interested in any of them at the moment, so I began panning around the room. When I got to the wall where the painting had been, it was still there. That couldn't be! I knew it to be at the location on Adeline Street.

I sat back and tried to think this through. Perhaps I had made a mistake with the timeline. I checked the data for the current image and verified it was the present. Then I checked Adeline Street again. The gizmo confirmed that the artwork was still there, and that image was also the present. The only obvious answer was that there were two paintings. One was an original and one was a copy. I verified that by having the gizmo go to the painting I had tagged in Milan. It would only take me to the Adeline Street location.

As I sat there thinking about the new information, I formulated a theory. The congressman must have had an exact copy made some time ago, including the frame, and then hung it on his wall. By now, innumerable influential people had to have seen it hanging there. When he acquired the real painting he could hang it up in plain sight and enjoy it. If anyone ever questioned his having it, he could say it was a forgery made to exacting standards and produce dozens of influential people whose testimony was beyond question and who would swear to having seen it hanging there many years before the real painting was stolen.

He must have been planning this robbery for a long time— years at the very least. Although he had his alibi all set up, he must have gotten spooked and moved it off his property so it couldn't be associated with him just in case the police came and impounded the painting for testing. His attitude when I'd seen him on the phone today was understandable.

I made a note of the Adeline Street address and then decided to work on something I had procrastinated doing until now.

The man who tried to kill me had to have been hired by someone, and I knew it was going to be a time-consuming search that may never yield results, but I had to try. Now that most of the paintings had been recovered, I could afford to make an effort at finding his connection to the case and who had hired him.

I went back to the time just before he had tried to bust into my hotel room and tagged him with the gizmo. Then I went back and tagged the two thieves. I checked to see if they had ever met with the hitman but came up dry, so they might not have sent him. Then I tried to link him to the congress-man but struck out again. That didn't mean that neither the thieves nor the congressman were behind the attempted assassination; it only meant that they hadn't dealt with him face to face.

I again started back at the hotel just prior to the attack and went backwards a little at a time as I tried to learn who the assassin's contact might have been. He'd had contact with a lot of unsavory-looking characters during the previous days, but I wasn't familiar with any of them. The only one I tried to identify was the guy who had handed him the gun.

It turned out that the guy who provided the gun would sell to anyone with the money, so it was unlikely he had been behind the assassination attempt. As in New York City, if a person traveled in the right criminal circles and wanted a gun, they were readily available when they flashed the cash. It was only the law-abiding citizens who usually didn't have easy access to handguns, unless they were in law enforcement.

I'd known it was probably going to be a waste of time, and by bedtime I still hadn't a clue to the identity of the person who hired the leg-breaker to kill me. He'd talked to so many people in the prior days that I could spend months just trying to identify the individual, and even then I probably couldn't be sure because I couldn't hear the conversations.

◆ ◆

Although I knew where the last painting was, and I had confirmed it was still there when I got up and began my day, I hadn't called Saul yet. It was the usual dilemma I faced. I was anxious to be on my way home and then to Greece, but I had to play the game of withholding information for as long as I could so it seemed more reasonable that I had learned it by using proper law enforcement or deductive reasoning techniques.

That thought led me to wonder if perhaps I had chosen the wrong field of endeavor. I was really, really tired of people shooting at me, and the attempts on my life seemed to be increasing. The odds that I was going to catch a bullet that would end my life increased with every encounter.

It's true that I never would have met the love of my life if I hadn't followed the pathway into the recovery of stolen art that had taken me to The Netherlands. And there had been no guarantee that Kathy and I would have been happily married, or even married, if I'd remained a poor author, an IT person, or whatever other 'safer' career choices I could have made. And I'd probably still be living in that third floor walkup on the West Side of Manhattan instead of the multimillion dollar co-op I now owned across from Central Park.

But— would I have been happier if I'd limited myself to just tracking down bail skips for my livelihood? And would I have been any safer? Those folks know how to hold a grudge. I'd looked at all of the various career options I could choose from once I'd acquired the gizmo and selected the one with the greatest rewards, but it was also the one that presented the greatest dangers. So maybe it was time to 'hang up my spurs' as they used to say in the old westerns. I knew I'd never be able to 'hang up my guns' while Delcona was alive and free, but just not making any new enemies who wanted me dead might improve my quality of life while also extending it.

Perhaps Uncle Yannis would offer me a position in the shipping business, although from what I'd learned from Mia, that might be just as dangerous as what I was doing now. The home on Thasos had obviously been built like a fortress for a reason. It wasn't too difficult to imagine everyone in the family ducked down behind mattresses with their Uzis at the ready as the minions of a competitor scaled the compound walls.

Perhaps I had just begun to see the world from a different perspective since the first determined attempt on my life aboard the ferry from The Netherlands to the U.K. Or maybe it was the second attempt, in Spain. The leader of that gang, and also the minion I'd always thought of as an 'anxious wannabe' killer, hadn't been apprehended yet. There was always the chance I could run into them again one day in Europe or elsewhere. I had, after all, 'robbed' them of their fifty million dollars in stolen artwork, and I imagined they still held a grudge.

I was still thinking about my future when Saul called.

"Hi, Saul."

"Colt. I haven't heard back from you. Were you able to learn if the painting is still where it was?"

"It's not where it was. I can't tell you where it is right now, but it's definitely not hanging on the wall anymore. So I wouldn't pursue that search warrant."

"I'm glad you told me. With the picture being in Oakland, I think we might have found someone willing to execute a search warrant. You have no idea where it is now?"

"I hope to have some new information for you tomorrow. I'm waiting to hear from someone."

"I don't know how you do it, Colt. Uh, can you at least give me a hint?"

"You've heard the old saying that there's no honor among thieves, right?"

"Of course."

"Well, I can verify that. And I can promise that part of the thirty million you're going to owe me for this recovery will be money well spent."

"You've turned somebody on the inside?"

"When a million dollars is talking, someone with information doesn't need a whole lot of convincing."

"I'm sure you wouldn't tell me who you've turned, so I won't ask. I just hope you get the information quickly."

"I should know by eight a.m. Pacific Time tomorrow. Can you have your people lined up and ready to go at that time?"

"I'll have them ready."

"Okay, give me a call then. With luck, I'll be able to give you the location of the twelfth painting. But I'm afraid I won't have anything to convince a jury that the congressman was involved."

"It's more important that we get the painting back. Fasko and his people can worry about building a case— if they even try. They deserve having the likes of that congressman in their backyard."

"I'll be talking to you, Saul."

I hadn't actually lied to Saul. I just talked in generalities that would make him think I had a well-paid snitch who was passing along information about the paintings. By making him think that, he wouldn't press too hard to learn more, and he'd know that he would never have an opportunity to interview the 'witness.'

I spent the rest of the day trying to learn who had set the assassin on me, but at bedtime I didn't have any more information in that regard than I had when I'd started.

◆ ◆

As soon as I awoke in the morning, I checked to make sure the painting was still where it had been for the past couple of days. It was— so I ordered breakfast.

Saul called exactly at eight a.m. Pacific.

"Good morning, Colt. Have you got good news for me?"

"Yep. Got a pen and pad handy?"

"Go."

I gave Saul the address of the building where the painting was located and described exactly where it would be found. "I suggest you get your people out there to surround the building while they wait for the search warrant to be signed by a judge. Right now the building is being watched to make sure that if someone removes the painting before the police arrive, we'll know the make, model, and license number of the vehicle, but if police are surrounding the building, no one will try to remove the painting."

"Is that how you knew the eleven paintings had been removed from the other location and were on their way out of the state?"

"It's a good system, don't you think? I don't have any police powers but, as far as I know, there's no law against observation by a private citizen as long as you're not illegally trespassing on anyone's private property. It's amazing how small the wireless video cameras have become. They even have them on lightweight drones that can hang suspended over an area and see everything that's going on."

"So you're using drones now?"

"I've always been sort of a technology nerd, and I use whatever's necessary to find the stolen goods and get the job done. Crooks are using technology to the max, so law enforcement must do the same, as long as we take care not to violate the rights of honest citizens."

"I agree. Thanks for the info, Colt. I'm going to get our people on this right away."

"Okay, Saul, I'll be standing by in case you need me."

I didn't think it was really necessary but I took out the gizmo and put it on the wall over the desk, then checked once more to verify the painting was still there. It was.

I'd had a reason for telling Saul the building was being watched. If he passed that information on, it might stop anyone from trying to remove the painting when the search warrant was requested if there *was* someone in the know passing on such information. We were in another law enforcement jurisdiction now since the painting was in Oakland rather than San Fran, but one never knew who or how many people were accepting payoffs from crime figures to provide such information. All it took was one temporary secretary to ruin an investigation that had taken months to set up.

I moved the view provided by the gizmo to outside the building so I would know when the police arrived. I estimated it would take several hours before there was any noticeable activity. First, Saul's people would have to communicate the information and convince the Oakland police that it was accurate. Then the police would check the ownership of the building to see if the individual or company had any history of crime involvement. Then the police would have to approach a judge and present their evidence to him or her to convince the judge to sign the search warrant.

During the past couple of years my name has been increasingly linked to high-profile theft cases with successful conclusions, including the very recent recovery of the first eleven paintings and the attempted assassination attempt by a known underworld thug, so I knew it would be used repeatedly at each step of the process. That was fine with me if it helped grease the wheels of justice.

◆

It was almost one p.m. before the first police car showed up outside the building where the painting was hidden. In seconds, additional marked and unmarked cars arrived, and officers spread out to cover all the exits. A half-hour later an unmarked car arrived and the small group that emerged from the vehicle walked to the main entrance and pounded on it. When no one responded, they used a ram to break it open, then entered the building with guns drawn.

I imagine they first searched to make sure no one was hiding inside before looking for the case holding the painting. About fifteen minutes after arriving, one of the plain-clothes officers emerged with the case. I thought I could hear the sounds of Greek music playing in my head. I hoped the police had had the good sense not to open the case.

I lost interest in watching after that. The gizmo told me the painting was inside the case, so it was just a matter of time until it was authenticated by the museum experts. I didn't really care if the congressman was ever connected to the robbery or not now that we had the painting back. But I had to admit to being delighted that I was responsible for destroying his dream of acquiring the real painting. He would just have to settle for staring at his very high-quality forgery.

Perhaps one of these days I would feel like continuing my investigation into who had sent the leg-breaker to kill me, but at the moment all I wanted to do was get on a plane headed east.

Since I knew the painting had been recovered, there was little sense staying overnight in San Francisco to get the official word from the museum, so I called and made reservations on a red-eye flight out of San Francisco that would get me into New York City around eight a.m., then sat back to relax. I would have called Mia to give her the wonderful news that I had completed my work here and was leaving tonight, but the ten-hour time difference meant it was almost midnight on Thasos. I would call her when I reached New York in the morning.

I might have gone sightseeing to kill the rest of the day, but the prospect of facing the media people everywhere I went squashed that idea. So I turned on the cable news to see what drivel they had chosen to deliver this day while ignoring most of what I believed were the really important news stories happening around the world. I was soon bored but hung in there until the replays began an hour later.

Since I didn't know how much sleep I could count on during the overnight flight to New York, I decided to get some before I left.

CHAPTER TWENTY-FOUR

The flight to Kennedy Airport in New York was one of those fortunately infrequent turbulence-filled trips that felt like driving on a wilderness road in an off-road vehicle with-out springs or shock-absorbers, and where it was impossible to miss rolling over a boulder every few seconds. As a result, I didn't get any sleep on the plane. I was glad I had grabbed a long nap in the afternoon.

As I stepped out of the cab in front on my co-op building, I thought how great it was to be home. I intended to stay here overnight and then head to Europe tomorrow afternoon.

Upon entering the lobby with my suitcase in tow, I smiled slightly as I nodded at the security guard. They all knew me by now, and while I didn't know all of their full names, I at least knew their given names. The first name of the man on desk was Pete, but I didn't know his last name.

As I started to pass the security counter, he said, "Special Agent James, there's a note here for you. It's from your car dealership. They've called several times looking for you."

I took the note Pete was holding out and looked at it. There were three different dates on the paper representing three different phone calls.

"Thanks, Pete," I said as I stuffed the note in my pocket. "I'll give them a call when I get upstairs."

"We heard about the shooting in San Francisco. It sounded like a close one. We're glad you're okay."

"Thanks. I appreciate that."

Like Dorothy said in the *Wizard of Oz*, 'there's no place like home.' As much as I was looking forward to returning to Thasos, a small part of me longed to stay home, at least for a short time. That was probably why I'd chosen to come here rather than immediately continuing on to Europe. I felt I needed a day to rest up after the frustration I'd experienced in San Francisco. The friendship— or perhaps I should call it an acquaintanceship— I'd formed with Ron Hooper had helped offset the negative feelings about the SFPD that I'd begun to develop after meeting Fasko.

I unpacked my suitcase and put the soiled clothes in the appropriate hamper. I'd repack tomorrow with all clean clothes before I left again.

As I emptied my pockets, I pulled out the note from the car dealership. I intended to grab a few winks, but I called the dealership before getting into bed.

The call was answered by a man who identified himself as William after naming the dealership.

"Good morning, William. This is Colton James. I just arrived back in town, and I understand you've been trying to reach me."

"Yes, sir, Mr. James. You haven't had your car serviced since it was new, and the warranty requires that it be checked over in order to keep the warranty in effect."

"I haven't actually driven it much. I've only put a couple of thousand miles on it."

"Yes, sir. I understand. That's common with car owners living in Manhattan. But the warranty is both for mileage and time of ownership. Even though a car is not being driven very much, it's still important to change the oil and check the fluids. Our inspection team also runs a complete engine diagnostic to help spot any potential problems before they become serious. The manufacturer requires the checkup, and I'm afraid your warranty will be voided if you don't have it done by us or another dealership within a month's time."

"I'm going out of town again tomorrow afternoon and I won't be back for a couple of months, so I don't have time to make an appointment."

"We can squeeze you in tomorrow morning, if you wish. We can pick up the car at your building at nine and have it back to you by noon."

"You're sure you can do it in that time window? Because if you can't get it done, you'll have to hang onto it for a couple of months until I get back."

"Have you been experiencing any problems with it?"

"None at all."

"Then I'm sure we can have it done in that time. It's highly unlikely that there's anything wrong with it. We'll change the oil and the filters, check the other fluids, tires, and tire pressures, and have it back by noon. If they find anything unusual, you can have us pick it up for service when you return. At least this way the warranty remains in effect."

"Okay. What time will your man be here?"

"He'll be waiting at your front door at nine a.m. He'll have a dealership jacket on to identify him."

"Okay. The car is in my underground parking garage. I'll drive it out and turn it over to him. You'll call before he drives it back?"

"Of course, sir."

"Let me give you my cell number."

After giving him the number, I ended the conversation. And as the coffee maker began to gurgle and pop while steaming coffee dripped into the glass decanter, I headed for the shower. The coffee might invigorate me a bit, but the shower would drain away all the tenseness in my muscles. I figured I'd still be alert afterwards, but it would be a more relaxed alert.

◆

"Hi, baby," I said, when Mia came to the phone.

"Darling, where are you?"

"I'm at home. I just got in this morning."

"Aren't you coming here?"

"Of course. I'll be on a flight out of New York tomorrow afternoon. I need a day to rest up and unwind before I continue on. It was an exasperating time in San Francisco."

"I'm so glad you got out of there before anyone else decided to shoot at you."

"Hopefully it'll be a long time before that happens again. How are things over there?"

"Not too good. As you probably know, the government agreed to make a number of austerity concessions and was able to get the bailout loans needed to reopen the banks, but the people are still angry because pensions have been cut a little and the social programs are being cut back. I hope everything will work out. Although they don't like it, most people understand you can't keep giving away money you don't have and that it's important that the country get a tighter rein on fiscal matters. The money the government will have to pay in additional interest payments could be better used to help our people."

"I just hope our politicians here learn that before it's too late. They just keep upping their credit line by raising the national debt limit so they can keep writing checks for money the country doesn't have and will never have while the current giveaway programs continue unabated and new ones are created. The half-trillion dollars the U.S. is presently paying annually in interest expense on the over eighteen trillion dollars of debt they've racked up, could be much better spent on social programs if the politicians would stop their foolish games and put some stability back into the economy. Sooner or later the chickens are going to come home to roost here, and, like Greece, we'll be in a whole lot of trouble. But I meant, how's the family? Everybody healthy?"

"Yes, just as healthy as when you left. Uncle was able to get the divorce decree set aside. It won't become official, so I don't have to worry about being excommunicated from the church."

"That's wonderful. I'm so happy for you."

"I keep thinking about poor Marcus. After we were married, I learned that he was such a spoiled little boy in so many ways, but he always thought he was so grown up."

"Don't grieve for him. There was nothing anyone could do. He was responsible for his own life and ultimately for his death."

Mia and I spoke for another twenty minutes, but I managed to shift the conversation away from Marcus. She seemed to be happy on Thasos, and I wondered how that would affect us in New York. When we returned from vacation, she might not want to come here. She had been a prominent member of the jet set, but I think that was mostly because of her strained relationship with her family. Now that she was back with them and all past differences had been forgiven and forgotten, would she want to stay with them most of the year?

I couldn't fall asleep, so I was watching an old movie I had on DVD in the hope that it would make me sleepy. My phone rang and announced it was Saul calling.

"Hi, Saul."

"Colt, I'm delighted to say that the twelfth painting has been evaluated and authenticated. The San Francisco museum is delighted because their exhibit can proceed as planned. The museum in Milan is delighted that you were able to recover their priceless artwork, and the Board is delighted that we won't have to pay out three hundred million."

"But there's still the thirty million."

"I neglected to remind them of that during the meeting— intentionally. I prefer they bask in the good news."

"So everyone is happy except Fasko."

"I told the mayor out there that if he was smart, he'd replace that idiot."

I chuckled. "I bet that went over big."

"Yeah, I've learned since then that Fasko is his cousin."

"You can't pick your relatives, but you don't have to put them in responsible positions. Okay, Saul, down to business. I owe about thirteen million on the mortgage so I'd like you to apply whatever it takes to pay that down all the way, and then put the rest in my bank account so I can send it to the government."

"Does this mean you'll be ending our retainer arrangement?"

"Not necessarily, but we may have to rewrite it to exempt me from being required to jump when you call if I'm out of the country on vacation. I'm just glad the trip to Fiji had been postponed because of Mia's divorce efforts. Otherwise I would have had to leave her on the beach while I went to San Francisco. That would not have pleased her at all. You'll still get first access to my services otherwise."

"Did she get her divorce?"

"Yes, but she didn't need it. Her ex was killed in the Bronx while I was down in Memphis."

"He was the white guy that had his head caved in and was then run over?"

"Yeah, and I'm sure glad I had an airtight alibi."

"It could have been difficult if you hadn't been in Tennessee. So when's the wedding?"

"We're still talking about that. No decisions yet."

"Okay, Colt. Have a nice vacation. Are you coming back to New York first?"

"I'm already here. I came back on a late night flight and arrived this morning."

"Before you even knew if the painting would be authenticated?"

"I knew it would be. Too bad they couldn't get it while it was still hanging in the congressman's basement."

"The investigation isn't over yet. They found a number of fingerprints on the painting and frame. The museum folks never touch it unless they're wearing cotton gloves, so the prints had to come from someone in San Francisco or Oakland. Apparently they were in such a hurry that they got careless and didn't wipe it down very well."

"That's the best news I've had since I learned they had recovered it. Maybe the prints belong to the 'congressman's armed bodyguards. I'm sure their prints will be on file from when they got their firearms permits. It would be better yet if they belonged to the congressman."

◆   ◆

I was dressed and ready to leave the apartment before nine the next morning. I had been sitting around too much lately, and I planned to walk around in the park and get a little exercise until my car was due back. But first I had to turn it over to the guy from the dealership, so I rode the elevator to the basement garage.

After exiting the elevator, I turned to the right to where my two parking spots were located. I was thinking about Mia, and wasn't as alert to danger as I should have been because I hadn't walked more than a few feet when a man stepped out from behind one of those enormous concrete supports used to hold buildings up. He didn't say anything at first, but I stopped walking because he was holding a handgun. And it was aimed at me. He looked familiar, but I couldn't place him.

Then a second man stepped out from behind a pillar on the other side of the drive-through aisle, and I immediately realized why the first man had looked so familiar. He was Weasel and this was Ox, the pair I had first seen at Billy's funeral and who I had assumed were part of Delcona's mob. Ox also had a gun aimed at me, and like Weasel, he was only about forty feet away.

"Take your gun out real slow, James," Weasel said. "Use just two fingers and place it on the ground in front of you. One false move and we shoot."

"Who are you?"

"You don't hear so good, do you? That wasn't a request. I gave you an order."

Since they hadn't already started shooting, I figured Delcona must have given them orders not to shoot me unless they had to. That gave me a slight edge, at least early on.

"I'm an FBI Special Agent," I said. "I order you to put down *your* weapons and put your hands up."

That struck them as being extremely funny— just as I'd hoped. When Ox laughed, it was my cue to make my move. I flung myself to the left, aiming to land behind the large building support closest to me, but I didn't quite make it. I heard two shots ring out as I hit the ground, but I kept on rolling because I wasn't all the way behind the support. Two more shots rang out, but I was behind cover by then. One ricocheted off the concrete support, sending a bit of cement flying in a puff of powder. I thought I heard a window shatter behind me, so I figured at least one of the slugs had hit somebody's car.

"Give it up, James," Weasel yelled. "You can't win this one. It's two to one. One of us is going to get you."

"All I have to do is stay low," I yelled back. "This garage is monitored by the security guard at the lobby desk. By now he's probably already called the NYPD."

"I guess you didn't stop at the lobby on your way down."

"Why should I have done that?"

"No reason, except that if you had you'd know your rent-a-cop isn't at the desk watching the monitors."

"No? Where is he?"

"He's out in front of the building. You see, at about the same time you were coming down to get your car, he was trying to roust a dozen homeless guys who set themselves up to beg for money from the building's residents as they came and went. Your rent-a-cop is probably still trying to get rid of them politely, but it's not going to happen. We're paying them fifty bucks each if they don't move for an hour. And if the cops do come and arrest them, we've promised to bail them out and still give them the fifty bucks each. So you see, you're on your own."

"Then we'll just wait for that hour to be up."

"That won't help you. Our orders are to bring you in alive, if we can. But if we can't do it in half an hour, our orders are to kill you. So at most you've got thirty minutes one way or the other."

From the sound of his voice I knew he was getting more anxious by the second. Time was not his friend.

"I'll just wait for the cops. If you want me, come and get me."

"Make it easy on yourself. The boss just wants to talk with you. You won't be harmed if you come peacefully."

"Sure, I come peacefully and wind up tied to a chair while some goon like your pal there beats my face to a bloody pulp. Tell me, were you there when Morris Calloway was beaten senseless and then strangled?" I knew they weren't, but I was sure they knew of it.

"Who's Morris Calloway?"

"The scientist you guys killed and then dumped into the Hackensack River."

"Never heard of him," Weasel yelled back.

"Who you calling a goon?" I heard Ox yell. I guess it had taken him a minute to realize I was talking about him.

"Shaddup, Ernie," Weasel said. "Listen James, I don't know who's been filling your head with such nonsense, but you should stop listening to them and get smart. I'm offering you your one chance to live."

"I still prefer to wait for the cops."

Until then I had stayed completely hidden from their view, and thus their line of fire, but I heard a sound like 'Psst' and figured Weasel was trying to get Ox's attention. He probably wanted him to try sneaking up on me. I moved to the edge of the pillar and peered quickly around it with my Glock leading, then pulled back. I had seen that Ox was tiptoeing towards my location. He was about thirty feet away but fully exposed and looking down at his feet. At this distance it would be difficult to miss such a big target. I moved to my right a couple of inches so my Glock was almost in the clear.

I waited a few seconds and then peered again. Ox was almost directly behind my car. I pressed the button on my key ring fob to unlock the doors and the car's horn sounded twice. At the sound I moved to my right. Ox had been startled and had turned his head towards my car with his gun also aimed in that direction. Most of my body was still completely hidden from Weasel as I fired three rounds. Ox fell over backward and landed like a three-hundred-pound sack of rice. He moved once, groaned, then didn't move again. I pulled back behind the support column.

Weasel began shooting in my direction while screaming, "You hit Ernie, you bastard. You're dead. All bets are off the table. I'm going to kill you, you son of a bitch."

Weasel had never really had a shot because Ox had been off to my right while Weasel was on the left. It's possible he hadn't even seen my gun as I fired at Ox. But to get a shot at Weasel I would have to expose myself to his fire a bit. I let him empty his magazine before I moved further to my right than I had with Ox. I was able to see Weasel's form through a car's rear and side window as he reloaded, but I didn't have a shot.

I had evened the odds but didn't feel much better about my chances of getting through this intact. The difference between Weasel and the gunman in San Francisco was that Weasel seemed to know what he was doing. He had extra ammunition clips and had changed the first one out in about two seconds. I knew the only way Weasel could get me was if I exposed myself or he came for me. I strained to hear any sound he might make.

When I heard what sounded like the sole of a shoe scuffing on concrete, I started to move around the pillar for a look. But Weasel was waiting for that. He might have even made the sound intentionally to draw me out. He fired before my head had moved far enough to see him. Apparently my Glock was more exposed than I realized, because when the shot rang out the gun was knocked from my hand. Weasel's shot had hit the pillar and a chunk of concrete had separated, striking the gun. When I pulled my hand back, it was bleeding and hurt like hell. The skin on the back of my third, fourth, and fifth fingers was ripped up from where the concrete had hit them. I looked around for my Glock and spotted it out in the drive aisle about six feet from the pillar. To get it, I would have to expose myself fully.

"Well, well, well," Weasel said. "It seems you've lost your weapon, Mr. FBI Special Agent. Tell you what. I'll give you a two-second count to get it before I fire. Go get it, James."

I knew I would be exposed for at least three seconds if not four as I bent to pick it up, then three more to get behind cover again. If I fell towards it, figuring to pick it up and fire before returning to cover, he would still have a clear shot at me. And his fire had been accurate enough that I didn't figure he'd completely miss.

"Well, James, what's it to be? Try for your gun or simply step out and let me put a bullet in your brain? The 'come along peacefully' option ended when you killed my friend."

"I'm still betting the cops will be here any second. If you were smart, you'd be running for the exit as fast as your legs could carry you."

"Get over it, James. NYPD ain't coming to your rescue. Nobody is coming to your rescue."

The inflection in Weasel's voice sounded different. It seemed softer than it had a few minutes ago when he had been speaking from behind a car some fifty feet away. I moved carefully to my right enough that my right eye could see around the pillar. I stopped when I saw the extreme left side of Weasel's body. He was moving towards me as quietly as possible. I saw his left foot come down slowly as he put his weight on it and saw his body shift as he balanced himself on that leg to raise his right foot. He was only about fifteen feet away. I waited until he had lifted his left leg again and was balanced on his right leg before I moved. With my right arm leading as I leaned around the pillar, I squeezed the trigger of my Glock three times.

CHAPTER TWENTY-FIVE

As my backup Glock, the same weapon I'd used on Diz and his pudgy friend, bucked in my hand, Weasel's smug look changed to one of surprise. He fell backward without ever getting his left leg down and landed in a deflated sitting position like a stringed puppet dropped by a child.

He stared down at his chest for a second before collapsing backward to the floor of the garage. As the three crimson stains on his chest merged into one large spot, blood began pooling around his body. His open eyes stared unblinkingly at the ceiling overhead as I remained concealed behind the pillar with just part of my head exposed until I was reasonably sure he wasn't going to be able to fire at me again.

After what seemed liked minutes but was probably only seconds, I stepped out from behind the pillar and walked cautiously towards Weasel with my Glock aimed at his head the whole time. If his gun moved the slightest bit I would put a round into his face without regard for what Philbin or anyone else might say about my 'decorating the garage with his brains.' But as I reached him, I knew he no longer represented a danger to me. I kicked his gun well away from his hand anyway.

Ox hadn't moved since he had fallen, so I figured he wouldn't be moving ever again, but I approached him in the same cautious way, with my Glock aimed at his head. I kicked the gun from his hand as I reached him just in case my assessment was in error. Only then did I let my right arm drop to my side. My right hand was dripping blood pretty good by then, staining the right leg of my pants and spattering my right shoe with blood, so I reached into a pocket and pulled out my handkerchief.

After wrapping my right hand tightly, I changed the clip on my backup Glock and replaced it in the ankle holster. Then I retrieved my service weapon and checked it over. It had a few scratches where it had been hit by the chunk of concrete, and it had a few dings from where it had landed on the concrete floor of the garage, but it appeared to be fully serviceable. I wiped it off with my hand, replaced the clip with a fresh one, and slipped it into the holster beneath my left arm.

No one from building security or NYPD had yet arrived in the garage, so I used my cell phone to call the Bureau's office downtown to report the attack rather than spending fifteen minutes trying to get any kind of a response through 911.

As I finished the call, I walked over to my car and raised the automated rollup gate using the remote fob on the key ring. There didn't appear to be any damage to my car from the gunfire. I was pretty sure that at least one car on this level had been hit, and it was reasonable to assume a few others in the line of fire had been struck as well.

I was thinking about my incredible luck of only having a few skinned knuckles when I heard some muffled sounds. My ears had been ringing since the first shots were fired in the enclosed area, or I might have heard it earlier. I followed the sounds to a Cadillac in the next aisle over, and then pinpointed their precise location as coming from the trunk.

I'd read a story once where an assassin always hid in the trunk of his victim's car, and then made noise when the victim entered the car to drive away. When the victim opened the trunk to investigate, the assassin fulfilled his contract. I had no idea who might be hiding in the trunk, but I intended to be ready for anything. I pulled out my service weapon.

While standing on the passenger side of the car and leaning over towards the center, I knocked on the trunk twice with my undamaged left hand. Nothing happened at first, except the noises stopped, but then I heard someone yell, "Help!"

"Who's in there?"

"I'm Michael Townsend."

"What are you doing in there?"

"Suffocating. Can you get me out?"

"Stand by."

The driver's door was unlocked, so I checked the ignition but the keys weren't there. I returned to the trunk.

"The keys aren't in the car," I yelled.

"There's a button in the glove box. Press that."

I walked to the passenger side door and opened it, then pressed the knobby protrusion that dropped the glove box door. I saw a button switch along the left side, so I pressed it and the trunk lid started to rise. Without closing the door, I quietly walked back along the car with my Glock at the ready. I heard some grunting noises from the trunk, and as I reached the rear of the vehicle, a man started to climb out.

"Freeze," I said. When he did, I said, "Okay, come out slowly and stand up with your hands raised over your head."

As he stood upright in the garage, I saw a man who had the innocuous look of actor Woody Allen in most of his movies.

"Who are you?"

"I'm Michael Townsend, as I said."

"What are you doing in the trunk of this car?"

"Two men stopped me as I was pulling out of the garage elevator at street level. One of them flashed a badge. I thought he was a cop, so I rolled down the window. He stuck a gun in my face and ordered me to move over. I did, and he climbed into my car. Then he unlocked all the doors and another man, a big man, climbed into the back seat on the passenger side. The smaller man drove around the block and then entered the garage elevator again, using my parking garage ID to get us back down here. After he parked, he made me get in the trunk and then warned me that if I made a sound, he'd kill me. You're Mister James, aren't you?"

"Yes."

"I live in ten-oh-four. I was on my way up to Westchester to meet with a client. Where are those men?"

"You don't have to worry about them anymore."

"They got away? Damn."

"They didn't get away. They're still here."

"Where?" he said, looking around anxiously.

"In the next aisle. Don't worry. They can't hurt you."

"Was that shooting I heard?" Looking down at my hand and then down at the blood on my pants leg and shoe, he asked, "Are you bleeding? I want to press charges for kidnapping."

"The police should be on the way," I said as I started to walk away. I took out my ID so I would have it handy for whoever arrived first— probably NYPD— and demanded to see it. "You can tell them what happened when they arrive," I said over my shoulder.

Townsend followed me and asked, "But you're FBI. Isn't kidnapping an FBI crime?"

"If you were missing, it would be. So far all I've seen is that you were threatened and locked in your own car. You have grounds for assault, carjacking, perhaps false imprisonment, and a whole bunch of lesser crimes— if the DA wants to proceed at all."

"Why wouldn't he want to proceed?" Townsend asked as we reached the aisle where Weasel and Ox were lying, but Townsend had been looking at me and hadn't noticed them yet.

"That's why," I said, pointing to the two thugs.

"Are those bodies?"

"Those are your carjackers. But they won't bother you again. And they're beyond worrying about whatever charges could be preferred against them."

"I think I'm going to be sick," Townsend said as he turned away and put his hand to his mouth.

"Freeze," I heard from the direction of the elevator.

I froze before loudly saying, "FBI."

"Turn around and let me see some ID."

I turned slowly, raised the ID wallet I had been holding in my hand, and let it flop open.

"He's okay," I heard from the elevator. "That's Special Agent James. He's a co-op owner here." The voice belonged to one of the building security guards.

The cop walked over and took my ID while his partner remained where he was with his weapon pointed at me.

After looking at my ID and my face, the cop said, "He's okay, Barry. This is the local FBI guy who gets all the publicity."

The other officer lowered and holstered his weapon, then walked towards us.

"What happened here, Special Agent James?" the first NYPD officer asked.

"I came to get my car, and these two thugs tried to take me down. They had carjacked Mr. Townsend there from ten-oh-four to gain access to the garage. His story is more interesting than mine."

Townsend was shaking as he stood there with his arms still raised.

"You can lower your arms, Mr. Townsend," the second officer said.

"Didn't you just kill a guy in San Francisco?" the first officer asked me.

"Uh, yeah. I was standing in my hotel suite, discussing my current case with Detective Lieutenant Hooper of SFPD, when an assassin burst into my hotel room and tried to kill us. We *both* drew and fired, managing to stop him— permanently."

"And you also took down those two guys over on the West Side here in the city. How many does this make now?"

I took a deep breath and said, "In total, the score is seven-and-oh."

◆

Over the next half-hour the number of law enforcement people in the garage grew appreciably. There were no less than a dozen uniforms, half a dozen plain-clothes, of which at least two were from homicide and one was a lieutenant, and four Special Agents from Federal Plaza. I learned that while I was fighting for my life in the garage, the building security had indeed been outside trying to move a group of indigents who had plopped down on the sidewalk in front of the building and refused to budge. But at least the security system had recorded everything that had occurred in the garage with multiple cameras.

I had to shake my head because the video records would have provided enough evidence to put Weasel and Ox away for many years if they hadn't died in their attempt to kidnap me. While some of the mice seemed to be getting smarter, many others seemed destined to get caught in those better mousetraps.

I was having my hand bandaged by a paramedic when Osborne and Snow arrived. I shrugged as Osborne grinned and shook his head.

"For someone as smart as Sherlock Holmes," Osborne said, "you sure don't seem able to avoid gunfights."

"I wasn't out looking for trouble. I was just on my way to get my car and drive it outside so I could hand it over to a dealership guy for servicing."

"Well, no time for that now, so you won't need your car. We'll give you a lift downtown."

"Oh come on, guys. I just got back from San Francisco, and I'm supposed to catch a flight to Greece this afternoon."

"Sorry," Osborne said. "Orders. You know the drill."

"Yeah, yeah, yeah. I know the drill." As I pressed the button on my remote that would lower the open gate at my parking spot I said, "Let's go."

"Hang on a minute," Snow said. "I need to notify the NYPD guy heading this investigation that we're taking Sherlock downtown."

While Snow went to speak to the lieutenant in charge of the investigation, I pulled out my cell phone and tried to call Mia. I wanted her to know I was alright and that I might be delayed slightly, but I couldn't make a cell tower connection from where I was standing. Rather than wandering around the underground garage until I found a spot where the cell tower signals weren't blocked, I decided to call her once we were aboveground.

When Snow returned, he said, "Okay. NYPD is cool with our heading downtown. The lieutenant said that one of his guys had already scanned the security videos. It appears to have gone down exactly as Sherlock told him. The two dead guys tried to kidnap him when he entered the garage to get his car."

"We still have to go downtown," Osborne said.

As we entered the elevator, I used my key to take us to the eleventh floor.

"Hey, what's up?" Snow asked. "We have to go downtown."

"I know. I just want get my suitcases. If we get done early enough I might still be able to make my plane to Greece. But if I have to come back up here to get my suitcases, it lessens the chances of that happening."

Ten minutes later we were headed down to the lobby. I could probably get a cell tower connection in the elevator, but I decided to wait until we were in the car.

◆

"Mia?" I said as the connection completed.

"Darling, where are you? Are you coming?"

"Yes, but there might be a tiny delay. A couple of hoods jumped me."

"Are you hurt, dearest?" she asked with concern in her voice.

"Just some minor cuts to the knuckles on my right hand. It's been bandaged."

"How long a delay are we talking about?"

"I don't know yet. There's still a chance I might catch the plane this afternoon. I'll let you know as soon as I know. I just didn't want you to be worried if you heard something on the news about me being attacked."

"Okay, darling. I love you."

"And I love you, baby. I'll talk to you later."

As I put the cell phone away, Osborne said, "You've become quite the lover, Sherlock. When's the wedding?"

"Nothing planned yet, guys."

◆

As we entered the lobby of the Federal building, all eyes turned in my direction. The last time I'd entered here dragging suitcases, I was a bloody mess. This time I had changed my blood-stained pants and shoes when we stopped into my co-op to get my suitcases. The only evidence of battle was my bandaged hand.

I dropped my suitcases off in the locker room before we headed up to the interrogation rooms. When we arrived upstairs, we were directed to a room, and all three of us entered and took seats around the table. I sat facing the two-way mirror because I knew it was expected.

We sat there without speaking for about five minutes before Philbin entered. That was the cue for Osborne and Snow to leave.

"Back again, I see," Philbin said. "You just can't stop murdering people, can you?"

"You've got me all figured out, eh Philbin?"

"I know you like to kill."

"Don't start, Philbin."

Philbin grimaced before saying, "Okay, tell me your story. What happened in your co-op building garage?"

I related the story in excruciating detail from the moment I stepped out of the elevator on the garage level until the two NYPD officers showed up. When I was done, I leaned back in the chair and stared at Philbin. I knew what was coming. He would try to confuse me by asking questions with facts I had given him after slightly altering them in the hope he could catch me in a lie.

"So you've never seen either of these two men before?"

"As I told you, I had only seen them once before. That was in Binghamton."

"Oh, yeah. You saw them in the church at your friend's funeral."

"Nooo. I saw them at the graveside ceremony and burial."

"Oh, yeah, right. And you didn't know who they were?"

"I figured them to be part of Delcona's mob."

"Why would Delcona send men to watch you?"

"I originally thought they were there to tail me back to Manhattan to learn where I was staying. But I never saw any-one tailing me— and I was looking hard."

"When did you learn their names?"

"I didn't. I still don't know them."

"But you called one Weasel and the other Ox."

"Those are just names I made up based on their physical appearances. As I told you, I don't know their real names."

"But you believed they were part of Delcona's mob?"

"Yes."

"And you think they were there to kidnap you and take you to him?"

"They said their boss wanted to talk with me."

"And you assumed that to be Delcona?"

"Of course."

"Why 'of course?'"

"I killed two of his 'boys.' I'm sure you remember that incident. Any talk with Delcona would probably end with me being dead."

Philbin stood up and circled the table twice while I just sat calmly. I imagined he was racking his brain to find a way to trip me up. So far he hadn't been able to cast any doubt on the truthfulness of my deposition. But that was the difficulty when questioning someone who was innocent and hadn't tried to conceal anything.

Philbin finally stopped walking when he reached a point across the table from me and said, "I'm surprised you didn't shoot the man who was hiding in the trunk of the car."

"Why should I? He wasn't a threat and he wasn't hiding. He was an innocent bystander whose car had been carjacked, probably so Weasel and Ox could gain entrance to the below-ground garage. Townsend wasn't associated with them at all. He lives in my co-op building."

"But you didn't know that while he was locked in the trunk of his car, did you?"

Philbin was grasping at straws now, trying to find something that would make me angry enough to slip up. He was wasting his time, and he should have known it. Perhaps he did, but he had a job to do.

"Are you about through trying to make me lose my temper?"

Philbin glared at me, then grinned. "Wait here," he said as he headed for the door.

I took a deep breath and relaxed. I assumed the interrogation was over. If I was right, I might make my flight to Greece after all. It would all depend on the NYPD. If they decided there had been the slightest bit of wrongdoing on my part, they could decide to charge me with something. But as far as I could see, the only thing I was guilty of was littering the garage with spent brass cartridges. And since it was on private property, of which I was a part-owner, I didn't think they could make a charge like that stick. But if paying the fine for littering got me on the plane today, I'd pay it in a heartbeat. I needed to get away from people who wanted me dead.

Philbin kept me waiting in the interrogation room for more than half an hour, but I knew he had to report to senior level managers and wait until they decided what action to take, if any. When he returned, he said, "You lucked out again. NYPD has decided there was no wrongdoing on your part and won't be filing any charges."

"Are we done here?" I asked as I started to stand.

"Yes. By the way, you were wrong about those two you killed being from Delcona's mob."

I stopped moving before I had completely straightened up and looked at Philbin, then slowly finished straightening up. "Then who were they?"

"They were allegedly part of a gang controlled by Igor Samethovsky, better known as Fast Sammy. Any idea why he'd want you dead?"

CHAPTER TWENTY-SIX

"**N** one."

"Then perhaps he really did just want to talk to you."

"When the invitation comes at gunpoint, it's called kidnapping. Perhaps his outfit was involved in the art theft case I just wrapped up and he was looking for revenge, after gloating a little that he was about to end my career."

◆

After retrieving my suitcases from the locker room, I left the building and hailed a cab to take me to the airport. The traffic was just as miserable as it always was in any major city during mid-day, but I still believed I could make my flight out. I sat back and lost myself in my thoughts.

I knew from the news reports that Fast Sammy allegedly owned a considerable number of illegal card parlors in New York City. That, in and of itself, had nothing to do with me or my investigations. It's possible that one of the skips I'd helped recover had convinced Fast Sammy to take me down. It was even possible that Fast Sammy had taken a part in the recent art theft. Someone had to have arranged for that shipping container at Newark to be modified and then get it onboard the right plane with the two thieves and the phony art cases inside.

But what seemed like the most likely scenario is that Fast Sammy had learned of, or heard rumors about, the gizmo's existence. Such a prize would be worth the elaborate scheme to take down an FBI Special Agent. Or perhaps he just wanted to ensure that Delcona never got his hands on it. With the gizmo, Delcona could control all crime activity in the country. Hell, he could control all organized crime on the planet. Anyone who refused to bow down to him would find their illegal drug shipments being confiscated, their planned thefts foiled, and all of their operations under police scrutiny. His being in control of all crime in the world might even be worse than politicians getting their hands on the gizmo. Well, no, probably not.

Without the ability to whip out the gizmo and begin investigating Fast Sammy's illegal activities, I was powerless at the moment. So I turned my attention to the recent attempt to kidnap me. The plan had centered around my being in the garage at the correct time. And that could only have been known if Fast Sammy had someone inside the car dealership who had known of the appointment. In fact, the call may even have been arranged by Fast Sammy or someone in his organization. And I had called a number that was given to me without first verifying that it came from the dealership. The dealership might know nothing about the arranged appointment. The call could have gone to a cell phone owned by Fast Sammy's operation. If so, it had probably been smashed and thrown in the garbage after the plan failed, so it would be untraceable now.

Since I was powerless at the moment to do anything about the most recent attack on my life, my ruminations just increased my frustration with each passing city block. I finally turned my thoughts to other events and found myself thinking about all of the loose ends I had left in my investigations and recoveries. Some of those loose ends had to be people who would love to see me dead. As my personal fortune had grown, the personal fortunes of the people who had lost their ill-gotten goods had shrunk. That was a powerful motive for revenge, and I'm sure some of them wished to exact the maximum.

Perhaps, as I had mused in San Francisco, it was time to call it a day and cease my crime-fighting activities. I had repaid the mortgage on the co-op and had no other debts. And I had a girlfriend with an inherited fortune containing so many zeros at the end of the number that it was dizzying. But that would make me no better than Marcus, and I never wanted that to happen.

◆

Despite the midday traffic, we made it to the airport with plenty of time for me to catch my flight out. I checked my bags and then went to stand in line at the metal detector station. I held up my FBI identification so the TSA security person manning the metal detector could see it before I entered the device and set off alarms. He walked over, looked at my credentials, and then invited me to step around the detector. I thanked him and continued up the hallway towards my gate.

From that point until I passed out of the customs area at Athens airport, I should be safe from armed attack. So during my leisurely stroll to the gate, I stopped to pick up a book at a small concession stand. Then it was just a matter of sitting and reading my book like so many other travelers until it was time for the plane to begin boarding passengers. But before I opened the book I called Mia and informed her I was at the airport and waiting for my plane to board. I confirmed that the flight information I had given her yesterday was the same. We then spent about ten minutes talking and ended the call with our usual intimate words of affection.

◆

Unlike the bumpy ride from San Francisco, the flight over the Atlantic was calm. It did get a little bumpy at times when we reached Europe, but most of the turbulence over land was minor. Overall, it was a great way to begin my vacation. I had already made up my mind that if Saul called, I wasn't going to return his calls until after Mia and I returned from Fiji. I still had an obligation to respond immediately, but the mortgage was paid in full, so I wasn't worried if he wanted to cancel the retainer agreement. I didn't know if I would continue in law enforcement or recovery work, but I did know that I wasn't going to delay my vacation plans a second time and dis-appoint Mia.

I had managed to get some sleep during the flight so I felt well rested when the plane arrived in Athens. After getting my bags, I walked to the customs stations. I recognized one of the inspectors as the customs man who had checked my bags and credentials during my last entry into Athens, so I joined the line of people waiting to be checked by him. I thought that since he had cleared me once there might be less interrogation of my travel plans and reasons for concealed weapons a second time, if he remembered me.

When it was my turn, the customs inspector looked up as I handed over my passport and gun permit papers. I saw recognition in his eyes and perhaps even a slight smile.

"Welcome back to Greece, Special Agent James."

"Thank you," I said with a smile. "I'm happy to be back."

"Your destination here is the same?"

"Yes, Thasos Island."

"And are you carrying only the same weapons as on your previous visit?"

"Yes, sir, that's correct."

After a glance at my passport and a perfunctory look at the contents of my luggage, he said, "I wish you an enjoyable stay."

"Thank you."

As he handed me my papers, he said, "I read about your recovery of the priceless paintings belonging to the Milan museum. Very well done."

"Thank you. The paintings are once again available for the general public to see, marvel at, and enjoy."

As I passed out of the customs area, there was a young man waiting with a sign that read 'James.'

"I'm Colton James," I said to him. "Are you from the air-taxi service?"

"Yes, sir. May I take your bags?"

"We'll each take one."

"This way to the cart, sir."

A few minutes later, my bags and I were securely aboard the electric cart that would transport us to the waiting air-taxi. My young driver wasted no time and spared no ohms as he whisked us through the terminal and across the airport grounds like an experienced hack driver.

As he pulled up next to a helicopter and carefully set my luggage on the ground, I handed him a twenty. His face lit up with a smile as he thanked me. Then, in a mild squealing of tires, he was gone. The air-taxi pilot hurried out of the hanger and loaded my bags into the helicopter's luggage area, then invited me to climb aboard. I sat back to relax and enjoy the ride.

◆

With each passing mile in the hour-long ride, I grew more relaxed. I was thinking of my beautiful destination, the friendly family with whom I would stay, and the beautiful woman anxiously awaiting my arrival.

But as we neared the compound, I grew concerned. There wasn't a hint of activity anywhere on the grounds. The last time I had come to the compound, there had been at least a dozen people visible inside the walls. I reached under my left arm and momentarily wrapped my hand around the handle of my Glock. It gave me a reassuring feeling that I was ready in case there was trouble. Of course, Mia would have called to warn me of problems, if she'd been able.

The pilot expertly set the helicopter down and shut down all systems before jumping out to remove my luggage from the storage area. I followed, while keeping a wary eye out for any signs of danger.

When my luggage was sitting at the very edge of the landing pad, well away from the helicopter's spinning blades, I handed the pilot a hundred dollar bill. He smiled as widely as the cart driver at the airport, then climbed back aboard the aircraft and started the engine.

As the air-taxi lifted off the pad, I was left alone with my feelings of dread. I made a decision to leave my bags where they were and approach the entrance to the compound in the same way I approached my co-op door when I wasn't expecting someone—that is to say, with my Glock drawn.

Suddenly, Mia appeared at the corner of the compound walls and began running towards me, but I could tell she wasn't afraid or anxious.

I felt all of the tenseness immediately wash from my body, and I let the smile on my face reflect the joy I saw on hers.

~ finis ~

A Message to My Readers

I hope you've enjoyed this book. If you have, watch for new books on the websites of all major book sellers, check my website: www.deprima.com, or, sign up for my free newsletter to automatically receive email announcements when future books are released.